Shadow

Karin Alvtegen

translated from the Swedish
by McKinley Burnett

W F HOWES LTD

This large print edition published in 2012 by
W F Howes Ltd
Unit 4, Rearsby Business Park, Gaddesby Lane,
Rearsby, Leicester LE7 4YH

1   3   5   7   9   10   8   6   4   2

First published in Sweden in 2007 by Natur och
Kultur, Stockholm

First published in the United Kingdom in 2009
by Canongate Books Ltd

A CIP catalogue record for this book is available
from the British Library

ISBN 978 1 47120 293 3

Typeset by Palimpsest Book Production Limited,
Falkirk, Stirlingshire
Printed and bound in Great Britain
by MPG Books Ltd, Bodmin, Cornwall

MIX
Paper from
responsible sources
FSC
www.fsc.org   FSC® C018575

To my family,
the very foundation

CHAPTER 1

'When you hear the tone – ding-a-ling – it means it's time to turn the page. Now we'll begin.'

The voice on the tape had changed. It almost sounded like a man now, although he knew it was a lady. Once again he opened the Bambi book to the first page and listened to the story on the tape player. He knew it by heart. He had known it for a long time, but today he'd listened so many times that the lady's voice was beginning to turn dark.

It had begun to grow dark around him as well; not as many mammas and pappas with kids and balloons were coming by any more. He was hungry. The buns he'd been given were all eaten up and the juice had made him want to pee, but she had told him that he should stay here, so he didn't dare move. He was used to waiting. But he really had to pee now, and if she didn't come and collect him soon he might wet himself. He didn't want Mamma to get that look. The one that made him hurt and sometimes made her leave him alone in the dark. He put his hand on the sore spot he'd got yesterday when he didn't want to go with her. Her eyes had

1

turned so angry and she'd told him he was being naughty. And then his back had hurt. She wanted to go to that house so often. First take the bus and then the long walk. Sometimes she stayed with him out there, but sometimes she was gone for a long time, and he wasn't allowed to bother her. There was a strange house of glass in the garden where it was rather fun to play, but not all the time and never alone. There was a little shed with wood in it too, where he could carve things even though he wasn't allowed to play with knives. Sometimes she took such a long time it got dark. Then the ghosts came creeping out, and the thieves. The knife in the woodshed was his only protection. And the magic floorboard with the dark spot that looked like an eye. If he stood on it with the knife in his hand and sang 'Twinkle, twinkle, little star' then they couldn't get at him. Before, she used to say they were going to live in that house someday, not in the glass house or the one with the wood, but in the big one, and then he would have his own room. Everything would be all right then, she said.

He looked around. He was sitting at the top of a wide staircase, and behind him there was a pond with birds in it. For a moment he wondered whether he dared leave his spot and walk up to have a look, but he remembered what he'd been told and stayed right where he was. The stone step began to feel cold. The voice on the tape player was speaking more slowly now. It almost sounded like she was falling asleep inside. Finally the button popped up and the voice stopped altogether. He suddenly felt lonely. And soon he wouldn't be able to hold it any longer. He didn't know where there was a toilet, and now he began to feel a little sad too. He didn't want to sit here any more. He had waited so long and now he had to go and pee and after that he wanted to leave.

'Hi.'

He jumped at the sound of the voice. In front of him stood a man dressed in green. It looked like he was wearing a police uniform but it was the wrong colour. There was writing on his chest just like a policeman's shirt.

'What's your name then?'

He didn't answer. Mamma had told him never to talk to strangers, and he lowered his eyes and stared hard at the stone step.

'We're closing now, so it's time for everyone to go home. Where are your mamma and pappa?'

The man's voice didn't sound angry. It sounded rather nice, but he knew he wasn't allowed to answer. At the same time he couldn't be rude, and suddenly he didn't know what to do. Two big drops landed at his feet, making dark spots on the stone. And then two more.

'Are you here with your mamma or pappa?'

He shook his head slowly. That way he wouldn't have to talk.

'So who are you here with?'

He shrugged his shoulders.

'Don't be sad. My name is Sven and I'm the guard

here at Skansen amusement park. Anybody who needs help in here can come to me. If you've lost your parents or can't find your way or need help.'

It was quiet for a moment.

'How old are you?'

Cautiously he held out the fingers of his left hand, and with his other hand he folded down his little finger and thumb.

'Are you three??'

He shook his head a little.

'No, four.'

He clapped his hand to his mouth. Now he'd spoken to him. What if the old man told his mamma?

He sat in silence, his eyes fixed on the ground. Then he glanced at the man to see if he looked like somebody who would tell. The man smiled at him.

'If you want, you can come with me to the little house down there where I work. We can wait there until they show up.'

He had to pee so badly. Soon he was going to wet himself, and then Mamma would be even angrier.

'I need to pee.'

The man nodded, still smiling.

'The toilets are down there. You run along, and I'll watch your things. Do you see the door there?'

He hesitated a moment before doing as he was told.

Sven Johansson waited on the steps, concerned as he watched the little boy running off towards the toilets. He had noticed him earlier that afternoon, and now he was worried. When the boy disappeared

4

into the toilet, he squatted down and had a look at his belongings. A tape player, a Bambi book, a clear plastic bag with crumbs in it, and a small juice bottle with a yellow plastic top and a few drops of juice left inside. He opened the book to see if the boy's name was written in it. A folded piece of paper fell to the ground. With a sense of foreboding he unfolded it and his worst fears were confirmed. The brief message was written in a flowing script:

'Take care of this child. Forgive me.'

CHAPTER 2

The key to the flat had arrived in a padded envelope from the police. A brown-veneered door in an old-fashioned stairwell that had been gnawed by time. Gerda Persson had lain dead for three days by the time the home help discovered her body. After ninety-two years and a little more than three months she had filled her lungs one last time and turned into a memory. That was all Marianne knew. And since she was the one now standing outside the door of the flat, it was also clear that neither the police nor the home help had managed to find any relative who could take care of all the details required when a life came to an end. That was why the task had landed on Marianne Folkesson's desk. A stranger's key to an unknown life whose past she'd been assigned to retrieve.

She had been in the neighbourhood before. The blocks were full of small flats, and many of their residents were in contact with Social Services' care for the elderly. Sometimes, when one of them died, there was no one to contact. No one except the district commission's estate administrator, Marianne Folkesson.

She opened her bag and took out the thin plastic gloves, but left the mask. She never knew what awaited her behind these strangers' doors, but out of respect for the deceased she tried to go in with an open mind. Sometimes the home was as neat as a doll's house, left to posterity in spotless condition, with meticulously cared-for possessions that no one would ever want. But sometimes among the belongings that filled the home of the deceased there was an inexplicable feeling of *presence*. In a way, her own arrival was an encroachment, and she didn't like to make it worse by wearing an ugly mask. She preferred to think of herself as an ally, come to close up with respect and dignity the lives hidden behind the unfamiliar names that landed on her desk. To gather the objects she found, and if possible locate the people to whom they would mean something. Death was no longer something that scared her. After twenty years in this job she had realised that it was a natural part of life. She no longer sought the meaning of life, but that didn't mean she thought she had found it. Since the universe had taken the trouble to exist, there must be a reason for it. And with that she had to be content, willing to trust in the mystery.

Life. A tiny moment between two eternities.

Far from all the cases she worked on spoke of lonely lives, even though the circle of friends may have diminished with time and the final years spent in loneliness. But some homes were the opposite of the neat doll's houses – where the chaos and filth were so pungent that her body recoiled from stepping across the threshold. Ripped wallpaper and broken furniture that loudly proclaimed the desperation felt by the deceased. In those cases her report was a portrait of a mentally unstable person without a social network who got by as long as psychiatric support was available. Perhaps the person had lived in a home, but eventually felt better and was then considered too healthy to take up one of the few places offered by the state. Then he was expected to take care of himself and was provided with his own flat, where isolation quickly allowed the disease to regain lost ground. A lonely person who had been in need of care but, once rejected, had not had the strength to beg or plead. Then it was her duty to provide some form of redress, to do everything in her power to track down a relative who at least would come to the funeral. Sometimes there was no one. Just her, the pastor, the funeral director and the cantor who followed the deceased to his final resting place. In that case she had to try, with the help of photographs and mementos, to get some sense of the person, to give the funeral a personal touch if possible. Whenever she was the only one placing a flower on the coffin, she always prayed for forgiveness for society's incompetence – that it had allowed this person to endure his misery without any intervention.

She turned and gave her companion a pair of

gloves. On the first visit someone from the county council always had to accompany her. There should never be any question that everything had been done properly. Various colleagues took turns coming with her, depending on who had time. Today it was one of the aid workers from care for the elderly. Marianne knew the woman's first name, but right now she couldn't remember her surname.

Solveig pulled on the gloves, and Marianne put the key in the door. The hall floor was covered with flyers and a handful of copies of the free local newsletter. There was no stench, only a musty smell that needed to be aired. She glanced through the post as she gathered it into a stack and put it all on the hall table. As far as she could see, there were no bills to be paid or magazine subscriptions that needed cancelling. Only one letter was personally addressed to Gerda.

An offer from a broadband provider.

The flat seemed to be in order, but a thin coating of dust lay on all the clear surfaces. From the home help she had learned that someone came by to do the cleaning for Gerda every third week and to shop for food every Monday. She had declined other assistance, wanting to take care of herself. The dust was certainly no sign of negligence but rather a sign of poor eyesight. Marianne had witnessed this before: the flats of old people where everything was in order but the dust was allowed to settle undisturbed.

In the kitchen a plate and a glass stood in the dish-rack. Otherwise it was empty. A kitchen towel hung over the radiator, and the little table with two chairs was cleared, except for a wicker basket sitting on an oilcloth with a pattern of tiny flowers. She opened the refrigerator. The stench of rotting food rushed out. Marianne found the plastic rubbish bag she'd brought along. Two weeks had passed since Gerda had died, and after the ambulance took away the body, the home help had been forbidden entry to the flat. An open carton of low-fat milk, a tub of butter, caviar and a rotten cucumber were all consigned to the plastic bag, which she quickly sealed and set by the front door.

'Look at this. She has books in the freezer.'

Solveig was still standing by the open refrigerator door when Marianne came back to the kitchen. A thick layer of ice had formed around the books, which were sealed in clingfilm and neatly stacked at the back of the freezer compartment. In one of the kitchen drawers Marianne found a spatula, which she used to prise the books from their prison. The plastic was frosted over, and she scraped her fingernail along the spine of one of the books. *Let the Stones Speak* by Axel Ragnerfeldt. One of the greatest. Not his most famous one, but then all his works were considered modern classics.

'There might be money hidden between the pages,' her colleague said. On several occasions Marianne had found banknotes hidden in the strangest places. But this book was empty, as were the others. All of them were by Axel Ragnerfeldt, and with some astonishment she discovered that they all had handwritten dedications. *To Gerda with affection* and *To Gerda with the warmest thanks.* And then an ornate signature above the printed name of the author. Marianne felt a warmth in her chest. As always she was glad to discover signs that this person who lived alone had at one time been part of some sort of community. That her life had not always been so solitary. In this case Marianne felt doubly satisfied. Generally, if no assets and nothing of value were found, there was little chance of a nice funeral. But these books could certainly be sold for a good price because of Axel Ragnerfeldt's personal dedication, and she would see to it that as much as possible went towards the decoration of the church and a beautiful headstone. A testament of respect for the person whose life had now ended.

'They don't seem to have been damaged by being frozen. These books must be really valuable.'

Marianne nodded. The shy Nobel Prize-winner had achieved fame that was without precedent in the cultural life of Sweden, but he had seldom given interviews. She couldn't remember hearing a single detail of his private life.

'Gerda Persson was ninety-two. They must have been almost the same age, don't you think?'

'I didn't realise he was that old. Do you really think so?'

Marianne wasn't sure. And the book jackets

provided no clue. They had been printed before the era of the cult of personality, back in the days when an author's words were more interesting than his face.

The flat consisted of two rooms and a kitchen. They went into the hall, past the living room, and into the bedroom. A Zimmer frame lay on its side on the floor. The nightstand had been knocked over and the sheet torn off the bed. The rug was in a heap and on top of it clothes and magazines were jumbled together. A water glass lay on its side next to a tube of hand cream and a box of valerian. In the midst of all this an alarm clock kept on ticking. Marianne straightened up the nightstand and replaced the bedside lamp. In the little drawer there were magazine clippings, throat lozenges, a Bible, a necklace, some envelopes, and a small pocket diary. She turned to a page at random. *Woke up at 6 a.m. Potatoes and meatballs. Hedda Gabler on TV.* Most of the magazine articles were about heart disease, and the dates showed they'd been collected over a long period. Some were poems from obituaries with the names cut off. The first envelope contained a fifteen-year-old gift voucher for podiatric care, the second a card offering congratulations on her seventy-fifth birthday from her friends in the library pensioners' group. The third envelope was thicker and well-thumbed. Marianne looked inside. Solveig opened a wardrobe but closed it again when she saw it contained only clothes.

'How much is in there?'

Marianne took out a bundle of banknotes and counted them.

'Eleven thousand, five hundred and seventy kronor.'

She closed the drawer but kept the envelope with the cash. After she had finished her search of the flat she would have to fill out an inventory form on which furniture and objects of value had to be listed along with any other assets found, such as cash. Any property belonging to the deceased would go firstly to pay for funeral expenses and a headstone, and secondly to the settlement of the estate. Whatever remained would go to any creditors.

Solveig took a quick look through the other wardrobe, then they both moved into the living room. This room was mainly furnished with older pieces. A bureau, a bookshelf and a more modern sofa – nothing that would generate large sums for the estate. A bed had been set up in front of the TV, and on the table next to it lay a TV guide, two scraped-off lottery tickets with no win, and a considerable array of medicines. They stood lined up on a piece of paper, cross-ruled with hand-written dates: Imdur, aspirin, Bisoprolol, Plavix, Plendil, citalopram, Pravachol.

It was amazing what society would do to keep people alive. Not to mention the enthusiasm of the pharmaceutical industry.

Like an exclamation mark amid the old-fashioned furnishings, a red push-button telephone sat on a small table inside the doorway. Marianne went over and leafed through a small stack of papers. A handwritten list of postal giro account numbers for radio service, telephone company and insurance. A notice from Söder Hospital. A supermarket flyer. A brochure from the chemist's about the use of Bisoprolol. At the bottom lay a dog-eared address book. Marianne looked up the letter A. A handful of names and phone numbers were written with different pens, and all but two were crossed out. The sum total of a lifetime of acquaintances collected in a little book. One by one the links to the outside world had vanished and were then deleted.

Address books were her best tool in the search for relatives. She would ring all the numbers she found, in the hope of persuading someone to come to the funeral. When older people died, the numbers were often disconnected with no forwarding number. Occasionally so much time had passed that new subscribers had taken them over.

A sudden thought made her turn to the letter R. At the top of the column of names she found what she was looking for. Ragnerfeldt. The name was not crossed out.

'Here are some photos.' Solveig was kneeling in front of the old bureau with a brown envelope in her hand. Marianne put the address book in her bag and went over to her colleague, casting a glance inside the open bureau doors. Piles of neatly ironed tablecloths, crystal glasses of various designs, a Chinese-inspired coffee service. A red cardboard binder labelled *Household Accounts* on the spine. Marianne pulled it out and stuffed it into her bag.

'I wonder if this is a picture of her? Looks like it's from a birthday.' Solveig turned it over. 'Nothing written on it.'

She handed Marianne the picture. A faded colour photo of an elegantly dressed woman sitting in an easy chair surrounded by vases of flowers. Her hair was brushed back and fastened in a bun. Her face wore a serious expression, as if she wasn't comfortable being the centre of attention.

Solveig took out another photo.

'Look, here he is. That's him, isn't it?'

Marianne looked at the picture. Black-and-white this time. Axel Ragnerfeldt was sitting at a wooden table staring into the distance with a coffee cup in his hand. A woman of about the same age and two small children were also at the table, looking into the camera. A girl and a boy. The boy was a few years older.

Marianne nodded. 'That's definitely him. I didn't even know he had a family.'

'Maybe it's not his.'

'It looks like a family photograph.'

Marianne put the photo back in the envelope and stuffed it into her bag.

Solveig moved on to the bookshelf. 'Here are some of his books.'

Marianne followed her.

'Signed?'

Solveig opened a book. The florid signature

flowed above the printed name, but this time without a personal greeting. Marianne pulled out another and flicked through the pages with her thumb. She gasped when she saw that all the pages were crossed out with a thick red marker. In certain places the text seemed to have particularly incensed whoever held the pen. Those pages had been obliterated with such force they were unreadable and the paper was almost torn.

'Why the hell did she do that?'

They checked one book after another, and they had all been subjected to the same fate. The red lines shone blood-red on the pages, and here and there the pen had made small punctures. Marianne pulled out a book by a different author but found the pages untouched.

'Hmm.' She didn't usually make comments, especially not about things that had taken place in the person's own home and didn't harm anyone else. But she found it odd, to say the least, that someone would intentionally destroy a signed book by Ragnerfeldt. Particularly in a home like this where the extra income from the sale of a valuable item might have been welcome. Perplexed, Marianne shoved the book back in place.

'So, what do you think?' said Solveig. 'Do you have everything you need for now?'

Marianne opened her bag and took out the folder of inventory forms.

'We just have to fill out one of these now.'

★   ★   ★

When the form was completed and Solveig had left, Marianne remained standing at the living-room window. She took in Gerda Persson's view. A tree, a lawn, the dull green façade of a block of flats in the background. Behind those windows the lives and secrets of other people.

Everything she needed for the time being was packed into her bag. If no relatives contacted her after the death notice appeared, she would have to resort to the provincial records office and the church birth registry. And the names in the address book. She would do everything she could to find as many pieces of the puzzle as necessary to honour Gerda Persson at her funeral. Now her real work began. The hunt for Gerda Persson's past.

She had already found one name.

Axel Ragnerfeldt.

CHAPTER 3

'No one had a greater influence on my father and his work than a man by the name of Joseph Schultz.'

With his finger poised over the name in his lecture notes, Jan-Erik Ragnerfeldt paused dramatically and gazed out over the large auditorium.

'I don't recall how old I was when my father first told me about Joseph Schultz, but I grew up with the story about the choice that he made and his fate. Joseph Schultz was my father's ideal, his great model for humanity. And I remember that every time my father told me about him, I understood even more that although it's good to think good thoughts, *genuine* goodness emerges only when one takes action.'

The spotlight was blinding him. He could only see the people in the front rows, but he knew that the rest were out there. An anonymous audience waiting devotedly for him to continue.

'So who was this remarkable Joseph Schultz? Is there anyone here who has heard his name?'

He shaded his eyes with his hand. A woman was sitting in the front row over to one side of the

18

stage. He had already noticed her, but now he took the opportunity to study her more closely. Lovely chiselled features. Her breasts swelled under a shimmering blouse with taut buttons, a little opening where they failed to close. The dark gap aroused his interest. He lowered his arm.

'Joseph Schultz was a young soldier in the German Wehrmacht during the Second World War. On the twentieth of July 1941 he and seven of his fellow soldiers were in Smederevska Palanka on the Eastern Front. Their mission was to suppress the partisans' resistance. It was the height of summer, harvest time, and Schultz and his detachment had been sent out on what they thought was a routine patrol . . .'

He stood quite still. A sudden movement would have broken the atmosphere he was building up. He had become very skilled at this; experience had fortified his self-confidence, and now he could do exactly as he liked. The privilege of success. The more confidence he had, the more charisma.

He shifted his gaze and let his eyes meet hers. He had made his choice. She was the one who would carry him through the evening, and he made it obvious enough that she would notice. That she had been chosen. And he felt the longed-for tingling sensation that came from standing there on stage and having the power to choose, while all she could do was acquiesce.

'After a short march they realise that the day's mission is something different from what they're used to, because suddenly Joseph Schultz and his detachment are stopped by a command.'

She lowered her eyes, but too late. She had given herself away. A stray smile had showed she was enjoying his attention. Like all the women he met, she had fallen for his position of power.

The game had begun.

'The local people are busy bringing in the hay. Provisions for the winter must be stored away, because even in wartime people have to eat. Daily activities must go on. In front of one of the haystacks, fourteen civilian men have been lined up. All of them are blindfolded, with their hands tied behind their backs. Schultz and his seven comrades realise that they are about to become an execution squad.'

She was resisting, not wanting to seem too easy. Instead of looking him in the eye she fixed her gaze on something off to the side.

'Eight young men who, legitimised by the law of their uniforms, receive orders to kill fourteen innocent fellow human beings.'

Someone coughed. Irritated, he saw that the spell he had created was momentarily broken. Some of the audience had begun shifting in their seats. Then her eyes were back on him. More assured this time, the bond established. In a hall of three hundred people they both felt it. Anticipation was aroused. A frisson.

Which could never be satisfied.

'Seven of the eight in the patrol do not hesitate.

They are ready to follow orders and raise their rifles. But Joseph Schultz suddenly feels that he has had enough. In the silence that ensues he drops his weapon on the ground and slowly walks over to the haystack. There he takes up position next to the line of the condemned.'

He clicked on his PowerPoint. The black-and-white photograph of the event that took place sixty-five years before was projected onto the screen behind the stage.

'No one would remember Joseph Schultz and his heroic decision if one of his comrades had not taken a photograph of the event. How was it possible for a human being to make the choice that Joseph Schultz made? What was it that separated him from the rest of the patrol? The ones who were not only ready to execute fourteen unknown civilians, but also their comrade Joseph Schultz.'

He let the question sink in as he took a sip of water. Her eyes were on him the whole time, and he felt himself grow. There was no man sitting next to her, but that didn't necessarily mean there was no man in her life. The audiences who came to the literary evenings out in the countryside were always predominantly women, and they tended to come in groups, leaving their husbands at home. His experience whispered that a spouse ensconced at home need not present a problem. The power of the stage worked wonders, opening doors that had never before been opened. Her gaze revealed that the lecture would be worth the effort.

'This was the question to which my father devoted his whole body of work, trying to depict it. And notice that I do not say "answer", but merely "depict". My father's sole driving force as an author consisted of an attempt to disseminate the essence of Joseph Schultz's action – what it was that made Joseph refuse to be blinded by the despair inherent in the idea that our choices are without meaning, and instead recognise that it is precisely our choices that make all the difference. Refusing to be cowed by the fear and selfishness we all detest but which continually seem to leave their mark on us and our decisions.'

He paused. He usually did so at this point in the lecture, and as always his audience now sat spellbound by his words, actually perhaps not *his* words, but his father's. Yet now it was he, Jan-Erik, who was conveying those words. Their voices were similar, and after years of giving lectures he had smoothed away the differences. By now their voices were scarcely distinguishable. Recordings of his father's legendary readings could be found in every home; his voice had become a national treasure. But the precious recordings were now the only remnant of Axel Ragnerfeldt's voice. A stroke five years ago had silenced him, and it was Jan-Erik's turn to carry on his cultural inheritance. The books had been translated all over the world, and each year the royalty payments poured into the family business, which over the years had turned into a small empire, with foundations and grants for charitable works. As well as a considerable salary for Jan-Erik, who was the president of the corporation and saw to it that everything ran smoothly. He had more requests to give lectures than he had time for, but he took on a good number of them. He enjoyed travelling. A euphemism for the fact that he felt no great eagerness to stay at home.

He had grown from the task. It had made him significant.

'Perhaps Joseph Schultz realised that death would take him even if he chose to remain with his comrades and fire his weapon. Perhaps he realised that if he chose the easy way out and obeyed the order, he would execute not only those fourteen men but also the last little sliver inside himself that made him a human being. That last little part of us that has to remain intact so we can face ourselves in the mirror when we get up in the morning. Perhaps he realised that once it was gone, he would no longer be truly alive. He would merely *survive* until death finally caught up with him.'

He clicked on the mouse and the photograph of Joseph Schultz's heroic act vanished. In its place appeared a close-up of his father, one of the few he had ever permitted his publisher to use.

'Joseph Schultz's action in wartime never conquered any country. He saved no lives; fifteen men died instead of fourteen. His unique spirit and civil courage never won a medal for bravery on the battlefield. His name is unknown to most people, while that of Hitler, Göring and Mengele have taken their places in the history books. But perhaps the most surprising thing of all is that sixty-five years later Joseph Schultz's decision arouses more wonder than that of his comrades-in-arms. His action seems astounding, despite the fact that all he did was what most of us realise was the right thing. Because if we were to choose, who would we rather be? Joseph Schultz or one of the others in the patrol?'

Silently let your gaze sweep over the hall.

'Who besides me wants to be like Joseph?'

Jan-Erik sensed the wave that swept over the audience. The spotlight was hot on his face. Every pore in his body was wide open, welcoming the feeling that filled him. As usual, just after these words, he left his notes on the podium and walked slowly to the centre of the stage, standing on the spot he had marked in advance and keeping his eyes on the floor at his feet. Apparently vulnerable and without the protection afforded by the podium, he seemed to join with the audience as he slowly raised his eyes.

'My father and Joseph Schultz both knew that our actions are like our children. They live on, and they continue to have an effect independent of us and our will. Joseph Schultz and my father belong to the minority who realise that the reward for a good deed is the very fact of having done it. That is important, very important. They have shown that by conquering our own fear we also conquer our mightiest foe. I am eternally grateful to have a father like Axel Ragnerfeldt, and to have the opportunity to continue to spread his message.'

The applause was spontaneous as always. He had opened himself up and made things personal, made the audience believe that they were all basically the same, like one big family. But he was not finished.

'My motivation for coming here tonight is to continue to spread this message. So let us follow in my father's footsteps and make Joseph Schultz our example.'

He gave her a searching glance and everything was in place. He was pleased to hear that her applause was different from the others'. A bit slower, a bit more considered, a bit more *you're fantastic, but don't think you can get what you want.* Precisely the signal that proved he could get exactly what he wanted. He smiled to himself at his success.

It was time for questions. The lights came up in the hall and he could finally see his audience. The unidentifiable sea suddenly became faces, and he retreated to his place behind the podium. He closed his eyes and tried to enjoy the moment. The one moment that remained before his father would recapture everyone's attention. Liberated from the nursing home where he physically resided, his spirit would sweep into the room and obliterate the evening's performance.

Axel Ragnerfeldt, who had reached the level of success that most parents wish for their children.

An older man at the back of the hall held up his hand and Jan-Erik granted him the floor. *Don't point like a woman. Use your whole hand.*

'I'd like to ask about the book *Shadow*.'

The man spoke with an accent. The novel he wanted to ask about had resulted in the Nobel Prize. It was the one Jan-Erik got the most questions about; the last book in a series of literary triumphs that had finally convinced the Swedish Academy. In the year 2000 the novel's main character Simone had been voted the twentieth century's best literary portrait of a woman, in stiff competition with Vilhelm Moberg's Kristina in *The Emigrants*.

'As everyone knows, countless articles have been written about the book, but I'm fascinated that he could make the story so true to life. I was fourteen when I was released from Buchenwald. For someone like me who experienced a concentration camp it's hard to understand how a person who was never a prisoner could describe it so precisely. Your father must have done a huge amount of research, since the book is full of so many facts that match reality. I'd just like to ask how he went about this.'

Jan-Erik smiled. The answer was actually short and simple. *I have no idea.* But he couldn't say that. It took a bit more to satisfy the public interest.

'My father was very private about his work

26

methods and never shared them with anyone. Nor has he ever talked about his research or where his ideas actually came from. My father called his writing time "a condition in which he found himself" when the words simply came to him; he considered himself merely a recipient.'

That may have been true but it offered no real explanation. He had always wondered the same thing himself.

More questions followed. None of them was out of the ordinary. During the entire session he avoided her eyes, wanting her to have to wonder for a while, afraid that she had lost him. But the whole time he was conscious of her presence. At the edge of his field of vision he noticed every movement.

He always concluded by reading aloud, knowing that their similar voices were the best way to dupe people. The lights went down and the picture of his father in the background faded away. The little reading lamp on the podium was the only light required onstage. He often read the same passage. He had studied his father's recording and learned his intonation and rhythm. Now and then he raised his eyes and looked at her over the rim of his reading glasses. Outside these events he always wore contact lenses, but glasses made him look more like the original.

He knew the final sentences by heart. He had read them so many times, and now he could gaze out over the audience.

'But when the deed was done and the evening came, she was no longer sure. Like a lost soul the anxiety appeared and made camp by the same fire. No matter whether your action is evil or good, it spreads like rings on the water. Over vast expanses it will travel, finding ever new paths. That is why your influence is infinite, and also your guilt.'

The lecture was over. He slowly closed the book. The lights were turned up. When his voice faded away, all was quiet, and in the interval that followed, the fear managed to creep in. The ever-present horror that this time it would happen. The audience would rise as one body and with a deafening roar scream out their disappointment. At his incompetence. His mediocrity.

The sense of relief when the applause came, the kick that pulsed through his veins. The sound of all the enthusiastic hands surrounding him like a loving embrace.

He was fantastic! Everyone admired him.

And then the longing for the relaxation that only the minibar in his hotel room could provide.

He gave her a long look before he left the stage. *Come to my dressing-room afterwards.*

There were three messages on his answer machine. The first was from his daughter Ellen. He knew that he'd forgotten to ring as he had promised. The second from his wife Louise, who sounded angry because he'd forgotten to ring Ellen. And then the third, from a Marianne Folkesson who wanted to speak to him regarding Gerda Persson. The house-keeper from his childhood who was always there. It was years since he'd had any contact with her, but the Ragnerfeldt Corporation was still paying out a sum of money to her each month, a sort of pension after long and faithful service – on direct orders from his father. He jotted down Marianne Folkesson's number and was just about to punch in the numbers to his daughter's mobile.

A discreet knock at the door.

He flipped shut the phone and opened the door.

All those prize-winning words were finally super-fluous. In the arena that remained he was the one who was the star.

He would not have to suffer through the night alone.

CHAPTER 4

*E*xcellent.

The word was the first to cross her mind when she woke up and opened her eyes; she couldn't for the life of her understand why. If the word had been *exhausted*, or *corrode* or some other unpleasant-sounding one she would have been less surprised, but it had been *excellent*, and that was a word she had not felt the occasion to use in a long time.

Louise Ragnerfeldt sat at the kitchen table eating breakfast and listening to the sound of her daughter getting ready for school.

At close range, gradual change looked like a standstill. Only with the sharpness of distance did the successive disintegration become clear. Because that's what it was, a disintegration; there was no closing her eyes to it any longer.

Time passes. It was probably all right. Could be worse. But this assessment no longer applied. Not when she was about to turn forty-three, half her life already spent and now fully aware of how fast it had gone. Her twelve-year-old daughter was living proof of how fast the rest would go. So the word 'excellent' was needed regularly, but in order for the word to apply it had to come from the heart.

She sighed when once again she got his voicemail and hung up without leaving a message. Sometimes she would imagine it was her father-in-law she heard on the other end; their voices had become so similar. Every time she was appalled. It reminded her that her husband was as much a stranger to her as her father-in-law was, and would always remain. Maybe it had been partly her own fault that she never got to know him before the stroke. If so, it had not been intentional. She could normally talk with anyone, but had shrivelled in Axel Ragnerfeldt's presence and become silent and dull. She had chosen her words so carefully that in the end none of them was worth saying. On the occasions when she mustered her courage, her sentences would be hopelessly stilted, full of 'sort of's and 'maybe's, most of them sounding like questions rather than statements. In the end his scrutinising stares had made her mute.

Her reaction had surprised her. Maybe she thought that the sheer physical departure from her childhood home in Hudiksvall would have taken her farther. She was the first in her family to go to university. Her parents had supported her even though she sensed their vacillation when they had to defend her against those who thought she'd turned uppity. In her parents' house, they only spoke about concrete things, and words were not to be wasted. Thoughts were something you kept to yourself, and the general view was that everything got better if you didn't talk about it. Books were something that educated people read, of a different class of society more elegant than their own – teachers, doctors and managers. Respect for the powers that be had been passed down for generations and was a natural part of life. It was thought best to keep to their own sort, which seldom required any expansion of their horizons. There was no bitterness; a great sense of solidarity with the other families in the area prevailed, and even when times were hard, people helped each other out in any way they could. And had a booze-up on the weekend to recharge the batteries. But they were always at a disadvantage to those allied with words. Lowered heads and caps in hand at PTA meetings and visits to the doctor. And anyone who tried to make his way beyond his circle, as though it wasn't good enough, was regarded as a traitor. Writers were something mysterious and other, with a distant, elevated mystique. Like magicians, they knew about things that were impossible for other people to grasp; they could capture the unattainable and describe what nobody else could see.

She remembered how proud she was at first to bear the Ragnerfeldt name. Her friends would get a dreamy look in their eyes whenever he was mentioned, and they wanted to hear all about what he was like. But when they noticed her ambivalence and lack of enthusiasm, she was met with suspicion, as if her words had sprung from envy. No one wanted to hear anything negative about Axel Ragnerfeldt, the national treasure. With all his wisdom about good and evil he had chiselled such astonishing stories out of their Swedish language. She stopped saying what she felt and wholeheartedly joined his crowd of admirers, at least outwardly. It was easier that way. The tremendous awe she felt for her father-in-law had made her tongue-tied, and she had never got to know him. Now he was the one who was mute, and even though she would never in her life admit it openly, it sometimes felt like a liberation.

'I'm off now.'

Louise got up from the kitchen table and tightened her dressing-gown belt. 'Wait a second!'

'But I have to be there in ten minutes.'

She rushed through the flat and caught up with her daughter in the hall. She hugged her quickly and zipped up her jacket.

'Bye then. It was at seven o'clock, wasn't it? Did Pappa ring you?'

'No.'

Louise swallowed and struggled to smile. 'He'll show up, you'll see.'

Ellen didn't reply. The door closed and Louise was left standing there. She closed her eyes and cursed the fact that she'd become part of this. Her own suffering was nothing compared to what she saw in her daughter's eyes. The appeal for attention. That just once he might notice her.

*   *   *

Thirteen years had passed since they first met. She was thirty then and Jan-Erik was thirty-seven. Two years earlier, after an eight-year relationship, she had been left by the man she had thought was the one. Her biological clock was not yet ticking, but the sadness and humiliation she felt at being dumped had made her wary. Then she had met Jan-Erik. His courtship had been the symbol that great true love arrives as suddenly as lightning. His determination had overwhelmed her. Nothing had been too expensive, no road too far to travel, no phone conversation too long. Eagerly, almost furiously, he had swept her up. Beyond all doubt and all suspicion, as if they were running a sprint. She interpreted his haste as a proof of genuine passion. The days were filled with surprises, and at night he slept close to her. As though he were a child afraid that she might disappear if she didn't hold on to him. His glowing devotion made her dizzy, and after having been rejected and dumped she now felt restored, the centrepiece of Jan-Erik Ragnerfeldt's universe.

A little over a year after they met, Ellen was born.

With that result achieved, Louise realised that he had been courting her the same way an estate agent impatiently hurries a prospective buyer through the rooms of a dilapidated house.

She went into the bathroom. Stuck her hand in the shower, turned on the water, and stood on the pleasantly warm floor waiting for the water to heat up. The bathroom had recently been renovated. Jan-Erik had given her carte blanche to make it just the way she wanted. She would have preferred to discuss how *they* would like it, but Jan-Erik hadn't had time, and she didn't know him well enough to know what he liked. It was a vicious circle. Their outgoings demanded that he work a lot, but the more he worked, the greater their outgoings seemed to pile up. She looked at the three specially commissioned nameplates above the towel racks: Ellen, Jan-Erik and Louise. If she didn't know better, she might think that those three names belonged together in one family.

She hung up her dressing gown and stepped into the shower.

Maybe Jan-Erik had seen her as an attractive prize. She had just had her fifteen minutes of fame when he whirled into her life. At least in the direct spotlight that prevailed in the world of high culture, the world to which the subsequent disintegration had shown it was so important for him to belong. After the wearisome separation from her by now ex-boyfriend, she had suddenly felt a need to write her story, even though she'd never before seriously concerned herself with words. In a moment of self-confidence she had sent off her efforts to a publisher. The poetry collection had attracted great attention, and the now yellowing clippings from the newspapers' cultural pages were filled with words of praise. An exceptional debut, they had written. A promise for the future, she had been called. But during the thirteen years that had passed, both her existence and her writing skills had fallen into oblivion. If she had believed in her naïve stupidity that her new surname would help her literary ambitions, she soon realised that she was mistaken. Her creation had been sucked into the black hole that surrounded the name of Axel Ragnerfeldt; any attention that might compete was effectively shooed off into the wings.

She turned off the tap and reached for the towel. She dried herself and methodically rubbed in moisturising lotion.

With hindsight it was difficult to discern the various twists and turns. Or know which tiny steps had inevitably led them to where they found themselves now. She believed that Jan-Erik's attention had faded at the same rate as her name had vanished from the newspapers. Maybe it was a trophy he sought, something to decorate the Ragnerfeldt family living room. But when the plain pine of her talent was revealed it turned out to clash with the elegant mahogany of the bookshelf. Once the centre of Jan-Erik Ragnerfeldt's universe, she had been relegated to the caretaker in his empire.

She looked at her breasts in the mirror. Round and just the right size, precisely as she had always wanted them to be. The scars were no longer visible. She had got a good price because it was a friend's husband who had operated on her, and Jan-Erik didn't know a thing about it. Why should she tell him? Her breasts were about as interesting to him as the boy next door's guinea pig. Perhaps even less.

She recalled how things had been in the beginning. Any occasion could lead to a passionate scene on the carpet in the living room, on the kitchen table, or anywhere else the mood took them. He had been a fantastic lover. His desire to give her pleasure, to put his own needs aside, to satisfy her at any cost, had astounded her. When she tried to reciprocate he quickly took back the initiative; sometimes it felt like he enjoyed her pleasure more than his own. He was like a ringmaster, skilfully performing his tricks, and she came to feel that her orgasms were proof that she really loved him. She abandoned herself to pleasure, almost ashamed of her own passion. But eventually it struck her that their conversations were becoming fewer and farther between; no matter how much sex they had she felt the distance between them growing. Finally she realised that all communication took place between their erogenous zones.

She tried to talk to him about it, but it was no use. If communication was difficult for them in general, words were hopeless when it came to sex. As if everything they had devoted themselves to without embarrassment lacked any sort of name. He took her tentative objections as a criticism of his ability, and the only way to prove the opposite was to let the conversation devolve into yet another act of intercourse. Then one evening – it was one of those evenings when she had wanted to talk – he couldn't get an erection. She assured him that it didn't matter, she just wanted to hold him close, but her words had no effect. Most of all she remembered the rage in his eyes when he pulled away like a beaten dog and locked himself in his office. The months that followed became silent in every respect. At first, she thought the words that might have helped them had simply gone missing, but soon she realised they had never been present at all. She had mistaken the strong feeling of connection that arose when they had sex for love, when actually she hardly knew him. She had waited for ever for him to return. His reluctance became obvious, his surliness left her in despair. She tried everything. Romantic candlelit dinners, beautiful clothes, theatre tickets. Nothing had brought them closer together. Her failed attempts only intensified the problem, and the distance between them grew even greater. Then, after a dinner with her in-laws, long after she had given up hope, he had unexpectedly crawled over to her side of the bed. Wordlessly and with the bedside lamp turned off, his fingers fumbling from the wine, he had prepared the way, and with aggressive thrusts forced himself to climax.

That had been the last time. Eleven years had passed since then.

Her expectations had readjusted to their new way of living, in which physical closeness might extend at most to a pat on the shoulder when it couldn't be avoided.

She looked at her naked body in the mirror. A little older, more mature, but well-kept after the surgery and hard workouts.

Desired by no one.

With each day that passed her longing became more unmanageable. A desire to once more experience the intensity of passion. A brief moment of balancing on the knife edge where life was at its most intimate.

She cupped her hands round her breasts and closed her eyes. To be able to give in. To be forced to acquiesce to the life force of passion and surrender. And then to rest in an embrace that assured her she was good enough.

At exactly ten o'clock, after a brisk walk, she put her key in the door of Boutique Louise on Nybrogatan. The Ragnerfeldt Corporation was the landlord of the shop. With Axel's permission Jan-Erik had arranged it for her seven years ago, when her writing talent had ceased as suddenly as it had begun. Exclusive designer clothing for rich customers, most of them living nearby. She had done her best to adopt the lifestyle that was expected of her, but at ever greater cost to her soul. She had trained as a civil engineer in information technology, but after her maternity leave she had never returned. With all the rapid developments in the computer field, she had never caught up. Besides, Jan-Erik thought that being the proprietor of a boutique was better, and perhaps she had even let herself be enticed for a while. The truth was that the boutique was a luxury hobby. Sales were few and did not contribute much to the household budget. But at least she had something to do, so that Jan-Erik could in good conscience devote himself to his own interests. And every time she pointed out that he was working too hard, she was told that it was necessary for the family finances. She was completely dependent on Jan-Erik and the Ragnerfeldt Corporation.

She hung up her coat in the alcove behind the counter and took out her mobile phone. Jan-Erik still hadn't called, even though she'd left a message to remind him of their daughter's show that night. She gave a heavy sigh and dialled Alice Ragnerfeldt's number instead. It rang many times, but that was not unusual. Her mother-in-law sometimes suffered from vascular cramps and claimed that the doctor said that a capful of whisky each morning was good medicine. Louise had no idea how big a cap was on the doctor's bottle, but the one on her mother-in-law's was clearly enormous. After the twelfth ring she answered.

'Alice Ragnerfeldt.'

'Hello, it's Louise. How are you feeling today?'

There was no reply at the other end. Louise regretted her choice of words. She already knew the answer.

'Fine, thanks, pretty much as usual.'

Louise hastened to reply before the detailed report began.

'I wondered whether you wanted to accompany me to a play at Ellen's school this evening.'

'This evening?'

'Yes. At seven.'

There was a long silence. Louise could hear her mother-in-law's heavy breathing. And then the question that she knew would follow.

'Is Jan-Erik going?'

'I don't know whether he'll be home in time. He gave a lecture in Göteborg yesterday, so he'll be coming back by train sometime in the afternoon or evening.'

Even as she answered she wondered why she didn't just tell Alice the truth. Why did she always instinctively defend him? It was as though a switch was thrown in her head each time she was confronted with her in-laws. A pretence that needed to be maintained to avoid insidious attacks and to prove that she fitted in. If her relationship to Axel was non-existent, then her relationship to Alice was more highly charged. At first openly displeased, over the years her mother-in-law had resigned herself to accepting the marriage. It was better than nothing, and something in Louise strove for that acceptance, to be admitted in earnest. To be a real part of the Ragnerfeldt family and not merely basking in their radiance.

For the moment Alice Ragnerfeldt could not give an answer and asked Louise to ring back that afternoon.

★   ★   ★

41

As expected, Jan-Erik did not show up at the play. Her maternal heart was filled with holy fury when, as so many times before, she saw her daughter survey the audience expectantly, how her eyes searched for him, her hopes extinguished when his seat remained empty. The anguish Louise felt afterwards, as she tried to reduce the sense of betrayal and soothe her daughter's disappointment. Her anger and power lessness had thwarted all possibility of enjoying the performance.

She couldn't live this way. Not really. Not if she ever again wanted to be able to use the word 'excellent'.

He didn't show up until around eleven. Ellen had gone to bed, and Louise was sitting with an anaesthetising drink in the easy chair by the bay window.

'Hello!' she heard the cheerful voice from the hall.

She wished she were in bed already, hiding in the dark with her back turned so she could avoid seeing him. She was so utterly sick of what she'd become.

She heard his steps approaching and then he appeared in the living room. He looked tired. His face was puffy.

'Hi.'

'Hi.'

She looked down and hastily brushed some non-existent fluff from the arm of the chair.

'I'm sorry I didn't make it to Ellen's play. The train was late.'

'You seem to have bad luck with trains. I thought it was last night you gave the lecture.'

He went over to the little gilt table with the bottles of spirits. With his back to her he poured himself a whisky. He was doing that more often lately. At night when she returned to the bedroom from the toilet, she would be met by the distinct odour of his breath. But considering what she was holding in her hand it was hard to raise objections.

'I had a couple of meetings booked today with some companies in Göteborg. About fundraising for the clinic in Somalia. Anything new here?'

No. Not if you ignore the fact that you've broken your daughter's heart again, she wanted to say.

'What clinic?'

He turned to her in surprise.

'Don't you know? The clinic we set up last year.'

'No, I don't know. How could I know if you never told me?'

Her voice was hard and prickly. She hated the bitterness that had crept into her, so slowly and silently that she didn't discover it until it had already taken root.

'Then I apologise. I thought I'd told you, or perhaps I thought you wouldn't be interested.'

She looked out the window across the tops of the trees towards the church tower. It was true what he said, she wasn't particularly interested. She knew that financially they depended on his work and it was useful; that the foundations and orphanages he established in Axel's name saved lives out there in remote places. But to be interested in his work was like legitimising her own tormentor. To always be rejected. Something else was always more important and took precedence over what she and Ellen had to offer. Maybe she was selfish. Otherwise she might have been able to set Ellen's and her welfare aside for a greater cause. But she was not that better person.

'I asked your mother if she wanted to go to the play with us.'

'That was nice of you.'

'No, not really. It wasn't for her sake, it was for Ellen's. But she couldn't come. She had to stay at home and take care of her leg cramps, her bad hip and the tinnitus in her ears.'

Jan-Erik drained the last of the whisky in his glass and poured another one.

'It's not easy for her. She did turn eighty this year. We'll have to hope that all three of us can go next time.'

She looked out of the window again. Wishing instead that she were on the other side of one of the windows across the street.

'Yes, that would be nice. A real Ragnerfeldt onslaught. Ellen would certainly appreciate not being the child who draws the smallest crowd for once.'

She loathed every syllable that came out of her mouth. Hated having turned into someone whose

44

last chance for satisfaction was to think she had the right to utter those words. Often they were trivialities that actually meant nothing; she used them merely to vent her frustration. Complaining about the way he left his shoes in the hall, the way the crockery was arranged in the dishwasher, the way the cushions on the sofa weren't in the right place. What she hated most was that Jan-Erik refused to be provoked. Like one of those invincible figures in Ellen's computer games he would rise unscathed after each mortal blow, always ready for more. His equanimity drove her crazy. She wasn't even important enough to cause a row.

He set down his empty whisky tumbler on the glass table top.

'I'm going to bed now. I have to see Mamma tomorrow. Gerda Persson has died.'

'Oh, really? And who is Gerda Persson?'

For a moment he looked surprised.

'Our old housekeeper.'

Gerda Persson. She had never heard the name before.

'Somebody called from the council wanting to discuss the funeral. I presume we must be the closest acquaintances she has. Or had. She was part of our household for my entire childhood and stayed there until 1979, maybe 1980. So it's not too much to ask that we help out with what we can. Mamma knew her better, so I'll have to discuss it with her.'

He walked out and soon she heard the bathroom

door close and lock. As if he were making sure that she wouldn't suddenly storm in and assault him.

She was living with a stranger. Gerda Persson had lived in his house for his entire childhood. And he had never before mentioned her name. Yet another sign of his success at keeping her out of his life. Present and past. And she had no idea what he thought about the future.

Her life was divided into two compartments: one was full of longing to recapture her own dreams; the other of bitterness over the way everything had turned out, including Jan-Erik's complete indifference. It was between these millstones that everything was being ground into a fine dust that was slowly settling over her life. Of course there was a way out. Many people had chosen it before her. Divorce figures were so high that grocers were giving out queue tickets for packing boxes. But there was a chasm one had to cross between *I would really like to* and *Now I will*. Ellen was part of that chasm. How could she allow herself to make a decision that would also affect her daughter so much? The other aspect was financial. Everything of value in her life belonged to the Ragnerfeldt Corporation, and its owner was still Axel Ragnerfeldt: the flat, the car, the shop. In a divorce she would be left destitute. But only as long as Axel was alive. She thought about it sometimes, and more and more often lately, the fact that her situation would be different the day the inheritance was divided up. She had begun to sense what was actually lurking beneath the bitterness; sometimes it would stick out a rough hand and grab hold of her. A tremendous sorrow over their unforgivable failure.

If no decisive change occurred, divorce would be the only way out, as soon as Axel died.

The alternative was to stay and for ever eradicate the word 'excellent' from her consciousness.

CHAPTER 5

He had learned to breathe so it sounded as if he was asleep. As he lay in his pyjamas on his side of the double bed he listened to Louise's bare feet padding across the oak parquet floor, then her hanging up her dressing gown, sitting down on the edge of the bed and removing her necklace, rings and earrings. He heard the clatter when the jewellery landed one by one in the little crystal bowl on the nightstand. He heard her pull out the drawer, unscrew the lid of the moisturiser and finally the sound of her rubbing it carefully on her hands. Night after night – the same routine. If the word 'boredom' could be visualised, this was a precise example.

He hadn't slept much the night before, yet he couldn't get to sleep. His heart was pounding unpleasantly, and he wished that he could sneak out of bed unnoticed and have another whisky. And besides, even though Louise thought him incapable of it, he felt guilty at having missed Ellen's play. Again. It hadn't been on purpose. He had planned to take an earlier train. But then the woman had asked him to stay another few hours, told him that she could get off work, and he hadn't been able to resist. As usual, his judgement had slipped down between his legs, and for a couple of hours he had watched with delight the effect of his talents, felt the satisfaction of his own ability when he made her whimper in ecstasy. The instant it was all over, he had been filled with self-disgust. A distaste so strong it was as if she'd suddenly sprouted tentacles.

But he missed the train.

He heard Louise's breathing deepen and presumed she was asleep. But maybe she could fake it as well as he could. They really ought to get separate bedrooms; then at least they could read in peace in the evenings. But to achieve that they would have to lay their problems on the table; open confrontations were something he hated. They could easily overflow and suddenly involve something altogether different from what one had intended in the beginning. It was much too risky.

The guilt he felt was hard to describe. He wouldn't be able to stand his home at all if he couldn't travel so often. And yet he had the same sense of relief each time he came back. On the verge of tears and with a heavy conscience, he wanted more than anything to be on good terms again. Like a boxer's punchbag that silently takes blow after blow, he was willing to endure her sarcasm. So often he vowed to himself that everything was going to be different; he was going to be a better person, drink in moderation, keep his cock in his trousers. But despite all his good intentions, restlessness soon caught up with him, and the itchy sensation in his body was impossible to quell. Then he would go out and it would start all over again. It was his only means of relief.

He took a swallow of water from the glass on the nightstand. A strip of light from a street-lamp came through the Venetian blinds and fell across the bed. He looked at Louise, who seemed to be sleeping, turned away from him.

Thirteen years ago, he had been certain. After an endless series of brief affairs and one-night stands, he had finally found the woman he was looking for. The one who would take away the grinding feeling of emptiness and make him whole. He had tried before, but those women had never come up to expectations. This time everything would be different. He was tired of the life he was leading, and more and more often he would see that look in the eyes of younger women – he was starting to become pathetic. Thirty-seven years old. It was high time he ended this late teenage rebellion that had started when he came home from the USA as a twenty-one-year-old. All the nights in bars, the drugs, the money that was frittered away as fast as it appeared. All the strangers lying next to him when he woke up in the morning, never as attractive in the morning light as they'd been in the intoxication of the night before. Louise would be the armour he needed. The one who would make him want to create some sort of structure in his life and finally prove that he could do more than shelter in the shadow of his illustrious surname. She had fitted perfectly. Stylish, beautiful and a celebrated poet. His father would be impressed. His mother, of course, would never be satisfied.

He cautiously pushed back the covers and with a wary look at her back got up with infinite slowness so that he wouldn't rouse her. She didn't move. He took his robe and quietly closed the door behind him. He had learned how to sneak across the squeaky floorboards. Ellen's door was ajar and her red lava lamp was on. For a moment he stood looking at her, not really knowing why. It was just so much easier to release the love he felt for her when she was asleep. Her duvet had slipped down, and he tucked her in carefully before he moved on.

He had a bottle of whisky hidden behind the books in his office. He left the door open so he could hear if anyone was coming and took a few gulps straight from the bottle. He looked through the business post but left it unopened. Two of the letters looked like fan mail. His father still got a couple every week. Jan-Erik usually answered them with a photograph and a rubber stamp of Axel's signature.

In the bathroom he brushed his teeth, carefully

scrubbing away the smell of alcohol. Then he moistened a little toilet paper and wiped off the white spots on the bathroom mirror. A simple effort to avoid being reprimanded.

Then he crept back into bed.

Everything had started so well. He couldn't get enough of her. For the first time he thought he'd found the woman who could hold his glance like a magnet instead of letting his eyes stray to look at other women. Louise was his grand passion. Enveloped in mystery, she had at first rejected his advances, and her resistance had brought him to the edge of insanity. It was like throwing himself into a whirlpool. Everything about her intensified his ardour. He always wanted to be near her, to know what she was thinking when she was silent, to smell her scent, make love to her, hold her tight and never let her go. Finally she had capitulated.

The enemy had held back a bit longer this time. It had prowled about once in a while and then retreated. Jan-Erik had believed that he had finally won. He didn't notice how it slowly but surely tightened its circles until once again he was surrounded. She began to demand too much, take up far too much room. He felt a greater and greater need to dilute her. Phone calls came when he least expected them. Intimate dinners by candlelight, when she inquisitively dug for secrets and without being invited shared some of her own. Little presents and surprises that compelled his gratitude. There were longer and longer detours to sort out day-to-day trivialities before he was given a chance to demonstrate his prowess in the bedroom. His suspicion grew; he saw clearly how she was trying to wriggle her way farther and farther in to make herself indispensable. And then it was all over. As always, the mystery was transformed into knowledge, and everything exciting became routine. Her secret underwear, which had occupied his fantasies for entire days, suddenly hung on the clothesline under fluorescent light when he shaved in the morning. Her beauty that had captivated him was organised in small labelled jars and bottles in the bathroom cabinet. Her thoughts that filled him with such wonder turned out to be just as ordinary as everyone else's. A woman was like a distant city in the night. From far off the lights glittered like magical jewels, tempting and enticing with all their promises and possibilities. But close up the city looked like all the others. Full of buildings that needed renovation and with rubbish along the kerbs. It was not companionship he sought; that gave him no relief. What he wanted was glowing passion and uninhibited sex, and he was furious with her because she had duped him. His love had once again turned out to be a disappointment. Like a cocaine buzz. He had been high for a while, and then irrevocably plummeted even further into restlessness.

He had planned to break off the whole thing

without explaining why. Just go out for cigarettes and never come back. That same evening she asked him to sit down on the sofa, took his hand, and with a happy smile told him they were going to have a baby.

He woke up before the alarm clock rang. Quietly he went over to Louise's side and turned it off before he went to wake his daughter. He wanted so much to have a moment alone with her, have a chance to ask her forgiveness for missing the play.

'Ellen?'

She stirred a bit.

'Ellen, it's time to get up.' He put his hand on her head and patted her awkwardly. She opened her eyes and looked up at him.

'Hi.' She sounded truly happy and started to stretch up her arms. He gave her a smile and wanted to say something.

'I'm making a little breakfast. What do you usually have?'

'Just some milk and a piece of bread. With cheese.'

He intended to apologise now but couldn't find the words. He stood there for a moment, searching, before he gave up and left the room. Once again he was struck by how hard it was to know how to behave. He loved his daughter, but she also scared him. Her obvious dependence and need of him made him feel anxious. As if he were forced to defend himself. He was incapable of giving her what she wanted from him. He simply didn't have it in him. She was an ever-present reminder of his inadequacy.

He made her bread and cheese then fetched the morning paper. When he returned she was sitting at the kitchen table. He sat down opposite her. Now. Now he would apologise.

'How's school, then?'

'Fine.' She kept eating.

'Do you have a lot of tests?'

'Some. Not that many.'

She drank her milk and got up to get more from the fridge. He realised that time was running out. He made another stab.

'I just wanted to say that, that, uh, if you want another piece of bread I can get you one.'

'No, thanks. Where's Mamma?'

'She's still asleep.'

'I can't find my green hair-slide.'

In a single gulp she finished her milk and put the glass in the dishwasher. Before he could say anything else, she vanished towards their bedroom and he could hear murmuring voices. Private conversations that never included him.

Ellen was one of the reasons why he had stayed. He would lose her if they separated. The bond between them was much too fragile to compete with the chain that Louise had managed to forge. But there was also another reason, so secret that only he and his father knew about it. It had to do with appearances.

Ragnerfeldts did not get divorced.

At the time Ellen was born, his father had not harboured particularly high hopes regarding Jan-Erik's talent for marriage, and even though the criticism could now only flash like lightning from his eyes, it would become quite clear the day he died and the inheritance was distributed. Jan-Erik could not be denied his legal right of inheritance, but his father had always been clever at manipulating the law. With his deft pen he had seen to it that Jan-Erik's share would be as small as possible if he wasn't living an honourable life on the day the will was read. Jan-Erik himself had been allowed to read the document. It was dated on Ellen's first birthday, and in impeccable legal language his father had confirmed his supremacy. With words oozing with contempt he had bequeathed large sums to Louise and Ellen. As long as the marriage was intact nothing would change; Jan-Erik would remain the executor with the obligation to render accounts to the auditor. But in the event of a divorce, everything would be disclosed, and Louise would be the major beneficiary.

'It's for Ellen's sake,' his father had explained. 'She's our bequest to the future.' They had returned to the dinner table, and Jan-Erik had got drunk on vintage wine. He had joined half-heartedly in the harmless chatter that hid the rage he was feeling. Why had the important future heritage skipped a generation?

That evening he had tried to overcome his aversion and have sex with Louise.

It had felt like fucking his jailer.

CHAPTER 6

Alice Ragnerfeldt didn't need an alarm clock to get up early in the morning. Even though she would rather stay asleep. She'd always said she preferred the night-time, revelling in the space those sleeping left behind. But being awake and having insomnia were two different things. Nowadays she wanted nothing more than to be able to sleep, but the sleeping pills only worked for a few hours. In the small hours she would wake up with vascular cramps. A heaviness around her heart, as if all the world's horrors had landed on her chest. Getting old was nothing but one long, drawn-out torment. The face of a strange old woman in her mirror. The anticipation of youth had been transformed as if by magic into the bewilderment of old age. The realisation that everything had gone so fast and so little had been accomplished. Chance occurrences that imperceptibly slid over into conditions that could not be budged. Decisions were made even though she could never remember being involved. People appeared, briefly kept her company and then departed.

Everything had become dispersed but nothing had been lost. The essence of her life remained, like preserved fruit from a season long gone.

Yet it wasn't the vascular cramps that woke her this morning, but a pain in her right calf. She had been waiting for it, and as she stretched out her foot to alleviate the cramp, she turned on the light and pulled out the newspaper clippings from her nightstand. Taking them out of the plastic sleeve she immediately found the right one. *15 September. 900,000 Swedes are struck by kidney disease – most of them without knowing it. A simple test can reveal kidney failure.* She read through the list of symptoms again: headache in the morning, fatigue the first and most common sign, itching, swollen legs, then at a later stage nausea and vomiting. There, there it was. She knew she had seen it. *Leg cramps are also common, probably because of the disturbance of the salt equilibrium.* She would ask Jan-Erik to drive her to the clinic. Ring and get an appointment. She would demand that they take a new sample, even if she had to pay for it herself.

She stood up and raised the window blind. Outside it was still dark. She put on her slippers and dressing gown, and went out to the kitchen. Tore a page off the calendar and filled the coffee-machine with water. Not just one cup today. Jan-Erik and a Marianne Folkesson were supposed to visit around ten, so she might as well make the coffee now. And she needed to see if she had

59

anything ironed to wear, now that someone from outside the neighbourhood was coming to have a look at Axel Ragnerfeldt's wife.

Gerda Persson.

She hadn't a clue why they should have anything to do with Gerda's funeral, but Jan-Erik had insisted. She poured a glass of water and took her pills. She skipped her little shot of whisky today; she didn't want to smell of booze when Jan-Erik arrived. He didn't come very often, as he was so busy. It was mostly Louise she heard from these days. Imagine, he was already fifty years old. Her Jan-Erik. How the years flew by. Annika would have been forty-five. She clenched her jaw. It happened less and less, but now and then the memory would flit past uninvited. The tyranny of age. The slowness of the present speeded up the past.

As a young girl she had known everything. Strong-willed and choosy, she'd had definite ideas about the way life should be. Influenced by the feminist movement, she'd be damned if she'd follow the paths that others had taken before her. The modern woman had to be strong and take responsibility for herself, demand more of herself but also of men. Together men and women would create a better world. That's what the feminists had written, and Alice had agreed with every word.

As the third in a family of five children, she'd obediently helped out with chores on the farm, trying out of sheer self-preservation to adapt to the little community in which the path one was expected to take was blatantly clear. But in secret she harboured a hope for something greater. She had been the odd one out in her childhood home. She wondered why she couldn't be satisfied like her siblings. Why she could never fix her eyes on things within sight, but always felt compelled to direct her longing towards the horizon. Away from the crunch of the gravel path under her bicycle wheels and the distant cries from a football pitch. Away from the smell of new-mown grass and the familiar faces in the little town. Away from the security of the season's recurring daily chores.

Books had been her refuge. And she had counted the days until she could head off for the big city and all its opportunities.

She poured herself a cup of coffee and put the rest in a thermos. Sitting down, she looked at her legs. They were a bit swollen, especially the right calf where the cramp was. She would ring the clinic as soon as it opened. She glanced at the kitchen clock. In three hours Jan-Erik would be here. Before that she'd put her hair in curlers so she'd look nice when he arrived. As nice as she could look, these days. Her thick, chestnut-brown hair was also a thing of the past, but she could always amuse herself by thinking about it.

Back then, in the late forties, she had worn her long hair pinned up. She had turned twenty-one, thus was of age, and her parents could no longer force her to stay at home. Even so, her departure had occurred with much commotion, and she had left with only ominous warnings in her bags. She took lodgings with an angry lady in Vasastan, in the centre of Stockholm, and went out looking for a job; what sort was not important. She wanted to write, and all hardships were acceptable since she knew where she was headed and nothing could stop her. Damned if she wouldn't show her family back home that she'd made the right decision. On the second day she was hired as an assistant at a Wassberg's beauty parlour in the City Palace building at Norrmalmstorg. Her duties were to wash the customers' hair, make coffee, and keep all the hairdressers' equipment clean, the brushes combed out. She could perform most of her tasks while listening to the rich conversations between customer and hairdresser. Sometimes usable as inspiration for the stories she wrote at night; in the best cases for small articles that she sold for cash to some newspaper.

As a new immigrant to the big city she quickly discovered the places frequented by similar-minded people. Those with extravagant dreams and empty wallets whose genius would be discovered any day now. Those who considered themselves gifts to the world and whose distinctive characters would in future appear in cultural history; young women and men, lingering over glasses of beer or wine, artistic equals and presumptive bed companions. The war was over and the future one long avenue of possibilities. The restaurants Tennstopet, W6, Pilen and Löwet. They would spend every evening smoking Gauloises to compensate for not being in Paris, preferably near one of the tables where the journalists from the big dailies drowned their sorrows. Axel had been one of that crowd of young people, someone she hadn't noticed at first. Nor had he shown any particular interest in her.

She got up and went to the refrigerator, checking she wasn't out of milk. Jan-Erik always took milk in his coffee. She drank it black, a habit from the days when it was supposed to help her stay alert even though she was cross-eyed with fatigue. When the days were filled with hair and the nights with pounding on her portable Royal typewriter that she had bought in a second-hand shop for seventeen kronor. At least that was her routine until the angry landlady forbade her to use the noisy machine and forced her to write in longhand. The waste-paper basket filled up with crumpled pages and returned manuscripts from publishers and magazine editors. In the evenings anguish could be shared and diluted with red wine, only to reappear with the next rejected manuscript.

No replies came to her letters home, despite her reassurances that everything was going well. She received a single note from one of her older siblings, a printed greeting card with wishes for a Happy Christmas and New Year. When things were at their worst she sometimes wished she were back down on aching knees amongst the weeds in the turnip fields, or feeling the sweaty prickle of hay on the drying racks: tangible results of an honest day's work instead of feeling her mind rambling on endlessly. She was just about to give up when it finally happened. A few sentences in a letter, proving that her literary turnip fields were cleared and the drying racks were ready.

She smiled at the memory, remembering how she strode into Tennstopet restaurant like a queen and announced that her novel had been accepted. She felt as if she were physically raised above the crowd. Her personal, meticulous choice of letter combinations had been judged as more skilful than those of all the others. Her door had opened, while the others were still knocking on theirs. The smiles – some honest and happy for her sake, but most of them filled with distrust. How could the world be blind to their greatness yet take notice of her insignificant scribblings? From across the table, Axel's blue eyes had burned into hers, taking her breath away. He was the only one not smiling, not toasting and congratulating her. He just gave her a look that screamed that he wanted to have her. Have her right then, if only she would stop lowering herself to the level of the riffraff surrounding them and follow him out of there. The thought had been dizzying: for once to say to hell with all obligations and let herself be swept along; finally to live the life for which she was destined. After that evening they had made a pact. *Art above all else.* Together they would realise their dreams and give the world what it had always longed for; nothing would stand in their way. And with a passion that almost killed them they had set to work.

At first everything had been wonderful. Too good to be true. She recalled how she often had that very thought. As if all her childhood dreams about how things could be had come to pass. She wrote long letters home and told them all about it, no longer as compliant, but still she got no reply.

They stopped going out with the old crowd. Hidden from the world they gave themselves over to their creativity. She received a small advance from her publisher, and occasionally they managed to sell a poem or short article to some magazine, which made their scant income stretch a bit further. Through Axel's contacts they were able to rent a little house with two rooms and kitchen just outside Stockholm. Each had a room with a desk and bed. Being a couple made them bold, and what before had felt lonely and vulnerable now became a bulwark against mediocrity; two co-conspirators wrapped up in their separate worlds but at night reunited in the heat of passion.

She sat down at the kitchen table again and stared at her coffee cup. It had been bought by Gerda some time in the seventies. Maybe she should tell that to the woman from the council so they could mention it at the funeral. Always something. She hadn't taken much with her when she moved to the flat after Axel had his stroke. She had no idea why she'd brought the coffee cups along. She hadn't been able to get away fast enough, and Jan-Erik and Louise were left to pack most of the things. Maybe this was the reason – the cups were quite ugly when she inspected them more closely.

She played with her wedding ring. Slid it down her finger and looked at the impression it had left. For fifty-four years she had worn it, and it had carved its way deeper and deeper into her finger. Just the two of them and a minister; no guests were invited, not even Axel's parents. She knew he'd regretted it later, but since her parents refused to put in an appearance, his shouldn't be there either. Fair's fair.

Or that's what he'd said back then.

In order to demonstrate their union they had both renounced their surnames and become united in the joint name 'Ragnerfeldt', the name that would bear their words out into the world. They both had novels published, first Alice and then Axel immediately after. Their new name became a constant on the arts pages. Their youth held the critics back, but more and more words of praise crept into the reviews. With genuine interest they participated in each other's creations, following each other's meandering thought processes, offering suggestions when needed and words of encouragement when things were going badly. After they both published a second novel, their affiliation was secured, but it brought higher expectations as well. Their books did not sell in great numbers, and they were utterly dependent on the publishers' willingness to pay advances. The increased pressure made it harder for them to write. It had been so much easier to be new and to surprise people than it was to live up to expectations. They were both afflicted by writer's block and retreated into their own work, becoming indifferent to the other's. Fewer words were written when they met in the evening, and their reunion half-hearted since they both became mired in frustration over what had not been achieved. But even half-hearted seed is good enough to conceive a child. A year later they bought the house in Nacka, and Jan-Erik was born. Contact with their old friends ceased completely since their new bourgeois life in the wealthy suburb aroused only contempt or disinterest. And a new era began. Their creativity was hampered by wakeful nights and hazy days. The baby demanded new routines that conflicted with publishers' expectations. Where mutual consideration had prevailed, it now became necessary to guard their own territory. The fictional characters of the novel suddenly invaded reality to compete with the shrieking baby who demanded constant attention. They were not content with the occasions that arose when Jan-Erik was sleeping, or with the scheduled writing times that they finally had to establish to avoid arguments. And then, like a preliminary solution, Gerda came into the picture. At least to remove all the dirt and take care of the cooking and other daily chores which had forced them into a situation that left not the slightest room for creativity.

Gerda Persson.

Once again Alice felt irritated that she was expected to take an interest in the woman's death. It was odd what a fuss was being made. Money was so tight everywhere nowadays that the council must have more important things to worry about. What she knew about Gerda was not much, despite the fact that they'd lived under the same roof for almost twenty-five years, from the years Jan-Erik was a baby until the day Gerda turned sixty-seven and needed a housekeeper of her own. And she needed one even before that; she was quite slovenly, if truth be told. But Axel had refused to replace her and let a stranger into the house. He had thought that Alice was exaggerating her criticism. She in turn hadn't understood what difference it would make to exchange one stranger for another. It was a mystery to her how Axel could have any opinion about the household, since he was always cooped up in his office. Gerda was constantly there, padding through the house like a cat, but they hadn't really known each other. The boundary between the gentry and servants was clear as glass, and they had both been equally inclined to maintain that distance. But Gerda always had a front-row seat. She had witnessed Alice's transformation from Axel's companion and artistic equal to representative wife who was expected to stand by his side and be happy for his sake, watching as he received his honours. Gerda had been along for the whole ride, and Alice begrudged the fact that Gerda knew that she knew that she knew.

Because in the end it had all turned into a perpetual power struggle. By then Annika was already growing in Alice's womb, and with her birth the fight was over. The schism that Alice felt had stifled the last remnants of her creativity and put her permanently in Axel's shadow. She had tried to fight her impulses but couldn't tell whether they were coming from inside or had been sparked from the outside. While Axel felt legitimised to pursue his dreams, her duty had been to renounce hers. The children and what they demanded of her became a threat to all that had once been her destiny: their shouts that disturbed her in the middle of whatever she was doing; their tears that she was expected to soothe; their dependence that ensnared her.

Alice Ragnerfeldt swallowed hard and stared into space. Only the eternal ticking of the kitchen clock held her in the present.

Because what was threatening to suffocate her and had been so obvious again and again was

69

actually only a glimpse. A glimpse that forty-five years later she would give anything to experience again.

To have another chance. To do better.

CHAPTER 7

Jan-Erik was still sitting there with his morning paper when Louise came into the kitchen. Louise had said goodbye to Ellen then had spent a long time in the bathroom. When she reappeared, her face was made up and she had a towel wrapped round her head. He followed her with his eyes as she walked over to the freezer, took out a bag of rolls, and put two of them in the microwave. Efficient movements and small hard smacks as she set things down.

He turned a page of his newspaper without having read it.

'Coffee's ready, it's in the pot.'

Stupid thing to say. Where else would it be? She didn't reply, just took a cup out of the cupboard and poured, took the rolls out of the microwave when it pinged, and put cheese on them with no butter. Sitting at the table she pulled out the arts section of the paper and took a bite of the roll.

The mood was like day-old ice; a brittle surface over deep water that had to be traversed, with each step tested cautiously. Two people, so intimate that they ate breakfast together in their bathrobes, yet the chasm between them so great it was perilous to try and bridge it. There was nothing to say, about anything. Not even if he made an effort. He was able to make conversation with anyone if he had to, with anyone except her, this woman sitting across from him at the breakfast table dressed in her bathrobe.

The restlessness made his whole body itch. It was twenty-four hours until his next trip.

She turned a page of the newspaper. Drank a little coffee. Scraped up the crumbs from the roll and gathered them in a neat little pile.

The silence was paralysing. It made his heart pound. He had an urgent need to say something to normalise the mood, but there was nothing to say, absolutely nothing. When he could no longer stand it and was just about to get up and leave, his glance happened to fall on the crumbs, a dry heap a moment ago, now wet and flat. He sat there transfixed on the crumbs. The next moment his misgivings were confirmed when two more tears landed right next to the spot. What he had found intolerable a moment ago was suddenly nothing compared to the dilemma in which he now found himself. Louise was crying. His cool wife who never showed any emotion except varying degrees of irritation was sitting across from him and crying so that tears were falling. But what aroused greater horror was the realisation that he was expected to console her. He had no idea how to handle such a situation, how to deal with behaviour that was beyond all personal experience. All he knew was that her tears had melted the day-old ice that a minute ago had seemed so deadly, but which he now realised had been shielding what was underneath, something that was even worse. Something that would now have to come to light as soon as he admitted that he'd seen her cry.

For a moment he sat in bewilderment, going over his options. More tears were falling from her cheeks, and soon the option of pretending he hadn't noticed and could flee would be no good. He never had a chance to choose. Without raising her eyes she reached out her hand and fumbled for her coffee cup. The next moment the contents were spilled all over the tabletop. The mishap was all that was needed to rob him of any possibility of salvaging the situation.

'Fucking shit!' she said. The sobs she had been trying to suppress took over completely.

His reaction was instinctive – he gave a slight laugh.

'It's only a little coffee.'

She hid her face in her hands and sobbed harder.

He sat stock still, waiting. He had never seen her cry before, had no idea what it meant or how he was expected to react. Minutes passed. Minutes in which she cried and he desperately tried to cope with the situation. Naturally he should get up, take the few steps round the table and embrace her. Try to soothe her pain. He couldn't do it. Her silent appeal made something knot up

73

inside him. He felt a rope come coiling across the table to ensnare him.

'We simply can't go on like this.'

He stopped breathing. Scrabbled about in his past but found nothing that could give any guidance. He so wanted to be able to get up and leave, simply pretend that he'd heard nothing and go on his way. Away from the tears and the conversation he didn't want to have.

'I don't really understand what you mean.'

The next moment her eyes were on his, and he shrank from the sudden contact.

'What do you mean, you don't understand? What is it you don't understand?' She quickly wiped her cheeks and rubbed her hand under her nose, almost urgently, as if she had just tossed a hand grenade and knew that the time she had left was limited. And yet he could see that she hesitated. That she wanted to say more but something was holding her back.

'I can't go on like this any more.'

He swallowed. The spilled coffee was soaking into the newspaper and turning the news brown. He wanted to fetch a cloth but didn't dare move.

'We never do anything together, we don't even talk to each other. It's as if Ellen and I were living here alone. You're never home. And when you are, then . . . We . . .'

She broke off. Looked down at the table and held her hands up to hide her face. She got up and went to get the kitchen roll. She blew her nose and ran a finger under her eyes. She had always been particular about her appearance, but right now she was dissolved, exposed, and he saw that she was suffering.

He was used to her anger; the sudden outbursts of wrath that justified him in keeping his distance and holding his armour intact. Now she had stepped straight through it. She had stopped fighting and acknowledged her weakness, begging for comfort and understanding.

He preferred her anger.

She came back to the table. Her tears had stopped flowing but her face was swollen. White streaks ran down her cheeks and mascara had smeared under her eyes.

'We never touch each other.'

Her voice was shy and he saw that she was blushing. Her throat was flecked with crimson and she lowered her eyes, fiddling with a well-manicured fingernail at the wet heap of crumbs that he cursed himself for ever noticing. He could feel his heart pounding. Everything he had avoided talking about for years suddenly took shape as a terrible bonfire between them. In his confusion he raised his arm and glanced at his wristwatch, and although her eyes were focused on the tabletop she noticed the gesture.

'Are you in a hurry or something?'

'No, no, not at all.'

He picked up his coffee cup and noticed his hand was trembling.

Across the table, she took a deep breath as if to take a running start.

'I'm prepared to fight for Ellen's sake, but I haven't the strength to do it alone.'

A few seconds passed in silence. The revulsion he felt was so intense it made him feel sick.

'I have a suggestion,' she said.

Now came the fear. To be forced into the bedroom and be expected to have sex with her.

'I want you to start going to therapy.'

'What?'

The phrase came so unexpectedly that his fear temporarily vanished.

'Therapy? What sort of therapy? Why should I do that?'

She didn't reply. Just looked at him for a moment too long, then released him and went back to her pile of crumbs.

'I've been going for six months, and it's helped me. Maybe it would be good for you too.'

The astonishment he felt was genuine.

'You've been going to therapy?'

'Yes.'

'Why didn't you tell me?'

'I didn't think you'd be interested. We don't usually tell each other things in this family. We're seldom even in the same room, and you never answer your phone.'

The caustic dig moved them quickly to familiar ground, where he at once found his footing. These endless reproaches. He worked his arse off to make ends meet, and yet she was never satisfied. Their spacious five-room flat, for which the seller had accepted a considerably lower price because their name was Ragnerfeldt. She seemed to have forgotten the difference between rights and privileges. He had pulled off the trick of putting food on the table by spreading memorable words through his lectures and starting up organisations to improve the world. He was useful. Both to the world and to his family. It was thanks to him that Axel Ragnerfeldt's unique prose was now associated with humanitarian aid efforts. What his father had written about had been transformed in his hands into something concrete; it was on his initiative that all these aid projects had been started. He had become someone that people listened to, and he was treated with respect. He had proven that he was somebody to be reckoned with. And yet all he encountered here at home were these constant accusations and sour looks.

'Another option is for us to go to therapy together, to a marriage counsellor. If you'd prefer that.'

No, he certainly would not. He didn't want to go to any therapy whatsoever and sit there gazing at his navel and digging through his childhood potty.

'And what if I don't want to?'

She seemed to sense his repressed anger and started at his new tone, yet her voice remained calm and composed.

'Well, then I don't know. Then it seems like you don't think this is worth fighting for. I really don't know.'

He was trapped. Chained hand and foot. His anger took over completely, at this woman who could sit there with her ultimatums without even realising what sort of leverage she held. The fact that he didn't have a choice, although she tried to make it sound as if he did. His rage purged his conscience clean, and he got up from the table. With all the self-control he could muster he pushed in the chair.

'Okay. I suppose I'll have to think about therapy then. But that doesn't mean I want to go or think I need it.'

She reached for her handbag hanging from the back of a chair. She took out her wallet and handed him a business card.

'I got this from my therapist. We can't go to the same one, but this is somebody she recommended who's a specialist in—'

She broke off and looked away.

'In what?'

She looked at him timidly and put the card on the table.

'In the sort of problems that you, or rather we, may have.'

He stopped short and stared at the card. He slowly reached out, picked it up, and lowered his eyes to read it. Robert Rasmusson. Licensed psychotherapist and sexologist. And then in smaller

78

type below: couples therapy, separations, sexual guidance and erectile dysfunction.

He clenched his teeth.

Without a word he left the kitchen and went into the bathroom. He locked the door and just stood there. His emotions raged between flaming anger and something else he didn't recognise. The need to go back to the kitchen and scream the truth in her face was so strong that he had to go to the sink and cool off his face with cold water. *I sure as hell don't have any problems with my erection! You're the one who's the problem! I can get it up with anyone I choose, as long as it's not you!*

He looked at himself in the mirror then splashed his face one more time.

The business card in her wallet. So clever, on the very morning she could no longer hold back her tears. She had fooled him once more. She had used the oldest female trick in the book to force him to listen to her. He read the card again, his wet fingers leaving dark spots on it. He resisted the urge to flush it down the toilet. Everything was suddenly a huge mess. It was five past nine. He would have to take care of all this later, try to work out a strategy.

He was due at his mother's flat in twenty-five minutes.

He was in a foul mood by the time he was walking up the two flights to Alice Ragnerfeldt's flat.

Marianne Folkesson wouldn't be arriving for half an hour. He had made a point of getting there in good time to ensure that his mother was not drunk before he let a stranger into the flat. After two short rings he fumbled for his keys, but then she opened the door. That was a good sign. She was dressed, her hair combed, and she was apparently sober.

'Hi, Mamma.'

He stepped into the hall and hung up his coat. Everything seemed to be in order. He held out the bag of cinnamon buns he'd bought on the way over.

'Come here, I have to show you something.'

Without taking the pastry bag she vanished into the kitchen. He bent down, pulled off his shoes and followed her. She was sitting on one of the chairs when he entered the room.

'Look at this.'

She pulled up the legs of her trousers and looked at him urgently. He peered at her feet and calves.

'Do you see it?'

'See what?'

'Don't tell me you can't see it.'

He leaned forward and looked more closely.

'What am I supposed to see?'

'It's swollen. The right calf. Can't you see it?'

She pointed. He kept his eyes on the linoleum and tried to hide how disgusted he was. She released her trouser legs and let them drop over her calves. Then she reached for a newspaper clipping on the table. Triumphantly she handed it to him. He straightened up and scanned the text.

'But you've already had your kidneys checked, and they didn't find anything wrong.'

'That was four months ago. I can feel that there's something wrong now. Everything matches with that list. See for yourself. Headache in the morning, fatigue, itching, swollen legs. I know something is wrong.'

He turned round and went to put the bag of buns on the worktop.

'I made an appointment at the Sophia Clinic,' she said.

With his back to her he closed his eyes. He knew what another doctor's visit would mean: the brave attempts by the staff to conceal their irritation over Alice Ragnerfeldt's constant demands for new examinations, which took away time from the patients who were really sick.

'Shall I put on some coffee?'

'It's in the thermos. The appointment's on the eleventh at 8.50 in the morning. Can you drive me there?'

He took out three cups and three plates from the cupboard.

'I'll have to check my diary.'

He had intended to finish the sentence by saying that otherwise they'd have to ask Louise, but he was instantly back to the morning's conversation.

The mere thought of her gave him heart palpitations.

'Otherwise we'll probably have to ask Louise,' she said. 'But I'd rather have you drive me.'

He didn't answer, just opened the bag and took out the buns.

'Where's your cake tray?'

Marianne Folkesson buzzed the intercom at exactly the appointed time. During the minutes that had passed between the cake tray and the intercom, they had discussed a mouldy smell underneath the bathtub. Alice claimed that it appeared every time water ran down the drain, and that her sore hip started bothering her when she tried to clean it. Jan-Erik had once tried to convince his mother that he should arrange for some cleaning help for her, but as usual she wouldn't hear of it. She didn't want some stranger snooping through her belongings. She thought all she needed was for Jan-Erik and Louise to help out with what she couldn't manage by herself. After all, they did live so close by.

Alice was sitting on the sofa in the living room when Jan-Erik let in Marianne Folkesson. He guessed she was about his own age, maybe a year or two older. Not bad-looking, but a bit too old for his taste. Anyway, his hunting grounds never encroached on territory occupied by his family.

Alice remained seated as they shook hands, watching discreetly. Jan-Erik invited Marianne to have a seat in one of the armchairs and served her coffee. His mother put a hand over her cup when the thermos came near. It had been difficult to convince her to attend this meeting. She didn't think there was any reason for them to get involved in Gerda Persson's passing. But he was more ambivalent. Naturally he had said yes when Marianne asked him, but there was a certain discomfort stirring in the shadows. Gerda belonged to a past time that he would prefer to leave undisturbed. The house that now stood empty was just as they had left it, but it still required attention and upkeep. The decision about its fate had been postponed with the excuse that his father was still alive. Sell it, turn it into a museum, move in there themselves – there were many options. It was a wonderful house. Built in 1906 with nine rooms and two kitchens, one on each floor. Three thousand square metres and within walking distance of the water. When Jan-Erik had moved back from the States, he had found his parents living on separate floors. He'd always had a feeling that it was because of Annika's death, but like so much else he had never asked. After the car crash her bedroom had been converted into Alice's kitchen. His parents had successfully done their best to avoid running into each other, except on public occasions when they presented themselves as a couple welded together, or at an occasional family dinner with Jan-Erik and Louise. But they never did get divorced. That was simply not done in the Ragnerfeldt family.

During Jan-Erik's childhood Gerda Persson had been the only person in the house who could always be counted on. She didn't say much, but there was a sanctuary in her silence. He knew it was safe and would not suddenly explode.

Marianne took a little sip of her coffee.

'I'd like to begin by saying that naturally I've read all of Axel Ragnerfeldt's books. They're really quite wonderful. Please tell him that from me and thank him for all the amazing reading experiences.'

'Oh yes, we most certainly shall do that. I'm sure he'll be extremely thrilled.'

Jan-Erik glared at his mother and cleared his throat loudly when he saw the crimson on Marianne's cheeks.

'Pappa has suffered a massive stroke, and we don't really know how much he understands of what we tell him. That's all that Mamma meant.'

'I see. How sad, truly sad. I didn't know that.'

Jan-Erik hoped that the look he'd given his mother would keep her quiet. Marianne took out a black notebook and pen from her bag.

'In any case, I'm here in my capacity as estate administrator first to try and track down any of Gerda Persson's relatives who might be entitled to her inheritance. Secondly, I'm here to arrange her funeral if no one else shows up to do so, and so far no one has. Do you know if she had any family?'

Jan-Erik left that question to his mother. He had no idea.

'No. I don't know very much about Gerda Persson. I haven't had any contact with her since the early eighties. I should think there must be someone else who is better suited to answer these questions.'

'Yes, that may be true. Unfortunately it's not always the case, and then we have to make the best of the situation.' Marianne was fighting back.

Jan-Erik felt even more depressed about the way the conversation was going. Alice stroked her hand over the burgundy velvet sofa cushion. He had never got used to seeing all this furniture here in the flat. It belonged at home on the top floor of the house in Nacka, and no matter how much he had helped her move it around, it still looked lost here. As if the furniture longed for home and refused to settle in.

'She was from Öland originally, I think, or maybe it was Kalmar. At any rate I know she had a sister, but she died in the late fifties, I believe it was. You were still small then.'

Jan-Erik nodded.

'I remember that she took a week off to take care of the funeral. Her sister was also unmarried, if I'm not mistaken.'

'But no other siblings that you know of?'

The tip of Marianne's pen rested on a line in the black notebook.

'No, none that she mentioned, at least.'

'And no children?'

'No.'

Marianne shifted position and leafed through some pages.

'I got one response to the death notice in the paper, a Torgny Wennberg who said he would come to the funeral.'

'Torgny Wennberg?'

His mother's voice was marked by suspicion.

'Yes. Did you know him?'

Alice snorted. 'I wouldn't say I *know* him. He was a detestable man who constantly came to visit Axel to bask in his glory. He had managed to get a few novels published that no one read, but he thrived on hobnobbing with more successful authors. Although what he should have to do with Gerda I have no idea; I didn't even know they knew each other. Of course they probably ran into each other when he came to the house, but that was more than thirty years ago.'

Jan-Erik remembered him. A reddish-brown beard and a big horsey laugh that didn't sound natural. Muttered voices behind the closed door of his father's office and from time to time that laugh. And oddly enough, sometimes laughter even from his father who seldom participated in that kind of manifestation of joy. The laughter always came more often as the evening wore on.

'He wants to come to the funeral at least.'

Alice snorted again. 'Yes, he probably thinks that

Axel will be there so he can ingratiate himself again.'

'Mamma,' he said, trying to appeal tactfully. Before, he had only needed to worry when she wasn't sober. Nowadays he was never sure. Inappropriate behaviour that previously had remained within the family now came out more and more often when they were with other people. He considered taking Axel along to the funeral. Get him into the wheelchair and take him there, no matter how much he waved his little finger, which was now his only means of communication. But he had no intention of having this discussion with his mother while estate administrator Marianne Folkesson was watching.

'If there's anything you need assistance with before the funeral, we'd be only too happy to help,' Jan-Erik said, with a kindly smile for Marianne.

'If you could think of some suitable music, I'd be very grateful, if you know the sort of music she liked. Or if there's anything else you think might make the funeral service more personal. Do you know, for instance, what kind of flowers she liked?'

'Roses.'

Alice shot him an astonished look. He had said that to beat her to the punch. He said the name of the first flower that popped into his head. He suddenly recalled an argument one afternoon over forty years ago. His mother out on the lawn, dressed as usual in her dressing gown, and Gerda standing silent with her head bowed. The shouting about the dandelions that he was afraid would be heard all the way to the neighbours'. His mother's rage that Gerda hadn't weeded them.

'Roses?' Drawn out and suspicious. 'Where in God's name did you get that from?'

'I remember her mentioning it once.'

His mother let the subject drop but gave him a look that said it was the stupidest thing she'd ever heard. Jan-Erik felt an increasing need to bring the meeting to a close. Something told him that his mother must have had a drink or two just before he arrived, and the effect was kicking in now.

Marianne was writing in her notebook. Then she leafed forward a few pages. Unaware of what was going on in the room, she was in no hurry to ask her next question.

'Do you know a Kristoffer Sandeblom?' she asked.

Alice gave a heavy sigh and braced herself to get up.

'Never heard of him.'

She headed for the kitchen and Jan-Erik watched her go.

'No, I don't believe so. Why?'

He knew what his mother was after, and he felt more and more anxious to get Marianne Folkesson out of the flat. She raised her cup and took a sip of coffee.

88

'He's listed as beneficiary in her will.'

He glanced at the doorway through which his mother had just vanished.

'I shouldn't think he'd get very rich on that,' his mother called.

Jan-Erik laughed to cover up the comment from the kitchen and wondered whether Marianne also recognised the sound of a metal top being unscrewed from a bottle.

'She stipulated expressly that all bills be paid first, but that what remained, including the proceeds from the sale of her possessions, should go to him. I was wondering if any of you might know who he is.'

'No idea. How old is he, approximately?'

Marianne checked her book. 'Born in 1972.'

Alice appeared in the doorway, standing with her arms crossed.

'Then perhaps it would be better to contact him instead of us, since he seems to have been on such close terms with her.'

'I've tried. I left a message on his answer machine but unfortunately he hasn't called back yet.'

Jan-Erik raised his arm and looked at his wrist-watch.

'If that's all for now, I'm afraid I really must be going.'

Marianne scanned a page in her notebook.

'There isn't anything else. Just the music, if you could think of something that would be suitable. Oh yes, I need a photograph of Gerda if you have one. I usually make an enlargement and frame it to put on the casket. We found one in her flat, but it's too blurry to blow up. If you have one I'd very much like to borrow it.'

Jan-Erik stood up. 'Of course. I'll see what I can find.'

They shook hands and Marianne thanked him. Alice said goodbye when they met at the doorway, then went back to sit on the sofa. Jan-Erik accompanied Marianne out to the hall.

'I'll be calling you soon. I'll see if I can find a picture.'

'Thank you, and if you think of anything else that might help, please give me a ring.'

Jan-Erik assured her that he would, and then she was out of the flat. He stood in the hall for a moment and looked longingly at his shoes. Just to walk. Walk somewhere far away from here. But the day was not over yet. There was one more filial visit remaining. It was important that his father's rehabilitation take place in close co-operation with the family, the doctor had said, and today it was time for another such encounter. Like pearls on a string the times kept cropping up in his diary, and he was the one who was family. His mother wasn't particularly interested, even though she'd gone with him once for appearance's sake.

He heard her calling from the living room.

'Darling, come and sit on the sofa a while with your old mamma, you can surely spare that much time. It would be so nice to talk with you a little. It's so lonely here in the daytime.'

He closed his eyes.

Tomorrow he would be able to leave on a trip. He was counting the hours.

CHAPTER 8

Kristoffer got up from his desk and went over to the window. A steady rain was veining the glass and obscuring the view over the cemetery at Katarina Church. He pressed his forehead against the cool window and closed his eyes, not moving until he found the words he was groping for. Then he hurried back to the computer and typed them out standing up. After that he sat down again at the desk, took a deep breath and began to read the words on the screen.

ACT 2
(The MOTHER and FATHER are sitting at a kitchen table set for breakfast. Around the table are four chairs. The mother is dressed in high-heeled red patent-leather boots, a micro-miniskirt and a tiny glitzy top. The father is wearing a pin-striped suit. The room is dark except for a number of TV sets of varying sizes, all showing different programmes. News, adverts, porno, action, music videos. The mother is knitting. The father is reading from a computer screen.)

(They sit in total silence for a minute.)

FATHER: What are you doing?
MOTHER: Knitting.

(They sit in silence for another minute.)

FATHER: What are you knitting?
MOTHER: Mittens.
FATHER: Why are you knitting mittens?
MOTHER: I'm going to give them to the collection for Rescue Africa.
FATHER: What do they need mittens for?
MOTHER: So they won't freeze.

(The SON, 13 years old, comes onstage. He is dressed in a Guantánamo-orange jump-suit, a black blindfold and a wide rubber shackle connecting his ankles so that he can only take short steps. From his ankles, chains connect to his hands, which are handcuffed.)

SON: Could you lock me up?

(The mother locks the handcuffs.)

MOTHER: Do you really have to wear those today?
SON: Give me a break.
MOTHER: It's below freezing outside. I don't want you to catch a cold.

FATHER: Just make sure that outfit is clean on Saturday when we go to the Svenssons' wedding.
MOTHER: You know what it cost? Four thousand kronor.
SON: I paid for it myself. With the money I got for Christmas.
MOTHER: Can you see anything at all?
SON: There are holes here, you know that.
(Lifts his cuffed hands as far as he can and points to tiny holes in the blindfold)
SON: Besides, it's sewn from organic material. Certified.

(The mother makes an open sandwich and feeds the SON. Helps him drink from a glass. Suddenly she turns to face the audience.)

MOTHER: Can anyone help me?

(The mother goes back to her knitting as if nothing has happened.)

FATHER: Our stocks in African Fishing Trade have gone up.
SON: I'm out of here.
MOTHER: Don't you have a late morning today?
SON: I won't make it if I don't leave now. (Points at the rubber shackle between his ankles)
FATHER: Watch out for cars and paedophiles.

(The son hurries off, taking little shuffling steps, and vanishes offstage.)

MOTHER: What stocks?

FATHER: The business concept is brilliant. Five hundred tons of filleted Nile perch per day are exported to Europe. They've managed to lower costs by using cheap Russian pilots and old freight aeroplanes. And the offal and fish-heads are left over for the local population, so those who say that the introduced Nile perch has killed off all the other fish in Lake Victoria will just have to shut up. Nobody's going to come and say that African Fishing Trade aren't doing their share. Besides, the young people can heat up the glue in the fish-crates and sniff it, so they'll sleep better in the alleys at night. Their parents have all died of AIDS anyway. It's a win-win situation for all concerned. We can thank our lucky stars we were in on it from the beginning and bought shares.

(They sit in silence. Suddenly the father turns to the audience.)

FATHER: Can anyone help me?

Kristoffer leaned back and clasped his hands behind his head. He wasn't completely satisfied. Something in the play didn't sound quite right, and there were only four weeks left till the deadline. His eyes left the screen and sought out the mobile phone, which was turned off. He picked it up and weighed it in his hand. For a week he'd been cut off from the outside world, but the number of pages he'd been able to produce was still alarmingly small. It just wasn't flowing. There was so much he wanted to say, but the words seemed stuck, as if screwed down in a space he couldn't access. Isolation was usually the key. The freedom that opened up after he shut off his telephones and stopped checking his e-mail. The feeling of independence. An inviolable wild man with the right to spew his bile over the societal structure from which he had chosen to remove himself. This time it hadn't worked. Instead he had felt lonely and cooped-up. And detached. Not detached the way he usually felt, when as an observer he registered what was happening though he wasn't taking part; and with his moral irre-proachability of the past three years, he had a right to criticise.

Instead he felt detached, as in lonely.

He wondered whether it had to do with the money. Each month a varying amount was sent to him from an anonymous giver, but this month it hadn't come.

He closed the screen on his laptop and went into the kitchen. Opened the fridge, then the freezer. The number of frozen meals had run low, and he needed to go shopping. Maybe he should give Jesper a ring. Grab a quick bite and talk for a while. Jesper, who at the risk of coming down with scurvy was struggling with his novel the way Kristoffer was struggling with his new script.

A year had passed since the little theatre had produced his first play. Provocative, some critics had called it. Others had claimed that it was insistent. He took that as a good sign. Several of the performances had sold out. He had sat there in the dark and mouthed the words spoken on the stage. No one could hear him, but in his head his voice had been exultant. And when the applause came he was always filled with the same wish.

Imagine if my parents could see me.

Now the theatre wanted a new play, and he had promised to deliver it in a month. It was a matter of producing something new yet retaining his distinct style. To attack, yet soften the blows so that only after a while would a hole open up and the criticism could slyly slink in. Human nature went on the defensive if it was ambushed. That was something in the genes. But the rage and frustration he felt about the state of everything made it hard to hold back.

He picked up the cordless phone from the kitchen worktop and punched in Jesper's number. He wasn't ready yet to turn on his mobile. Then the spell would be broken for good, and he needed to get down another few pages before he gave up for the day.

'Hey, it's me. Where are you?'

'I'm down at Café Neo. How about hanging out for a few?'

He hesitated only a second, then gave in.

'Okay, I'll be there in ten.'

He went out to the hall and pulled on his trainers and duffel coat. He left the umbrella after a glance out of the window; it had stopped raining. He locked the door and chose to walk down the stairs; he needed the exercise after sitting for a week. He let his hand glide along the banister. Let himself be filled by the ambivalent feeling at the thought that so many hands had glided there before his. That he was a part of the whole. That everything belonged together, but everyone had his own responsibility, and he had realised that he had to start carrying his own. It was the idea that had guided each step for the past three years.

His new journey had begun then, when as a 32-year-old bartender he was standing behind a bar in Åre and felt that he could no longer breathe. He realised that he was about to go under. He had looked about among the drunken people and ascertained that the total IQ in the pub corresponded to that in the ape house at Kolmården Zoo. With the crushing difference that the inhabitants of the ape house behaved with more dignity. It was as though a cloudy lens had been removed. He had suddenly felt like an alien from outer space who wanted to know how we intelligent humans lived our lives here on Earth. Everything had all at once become inexplicable. He had seen all the fumbling attempts. All the bullshit that never led anywhere except possibly to people staggering home to a rented hotel room where they could screw in drunken abandon.

The bunch of girls on the other side of the bar, the ones who had told him the night before that they were studying nursing together and were there on their annual trip; their shocking pink T-shirts with the slogan I'M HERE FOR THE GANGBANG; the conversation some of them were trying to have with three muscle-bound men who had a hard time standing up straight – all desperate padding, people who were trying to endure although something was missing. And he and his colleagues who facilitated the idiocy that was going on, dressed in uniforms emblazoned with distillers' names, they kept serving more shots, beer and brightly coloured cocktails to people who were already so drunk they could barely lift the glass to their lips. Yet they had chosen this condition voluntarily.

They were having fun.

The revelation that he was definitely one of them.

He stopped at a crossing and pressed the button. Across the street a van with a beer logo along its side had stopped to unload grey barrels outside a restaurant. Two men from the staff wrestled the heavy metal cylinders in through the door. In the next few days the contents would enter an unknown number of human brains in their hunt for peace of mind.

For thirteen years this had been his life. Visby in the summertime and Åre in the winter. Après-beach and après-ski parties were deceptively similar. Released on holiday, people had to make up for all the lost time; the caveman in them was set free for a while to get some air. After the workday was over he would join in the fun. Seasonal work was a lifestyle that possessed everything for maintaining a distance from a dull contemptible life, that of some faceless suit with a mundane routine. Parties that started at closing time and went on till morning, a few hours' sleep so you could handle the evening shift that lasted till the next party started. A superficial life in which he let himself float away like a feather on the breeze. It all went so fast, so fast, and depended on the whim of a second. A constant search for kicks, a blissful mixture of sex, alcohol and other drugs. Just as long as it heightened his sense of being alive and raised him above mediocrity, silencing what was tearing at his soul because he didn't want to acknowledge it. He was ready for anything, and if something did go wrong it was always possible to blame his blood alcohol level. He had taken the trouble to become a member of the 'ski club', the ones who had sex in the small gondola lift. He'd become a dangerous competitor in the beer-chugging contests and the riskiest off-piste runs. He'd stood in queues to hotel rooms where girls had set up a system with guys writing their names on condoms that were then placed in a cooler in the corridor while awaiting their turn. He'd taken penicillin for chlamydia and on one occasion was admitted to the hospital with kidney pains after weeks of hard partying. In countless places he'd woken up covered in his own vomit, yet he couldn't remember how he'd got there. He'd done things that afterwards had filled him with shame. But nothing had made him question his behaviour. Life had been a closed cocoon unaffected by the world outside. There was nothing but the night's escapades and the morning's remorse. The hellish anxiety that came with the hangover, which nothing but the hair of the dog could remedy.

And he had enjoyed the camaraderie with the other seasonal workers, who were equally homeless and flitted from summer to winter.

Almost as if he'd had a family.

On the main street he met an elderly lady with a dog. She gave him a fleeting glance and he broke out in a big smile. She hurried on with her eyes lowered, and Kristoffer continued in the opposite direction. He'd done it to amuse himself really. A friendly smile from a stranger always seemed to arouse confusion. But no good person thought that way. And he was good. Nowadays.

Years had passed and finally it had begun to gnaw at him, an uneasy feeling that something important had passed him by. The nagging thought he had every time he served an overbearing party of customers with reliable credit cards and receding hairlines. The reminder that genuine success also took time, at least if it was going to survive the in-crowd list on the slate behind the bar.

And the nagging feeling had spread. Not even alcohol had been able to drive it away, when he was drunk and in some strange way was able to talk to himself in a voice that came from somewhere else. The voice had suddenly begun to wonder where he was headed. *Is this really me?* it had asked. *Was it really me who just got up from the table, and if so, why did I do that?*

Up until now he had regarded his life as a temporary arrangement. Whatever was going to make it start for real had not yet happened. His naïve belief that he didn't have to initiate anything himself, that everything would fall into place if he just waited long enough. But then, when he began questioning this attitude, he had realised that this makeshift arrangement was not so easy to get rid of. Maybe it was the anonymous money that had been sent to him every month that had lured him into the delusion that his real life was actually going on somewhere else. During the black anxiety of his hangovers he had come to the conclusion that his life resided in the vacuum that existed inside the atoms of his body.

And no one, not even himself, knew where this body had come from.

It was the need for an answer to this mystery that legitimised his diversionary tactics during the waiting period. The monthly payments that proved there was somebody out there who knew.

He stopped at the window of Pet Sounds. He usually allowed himself a CD now and then, even if the price in his new life without tips was a bit steep for his wallet. Downloading music for free was not part of his world-improving ideology. The door opened and a guy in his twenties came out holding a chocolate bar in his hand. As he passed by he threw the colourful wrapper on the street.

'Excuse me, you dropped something,' said Kristoffer.

The guy gave him a quick look. 'It's just rubbish.'

'Yes, I can see that, but who do you think is going to pick it up for you?'

The guy stopped short. He looked about and gave Kristoffer an uncertain smile, as if to check whether he was kidding. Kristoffer stood there waiting, looking him straight in the eye, but this time he wasn't smiling. A few seconds passed before the guy bent down and picked up the wrapper, shamefaced. Only when he'd left did Kristoffer smile, pleased with himself and his action.

Nowadays these were the types of kicks he sought, since the ones he'd been getting from sex and alcohol were suddenly gone. Tortuous anxiety had already crept in before the new kicks had managed to soothe him. In despair he'd realised that he'd reached a blind alley, that the cost of the only thing that helped actually scared him as much as what he was trying to escape. Only then had he understood how hard it was to change his behaviour. How the alcohol and the other drugs demanded their place even though he didn't want them any more. What he'd thought was voluntary had proven to be a necessity. His most dangerous enemy lived inside him, feeding on his brain and preventing him from making his own decisions. The air that no longer reached down into his lungs, the restlessness that demanded constant motion even though he didn't dare. The longing for relief, to escape from his own thoughts, but at the same time the fear of what it would cost – the life-threatening anxiety of the hangover. The fee for a few hours of grace. He'd no longer had any defence against what was tearing at his soul. The panic of feeling something slowly break down, letting something ghastly force its way out.

He had left his place behind the bar and gone home to the cubby-hole he shared with another seasonal worker. He had sat for hours on the unmade bed, having a hard enough time just breathing. The thought of what his parents would think if they could see what he'd become.

The shame he felt. Over what he'd done, how for so many years he'd humiliated himself. The experience of being in debt, both to himself and to all existence. He had felt utterly flayed, lost and alone.

He had packed his bags and taken the train to

Stockholm. Made use of his many contacts after his years in the pub business and managed to find a flat. A sublet contract for an indefinite period; the owner was doing research abroad. Kristoffer didn't know what sort of research except that the books on the shelves suggested it was something in the natural sciences. The first few months he had locked himself in the flat and didn't dare go out. The days he'd been forced to go grocery shopping had been a nightmare. At least he had enough money in his bank account, after saving up all his tips, since his food and drink had been free. In the hope of leaving everything behind, he had broken all contact with his old life and alone had begun to fight his inner demon. One by one he had browsed through the books on the shelves, often incomprehensible, but at least they offered some distraction. At night he sat at the computer. He found an Alcoholics Anonymous chat room in and got help making it through the small hours. He had woken up each morning with the choice of giving in to his all-consuming longing, or making up his mind to get through another day. Tiny, tiny steps, which taken together led him forward.

After six months he ventured outside to take long walks around Stockholm. He walked endless distances as if trying to leave something behind.

He was standing on Fjällgatan when it happened. Enjoying the view. It was springtime and the shimmering green shifted in endless nuances. The white ferry to Slussen sliced through the water, which glittered as though strewn with diamonds. All this beauty had surprised him. An unexpected wonder. It couldn't have been there before, could it, since he'd never noticed it? It had come from deep inside, a tingling, dazed sense of joy, impossible to resist. Even though there were people all around him, he had let his laughter echo across the street and further out over all of Stockholm, and he had felt that finally, finally he was free. That everything before him held possibility. He'd always felt that he was meant for something great, and now the time had come. He would make a contribution, do something significant. Everything had now acquired a meaning. From the moment his consciousness opened, there was no turning back. Then each waking moment became a struggle for change, an eternal refusal to adapt or accept the way things were. The world was a swamp, and it was the responsibility of everyone to drain it. To become, like him, an advocate of humanity's self-defence, a champion against everything shallow.

Jesper was sitting in the far corner at the table where they always sat. He had finished his latte and on the inside of the tall glass the foam had dried in an irregular pattern. The first thing that struck Kristoffer was the lack of the obligatory notebook, Jesper's constant companion that he always placed within reach wherever he sat down.

The notes that were later spun into his attempt at a novel, *Nostalgia – A Strange Feeling of Manageable Sorrow*. Jesper was a lone wolf, just like Kristoffer. Maybe that was why they got along so well.

Kristoffer hung his duffel coat over the back of the chair. 'So. Would you like anything?'

Jesper shook his head, and Kristoffer went over to the short queue at the counter. He stood a little too close to the person in front of him. Just as a test. The man took a step forward and Kristoffer followed. The man's discomfort was apparent, but he did his best to hide it. He stood his ground, looking out of the corner of his eye as if he wanted to watch Kristoffer without being noticed. Why was it so threatening when a stranger got too close? Kristoffer had long pondered why it was so important to keep one's distance. Maybe it was precisely there, in the discomfort, that the unconscious touched upon the knowledge that everything that exists is a unity, that everything is interrelated. He had read that in the science books on the shelves in the flat, that atoms never die but only change form. It was enough to see a photograph of the earth taken from space to sense the truth. If that realisation were ever taken seriously, the prevailing worldview would come crashing down. No one would any longer be able to watch what was going on without being forced to take action.

The man in front of Kristoffer took another step to increase the distance. Kristoffer let him be. He ordered a double espresso, and while he waited he watched Jesper. He was still sitting with his chin resting in his left hand, drawing invisible figures on the tabletop with his right. Gloomy, Kristoffer thought. Not the first time. Jesper was an open book when it came to where he was on the emotional scale, and gloomy was not that unusual. Kristoffer thrived on clarity. There was nothing vague that could create brooding, only visible messages. He suddenly felt himself smiling as he looked at Jesper, struck by how much he valued their friendship. Jesper was a teetotaller for ideological reasons, which made their interaction easier. Since Kristoffer had stopped drinking he needed to avoid certain situations. Enjoying a whole evening in a pub was like being a diabetic at a cake party. He could still get thirsty, and sometimes he really had to steel himself not to take that first drink; the one that would produce that numbing sense of relaxation, the peaceful sensation that everything became smoothed out and tolerable, the feeling he used to spend so many nights trying to recapture, even though it passed so quickly.

Jesper was the only person he could call a friend. His lonely work sitting at the computer and his abstinence from pub life had not gained him a big circle of acquaintances since he'd broken off with the old ones.

But even to Jesper he hadn't revealed his secret. It was so fraught with shame that the very words refused to come out. Thirty-one years had passed, and he had not told anyone.

The fact that at the age of four he had been found on the stairs at Skansen amusement park.

That he had been rejected.

He went back to the table.

'How's it going, anyway?'

Kristoffer sat down at the table and began to sip his double espresso. Jesper didn't say a word. Gloomy, Kristoffer thought again.

'I don't know, I suppose I should be happy. But I'm not.'

'What is it?'

Kristoffer drank some more coffee. Jesper leaned back and stretched as if he wanted to shake off something unpleasant. And then he said the words that made the room turn inside out.

'They want to publish my book.'

Kristoffer froze, his hand in mid-air, and was shocked at his own reaction. He ought to be happy, ecstatic, jump up from his chair and buy a cake. The way a good person would react. His best friend, after all his struggles, had reached the goal of his dreams. But instead of rejoicing on his behalf Kristoffer sat as if paralysed, invaded by a huge, black envy.

'Well, that's fantastic,' he managed to say. And the blackness grew bigger.

'Is it?'

Jesper didn't look the least bit happy. Kristoffer gratefully welcomed the confusion that began to compete for space.

'Of course it is. Isn't it? Isn't that why you wrote the book?'

There was a moment's silence. Jesper wasn't one to say something unless he had first deliberated carefully. A trait that Kristoffer admired. The world would be a better place if there were more people who chose their words carefully.

'Mostly I think it feels empty somehow, almost as if I've been robbed.'

'What do you mean, robbed? Now you can start eating something besides noodles for a change.'

He could hear it in his own voice. That the words concealed what he actually felt.

'I don't mean the money, you know that. I mean, I don't know how to say it, my life has sort of been robbed. What the hell am I going to do now? I've been writing that fucking novel for so long that I don't know what I'll do when I can't work on it anymore.'

'Then you'll have to write another one.'

The idea did not seem appealing, and another silence settled in.

'But what if I can't?'

'Stop it. You can at least give it a try before you give up. Besides, you'll have to go out and promote the book, travel around and do interviews, go on TV chat shows and give readings.'

He could feel the envy growing. The dream of success. To be in demand and finally have your worth confirmed.

'But that's just it. How the hell do you think I

could manage to go on a talk show? Can you see me sitting there? Can you? Or doing interviews? What would I say? Read the book, you fucking idiot! Everything I wanted to say is in there. How do you think that would come across?'

Kristoffer didn't answer. He had seen Jesper get tongue-tied just trying to order coffee and realised that to some extent he was right. And yet he couldn't help being irritated at his whining.

'And anyway, I'm too ugly.'

'Give me a break.'

'It's easy for you to say, with that cherub face of yours.'

'It doesn't matter one damn bit what you look like.'

'Yeah, right.'

Jesper looked utterly hopeless. He put his head in his hands and sighed. Kristoffer finished his coffee and shoved his cup away. If only it had been him. Maybe he should write a novel himself. If Jesper could get his published, he could manage it too.

'It's obvious that I want the book to be read by as many people as possible, obviously I want that, that's why I wrote it. Because I want something. But I didn't think about what it would really involve. You know me, I can't cope with being the centre of attention. This was my way to try and say something anyway. I simply don't fit as a brand name. The people I met at the publishing company, I told them the truth, that

I didn't know if I could handle a lot of interviews and stuff like that.'

'So what did they say?'

'They didn't exactly jump for joy.'

'Well, shit, there must be some other way.'

'I knew they were disappointed when they met me. They were so positive on the phone after they'd read the book, but that was before they met me.'

Kristoffer stopped arguing with him and they sat quietly for a moment. He tried in vain to silence the thought that the publishers' reaction was a relief to him. Desperately he struggled to shove the envy back into the rubbish-heap it had crawled out of, because what sort of person reacted the way he had done? In an attempt to pull himself together he reached out and patted his friend's hand. The gesture was so unlike him that Jesper gave a start at the touch.

'I'm sure it will all turn out fine.'

Kristoffer pulled back his hand and smiled.

'Shit, I know a real author!'

But the words only intensified his envy. He had always been the one who was more successful; their respective roles had been well-established. Their entire friendship hinged on those unwritten rules, but now the balance had been disturbed. He wanted to go home and keep working on his play, see to it that every critic would end up prostrate with rapture.

'You'll have to think of another way to promote the book. Do something that nobody has ever done, so the book gets attention even if you don't put in an appearance.'

If you think it's too much trouble, he wanted to add, but didn't.

'What would that be?'

'I don't know, you'll have to think about it.'

They said goodbye out on the street, and Kristoffer headed off to buy groceries. He was weighed down by guilt, a despic able person who was incapable of being happy for a friend. The goodness and competence he had always striven for had at the slightest provocation yielded to the selfish instincts that belonged to a second-rate nature. He knew so well that moral value does not come from desire but from duty. And yet he had failed. In an attempt to rectify it he began to mull over Jesper's dilemma, trying to think of what would make the media notice the book. Inside the supermarket he stopped in front of the magazine racks and read the headlines: *I slept with 4,000 women / Booze, sex and total decadence – we were there / Get rich with file-sharing / Sin, gambling and strippers / We can only say Wow! when hot Emma takes off her wet blouse inside / Win a computer! Download all the porn you want!*

Kristoffer sighed. Since he was a man and the headlines were aimed at men, he felt humiliated. That just because he was a man he was expected to be an idiot. It wasn't that he had anything against naked women. Even though he wasn't proud of it, he did have some well-thumbed magazines in his flat. He lived alone, what was he supposed to do? But he found it insulting that his lowest instincts were appealed to without finesse. He picked up one of the magazines and looked at the masthead. Nothing but men in editorial. He wondered who these men were. Why had they no higher ambitions? And if they had, what was it they wanted? Once he had phoned a newspaper and asked this very question.

'We have an obligation to our shareholders to focus on what makes people pick up the paper,' he'd been told. 'Unfortunately world crises don't sell.'

Well, Jesper, he thought. This isn't going to be easy. A headline about Jesper Falk writing a thought-provoking novel about his generation would hardly cause a stampede at the news-stand.

He sidestepped and found himself in front of the shelves filled with women's magazines. *Beautiful eyes – get the sultry look! / Shopping frenzy – 500 best buys / How to walk in high heels / Are breast implants a good idea?* The whole thing was so confusing, the fact that all these magazines apparently did sell; the fact that so few women demanded more than this, to feel themselves enlightened.

On the far right he caught sight of the magazines for teenage girls. *All the dirt on celebrity girls' bitching / Vote for Hollywood's cutest puppy dog / 7 Miss Teens we want to diss / Tricks to make him fall for you.* All women in editorial, except for a man or two in production. He wondered how these women brought up their children. Whether in their private lives they were also inclined to stereotype all the gender roles and see to it that their daughters became infantile bimbos, or whether they just did the job as long as it paid.

One more time the thought raced through his head – where were the intelligentsia? Why was it that some people spent so little time thinking and had so few thoughts? Why did they make themselves so insignificant that they were convinced their actions made no difference?

Since the possibility of numbing his mind had been taken from him, he'd had a harder and harder time tolerating reality. Could it be that the human brain needed to be blunted occasionally, so that it could overlook all the stupidity and manage to feel some hope?

'Are you in the queue or not?'

He was roused from his contemplations and began putting his items on the conveyor belt. With a new supply of frozen dinners he headed home. His thoughts had given him a new idea, and he was feeling good again, ready to keep working on his play.

The door to his building was in sight when he decided to turn on his mobile. He had three new messages. One from the theatre, wondering how it was going; the second from Jesper. It wasn't until he listened to the third one that time stood still. He put down his bag of groceries and had to lean against the wall.

Something about a will in which he was named the sole beneficiary.

CHAPTER 9

The smell of an apple. To be able to reach out his arm and pick it up, move it towards his face and breathe in its aroma. The lightning-quick displacement to a lost time; a magical gateway to the realm which normally lay dimmed by decades of change, but which in an instant could be resurrected.

Axel Ragnerfeldt looked at the bright green apples lying in the fruit bowl. Just as inaccessible as if they were still in the land of their origin named on the little label stuck to them. He consoled himself with the fact that they surely no longer had any smell, injected and manipulated as they were to withstand the long journey halfway around the world. They were not like the apples of his childhood, carefully harvested from the lone tree in their allotment, to be converted into golden juice and holiday apple sauce. The meticulously tended garden with potatoes, turnips and other practical vegetables, and some occasional extravagances such as snapdragons, columbines and sweet violets sneaking into the rows. Mamma hurrying about her thousand tasks and father's steady hammer-blows, proud and precise. The little shed that slowly grew beneath his rough hands. Six square metres, but more precious than the most magnificent palace. He recalled the regulations posted: *The allotment gardens are primarily intended for the great number of labourers and their like who live in the city in poor circumstances and have difficult living conditions.*

'Bliss', they had named it, the little plot that like an oasis offered them solace from the cramped flat with one room and kitchen a stone's throw away: the little wooden city with its simple dwellings in the gap between Ringvägen and Blekingegatan streets, built as an emergency solution to the acute housing shortage after the First World War, though it remained until the end of the sixties.

Fill your head with knowledge, boy, it's the only thing that can take you out of here.

There was a knock at the door. He had never understood why they bothered. Since he'd ended up at the nursing home he could neither welcome anyone nor send them away, and he found their knocks insulting. As if rubbing it in. He heard the door open behind his back. Somebody came in but said nothing, so he didn't know who it was until she appeared in his field of vision. He didn't remember her name; everyday details often slipped his mind, perhaps because he wasn't interested. Only things that happened long ago had sharp contours. Maybe that was his brain's way of protecting him. His body had become a closed space in which he was locked inside. Without doors or windows and beyond all human contact. Monotonous days that came and went and had to be endured. His entire prize-winning intellect had moved into the little finger of his left hand, which sometimes obeyed his orders but lately had more often proved unco-operative. Trapped in a body he couldn't move, but whose sensations of pain were intact. After hours in the same position the pain was unbearable. And yet he couldn't ask for help. Then his only salvation was to escape into the past.

Though there were certain nooks and crannies he carefully avoided, to which his mind did not care to go.

'Hi, Axel, are you comfortable or should I move you a bit?'

A towel wiped off the saliva that had drooled out of his mouth. How did she expect him to answer? A movement with his finger meant yes. The question was beyond his resources. He wanted to sit up and scream, release the roar of rage that filled him. This was no life, it was a condition, and his feeling of humiliation was his worst enemy. He had always been selective about the people with whom he associated, and few had passed through the eye of the needle. Forced gatherings had always been refused, and over the years even the select circle of acquaintances had shrunk. At the same pace that his fame had increased, the people around him had changed; a few had remained themselves but most of them had turned deferential or obsequious. He had experienced a sense of being an outsider, which soon became incorporated into his lonely writer's life, and finally he could probably best be described as unsociable. Now he was fair game for unknown people. They came and went, and witnessed his humiliation. Strange hands that touched his body and became familiar with his most private parts. He was at their mercy and utterly dependent; he couldn't even die by his own hand.

She was still standing to one side behind his back and he sensed that she was waiting.

'Shall I move you a little?'

He concentrated but his finger refused to respond, even though his body was begging to be moved. Not until she turned and left did he see out of the corner of his eye how his finger gave a little twitch. He heard the door close and fled back into his memories.

How much had been made clear? He didn't know. Perhaps what the eye saw and the ear heard could be distorted, but never the experience. Everything fallen into an oblivion that still carved tracks. The neighbourhood of his childhood was long gone, but was immortalised in several of his early novels. Despite poor circumstances it had been a good place to grow up. Constant chatter about the weather in the stairwell and from the windows. The games that changed with the seasons, always outside because of the crowded living conditions. Skating in the winter on rinks they flooded themselves. The gigantic snow caves that turned into forts during the snowball fights. The toboggan runs where red-cheeked kids with chapped lips slid on sheets of cardboard and the seats of their trousers. When the snow melted the games began; treasured marbles constantly changed owners. He would be rich one evening and destitute the next. He remembered playing rounders and games with home-made footballs of paper and string. In the summertime swimming in Årstaviken and chasing after the water-sprinkler truck that kept down the dust between the cobblestones. His envy of those who were lucky enough to go to holiday camp or had relatives in the countryside. The autumn, when they all got together again. The season of hide-and-seek and ghost stories.

He remembered the smells. Always the smells. The aroma of dinner and fresh-baked bread, the rank smell from the rubbish bins and outdoor toilets in the courtyard. The smell of sweaty coats drying in the dark hallways. Horse-shit on the streets and newly chopped wood. The fleeting smell of freshly washed sheets in the drying loft.

The shops, all with their distinctive smells: the fishmonger, the butcher, the bakery, the wood and kerosene cellar. And all the sounds. In the streets the noise from cars and trams, pushcarts, iron-shod hooves and clattering wheels. The new and the old in a struggle for space.

He remembered the silent winter, when sound was absorbed by the snow and the grown-ups stayed indoors. Huddled in their tiny flats and then released in early spring when everything returned.

The radio. That magical box around which everyone gathered and which conjured away the walls, opening the room to the wide world.

Fill your head with knowledge, boy, it's the only thing that can take you out of here.

As a little boy those words had scared him; he didn't want to go anywhere. He wanted to stay there with Mamma and Pappa where things were familiar, with all the safe routines and monotonous repetition. He had wondered why they wanted to get rid of him. Why they were so eager to drive him away from the life which in the next breath they were so quick to praise. Hard work, fastidiousness and order. Unity gives strength. High morals and a conscientious life, a bust of Hjalmar Branting, Sweden's first Social Democratic prime minister, demonstrated their class affiliation from its place of honour on the bureau. One of the few objects in their home that was not utilitarian. So many times his memory had furnished this place. The kitchen, where his mother reigned until evening, and a bed made up for Pappa on the pull-out sofa. The room inside, which during the day stood empty but where at night he and his mother and his two-years-older sister slept. She was the one who had a good head for studying, but no notice was ever taken. Not even when her teacher took the time to knock on their door one evening to try and convince his parents to let the girl continue her studies after elementary school. They had stubbornly stood their ground. Axel was the one in their family who was going to study, and that had been decided long ago. He was going to be an engineer, a profession with a future. His sister had been filled with a bitterness that was constantly nurtured in the years that followed. She never forgave him, even though the choice had not been his.

The sun had reached past the window-sill and an irritating shaft of light struck him in the face. His eyes, which during the first year after the stroke would blink when he wanted them to and not merely when necessary, closed and left him in a reddish-purple darkness.

The fact that his parents had chosen engineering, of all things, had astonished him. Numbers had never been his allies. Nor was he particularly practical by nature. God knew that he tried; in his eagerness to impress his father he had done everything to become like him. His father's indulgent glance when his hand demonstrably lacked talent for the hammer when they were building the shed at Bliss. Doggedly his father pulled out the misplaced nails and simply put them where they were supposed to have gone. Never a harsh word, only the silent message that practice made perfect and that one should never give up. Hard work, fastidiousness and order. At five thirty every morning except Sunday the alarm clock would ring, because at seven his father started work at the sugar mill. His mother did her part by taking the tram twice a week all the way to Östermalm, where she cleaned a flat. And it was from that family's voluminous bookshelves that the treasures were gleaned, carefully smuggled out and then returned the following week – novels by Jules Verne, Alexandre Dumas and Jack London. He lost himself in the meandering stories, let himself be whisked away by the tales and continued the journey in his own words when he finished reading the books. His exercise book and loose sheets of paper were filled with fantastic stories about heroes and adventures. Both his mother and father read what he wrote, commenting on and evaluating his penmanship and spelling, but they never said a word about the content. The double message was imprinted early on – you in particular are expected to rise above the limits of your origin; but even so don't believe that you're anything special. When his stories finally were deemed far too verbose, the source of their inspiration stopped appearing in his home. The books that inspired his imagination, whose pages dripped with colourful fantasy, remained on the shelves in Östermalm; instead reference books and technical literature with bone-dry text were borrowed in an effort to usurp. All to prepare him for the day when he would take the exam for one of the free places at the Higher General Secondary School for Boys in Södermalm.

The door behind him was opened, but there was no knock this time. His eyelids refused to obey his command and remained as they were, a shield against the glaring sunshine. Only when he sensed the wheelchair moving and he ended up in the shade did they open, and he saw that it was Jan-Erik who had come.

'Hi, Pappa.'

Once again he felt the towel wipe his chin, where the drool still ran; the itching was driving him crazy. Jan-Erik's hand was tentative, not firm like that of the attendants. It revealed that his son was just as uncomfortable in this situation as he was, that he experienced it as equally unnatural.

'Would you like to lie down for a while? They said you'd been sitting up all morning.'

With all his strength he concentrated and finally managed to lift his little finger.

'Okay, I'll just go and fetch someone to help me.'

Out of the corner of his eye he saw Jan-Erik disappear. He realised he ought to be grateful, surely his son's visit was out of duty and not of his own free will, and yet he couldn't bring himself to feel grateful. He had never really understood his son, and to be honest he wasn't even sure that he liked him. His total lack of ambition. Born with every opportunity served up on a platter, yet he had never made use of a single one. Only hopped about half-heartedly without purpose or goal, without ever taking the helm. Axel himself had been born without any opportunities at all, but his parents' toil and his own indomitable will had propelled him forward. Against all odds. He remembered the shame he felt when he failed the scholarship exam, and his parents' disappointment. His mother and father, whose motto was 'Never give up', had not let themselves be deterred. Over the next eight years they had endured constant hardship to finance his studies to become a graduate of the secondary school, all to open the doors to the Royal Technical College where the final goal hovered like a mirage: his degree in civil engineering. No sacrifice had been too great. Both his parents had two jobs, saving every krona to be able to afford the tuition fees. Axel himself had spent every waking moment fulfilling their ambitions, trying to convince himself that those ambitions were his as well. But the school had been a foreign environment in which he slowly changed. Pupils from his social background were rare, and to get along in that setting he was forced to adapt. Here conflicts were not solved with fists like in the back courtyards; here it was always language that brought superiority. Unlike his own environment, the goal *was* to distinguish himself, to believe seriously that he *was* somebody. Difficulties arose when he had to switch back and function in his own neighbourhood, where the old rules applied.

His transformation led him farther and farther away from his origins, and also from his parents who had fought so doggedly for his cause. His language changed, his thoughts ventured outside their traditional realms. At home, where everything was done for his benefit, he felt more and more alone. He sensed that he was cherished not so much for who he was, but for what he would someday become. He began to regard himself as a project and not as a member of the family. His sister's bitter envy and the weight of his parents' expectations were sometimes so oppressive he could hardly breathe.

In his third year he was already having trouble with mathe matics. Words fell into place of their own accord, but he found no logic in numbers; they refused to yield up their secrets to him. He got the highest marks on all assignments in Swedish class, while he barely passed his maths exams. It was during the same period that his father had been called up; the country was being mobilised after the Germans had occupied Denmark and Norway. The lack of his father's income brought the family to their knees. Not only was there food rationing; in poor homes there was a lack of everything. He remembered the endless queuing in shops with empty shelves. The cold nights. How there was never enough wood, and how the dampness ate into the fabrics. How he and his sister went out in the evenings to try and find something to put in the stove. The blackout curtains, the frenetic voice on the radio and the terror that Hitler would come.

He concealed his failed maths exam, made sure the results were never seen by his eager parents, and when it was time to choose a major subject he was forced for the first time to go behind their backs. The scientific path with mathematics as a major focus was the one that would open the way to the Royal Technical College. Instead he selected the humanistic linguistic path, and thus the anticipated door was secretly closed.

Jan-Erik came back again with an attendant. Together they lifted Axel onto the bed. He felt the relief as the pain gave way and his body was straightened out on the soft bedding. The head of the bed was raised and some pillows were arranged behind him. Then came the constantly recurring question.

'Is that comfortable?'

No, he wanted to scream. No, it's not comfortable. I want you to bring me all the sedatives you have in this ward and pump them into my bloodstream so that I can go to sleep once and for all. But he could only lift his little finger and assure them that everything was fine.

Jan-Erik sat down in the visitor's chair, and the attendant left. His son usually brought along the day's paper and read aloud to him, and he had done so this time as well. Axel didn't understand why he had to be kept informed. How could anyone believe that he had the slightest interest in the world he had already left behind? He had to be kept company, and this was Jan-Erik's brave attempt. Their relationship was not constructed in such a way that the power balance would tolerate a shift. He couldn't explain his antipathy, why he had never felt close to his son. There was something about his compliant gaze, the fact that he never demanded his rights. Never burned so strongly for something that he dared take up a fight. And on the rare occasion he had tried, he had been so wrong. As if he had no concept of what was best for him.

Jan-Erik's voice droned on through the endless columns, and Axel returned to his own thoughts.

It was during the final year before graduation that the conflict inside him had erupted in earnest. A consuming anxiety about having to tell his parents that their engineering dreams would remain nothing but dreams. But also about the other matter that was becoming stronger and stronger. He knew that he had a talent, and the years of study had confirmed his brilliance. His lack of aptitude for mathematics had left room for another quality: he was drawn irresistibly to language, like a moth to the light. The temptation was irresistible. He could feel the stories jostling about inside him, waiting to be given life. But writing was not a real profession, it was a dissolute hobby that one might take up in free moments. There was every reason to be suspicious of literature that did not lead to concrete knowledge. He knew that his parents would never understand, and with each day that brought him closer to the conversation he would have to have with them, his fear grew.

It had been on the day of his final examination. They were sitting in the room next to the kitchen where in honour of the day they were going to have their coffee, watched over only by Hjalmar Branting. No guests had been invited; you shouldn't believe that you were somebody even though your son against all odds had just passed his final exam. But real coffee would be served, not that substitute they'd got used to during the wartime rationing. They were all dressed up, his parents beaming with pride and his sister joining them, although in silent protest. With excruciating clarity he recalled how something in their eyes was extinguished when he told them about his decision. The fact that there would never be a civil engineer in the family, but rather a writer. His sister's spontaneous guffaw. His father's slap that silenced her.

On that day he passed the fork in the road and went on to meet his calling.

Sixty-three years later he still didn't know whether he had done the right thing. He had followed his conviction, but with the years his perspective had changed. A nagging guilt had become his companion, constantly driving him forward. No matter how much fame he acquired, it would never sink in. He could stand and look at his books and all his fine prizes, but he had never been able to feel any pride. They were and remained mere mileposts that he needed to surpass.

And all his life he had felt uneasy every time he was unlucky enough to meet an engineer.

Young people believed there was a goal in life. He had believed it himself; on that particular day he had believed it, believed it blindly, when in spite of his parents' annihilating disappointment he had set off to write his book. And he had written his book. And he had become an author. And he had realised that life was an infinite journey. The redemptive goal had always turned out to be a new starting point by the time he managed to get there. It wasn't possible to reach any goal. Only an end. And when he finally arrived, much like before, so many things had forever been left too late.

He woke up when it was suddenly silent and realised that he'd fallen asleep for a moment. With a rustling sound Jan-Erik was folding up the newspaper.

'I have to get going now. I'll swing by the house and see if I can find a picture of Gerda Persson. She died about a week ago and they want one for the funeral.'

All of a sudden he was wide-awake. His eyes flew open. The name had taken him straight into the nooks and crannies of his mind.

'I thought I'd see if I could find something. You probably know if there's something in your office, don't you? Maybe in the cupboard where you saved everything over the years?'

He was having heart palpitations. Gerda was gone and he ought to feel grateful. Evidently she had remained loyal to the end. Now there was only one person left who could obliterate his life's work. If he was still alive. As long as Axel had been able to talk it would have been both of them dragged through the mud if the truth had come out. But since the stroke not a day had passed without his thinking of that man's name and what he might be capable of doing.

And then there was the cupboard in his office, where things were kept that nobody must see. He had begun to clean it out shortly before he had the stroke, suddenly aware of the insanity of keeping those things. Perhaps his unconscious had been warning him that time was growing short. But he hadn't finished. He wondered whether the rubbish bag was still there or whether Jan-Erik had thrown it out by now. He hoped

132

so. Even more he hoped that Torgny Wennberg was dead. The Devil himself in human form. If only these two wishes were fulfilled, the name Axel Ragnerfeldt would for ever be allowed to retain its radiance.

Then it would all have been worth the effort.

CHAPTER 10

The Rector's Sports Prize in the municipal school district, 1967. Silently he whispered the words to himself and felt an expansive, bright joy spread through his body. He, Jan-Erik Ragnerfeldt, had won, and it would be announced in the school's assembly hall in the presence of pupils, teachers and parents. The choir would sing and the rector would give a speech, and in the middle of the school's spring concert he was the one who would be called up on stage to receive the cup and a diploma.

Now only the hardest challenge remained, to make sure his father was in the hall when the solemn event took place.

He sat at the kitchen table eating a salami sandwich.

'Now eat so that you grow big and strong, and if you want more bread it's in the tin.'

Gerda stood at the worktop preparing meatballs for the following day. She cracked an egg on the edge of a stainless-steel bowl, and her hands began kneading the mincemeat. As so often before she hummed some melody that Jan-Erik didn't recognise. But he had enough to do with working out a solution to the dilemma occupying his thoughts.

'Where's your sister? Doesn't she want an evening snack?'

'She's probably in her room.'

'I most certainly am not.' A hand appeared in the corner behind the wood-stove that was no longer used, and the next moment Annika came creeping out.

'I declare, so there you are. You fooled me again.'

Gerda gave a long laugh as if she found it an extremely amusing trick, even though Annika was most often to be found in that space behind the stove, which she had fixed up as a little house.

'Well, I told you.'

Jan-Erik smiled at Gerda. It was so odd such things amused her – things that nobody else ever laughed at. Both he and Annika loved being in the kitchen. Partly because it was far enough away from their father's office that they didn't have to keep their voices down, but also because there was something comforting about Gerda. As long as no other grown-up was in the vicinity. As soon as one of their parents was present she changed and laughed as little as all the others in the house.

Someone rang the doorbell. Three short rings. It was Gerda's task to answer it, but right now her hands were full of the sticky meat.

'Go and get the door, Annika, if you would.'

Annika vanished down the hall. Jan-Erik heard

135

at once who it was, and all hope was extinguished. Now the evening would turn to night before he had a chance to ask his father.

Annika came dashing back into the kitchen and crawled in behind the stove. In the next instant Torgny Wennberg appeared in the doorway with his overcoat on, hat in hand.

'Hello, all, I see you're cooking. What sort of delicacy is it this time?'

'It's just some meatballs. I'll tell him you're here.'

Gerda went to the sink with her gooey hands.

'No, no, don't let me interrupt. I can knock on the door myself.'

And then he was gone. Jan-Erik wondered why a stranger who didn't even live in the house was allowed to do something that nobody else could do. Knock on the door while his father was working. The next moment he realised that now was his chance, now that the door would be opened even if it wasn't for him. As fast as he could he ran through the house to get there before it was too late. Torgny Wennberg was still standing at the door when he arrived.

'Yes?' came a voice from the other side of the door.

Torgny opened it and went in. Jan-Erik sneaked up and stood just outside the threshold.

'Well, hello there, Torgny, so it's you coming to bother me.'

'I thought you might need a little inspiration on a Tuesday evening.'

Smiles and handshakes, and then his father caught sight of him.

'Did you want something, Jan-Erik?'

'Yes, I just wanted to ask you something.'

'It'll have to wait, I have a visitor now, as you can see. Go and ask your mother or Gerda.'

He closed the door firmly.

Jan-Erik was sitting in the armchair in the living room. From there he had a view of the door to the office, and he hadn't left the room in two hours. Three times his mother had passed by, each time asking what he was doing. Nothing special, he'd replied, and she'd looked at him as though she thought he was lying. Now it was almost bedtime and the door still hadn't opened. Everything would be ruined if his father didn't come. Now that he finally had something to show him.

He heard her footsteps on the stairs and for the fourth time she appeared in the living room. This time she was silent. She simply went over to one of the bookshelves and ran her finger over the spines of the books as if searching for a certain volume.

And then with her back to him she said, 'Have you asked Axel if he's coming with us tomorrow?'

'No, I told him about it a couple of weeks ago, but he hasn't said yet whether he's coming.'

'And how long were you planning to sit here?'

'I'm just sitting and thinking a little. I have a geography test on Friday, so I'm trying to prepare.'

She turned to him. 'So where's your geography book?'

He could feel himself blush. 'Well, I know almost everything by heart. I'm going over my European capitals.'

That was all she said. But he noticed that she didn't take a book with her when she left and went upstairs.

Another hour passed. The ticking clock on the wall kept precise track of the time, and the soporific sound made him doze off. He woke up when somebody tugged at his sleeve. Annika had her nightgown on, and he could see that she'd been crying.

'You have to come, there's something wrong with Mamma.'

He looked at the door, which was still closed.

'Hurry up!'

Despite her fear she was whispering, and he ran down the hall after her and up the stairs.

Their mother was lying on the floor of her bedroom, in her dressing gown with her face to the floor. He was filled with a greater fear than he'd ever felt in his life. Annika began to sob. Jan-Erik hurried over and knelt down at his mother's side. He pulled on her arm and brushed the hair out of her face.

'Mamma! Mamma! Wake up, Mamma! Tell me what happened. Say something, Mamma, tell me what's wrong with you.'

She didn't move. Her arm was limp as he tugged and yanked at it. He felt the tears come. He put his nose to her mouth, but she didn't smell as sour as she did sometimes when she'd been drinking wine. This was something else.

'Mamma. Please, Mamma, wake up.'

He let go of her arm and pressed his hands to his face.

'We have to get Pappa.'

He was just about to jump up and rush off when she opened her eyes. She twisted round a bit and looked first at him and then at Annika.

'Annika, could you fetch me a glass of water?'

Annika ran off. His mother sat up. All at once she looked completely natural, as if she hadn't just been lying like a dead woman on the floor.

'So you do care a little bit after all.'

Jan-Erik froze. At first he didn't understand what she meant and just sat there. A tear was allowed to run down his cheek undisturbed.

His mother got up but he remained on the floor; following her with his gaze as she went over to the bed and sat down.

'What do you mean?' he finally managed to say.

'You're so anxious for Axel to come tomorrow, but you've hardly asked me.'

'But I want you to come too. You told me you would. I'm sure I asked you.'

'Are you quite sure you want me to come?'

He felt the tears again.

'Of course I want you to be there.'

Suddenly she covered her face with her hands and her shoulders began to shake the way they did when she was crying. Jan-Erik's tears ceased abruptly. He got up from the floor hurriedly and went over and patted her on the arm.

'I'm sorry, Mamma, I'm sorry. I do want you to come, much more than I want Pappa, I promise. I'm sorry.'

Annika came back with a glass of water. Their mother wiped her eyes and put the glass on the nightstand.

'All right then. We'll say that. I'll talk to Axel and make sure he comes too.'

CHAPTER 11

'There has been no improvement at all, rather the opposite. Axel is actually too ill to remain here. Our beds are intended for patients who can be rehabilitated. But since he is Axel Ragnerfeldt, we've decided to let him stay. It's not definite that he'd be able to get a private room anywhere else, and considering his celebrity and what it means for his integrity, we've decided to make an exception.'

That's what the doctor had told them during the meeting, and Jan-Erik had expressed his gratitude. Then he had spent an hour with his father and confirmed that the medical diagnosis was correct. It was becoming harder and harder to make contact. Jan-Erik had tried to update him on both the news and what was going on culturally, but the question was how much he actually understood.

He found the visits grim. For so long he had dreamt of gaining the upper hand, but when he finally did any sense of satisfaction failed to appear. Instead he was plagued by what would now never happen. He wondered how it would be the day

141

Axel actually died and was gone, how the grief would feel. Because how could he let go of what he'd never had?

He let the motor run and got out to open the gates, noticing that it was time to call the head gardener. The verges were brown with withered perennials, and everything was covered with leaves. One of the supports on the covered patio, built when he was in the States and which nobody had ever used, had blown over and was lying in the grass. The gravel path, the constant bane of his youth, had been infiltrated by grass, and he was thankful that his mother wasn't with him. She had kept an eye on the gravel and its border with the lawn as if keeping them separate were a matter of life and death, and it had been his task to maintain it – his and Gerda's and Annika's.

He returned to his car, drove in and parked in front of the house. There he sat for a while, feeling no hurry to go inside.

It had been a long journey. Perhaps not geographically speaking, but it felt as though life had gone through an endless number of twists and turns since he'd moved out of this house. Over thirty years had passed, and yet it was as if everything led him back here, no matter how he tried to escape its grip. Sometimes he was even homesick, though he didn't know why. But he only felt that way as long as he was somewhere else. Once he arrived he immediately wanted to leave.

He got out of the car and fished out his house

keys. The steps to the front door were covered with leaves, and he swept them off with the broom that had stood guard by the entrance since time immemorial. The ends were worn down from years of use and reminded him of a cheese that had been sliced crooked. Once again Louise appeared in his mind; cheeses cut like a toboggan-run always irritated her, and he had learned to use the cheese-cutter with precision. He sighed. He had placed the business card she'd given him in his wallet, but naturally he hadn't rung the number. He knew she would ask as soon as he stepped in the door at home.

He unlocked the front door and turned off the burglar alarm, wiping his shoes carefully on the doormat but keeping them on because the floors of the uninhabited house were cold. The heat was kept down to a minimum and was turned up only in the wintertime to keep the water pipes from freezing.

He went into the kitchen and placed the house keys on the wood-stove, looking about to make sure that everything was as it should be. Everything was unchanged and looked the same as always. Only a lamp by the window clashed with his memory, the one he had put there himself and hooked up to a timer. The refrigerator door was ajar with a kitchen towel in the gap, and all work surfaces were bare and clean. Everything lay fallow.

He knew the house inside out, except for the blank spot that made up Axel's office, an unknown world in all this familiar space. He left the kitchen and went through the silent house. Every nook was inhabited by memories: each door handle, each creaky floorboard, each tiny object. Except for the switches for the ceiling lights, which had been replaced in the eighties when the house was rewired. Every time his hand trailed along the wall and met the unfamiliar shape it was surprised, expecting a different one.

Most things had been left in place after Axel's stroke, when his mother felt that she could leave the house at last and move into the city. Some of the paintings and most of Axel's literary prizes, the ones he had received from near and far and which had stood on all the window niches and bookshelves, were now in storage somewhere safe until it was decided what to do with the house. The items that had been removed had left empty spaces behind, giving the house a desolate feeling. The walls were full of mournful borders, left by pictures that had been removed.

He lingered in what they called the library. Dark brown, built-in bookshelves teeming with literature. And yet they were insufficient; the books had escaped from the room and spread like a plague throughout the house with constant demands for new shelves. He hadn't read a fraction of them, and to be honest he hadn't even been particularly interested. Or else his indifference may have been a cautious protest, he didn't know. But he did know that each book represented sacrifices demanded from the family and friends of the author so that it could be written. And nothing else had mattered.

In the room was a framed photograph of Annika. In a gap in the row of books it stood wedged in next to a white porcelain figurine, a little boy who lay resting against a dog. Jan-Erik went over and took down the small frame. He rubbed his sleeve over the dusty glass. She was ten years old in the picture, with five years left to live. Her hair was in pigtails and she was smiling at the camera. He missed her, often wondering how everything would have been if she were still alive. She still felt so familiar, like a part of him; only no one could see her. In appearance she was always twelve years old, the way she was the last time he had seen her. But in his mind she had aged along with him. Or else it could be that in his internal conversations with her he was still back in the time when she was alive. What a person had shared with a sibling could never be transferred to anyone else. It was a relationship built on common experiences, the fact that they were in such close proximity during the stage of life when they had no choice of their own. The fact that they were marked by the same environment. Sometimes he would even type her name into Google to see if there were any others besides him who remembered her. He never got any hits.

She was fifteen years old when she was run over. The driver of the car had never come forward. He didn't know many details, because it had happened while he was abroad.

With the photograph in his hand he sank into one of the library armchairs. He stroked his finger over her face. He should never have left her alone.

At first it had all been like a dream, too good to be true – he had received a scholarship. His tennis coach, who recognised his talent, had helped him with the formalities. Without him saying a word at home, the application had been sent in and accepted. For three years he would study at a college in Florida and be part of the school's successful tennis team. Everything had been arranged when he had proudly come home to tell them. He had imagined the scene, how at the dinner table when everyone was gathered together he would take out the letter and pass it around. How he would silently read the astonished reactions on their faces. How his father would be ashamed that he hadn't understood, and regret that he had never come to watch a match. And finally he would realise that his son had his own rare talent, despite his inability to see poetry in the simplest objects. Unlike his father Jan-Erik was the type who simply saw a dustbin when he saw a dustbin, and not a 'vessel for unwanted memories'. And there had been a reaction, but not the one he had imagined. His mother congratulated him and then took another gulp of wine, which was to be expected. But his father's reaction he could not have predicted, not from this man who had never before cared. Sports were not something for intellectuals, Jan-Erik was informed; one might devote oneself to sports in order to keep the body in shape, to oxygenate the blood and thus facilitate the flow of knowledge. Tennis was a sport for the upper class, for spoilt rich kids, and he certainly hoped that his son was not turning into one of them.

Jan-Erik had sat there silent, incapable of matching his wild hopes with what was actually happening.

His mother got up from the table and glared at her husband.

'You're an idiot and you know it,' she said.

Then she refilled her wine glass and went upstairs. Annika followed right behind her. Alone, father and son finished dinner in indignant silence.

Several days passed, and for the first time he had dared take up the fight. In his seventeenth year he had finally opened hostilities. At first timidly, but after daring a few times he had begun to enjoy being able to slam doors, stomp up the stairs and in wrath say whatever he liked. He remembered Annika, the way she had sometimes slunk along the walls. He had no memory of his mother's actions during the war. Only the eternal dressing gown, which she wore more and more often. And Gerda's nervous comments – 'He only wants what's best for you' and 'Is it really worth all this?' And then the resolution, which on his father's part was a concession. Of course he could go to America if he wanted to, Axel had even arranged everything for him with the help of his contacts. American Field Service had a student exchange programme with the objective of promoting understanding, contact and friendly relations between students from Europe and the United States. It was a context in which a Ragnerfeldt belonged, and the tickets were already booked.

At that moment Jan-Erik had realised for the first time how much he hated his father, and staying in the house had seemed impossible. A month later he had left, his own plans defeated and travelling on his father's tickets. He ended up in a little dump of a town in the Midwest, living with a conservative middle-class family with Christian values. The Vietnam War was raging, and the family stood wholeheartedly behind their president. He himself had not been very involved. But around Christmas in 1972, being Swedish was enough to land him in the opposition camp. The prime minister Olof Palme had criticised the United States and compared the continuous bombing of North Vietnam to Hitler's attacks during the Second World War. In a rage President Nixon had refused to receive the new Swedish ambassador. Jan-Erik had done his best to be accepted anyway. He had devotedly assimilated American culture and set a new personal record for adaptation.

★　　★　　★

He jumped when his phone rang. The sudden sound in the empty house frightened him. It was Louise's number; she was ringing from the shop. He hesitated, wanting to let it ring and have the voicemail pick it up, but he knew that wasn't a good solution. He had used that trick too many times before.

'Jan-Erik.'

'It's me.' He didn't want anything from her so he said nothing.

'Where are you?'

'At the house. I'm looking for a photo of Gerda Persson.'

'How'd it go with your father?'

'Same as usual. No improvement, at any rate.'

'When are you coming home?'

She sounded different from that morning. He could almost imagine that they were having a normal conversation in which one could say anything that came into one's mind rather than having to screen things out.

'I have to look for that photo. I don't know how long it will take, I just got here.'

'Are you coming home after that?'

'Yes.'

There was a pause.

'You know, I just want to say that I'm glad we had that talk this morning, even though it was hard. I think something good can come out of it.'

He said nothing.

'Anyway, I just wanted to tell you that. I'll see you later then.'

'Sure. Bye.'

He hung up. Her new tone worried him; it had sounded almost like a rapprochement.

He got up and put the photo of Annika back on the shelf, adjusting the angle so it could be properly seen. It struck him that it had been a long time since he'd been to her grave, but he had never really felt any connection with the place. How could he? Her name on the headstone proved that she was lying there, but he had never seen her with his own eyes. His father had refused to pay for the trip home, since Jan-Erik had refused to use the return ticket he had already financed. Against his parents' will he had stayed in the States after finishing his studies, and for two years he had hitchhiked around with no goal except to avoid going home. It had taken him ten months to make enough money for a plane ticket, and in the meantime he'd missed both Annika's funeral and the Nobel ceremony for his father. But he did make it home in time to see Björn Borg win at Wimbledon. They had met twice as junior players. One time Jan-Erik had been close to beating him.

It had begun to grow dark outside when he opened the door to his father's office. His hand found the new light switch. He stopped in the doorway. About a month after his father had his stroke, when Jan-Erik had become used to the idea that no one was going to stop him, he had gone in and sat down behind the desk. He had sat there for a

150

long time, absorbing the feeling. Then he had carefully pulled out the top desk drawer, just to see how it felt, and then pushed it back in.

One wall was filled with bookshelves, most of them holding Axel's books translated into various languages. The opposite wall was covered with certificates and framed photographs, and here and there was a space where a signed picture had once been. He went over to the wall. None of the photos was of the family. They were all from some award ceremony or banquet with dignitaries. Believing that he would find Gerda anywhere was hopeless.

He went over to the cupboard door. He had only looked inside once before, and he'd found the key in the desk drawer. The darkness and raw cold struck him, and he realised that he needed a pocket torch. There was one on the shelf inside the door to the cellar; it had always been there. Removing it would have been ill-advised, since his mother had always been meticulous about everything having its place, and her reaction was unpredictable. Yes, the pocket torch was right where it should be, despite the fact that no one would ever be angry again, as if it had learned to obey all on its own. Nothing happened when he pushed the button on it. He went to the kitchen and pulled out the fourth drawer from the top – the drawer for batteries, elastic bands and clingfilm. There was an unopened packet. It occurred to him how strange it was to find charged batteries in the deserted house. As if they were the only things still alive. They lay there, ready, waiting for something that no one knew would ever happen. He changed the batteries and went back to the library.

There was a half-full rubbish bag inside the door. He shone the torch beam into it and saw printed materials and other papers. He would take those with him when he left – if his father had intended to throw them away they were undoubtedly rubbish. Axel had saved everything. Jan-Erik's mother had called his hoarding a disease.

The cupboard was bigger than the others in the house, and ran along one whole side of the room. Heaps of paper, magazines, folders, binders, fan letters, newspaper clippings and boxes. All in a godforsaken mess that could not have been systematic even for the person who had once stuffed it all in. It would take weeks to clean out, sorting through what should be saved. The rubbish bag was a sign that his father had already begun, but considering the small amount in the bag and the quantity left he hadn't got very far. The dream was to find an unpublished manuscript somewhere in the mess. After his Nobel Prize, his father had only published a few books; they were well received by the critics, but there was no real enthusiasm for them. It was clear to everyone that *Shadow* had been the high point of his career, a level he never managed to achieve again. But an unknown manuscript published after his death would bring in a considerable sum, even if it was from his declining years.

Jan-Erik began to dig through the piles, at a loss as to where to start. Notebooks, reviews, letters from admirers, programme flyers for author visits and the follow-up articles in the press. Much of what he found he was interested in studying further, but he knew this was not the right time. Even finding a photograph of Gerda might take hours. He opened a cardboard box full of old letters and to his relief found some old photographs. He took the box over to the desk and sat down. He moved the typewriter and set the box in its place. The first photo was an old black-and-white snapshot showing his father's parents; the next was in colour and more recent, and they looked just as he remembered them. They had come to visit occasionally, always formally dressed, his grandfather in a suit and tie and his grandmother in a dress. They had moved about the rooms cautiously as if they were afraid to knock something over. They would come on the occasion of some celebration, and he recalled that even as a child he had noticed the way his father changed. He had looked on in wonder as Axel suddenly lost his usual commanding presence and instead dashed about the house showing off his fine prizes and framed certificates. His grandparents had looked on wide-eyed but didn't say much, except for trivial remarks about some detail of a frame. Otherwise they had seemed to be more comfortable in the kitchen with Gerda, who on those occasions was always welcome to eat with the family in the dining room. And he suddenly remembered one Christmas dinner when they had been using the fine china, and his grandmother had tipped over her glass on the white tablecloth. Her face had turned crimson despite all assurances that it didn't matter in the least, and she hadn't eaten another bite. Not until Gerda happened to tip over a half-full beer bottle 'by accident'.

They had died in the mid-eighties, four days apart, and at the joint funeral Jan-Erik had seen his father cry for the first and only time.

He put the lid back on the box and went back to the cupboard, determined to start at a different corner. There was a box on the floor at the back. A tall pile of papers was stacked on top. He lifted them off and opened the box. The first letter was dated 1976 and was from a publisher, but the date showed that he was in the right time frame. He took the box out to the light in the office.

He found it somewhere in the middle of the pile, after he'd glanced through his father's name and address on countless envelopes and other items of mail. It was not at all what he was looking for, but the printed text up in the corner attracted his interest. A brown envelope from the police. He pulled out a folded sheet of paper, and everything he thought he knew became meaningless in an instant.

It was a police report.

Annika's full name, address, and Social Security

number. The words underneath made his body react as though he'd been startled by a sudden bang.

Immediate cause of death: Hanging.

Manner of death: Suicide.

CHAPTER 12

'When you hear the tone – ding-a-ling – it means it's time to turn the page. Now we'll begin.'

Kristoffer pushed the stop button on the old tape player. Many years had passed since he'd listened to the cassette. When he moved it had been packed in a carton and always had its obvious place among his belongings, but now he could no longer listen to it.

If a person had been waiting for a phone call for thirty-one years and that call finally came, how would that person be expected to react? Kristoffer didn't know. For five hours he had sat motionless on the sofa, incapable of feeling anything at all. The little scrap of paper on which he'd written the number lay beside him on the sofa cushion; occasionally he would turn his head to look at it.

Named as sole beneficiary in a will.

As long as he could remember, he had been afraid of the dark. He always slept with a light on when nobody else was around. Terror gripped him whenever what was revealed by the light disappeared into the dark; he had fantasies about what took shape when he could no longer see. Right now the room lay in darkness. Only the stubborn blinking from the closed lid of his laptop shone at regular intervals, pulsating like visual heartbeats. He hadn't eaten, hadn't called anyone, hadn't done anything at all. Just sat there motionless, trying to decide what to feel.

Biding his time.

He had always waited. And yet he was incapable of pressing down the numbers on the telephone. Like a magic formula they would transport him to the desired place, the place he had always dreamt of, though he knew nothing about it.

Who would he be transformed into once he did arrive?

His ego had been formed on two foundations. One was everything that it was possible to see, everything tangible with which he could have a relationship. The second consisted of what had always been out of reach, the hidden world where he belonged but to which he had always lacked access. Who was he? Why was he the way he was? Did he have any genetic traits? What had been affected by what?

Who was it who had once chosen his name?

And then the fundamental question, the one he'd carried with him like an invisible stigma: why had he been abandoned?

The missing answers had become a part of his identity. Time after time he had been forced to invent his background, altering details when the old ones had worn out, adapting it to new demands.

All the conversations he'd been forced to listen to; about hopeless parents and insufferable family get-togethers, Christmases that had to be endured and family squabbles about weeks of holiday in summer cabins that were a shared inheritance. Bitter battles, broken family relations and sick parents who required time-consuming care. He had always hidden behind the claim that his parents were dead. Someone had even had the bad taste to express envy because he had the freedom to do as he pleased without having to be subjected to a guilty conscience.

All around him was emptiness. Everyone else he knew was anchored to a clear chain in which the links could be followed. But he hovered freely with nothing holding him. He dreamt of finding the chain that was his, the one that would become whole when the missing link was finally rediscovered.

Kristoffer had been about four years old when he moved in with his foster family. Apparently they had handled the situation as well as they could. They had answered his questions to the best of their ability, but what could they say when there were no answers to give? The police investigation had produced no result. He had only been able to give a first name for his mamma, and everyone named Elina had been contacted with no result. He had never named a pappa.

At ten years old his foster parents had taken him to Stockholm and showed him the steps at Skansen. He got to meet the guard who had found him, who had never been able to forget the experience. But none of the questions Kristoffer asked him had produced an acceptable answer.

Sometimes a vague sensation would float by, a second-long feeling rather than a memory. Always torn out of its context, squeezed in between dim and incomprehensible thoughts.

He had created his own truth for himself, convinced that his real parents would soon show up. Overjoyed at finally finding him again, they would take him home to his real life, away from the life where he was simply waiting. They would explain how crushed they had been, how a horrible witch had locked them in a tower and refused to let them go. How they finally in spite of difficult hardships managed to escape, prepared to do anything to see him again. Over the years his fantasies had developed and the explanations became less like fairy tales, but the feeling that he was living in a temporary situation had never left him. He decided that it wasn't worth immersing himself in anything, since at any moment he would have to start over.

If only they would show up some day.

If he just held his breath until that car had passed, then they would show up soon. If he peeled the tangerine in one piece, then they would show up soon. If a man and a woman got on the bus at the next stop, then they would show up soon. As he approached each corner he would hope, and in every crowd he would search for his own facial features. He would stand for hours in front of the mirror. He memorised every detail of his face. Sometimes just for an instant he thought he saw someone else, one of the two unknown people who lived inside his body.

His relationship to his adoptive parents had been quite distant. They had done everything to win his trust, but he had never been interested. In secret he had even despised their ingratiating behaviour, the way they would back off instead of restricting his freedom to act. Sometimes he had even seen fear in their eyes, when he flatly refused to obey their wishes, although sometimes he did it out of sheer obstinacy. They were and would remain intruders in a space intended for others, and when he turned eighteen he left home and broke off all contact.

In January 2005 he had read their names in the paper in a list of missing persons after the tsunami in Khao Lak. He hadn't felt anything in particular.

He got up and turned on the desk lamp. The note was still lying on the sofa and his whole being was conscious of its existence. His mobile lay next to the keyboard, and he was just about to pick it up when the intercom buzzed. The unexpected sound made him jump; nobody should be coming unannounced. He decided to ignore it; he didn't want any visitors, not right now when everything was upside down. The next moment his mobile rang. It was Jesper. Not now, he thought. The ringtone stopped abruptly and then there was a beep for a voicemail message.

'Yeah, it's me. I'm standing in the street outside your front door, because I thought I'd ask if you could do me a favour and take some pictures of me. I've got a camera with me. I think I've solved the problem with the book promotion. Call me as soon as you hear this. Bye.'

Kristoffer deleted the message and pressed recall. Then he stopped and put down the mobile. Not a very nice thing to do, but these were special circumstances. Jesper would understand. Sometime in the future he'd explain. Besides, Jesper had sounded happier this time. No longer so gloomy.

Somebody had died. Maybe it was all too late. He sat back down on the sofa. Got up again, went out to the kitchen, drank some water out of the tap, turned and went back into the living room. He wanted a drink. Just a little one to get up the courage to dial the number. He brushed aside the thought, drove it off, but could feel how it stayed close by in case he changed his mind. He clenched his fist and smacked himself on the forehead, trying to pound in the courage he was lacking, and went back to the kitchen. He had to do it, he had to decide to do it right now, before he had a chance to change his mind. Resolutely he went back to the living room, picked up his mobile and went over to the sofa. Sat down and began to dial, put the phone to his ear, got up again. Seconds passed. Maybe the last seconds of his life as it had always been. Then an unfamiliar voice.

'Marianne Folkesson.'

'Yes, hello, this is Kristoffer Sandeblom. I got your message on my answer machine but I've had my phone off for a few days. That's why I didn't ring earlier, because I've just played your message.'

A little pause followed his speech. The nervousness had made him ramble. He sank back on the sofa.

'How nice of you to call. Yes, I'm the estate administrator for the county council, and I've been looking for you because Gerda Persson has unfortunately passed away.'

He could feel the rhythm of his heart. In his fingers holding the phone, in his thighs resting on the sofa. A regular pulse in his head.

Gerda Persson.

A woman, a mother. Not Elina but Gerda Persson. The name he had always been searching for.

'As I said in my message, she named you as sole beneficiary in her will.'

He couldn't speak. All his questions had stuck. For decades they had been practised for this very occasion, but now that it was here, no words would come out.

'Hello?'

'Yes, I'm here.'

'The funeral is on the twelfth at 2.30. I've begun the preparations since I haven't been able to get hold of any relatives, but of course I'd welcome your input, if you want to take care of it some other way.'

Gerda Persson. The name was taking up all the space.

Gerda.

Persson.

'Hello?'

'Yes, I'm here, that should be fine.'

'Then there are a number of decisions that have to be taken with regard to her flat. Perhaps you'd like to go over there and see whether there's anything you'd like to have before we clear it out?'

There was a long silence. Naturally he didn't say a word, and the woman on the other end seemed to have a hard time going on without a response. When she finally spoke, her tone was different. Less formal and more candid.

'I'm sorry to harp on about all the details, it really wasn't my intention to be insensitive. I'm sorry for your loss. I presume you were close?'

He got up and went over to the window. Looked out over Katarina cemetery. Was he really ready for this, did he really want to know? Of course he wanted to know, this was what he'd always been waiting for. But what if the waiting had actually become more important than getting the answers?

Everything had seemed so good the past few years. What would happen if all his assumptions were changed?

'It's like this, I—'

He stopped abruptly. For thirty-one years he had kept his mouth shut, and he now found it impossible to allow a stranger to be the first person he told.

'It's like this, we didn't know each other.'

Now it was the woman on the other end who was silent, and he welcomed the pause.

Here in Stockholm. Had she been so close?

'Okay . . . But you have been in touch?'

'I don't know.'

She said nothing, as if waiting for more. He realised that it would be fitting to say something, but he had nothing to add.

'It's a little odd,' she said, 'so I understand your surprise. But you must be the one she intended in the will. You do live in Katarina Västra Kyrkogata, care of Lundgren?'

'Yes.'

'That's the information I have.'

'But how could she know my address?'

'I don't know. You're the only one with that name, and as long as you're listed somewhere you wouldn't be that hard to find.'

And in a flash he understood. The money each month. The small sum that had appeared since he turned eighteen, wherever he was, and which he at first thought was from his foster parents. But

164

they had denied it after he'd left, when he once confronted them. The money that had not shown up this month.

Suddenly the word came down on him, the most shameful of all. Like a sharp glass shard it cut through all the evasive layers.

Foundling! You're a foundling!

Whatever was found had been lost by someone. But you didn't fasten little notes with instructions onto something that you lost by accident. It was deliberate.

He could feel something let go, and tears suddenly blurred his vision. He who never cried. With his hand over the mouthpiece he tried to collect himself; more tears fell and he sank deeper into the sofa. With all the self-control he could muster he tried to continue the conversation.

'So you have no idea where she could have got my name?'

'No, unfortunately. I can understand if it seems strange. I've gone through the personal records and I didn't find you in her family. She was unmarried, had no children, and the only family I found was a childless sister, but she died back in the late fifties.'

Seconds passed; everything was swimming around. He straightened up.

'How old was she, did you say?'

'The sister?'

'No, Gerda Persson.'

He heard her leafing through some papers.

'She was born in 1914, so ninety-two.'

He grabbed a pen. There was something that didn't add up. Ninety-two minus thirty-four was fifty-eight.

'A woman couldn't have a child at that age, could she?'

There was silence on the other end. Kristoffer realised to his dismay that all this dizziness had made him think out loud.

'What?'

'No, nothing.'

'At the age of ninety-two? No, I don't think so, even if science is discovering the most astounding things.'

Kristoffer cursed his clumsiness. She couldn't find out, nobody must find out! Not before everything was cleared up and it was possible to excuse what they had done.

'What happens next?'

'You mean with regard to the inheritance itself?'

He had actually been thinking of something more important. How he could find out more about Gerda Persson and how she knew about his existence.

'Yes.'

'It's not complicated. We can make an appointment to meet so that you can get some information about the estate, and then it's up to you what you want to do. I can tell you about various alternatives, but first I have to arrange everything for the funeral. The flat and the rest will have to wait until afterwards. Perhaps you'd like to come?'

Four weeks left till his deadline. The play suddenly felt very far away.

'Yes, maybe, thanks.'

'We'll talk more about things after the funeral. I've been in touch with the family who employed her as a housekeeper during her working life, and they've promised to help out with the funeral arrangements. It's the Ragnerfeldt family, by the way. If you like, I can give you the phone number of the son in the family, Jan-Erik; he's the one I talked to. If you'd like to ring him and ask a few questions, I mean. I did ask them if they knew of you. They said no, but at least you might be able to find out some more about Gerda Persson.'

He sat up in his chair. All the information was whirling past, seeking a foothold. He had an inheritance from Gerda Persson, and had finally found Mamma, but then hadn't after all. Instead, he had inherited from Gerda Persson, whom he didn't know and who was not his mother but who was probably the one who had been sending him money and knew that he existed, and then on the periphery there was Axel Ragnerfeldt. The greatest of the great. A man who almost didn't seem real, he was so brilliant.

He jotted down the phone number for Jan-Erik Ragnerfeldt, and they said goodbye. But to ring up the world-famous author's son seemed inconceivable.

Because what would he say?

*   *   *

His confusion was still there. Even more questions than before had taken shape. But a possibility had also arisen. The gate to his hidden world was standing ajar, a little gap had been opened. He just wasn't sure whether he actually dared go inside.

There was only one thing he was sure that he wanted.

To find an explanation that would bless him with the ability to forgive.

CHAPTER 13

'What the hell is this?'

Alice put down the crossword puzzle she was working on and looked at the piece of paper in Jan-Erik's outstretched hand. Without ringing the bell he had let himself in with his own key. She had managed to feel glad that he had come. The feeling had lasted until he appeared in the doorway and she saw the expression on his face. With shoes and coat on he was now standing on the other side of the living room table. There was something threatening about him, a rage she had never seen before. His unusual behaviour made her nervous. She reached for the paper and he stood there looking at her, as if wanting to observe her reaction. With unwilling fingers she unfolded the paper. It took only a second for her to see what it was.

She closed her eyes. Lowered her hand with the awful report and cursed Axel, who hadn't had the sense to throw out something that could only cause pain.

'Why the hell didn't you tell me about this?'

What could she say? Nothing. What had happened

169

had happened, but the lie they had chosen. Perhaps to be able to endure. A barrier had slammed down at first then all these strange feelings had surfaced to keep the pain away. What could not be admitted under any circumstances without allowing madness to take over.

'Answer me!'

'I'm trying.'

She had done all she could to forget. Made an effort to take long detours around details when the memory came too close. Spent aeons of time trying to suppress the remorse about not having understood how serious things were. But certain voices are never silent. They're still there, far away in the din. Nobody was ever whole after losing a child, especially not if the child died by her own hand. What could not be acknowledged at first had taken years to arrive. The conversation with her daughter that had never managed to get started, but which would now remain lost for ever. The thought of all the tiny, tiny steps that had been taken. The certainty that all the choices she had made, none of which was especially reprehensible, had added up and led to what could never be changed for all eternity.

She took off her reading glasses and placed them on the arm of the sofa.

'We don't know why.'

Jan-Erik shifted position, waiting impatiently for her to continue.

'What happened? Did she leave a note?'

Alice shook her head, rubbing her hand over her face. No, she hadn't left a note. Only a message clearer than any words could ever have expressed.

'But you must have noticed something before, surely? Something must have happened, or why did she do it? She couldn't have simply decided to hang herself from one day to the next without something happening, could she?'

'Don't you think I've asked myself that question? That I've cursed myself because I didn't understand how bad things were?'

'How bad were they?'

She sighed and put the paper down on the table. Took one of the embroidered sofa cushions and put it on her lap. Involuntarily her finger began tracing the intricate pattern.

'We never got a real answer. It came out of the blue, she was suddenly changed beyond recognition. She'd been acting the same as always, but one morning she simply refused to get out of bed.'

Alice tried to remember. Gather up all the bits that she had so conscientiously banished. All at once she realised that it was all intact, that the details were still there as if they had only been in a deep freeze.

It had been a beautiful morning. She'd been in an unusually good mood, sitting in the kitchen drinking her coffee. The garden had been bejewelled with glittering new snow, and the sheaves of grain that Gerda had set out were full of little birds. She had thought that Axel's gesture might be a turning point. That even he had finally realised that everything was untenable. She had viewed his initiative as a sign that he was making an effort.

'We were in the city the evening before and went to the cinema, Axel and I. You know how he would never do anything like that. It was even his suggestion.'

They had seen *Face to Face* by Ingmar Bergman. It was so rare they did anything together, shared any experience at all. Whenever he left the house it was on literary business: readings and banquets as guest of honour, and she went along only because it would attract attention if she didn't. Those occasions were merely reminders of her own failure. At home Axel was hardly ever seen, locked in behind the door to his office. But that evening he had suddenly suggested the cinema, despite the fact that there was only an hour to go before the show began.

'I was eating breakfast in the kitchen when Gerda came and told me that Annika was still in bed. We thought she was already at school. I remember that it was past ten o'clock.'

Alice had left the kitchen and gone to her daughter's room. Pulled up the blind with a snap and torn the bedcovers off the girl. She thought Annika was ruining everything, just when she finally felt a little joy for a change. She got a lump in her throat when she thought about it. The way she had scolded and scolded but got no reaction.

'At first I thought it was just something to do

with puberty, that she was just lying there out of sheer spite. Being difficult. But after a while I realised it was something else. She seemed closed off, as if she didn't even hear what I was saying.'

The days that followed: the worry; the frustration. Axel said nothing, withdrew, as if he didn't want to be involved in what was happening.

'I tried to talk to her, I really did. I asked her if something had happened, but she didn't say a word. She just lay there staring at the wall.'

Tears, so long bottled up, were spilling out along with the words. She remembered how she had tried and tried but finally lost patience. Gerda had cautiously suggested they should call the doctor, but Axel thought it was a family matter. And her vacillating between the desire to get help and the shame that their daughter was behaving like someone who was mentally ill.

Jan-Erik went over to the window, turning his back to her as if he wanted to be spared seeing her tears.

'How long did she lie there like that?'

'Four or five days. Gerda and I took turns looking in on her at night. Then one evening she suddenly began eating again, and naturally we took it as a sign that she was getting better.'

She needed a drink but knew that this was not the time. Jan-Erik seemed to have calmed down a bit, and she didn't want to provoke his wrath. It had frightened her.

'Afterwards I realised it was because she had made up her mind.'

'Didn't you ever talk to her friends? Did they not notice anything? What did they say at her school?'

Early on the lie had been formed. The fear that what had happened in the Ragnerfeldt home might cause a scandal had prevented them from asking any questions. The hit-and-run accident had been given as an explanation at her school as well, and it thus became the official truth.

'They hadn't noticed anything.'

Alice looked down at the cushion on her lap.

'Where did she hang herself?'

She couldn't stand it any longer. She got up and went to the kitchen. Blew her nose first on a piece of kitchen roll to create a diversion, and then quietly took the bottle out of the cupboard and unscrewed the top. When she turned round, Jan-Erik was standing in the doorway. Without a word he went over to the plate rack and got a glass. He took the bottle out of her hands and filled the glass to the brim, draining it in a single gulp and then setting it down on the worktop.

'So, where did she hang herself?'

Maybe they should have got a divorce. One's hand doesn't linger on a hot-plate that sears the skin. But the soul was allowed to atrophy slowly without relief. Naturally she had considered it then, as a last desperate attempt to have some influence. But only briefly. One did not get divorced. It was as simple as that. Even if there was reason enough, there were other things that were more intimidating. She had few friends, and all contact with her parents and siblings had been broken off, so where could she turn? As Mrs Axel Ragnerfeldt she at least enjoyed a certain status.

All the sacrifices she had made to maintain the illusion.

If only she had understood how unhappy Annika was. If only she'd had the ability to look beyond her own pain, to see that there were others to consider. Perhaps then everything would have been different.

'She hanged herself in Axel's office.'

Jan-Erik collapsed on a kitchen chair and put his face in his hands. She filled the glass he'd set aside and brought it gratefully to her lips. She took a large mouthful and tried to defend herself against what her memory had set loose, everything that was now running amok. Jan-Erik sat motionless; only his shoulders moved in time with his breathing.

It was Axel who found her. Annika had carefully unscrewed the light fixture in the ceiling and stood on Axel's desk. His scream woke her. On the way downstairs, fumbling to tie her dressing gown, Alice realised that the belt was missing. The sight of her daughter with the belt as a noose round her neck was eternally etched in her memory.

She filled the glass and knocked it back. No, that was enough of that. This was not something to dwell on. Thirty years had passed and nothing

175

could be undone. Drowning herself in guilt would do no good. She had done the best she could under the circumstances.

She put the bottle back in the cupboard and went over to the sink to rinse out the glass.

'Yes. That's how it was, so now you know. The best thing for all of us is for this to remain within the family. It's not something we should go round talking about.'

Jan-Erik's shoulders stopped heaving. Slowly he straightened up. She wished she could escape the look that he gave her. Then he stood up, went into the living room and fetched the piece of paper. Without saying a word he went out the front door.

Alice looked at the clock. The TV programme she was waiting for would be starting soon. Why dig up old memories now? They were better off left alone.

She went back to the sofa and reached for the remote.

CHAPTER 14

*I*t is by describing love that we rob fear of its power. Kristoffer stood in front of one of the gravestones in Katarina cemetery and read the inscription. He'd had to get out of the flat. He was restless and needed to get hold of something to keep his fear at bay. He knew what his body was longing for.

The odd thing about alcohol was that it could be used for so many purposes: to forget, to intensify a mood, to relax. To celebrate, go to sleep, be content, warm up, cool off, escape, find inspiration.

To summon courage.

Of all the drugs he had used, alcohol was the one he found most deceptive. Insinuated into and accepted in every environment, always available, enthusiastically promoted by the state and establishment. He was well aware of the discomfort he caused each time he said 'No, thank you.' The status these words conferred. People didn't want to have sober witnesses when they let go of their inhibitions; a guilty conscience sitting next to them, looking on.

He had read something once that stuck in his mind. He recalled the lines pretty much word for word, since he thought he'd found an explanation and maybe an excuse for his own earlier behaviour: *Since the human being as a species is extremely vulnerable, he must always be ready to defend himself. The human brain has increased in size during evolution. Consciousness is a refined defence system – a constant state of alertness that watches the surroundings to discover possible threats. Our strong sense of fear explains much about human nature and civilisation.*

Sometimes he thought this fear might be the explanation why alcohol was so tempting. To be able to shut down the warning system for a while and relax. To numb one's brilliant consciousness. In all cultures intoxicants are used; only the types are different. If one discovered an isolated tribe in a remote jungle, there were bound to be certain leaves or roots that could be chewed or smoked to achieve the desired intoxication. In the Western world alcohol had been chosen as the legitimate drug.

Sometimes he thought that evolution had made a mistake in developing such an advanced brain. Why else would so many people feel the need to numb it? Yet we see ourselves as being the crown of creation with a superior intellect and the ability to show empathy and moralise. Perhaps humanity was at a critical stage: intelligence had made it possible to eradicate the planet, while deep inside everyone was governed by powerful fears and primitive desires; an immense ongoing conflict hidden inside everyone.

Right now he was missing the solace of alcohol. For a long period it had been his best friend and ally, the one thing that had been allowed to take precedence over everything else. It had helped him to rob the fear of its power.

But on the gravestone before him it said 'love'. That sort of love, he was not familiar with.

He often took walks in the cemetery, even though he had no real reason to go there. He found it peaceful, and not even his fear of the dark kept him away. There was nothing to fear in a place where death already resided. There was only calm, and everything in comparison became small and surmountable. He was not even sure whether he was afraid of death. Sometimes he envied people who had lived their lives and were now allowed to rest. Not that he longed to die, but neither did he feel particularly keen to live. He envied the dead because they avoided the responsibility of continuing to struggle. They had escaped having to maintain the will to go on.

Rich, poor, good, evil, ugly, beautiful, smart and simple – the same fate awaited all. No matter how fast one ran, it was impossible to escape.

All those names and dates on the gravestones. Some of the people resting below had been dead for hundreds of years, but their memory had won out over wind and weather. Only the special ones were allowed to have their graves undisturbed and the stones left in place, the ones who were of importance. The graves of ordinary people were cleared out as they were forgotten, and their last resting place became someone else's. His goal was to be one of those who were left, one of those whose names were allowed to remain and remind new generations of their existence. He would be one of the special ones, one of those who had excelled, who had done something of significance. A true survivor.

Then death would no longer be able to get to him.

Herein lies that which belonged to the earth. Faithfully loving, eternally reunited.
The man had died in 1809, his wife in 1831. No one was now alive who had known them. And yet he was standing here 175 years later and knew that they had existed.

He liked reading the messages on the grave-stones and found them consoling. He would wander among the well-tended graves with flowers that were constantly replaced, and those graves that no one cared for any longer. Time came and went and priorities changed; stones with one engraved name stood next to a blank space waiting for the spouse still living. He wondered how it felt to stand there, knowing that one's name and a date would some day be etched there, and one would never see the result. He felt a flicker of jealousy that they at least knew where they belonged.

He continued along the illuminated gravel path, lured by the glow from the floodlights in the corner of the cemetery where the newer graves were located. On the way he passed several large stones with the inscription 'Family Plot'. One of the most beautiful phrases he knew.

Eternally reunited.

He had not been without offers. He was good-looking and had been considered, at least as long as he was drinking, to be interesting enough to spend time with. Now he no longer knew. He didn't frequent places where prospective speculators could show their interest, since that most often occurred under the influence of alcohol. But back then, when he was still participating in the mating dance of nightlife, he had seldom gone home alone. He had experienced sex so many times he eventually grew weary of it, but he hadn't really known love. Whenever something was about to develop, he had declined and returned to his waiting.

For the answer to who he was.

Then his life could begin.

His ringtone began to play in his pocket, and he took out his mobile. He recognised the number at once.

'Kristoffer here.'

'Hello, it's Marianne again. You know, it occurred

to me that a Torgny Wennberg RSVP'd for the funeral. I thought that if he knew Gerda Persson, then maybe he knows more, and you might want to contact him. I don't have his number, and I can't get online right now, but maybe you could check it out yourself. There can't be too many people with that name.'

'Torgny Wennberg?'

'Yes.'

'With a W or a V?

'I can't check right now but I'm pretty sure it's a W.'

'Okay. And he's coming to the funeral, you said?'

'Yes, at least he said he was.'

'I'll check it out then. Thanks for calling.'

Torgny Wennberg. He added the name to the address book in his mobile so he wouldn't forget it. Now he had those palpitations again. The feeling of wanting both to know and yet not know.

He had reached the new graves. Many of the dead resting here were children. Several graves were decorated with toys, pretty shells, teddy bears and small heart-shaped stones. There were almost always candles burning.

Eternally loved.

Words that appeared again and again. The endless care with which they looked after their beloved children's graves. The thought of his own parents. How deep their pain and despair must have been if the only possibility remaining to them was to abandon him.

A cold wind swept over the cemetery and made the dry leaves whirl around. He pulled his duffel coat tight at the neck and decided to head for home. There he heated up a vegetarian lasagne in the microwave and sat down in front of the computer. With his dinner beside the keyboard he began to search. There was no turning back now; the door was ajar and he would never forgive himself if he missed the chance to step inside. He started with Torgny Wennberg. His name produced 313 hits. He clicked on the first one and was taken to the Workers' Movement Archive. The heading was *From our collections – Torgny Wennberg (b. 1928), forgotten proletarian writer.* He skimmed through the text.

Torgny Wennberg was born in Finspång, Östergötland county. His father was a metalworker. Wennberg began as a metalworker at the age of 14. Early on he began to write stories. In 1951 he debuted as a writer with the novel It Will Pass. *The next year he moved to Stockholm.*

Torgny Wennberg is best known for his novels about the metalworkers in Östergötland. Keep the Fire Burning *is considered one of his best works, published in 1961. Wennberg has also written several plays for the stage and radio.* At First It Hurts *was his last proletarian novel; later books can instead be characterised as relationship novels. His last novel,* The Wind Whispers Your Name, *was published in 1975 and portrays a man's downfall after a love affair.*

Wennberg has published a total of twelve prose books and eight plays.

Kristoffer printed out the page. He went to another search engine, typed in the name and got a hit. There was a Torgny Wennberg living in Hantverkargatan. Kristoffer wrote down the phone number. He went back to Google and searched for Axel Ragnerfeldt. The name produced 1,000,230 hits. He hopped from page to page, reading a little here and there. He already knew much of the information. He had read all his books, some of them in school and the rest on his own. He added Gerda Persson to the search box but got nothing. Deleted Axel Ragnerfeldt and searched only for Gerda Persson and got 205 hits. It was impossible to tell which of them might be about the Gerda he was looking for. For the next hour he read selected pages about Axel Ragnerfeldt. Most of the hits led him to publishers and booksellers all around the world; there were also student projects and theses, but very few gave any clues to his private life. His wife Alice Ragnerfeldt was also a writer, and he spent a while reading about her books. Her last book was published in 1958, but from what he understood she was still alive. Many of the links were about the foundation that was established in Axel Ragnerfeldt's name. He read about a children's home in Chile and several clinics in Africa.

A true survivor.

The food on Kristoffer's plate had grown cold. He went to the kitchen and put it in the microwave. Standing at the sink he shovelled down the last of the food then rinsed the plate. He wondered whether Axel Ragnerfeldt would come to the funeral. Whether he would have a chance to meet the great icon. Jesper would be green with envy. He pondered over whether to invite Jesper, but rejected the thought at once. Even though it would be his first funeral, and the occasion was definitely out of the ordinary, he would rather suffer through it alone. As he usually did. The alternative was to tell Jesper the whole story, but his sense of shame felt like a barrier. The truth would put him in an unbearably vulnerable position, increasing the distance that Jesper had already created between them. It would prove once and for all that Jesper was his superior.

Because *his* parents had chosen to keep him.

Kristoffer went back to his computer. Jan-Erik Ragnerfeldt produced 768 hits. Most of them were information about lectures. *Jan-Erik Ragnerfeldt will speak about his famous father and his writings.* A lecture the very next day at 7 p.m. at the Västerås Theatre. He leaned back in his chair and read the information again. Not that far away. It would be easier to meet him there in person than to pick up the phone and ring. He glanced at the dark windows. He wasn't sure he could handle letting all his questions pile up and then ask them for the first time at the funeral. It would be better to get a general sense of him and be a bit prepared. He had no idea how Jan-Erik would react.

CHAPTER 15

One more and then he would go home. He ought to have gone a long time ago, and yet he couldn't bring himself to leave. Nor had he called home to let them know he'd be late, and he'd ignored the mobile ringing in his pocket. In his other pocket was Annika's death certificate, and several times he had taken it out to read. Trying to convince himself that he hadn't missed something, a word or innuendo that might give him an explanation.

Why did you do it? How the hell could you leave me here alone?

You'd already left. We had no idea where you were. You were the one who left me.

The woman behind the bar served him what he ordered. Maybe he was just imagining the contempt in her eyes; maybe his own opinion simply mirrored in her gaze. He'd already had too much to drink. There was a roaring in his ears, and the contours of everything around him kept blurring and then slowly returning to their original state. He asked for a glass of water and heard himself slurring.

They had never fought the way he understood

other siblings did. There had never been enough space for that. They had been forced to form a united front against everything that was unpredictable – Axel when he turned his back on them and Alice who would sometimes get angry and other times beg for more love than they were capable of giving. He couldn't comprehend how his mother had managed for all those years to keep the suicide a secret. Why she had never said a word about it. Not even when he finally returned from the States, more than six months after it happened. Back when he found himself a run-down bedsit and wanted to manage on his own and she kept popping up at his place of refuge, always unwelcome. Sometimes drunk, sometimes sober. Always begging for his affection. The bitterness about Axel that she dumped on him in an attempt to turn him into her ally. He had hated her tears. He wanted to be left alone, to cut all ties and have a chance to start his own life. To be honest, he probably hadn't made the proper sort of effort. Nor had he turned down the money she would foist on him, since his visits to the in-crowd hangouts cost a good deal. But he had mixed in the right circles, and there was always somebody willing to pay the bill. His surname had an astonishing way of making new contacts. Doors were opened, queues vanished. The letters of his name were a guarantee of Jan-Erik's splendid qualities. Not everyone had a father who had won the Nobel Prize for Literature.

'We're closing now.'

He couldn't raise his head but saw a hand and a light-blue cloth wiping the bar in circles. He grabbed his glass and raised it to his lips, downed the whisky and immediately felt like throwing up. He stumbled off the bar-stool and tried to get control of the nausea but couldn't. Something had to come out. Without looking round he rushed towards the door and made it about ten metres outside before the contents of his stomach spewed out on the pavement. He stood there leaning over with his hands on his knees and saw through his tears the vomit on his shoes. He couldn't go home like this. He'd have to walk for a while to sober up a bit. Most of all he wanted to go home to bed and sleep as long as necessary, so he could wake up and no longer feel the way he felt.

The streets were deserted and the city seemed different. What had been concealed in the bustle of the day became visible at night. He wandered aimlessly along the streets of Östermalm. Occasionally he would meet a bunch of youths on their way downtown, those who were in the process of finding a life for themselves. Now and then he saw a middle-aged night roamer who at the midpoint of his life had discovered that what he'd found was no good and set out to search again. And occasionally he saw one of those who'd got lost and was stumbling about with paper bags hoping only for a miracle, or death.

He grew increasingly cold and thirsty. Not until

the ground stopped pitching up and down and a mild headache set in did he dare head home. In the stairwell he went into the utility room and threw away his shoes. In his stockinged feet he walked up the stairs; the risk of meeting someone at this time of night was slim. As quietly as he could he put the key in the door and turned it. He stopped and listened. It was almost three in the morning, and if he was in luck she would already be asleep. Gingerly he pressed down the handle and opened the door a crack. Only the little lamp on the hall table was on; the rest of the flat was dark. He hung up his coat and went straight to the bathroom and put his mouth under the tap to quench his thirst. Then he tossed all his clothes in the laundry basked and got into the shower. The nausea had retreated, to be replaced by disgust. He should have come straight home instead of sitting in a bar. She would ask him where he'd been and why he hadn't called, and he had no intention of telling her. Confess to her that his sister had hanged herself and his parents had lied about it for all these years? He knew what she thought about his family and didn't plan to give her more grist for the mill.

He stepped out of the shower and dried himself, rubbing the towel harder than was comfortable. Then he drank more water in the hope of easing his headache. After brushing his teeth thoroughly and wiping off all the white spots on the bathroom mirror even more thoroughly, he stood and looked at himself. He had a hard time meeting his own gaze. He had to cut down on the drinking, he really did; he hated hangovers. It was already creeping over him. It would force him to suffer through the anxiety his boozing had postponed.

He unlocked the door and peered out cautiously. Everything was quiet. Only the unpleasant sound of his own heartbeat pulsated like the bass on a dance floor. He padded down the hall past Ellen's door and went into his office. Reached behind the books but changed his mind before his hand found the bottle. He wanted it, and yet he didn't. He went out to the living room. The door to the bedroom was closed and no light seeped through the little crack at the bottom.

On the table in the kitchen stood a candelabra with candles that had never been lit, and in front of the chair where he usually sat were a wine glass, a plate and half a bottle of wine. Two saucepans on the stove. He closed his eyes. It was just a matter of accepting that everything was untenable in the long run. It was only a question of time before it all began to crumble. Couldn't anyone tell him what to do? This morning's conversation came back to him, but suddenly all the rage had drained out of him. All he was appealing for was calm, all he wanted was to be forgiven. He would do better, see to it that there was a change, he really would! Imagine if what he had done tonight was the last straw, the final thing that made her decide. He suddenly found it hard to breathe. He pressed his hand against his chest. He would stop drinking, he would, and now he really meant it, because this wasn't worth it, not by a long shot. He went back out to the living room and looked at the closed bedroom door. So many times he had wished that she wouldn't lie in there waiting, but now, faced with the possibility of having his wish granted, he imagined for the first time in earnest that the room really was empty. That instead she lay in another bed next to some other man. That Ellen's room was empty and quiet and that another pappa who was better suited would take his place. All at once he wanted to cry, but no tears came and instead he got a cramp in his chest. Something broke loose inside and came bubbling up to the surface, from all the way down in the depths, where it had lain submerged in the blackest ooze.

An overwhelming fear that Louise would abandon him, leaving him all alone.

CHAPTER 16

Axel lay wide awake. Since not even one of the twenty-four hours made any specific demands, they were all interchangeable. He often lay sleepless at night. Waking hours that were compensated for during the day when he was still lying there. But tonight there was something else hovering over his wakefulness. Jan-Erik's visit and everything he'd said had dragged him away from where he wanted to be and left him with memories he didn't want to confront. Now they were streaming in from every direction, like old acquaintances happy that he'd finally got in touch. Eager to contribute what they could, as if they'd never been banished. Shadows crowded around the bed, all talking at once to fill in the gaps. Piece after piece was dragged out to complete the picture. Even the emotions he'd once felt, which he'd always wanted to forget. Because like spilled water one could never take back what one had once said and done.

The desire to be perfect. To know that not a single shadow could stain. To be able to lean on his life's work, and deep inside know that it was untouchable.

He was back in the little room where they gathered, where the bookseller was informing them of the order of events at Västerås Theatre.

'. . . and we thought that Axel should close the show. Then there'll be a book signing in the foyer, where tables and book displays will be set up, and when the whole thing is over we'll serve some hot food, canapés and sweets, and then the evening can continue as long as you like.'

Axel thumbed through his book and noticed that his hands were sweaty. This was the fourth Book Day event he had participated in this autumn, and as usual they wanted him to close it. Implicit in this was that he was the big name of the evening, a fact not always appreciated by the other authors.

'I hope there's a little something for the throat as well, and not just hot food.'

Scattered laughter followed Torgny Wennberg's comment. He was the one who had the honour of opening the evening.

'I don't think anyone will be disappointed.'

They were sitting in a room behind the stage. Book Day was a popular event out in the country, and the tickets were sold out. The authors had an opportunity to read aloud and discuss their books and perhaps sell a few copies. In the early seventies the book trade had fluctuated as book prices rose, sales dropped and bookshops closed. Now optimism had begun to grow, but publishers were still being cautious with their lists. Even though Axel was comparatively safe, he had sensed an undertone of concern from his publisher that it had been a long time since he had delivered a new manuscript. In the end it was his publisher who had convinced him to show up at some Book Day celebrations during the autumn, even though he had nothing new to offer. Axel had been reluctant. The book he was struggling with was far from ready, and he feared more and more that he might never finish it. For days he sat ensconced in his office without squeezing out a single word, and with each day he grew more frustrated. Worried that something had been lost. Before, creativity had been taken for granted, as if all he had to do was open up to the universe and take notes – a collaboration with a divine source that flowed through his pen. His duty and calling was to write down what came to him. He had a feeling of being chosen. The process was very delicate and required that he shield himself from earthly distractions.

Now he wondered if the gift had deserted him. Or maybe it was Alice's bitterness that lay like a cloud over the house and blocked the flow. After Jan-Erik had moved to the States she had become even more difficult to be around. It was as though the air itself was contaminated by her presence, which halted all creativity. It had contributed to his decision to say yes to travelling this autumn. The opportunity to breathe a little fresh air.

Despite his loss of creative power the promoters wanted him to close the evening. He felt neither joy nor pride. He hid behind old achievements, and it gave him as little satisfaction as the memory of a sandwich when he was hungry. Writing was what he lived for, and without it he was nothing. To lap up admiration from a stage only made him uncomfortable, as if the audience were secretly peeking at him through a keyhole.

'You're on in ten minutes.'

The evening's organiser left the room and only the authors remained. He had known Torgny for some time, while the other two were strangers, one a first-time novelist and the other a crime writer. The latter had apparently sold a good number of books, although it was incomprehensible to Axel that people read such drivel.

Torgny reached out his hand and grabbed the book that Axel had on his lap, eyeing it as if it might divulge a secret.

'Oh, that's right, you haven't published a new novel this year. This one's two years old, isn't it?'

He turned the book over.

'So you're going to read from this one, I suppose, since you won't say anything about your writing, as usual.'

He laughed but his taunt was clear to everyone in the room.

'Yes, I thought I'd read a few selected passages.'

'How's your new one going, then? Or maybe you can't tell me about it because then you'd have to shoot me.'

He cast a glance at the two listeners in the room who were obviously amused by this exchange, and by Torgny's disrespectful tone towards the famously shy author. Axel was aware of his reputation but had no intention of apologising for taking his creativity seriously. There were plenty of buffoons like Torgny, never missing a chance to draw attention to themselves. He came to visit sometimes, always without an invitation and always with a bottle in his pocket. Sometimes the visits would amuse Axel as a welcome break in the daily grind, but often he found them simply tiresome. They came from a similar background; both had made the escape from poor working-class homes. He suspected that Torgny's visits were prompted more by curiosity and a desire to stay up to date. With the starting blocks in the same place it was possible to pick a winner, and the race was always on. Axel knew very well that Torgny's indulgent friendship was feigned, since Axel was several lengths ahead in the race. His name had even been mentioned in connection with the Nobel Prize. The fact that he had not yet been elected to the Swedish Academy was remarkable and much discussed, and not merely an omission that was magnified by his own offended look.

'It's going well, very well in fact. I just don't

want to let go of it before it's done, so I'll hold onto it a bit longer and polish it up. Nobody wants to publish a book that's worse than the last.'

Torgny's latest novel had received bad reviews in the main papers. Axel had been somewhat amused by the sarcastic pieces.

Torgny looked at the clock.

'I think it's about time to go out.'

Axel remained seated in his chair. 'Quite right. You're supposed to lead off, aren't you?'

Torgny smiled, winked and raised his hand. He pointed his finger like a pistol barrel and aimed it at Axel. At least he had a sense of humour.

The performance, if that was the right word for the evening's event, was neither worse nor better than expected. Torgny's opening act contained many funny lines, and one burst of laughter from the audience followed another. He told them frankly about the agonies of writing and his sources of inspiration, ending with a reading. Axel's discomfort grew. The book in his hand seemed more irrelevant with each minute that passed, as if someone else had written it and he'd been sent to defend it. Now it was his turn to take the stage. He listened to the lyrical introduction and tried to step into the role of celebrated author.

'. . . who with his unique narrative voice and his shimmering prose has given us so many magical reading experiences. With the clarity of his vision into the depths of the human soul he leads us in a search for atonement in a hard and inhumane world. In the contrast between light and darkness his characters assume razor-sharp contours, and their fates continue to enthrall us. Tonight it is with great pleasure that I have the honour of introducing Axel Ragnerfeldt.'

He didn't recognise the man described. Only at his desk in the moment of inspiration was he this person. Not here and now, trembling in the wings, ready to show himself to the masses. Unsteadily he walked out on stage. The book in his hands was shaking, and he wondered if it was noticeable. A sea of expectant faces. Well-educated, intellectual, well-read.

Engineers.

At any moment he could be unmasked. He quickly turned to the first page and began to read. He read and read until his time was up and he was free to go. The audience's thunderous applause. Like a wave it crashed over him, on and on. The master of ceremonies standing next to him seemed pleased at the evening's success. Some in the audience stood up, pulling others with them, and there he was, Axel Andersson – now Ragnerfeldt – esteemed, celebrated, idolised by a standing ovation.

And it gave him nothing.

Nothing.

It was time for book signing; Axel and Torgny walked out to the foyer. There was no doubt which table was Axel's; the queue was already quite long. A few fans were standing at the other authors' tables, several more at the crime writer's, but it was obvious that Torgny had no intention of showing his envy. After a pat on Axel's back he went to his own table.

'Just say the word if you need any help.'

Axel sat down and began signing books. Several of his older titles were on the table, and some of them ran out before the end of the queue. What fantastic books you write, said the strangers standing before him. Time after time: how good you are. It made him feel worse each time the words were repeated. What did they know about what was good? he wanted to ask. What is it that's so good about my novels, can you tell me that? Anyone able to describe it would have the right to say the words, he thought, as he wrote his name in yet another book that would be read by yet another ignoramus. Someone who had no idea of the effort that lay behind the book. Who would rush through the pages without devoting the same care and time to each sentence as he had done.

The others had already filled their plates by the time he was finished and stepped into the room where the food was laid out. About thirty people were there, those involved in arranging the evening and specially invited guests. Everyone was already in high spirits.

He noticed her immediately. A perfect work of art among a pile of rejected sketches.

'Come and sit with us, Axel, we've saved you a seat.'

It was Torgny calling to him, a bit louder than necessary. He had always been keen on pointing out how well they knew each other, forcing his way in and taking advantage of the spotlight. The woman was sitting next to him, and the chair he was pointing to was facing her. Axel went over to the buffet and took a glass of red wine. His curiosity was aroused in a way that felt unfamiliar.

'Axel, bring a bottle with you, we need a refill.'

The request was so loud that all conversation stopped, but when nothing more of interest occurred the chatter resumed. Axel took a bottle of red and went over to the place Torgny had saved for him. He tried to act less interested than he was. But a true aesthete could not ignore her beauty. She was staring at him intently, and his eyes swept past hers not daring to stop. Torgny grabbed the wine and filled their glasses.

'Axel, this is Halina. She's here with me but she didn't want to come backstage to say hello before we started. She's a bit shy that way.'

Torgny grinned.

'I just didn't want to bother you.' She reached her hand across the table. 'Halina.'

Axel took her hand. It was cool and dry and he felt that it might break if he squeezed too hard.

'Axel.'

She gave him a little smile then lit a cigarette. He couldn't help it, her touch had affected him. Shy as a schoolboy he sat down on the chair and tried to direct his attention elsewhere. His reaction surprised him; at forty-eight he thought that sort of response had been lost. So many years had passed since he'd last felt it.

Torgny babbled on. For once his torrent of words was welcome. Axel exchanged a few words with a man from the city's bookshop, the whole time uncomfortably aware of her presence. Glasses were filled and emptied and the noise increased, chairs scraping on the marble floor as people moved around and changed places. Torgny stood up to get more food and fell into a conversation by the buffet table. She was the one who spoke.

'We've met before. Do you remember?'

Axel was taken aback.

'Really? I can't believe I'd forget.'

The wine had given him courage. Her eyes were dark brown, her face framed by curly dark-brown hair. She was wearing an embroidered green jumper, and he had noticed straightaway that she wasn't wearing a bra. Her make-up was subtle, if she was wearing any at all, and on her left wrist she wore some thin silver bangles that clinked when she moved.

'It was only a brief meeting, not particularly special, so it's no wonder you don't remember. At a writers' demonstration in '69.'

He certainly hadn't forgotten the event, but he didn't remember their meeting. In protest against the low payment they received for books borrowed from the libraries, the writers had gathered at the main branches of libraries in Stockholm, Göteborg, Malmö and Umeå. Together with sympathetic librarians they had emptied the shelves and driven off the books in buses, and hadn't returned them until a week later. He had felt invigorated, taken back to his working-class roots.

'So you're a writer too?'

She smiled and fingered her glass.

'I do the best I can, but I haven't had anything published yet. I'm struggling. What I'm working on feels like it could turn into something, but right now I'm stuck.'

Her voice was as pleasant as her appearance. Despite her foreign name he could hear no accent. Her fingers slid along the stem of the wine glass, and he couldn't stop following the movement with his eyes. He wanted to reach out his hand and touch her again, see whether her skin was as soft as it looked. It was so long since he had felt the nearness of a woman. Sometimes he would ejaculate in his sleep. Like a teenage boy. The body's desperate self-regulation when nothing else was available.

'Since you're the "master of good and evil", I have to ask you something.'

'Those are your words, remember.'

'But that's what people say about you.'

'Oh, that's something altogether different. But go ahead and ask, and I'll do what I can.'

Suddenly she was eager. She stubbed out her cigarette and took a pen out of her handbag, looked for something to write on and pulled over an unused paper napkin. She drew two parallel lines across it and then drew small wavy lines between them.

'This is a river full of crocodiles. No one can get across without a boat.'

She drew a square on one side of the river.

'Per lives here. He loves Eva who lives on the other side of the river and Eva loves him. One day Per comes down with a serious illness and he rings Eva and asks her to come and help him. He explains how sick he is and asks her to hurry. But Eva has no boat, so she runs over to Erik, who lives on her side of the river and has a boat. She explains the situation and asks him to lend her the boat so she can row across and help Per.'

Axel was following her words with interest and looking at the little map taking shape on the napkin.

'But Erik refuses to help Eva for free. He says that she has to have sex with him first, then he'll row her over to the other side of the river.'

Axel raised his eyes and looked at her face, following the movement of her lips as she went on with her story.

'Eva, of course, is broken-hearted, so she goes to Olof, who lives here . . .'

He forced himself to look at the napkin, where she drew another square between Eva's and Erik's houses.

'. . . and tells him what Erik said. She asks him to come with her and talk some sense into Erik. But Olof doesn't want to get involved and asks her to leave. So Eva sees no alternative but to do as Erik wants, and even though he's a disgusting old man she goes there and has sex with him. Then he rows her across the river.'

Torgny came back and leaned across the table to look at the napkin.

'Are you telling that one again?'

'Don't bother me, go away.' Halina shooed him off.

Torgny sighed and left, stumbling a little as he went.

Halina continued filling in details on the napkin. Axel preferred looking at her rather than her drawing.

'Is this the plot of the book you're writing?'

'No, it's a moral dilemma. Shhh. Eva finally arrives at Per's house and tells him what's happened. Per is furious that Eva had sex with Erik and throws her out. Eva then goes to Sven and tells him that she was forced to have sex with Erik so she could help Per, who then threw her out. Sven flies into a rage and goes to Per and beats him up.'

Halina looked up.

'Are you following this?'

'I think so. People seem to be on neighbourly terms in this town.'

She put down the pen and took out a cigarette, lit it, and blew smoke out of the corner of her mouth.

'What I want to know is which of them was most in the wrong. Grade them from one to five, with the one who was most in the wrong a five.'

'Am I supposed to decide?'

'Not decide. Just tell me what you think. This should be a topic that appeals to you.'

'I generally focus on asking interesting questions rather than answering them.'

'But you must have an opinion, don't you? Here's a taste of your own medicine.'

He pulled over the napkin and looked at her drawing. She had even drawn in a little crocodile, on the riverbank next to Erik's house. He glanced up again and could see her nipples under her jumper.

'What do you think?'

She leaned back and looked at him. Torgny's distinctive laugh resounded through the room, and both turned to look his way. He had sat down on a sofa with a glass in one hand and a bottle in the other.

Halina took a drag from her cigarette.

'I know what I think.'

'Who is it then?'

'Olof.'

'Olof?'

She nodded.

'But he's the only one who didn't do anything.'

'That's precisely why.'

For a moment he recalled the first years with Alice. All the dizzying conversations that had enriched their writing. The dialogue that had now broken off and fallen silent. He looked at Torgny, who was leaning back in the sofa with his eyes closed. He never would have believed that anything Torgny had would ever arouse his envy. But now he felt it, a painful jealousy. To have a woman it was possible to talk with.

'I was nine years old when the war ended and I was liberated from Treblinka.'

She pulled up her sleeve and showed him a row of tattooed numbers.

'My mother was shot as soon as we stepped off the train, but my sister and I managed to survive for three years inside the barbed wire. Just before the liberation she died of exhaustion.'

Axel searched for words.

'I don't know what to say. I'm so sorry for your loss.'

'Thank you.'

Neither of them said anything for a moment. Halina stubbed out her cigarette. All around them the partying continued.

'The evil I saw in the camp was inconceivable. It's impossible to understand how human beings can behave that way, how something like that can happen. But one thing I do know: many of the people working in the camps thought that they were doing the right thing; they didn't consider themselves evil. They were driven by their convictions and believed that the men who made the decisions and gave the orders possessed the truth. Because who decides what is good or evil? From what angle must one look to get the right view?'

Axel refilled their glasses.

'Perhaps by trying to see the whole thing through the eyes of an opponent.'

Halina snorted.

'And you think that people are capable of that? If we were, the world wouldn't look the way it does.'

'But that wasn't what your question was about. You asked how we should act.'

Halina raised her glass but set it down again without taking a drink.

'I believe that what is most dangerous for a society is when people turn over their responsibility to others. When they stop thinking and acting for themselves.'

She reached for the napkin and drew a circle round Olof's house. She crossed it out with repeated strokes.

'All those people who knew what was going on, who thought it was wrong but still did nothing, isn't that evil? You Swedes, for instance, who saved your own skin by letting the German trains pass through to Norway and even fed the soldiers along the way. Your king who apparently wrote a letter to Hitler congratulating him on his successes on the Eastern Front. All your banks and companies that continued doing business with the Nazis and made tons of money and never had to answer for it later. Isn't that evil? How many of the banks' or other companies' customers do you think care about that today? Or take Hugo Boss. He was the one who designed and sewed the uniforms of SS officers. That's not something they use in their advertising.'

She drew small circles on the napkin.

'I was only a child, and every day I waited for someone to come and rescue us. I was sure that if only someone found out what was happening, they would come for us. That's what hurts the most, finding out afterwards that so many people just let it happen, even profited from it. Afterwards they simply switched sides and went on with their lives as if nothing had happened.'

Axel listened as she continued her story, how she travelled alone, exhausted and malnourished to Sweden on a hospital ship. How she lived at first in a sanatorium where she regained her strength and then went to live with her grand-mother's sister, who had managed to flee to Sweden only a few days before her friends and family were shut in behind the walls of the Warsaw ghetto.

'And don't believe that we were welcome in Sweden, not with a J for Jew in our passports. She was smuggled in on a fishing boat and never dared register here, not even after the war was over, although I tried to talk her into it. She died of pneumonia in the late fifties because she was too scared to go to the doctor. When I finally got her there it was too late.'

He recalled the government's decision the year before the war broke out, even though he was too young really to understand and only afterwards grasped the cynicism behind it. A foreigner could be refused entry if it was suspected that the person intended to leave his homeland for ever. At the same time in Germany, the law was that a Jew could get an exit visa only if the person promised never to return. For an immigrant to be granted a residence permit in Sweden, financial guarantees were required, and at the same time Jews emigrating from Germany were not allowed to take their property with them. The opinion in Sweden had been clear. They wanted to prevent the risk that a great mass of fleeing Jews would come to Sweden. By the time the war broke out, Jewish immigration had almost completely ceased.

Halina fell silent and picked at the napkin. He wanted to put his hand on hers but couldn't pluck up the courage.

'Have you any other family in Sweden?'

She shook her head and took a gulp of wine. He watched her, fascinated. She was a survivor. And as beautiful as could be. He sat quietly and searched for something to say. Suddenly she shifted in her chair, as if she wanted to shake off what she had told him, let the conversation take another tack.

'You know, they've tried this moral dilemma on a great many people. Almost no one puts Eva at the top of the list.'

'Well, I'd say she's most likely to be thought of as self-sacrificing. Nothing she does is for her own sake.'

'But one thing is rather interesting. If instead of calling her Eva we give her a foreign-sounding name, the result is altogether different. I don't recall the percentage, but a good number of people suddenly think she's the one who is most in the wrong.'

'Can that really be true?'

'Yes, really. A foreign name is not an advantage, I can tell you that. A publisher I was in touch with who liked what I wrote told me straight out that I ought to write under a pseudonym if I wanted to get anything published.'

'I don't believe it.'

She said nothing, but looked at him for a long time. Then she gave a little smile.

'You're pretty naïve for someone who's supposed to be so wise and so brilliant.'

'I'm no more brilliant than anyone else; a rumour often grows larger than the source itself.'

A comfortable silence followed.

'So are you happy?'

He smiled and thought it over for a moment. 'That depends on what you mean by happy.'

She gave a little shrug. 'Happy as in content with life, I should think.'

'I don't know. Are you?'

With a resolute movement she crossed her arms.

'You never answer questions, do you? You just bat them back.'

'Do I?'

'You've just done it again! Is it so awful to let somebody get close to you?'

'That depends.'

Her arms relaxed and she leant forward, resting her chin in her hand.

'On what?'

It was so long since Axel had been challenged he no longer knew how to react. He felt both annoyed and excited. Annoyed because she was threatening his integrity, and most people refrained from doing that. Excited because she dared to do so, because she offered him a resistance that was worth countering.

'Nowadays happiness is looked on as a right, almost as an obligation. There's a great risk of being disappointed if one's expectations are too high.'

'So are you afraid of being disappointed?' The whole time she was smiling, as if she were teasing, her eyes fixed on his. Both of them were aware of what was going on.

'I don't know. Are you?'

'There you go again.'

'I'd already answered.'

She took a sip of wine. 'I read somewhere that someone who always puts caution first stifles the life he's trying to save.'

Suddenly her finger stroked his hand. A quick caress was all it took.

No one in the room paid any attention; they were all deeply involved in their own conversations. His cock was throbbing, and he needed to adjust his trousers, but didn't dare lower his hand. It had been so long since anyone had touched him, so long since he had touched anyone else. What he'd thought was dead had suddenly come to life, a glimpse of the man he had once been.

'What about you? Is Torgny the man who makes you happy?'

She pulled back her hand.

'Torgny is my friend, but not my man. We're not a couple or anything, if that's what you're thinking.'

She glanced at Torgny over on the sofa. He was asleep with his mouth open.

'He's . . . a little too shallow, one might say.'

The next moment her eyes were on his, and he felt her foot between his thighs.

'I like it better in deeper waters.'

White noise filled his ears. The others in the room were no longer there. Only her foot on his cock and the bra-less swelling under her jumper. There was no writer's block, no Alice, nothing was important any more. Only the goal of his desire, within reach on the other side of the table.

Why should he say no? Nobody would thank him. Least of all Alice, who no longer wanted him.

Why in the world should he say no?

CHAPTER 17

'No person has had so great an influence on my father and his writing as a man by the name of Joseph Schultz. He was my father's ideal and a great role model. I remember my father telling me about him and I suddenly understood that although it's certainly good to think good thoughts, it is only through action that genuine goodness is born.'

The stalls in Västerås Theatre were almost full. Kristoffer had taken a seat at the back, but only a few minutes into the lecture he wished he'd sat closer to the stage. He had finally found himself in a place where something important would be said, and he didn't want a bunch of fat necks and greasy hairdos between himself and the speaker. He listened attentively to Jan-Erik Ragnerfeldt's account.

'Seven of the eight in the patrol did not hesitate; they were ready to obey the order and raised their weapons. But Joseph Schultz suddenly felt that he'd had enough.'

Kristoffer looked around. The audience sat spell-bound. They appeared to feel as he did, amazed at finally having stumbled upon someone who was saying something important, who really had a mission. Someone who kept his head above water in the sea of superficialities and cynicism that was so typical nowadays. A person who dared to believe in his audience's ability to think, their will to be enlightened.

'How was it possible for a person to make the choice that Joseph Schultz did? What characteristic was it that differentiated him from the others in the patrol?'

Kristoffer was reminded of the science book he'd read several times by now. It said that what made it possible for human beings to leave the primitive stage and develop a civilisation was that the strong defeated the weak, the skilled the incompetent, the intelligent the slow-witted. He had wondered whether it might be true that this weeding-out was still going on. But in that case, why did the incompetent and slow-witted take up the most space and were heard the most often?

'Perhaps Joseph Schultz realised that death would strike him even if he chose to remain with his patrol and fire his weapon. Perhaps he realised that if he chose to obey the order he would also extinguish the last little fragment within himself, the one that made him human.'

Kristoffer smiled. He was meant to hear this; fate had reached out its hand and accompanied him to Västerås so that he could hear Jan-Erik Ragnerfeldt's words. The hope for humanity, so difficult for him to maintain, had acquired new strength, and feeling gratefully calm he let himself be touched by the rest of the story about Joseph Schultz.

To risk his life for his beliefs, to die rather than conform.

A true survivor and role model.

He had longed to be able to find someone like this. Everything he had heard convinced him he was on the right track. Maybe it was high time for the natural leaders to rise above the mediocre masses and take command. The creators of the new and the courageous who refused to let themselves be enslaved, who would promote what was genuine and were intelligent enough not to let themselves be duped. He'd read about people who bought environmentally friendly cars, but when the ethanol got a few pence more expensive they went back to using petrol. He had confronted customers who would walk right past the cartons of organic milk and organic vegetables, claiming that they were too expensive, while their shopping basket overflowed with soft drinks and sweets. Maybe it was genetically determined. Maybe some people were better suited from birth. So few people tried to set a good example and take responsibility. Now it was time for the visionaries to take on the task of crushing the tyranny and begin shaping the future. The others, those who had renounced responsibility and subjugated themselves, had to accept guidance. What was needed was a revolution, since the bovine masses didn't know what was good for them.

'My father and Joseph Schultz both knew that our actions are like our children; they live on, and they continue to have effect independent of us and our will. Joseph brought to life the proverbial phrase that the silent consent of good people is just as abominable as the outrages of bad people. He proved that, by conquering our own fear, we also conquer our mightiest foe.'

The applause that followed was spontaneous, and Kristoffer felt almost proud.. There was so much that united him with the man up on stage. Everything he had so often thought, and had made him feel so alone. Jesper was the only one he could share his thoughts with. Humanity was being killed by entertainment. Everything challenging, enlightening or the slightest bit thought-provoking was screened out. He was convinced there was a conspiracy behind all of it. That the Power sat pulling the strings, making sure the people were dumbed down and kept dim-witted and docile, and thus easier to control. Finally, finally, he had found a comrade-in-arms. Someone he could respect.

The lights in the auditorium dimmed and Ragnerfeldt began to read from one of his father's books. His voice was astonishingly similar to his father's. Kristoffer leaned back and enjoyed the shimmering art that arose in the spaces between the words.

He felt strangely consoled.

★   ★   ★

Afterwards it was time for questions. The house lights came on and a roaming microphone was sent out into the audience. Ragnerfeldt gave the floor to someone in the stalls that Kristoffer couldn't see. The voice was that of an elderly man.

'First of all, I would like to thank you for a very, very fine and thought-provoking reading. I actually had the honour of introducing your father on this very stage many years ago. It must have been in the early seventies, because it was before he received the Nobel Prize. I remember the audience being just as enchanted then as we have been here tonight.'

Ragnerfeldt smiled and bowed.

'Thank you very much. Yes, if I recall correctly, he did give occasional readings around that time.'

'I would like to ask what your father's doing today, whether he's still writing?'

'No, unfortunately he's not.'

Ragnerfeldt hesitated before he went on.

'He's been stricken with the infirmities of old age that prevent him from writing anymore. But he sent his good wishes to everyone here tonight, and I see him almost daily. Are there any other questions?'

Kristoffer was reminded of why he had come here this evening but naturally he couldn't ask him here and now. It would have to wait until later. All his nervousness was gone; the fact that he had ended up here tonight was a sign that he was on the right path. His questions about Gerda Persson had been transformed into an opportunity. A chance to get to know Jan-Erik Ragnerfeldt.

He remained in his seat after Jan-Erik left the stage and the auditorium began to empty out. He was slightly hesitant now that the time was at hand. He would let Jan-Erik have a moment to himself at least before he went backstage; he knew that actors in the theatre usually appreciated being left undisturbed straight after a performance.

Finally he and a woman who'd been sitting in one of the front rows were the only people left. Kristoffer pretended to be searching for something he'd dropped. He glanced at the stage and saw the woman go up the stairs at the side of the stage and disappear into the wings. He sat back down and looked at his watch. He had an hour and a half before his train left. There was plenty of time.

He sat there for a good while. Then he realised that Jan-Erik might leave if he didn't do something soon; yet he waited and let the minutes pass. What was easy to do in his mind was not always as easy to carry out. He tried to convince himself that his mission was important and that Gerda Persson was a sufficiently strong bond between them. It should be of some interest even to Jan-Erik Ragnerfeldt. Just as he was about to get up, a man came out on stage. He walked over to the podium and suddenly noticed Kristoffer.

'Are you waiting for someone?'

Kristoffer stood up. 'I'd just like to have a word with Jan-Erik if possible.'

The man looked towards the wings and then back at Kristoffer.

'Does he know you're here?'

Kristoffer hesitated for a fraction of a second before the lie took shape on his tongue.

'We're good friends and I wanted to surprise him.'

The man relaxed and began unscrewing the reading lamp.

'Well, go through the door at the back and then turn left. It's the second door on the right.'

Kristoffer hurried to the stage and followed the route the woman had taken. He gave the man at the podium a friendly smile and felt his way behind the black curtains. The lie had been justified. Sometimes the boundaries of truth could be stretched in the service of a higher goal.

Outside the door he hesitated. He was standing in an empty corridor, but he could hear voices. He put his ear to the door but there was no sound behind it. He knocked cautiously. Nothing happened. Maybe Jan-Erik had already left. Cautiously he pushed down the handle and opened the door a crack. There was a light on and he saw a coat hanging on one wall.

'Hello?'

He heard a sound and in the next moment Jan-Erik appeared. His shirt was untucked and he had red spots on his throat.

'Yes?'

Kristoffer sensed impatience in his voice.

'I'm sorry to bother you, but my name is Kristoffer Sandeblom and I wonder whether you might have time to chat for a moment.'

Ragnerfeldt glanced at something hidden behind the door. Kristoffer suddenly felt uncomfortable in front of the great lecturer.

'What's it about?'

He tried to find a way to describe why he was there as quickly and concisely as he could.

'It's about Gerda Persson.'

Jan-Erik's face changed. Once again he glanced behind the door.

'I just want to ask a couple of questions, if possible.'

Jan-Erik seemed to have trouble making up his mind, but then he turned and went over to the coat on the hanger and took something out of the pocket.

'Darling, just go on ahead and I'll be there soon.' When he turned round he had a perforated plastic card in his hand. 'It's room 403.'

Now Kristoffer understood what was hidden behind the door. The woman he had seen disappear into the wings emerged and took the card from Jan-Erik. Her finger stroked the back of his hand.

'Just don't be too long.'

Kristoffer looked the other way and felt even more uncomfortable. The woman took her jacket and smiled at him as he took a step into the room to let her pass. She closed the door behind her.

'I didn't mean to bother you.'

'It's no problem. That's my wife – we'll see each other later. She comes with me sometimes when I'm out lecturing.'

Jan-Erik stuffed his shirt into his trousers and asked Kristoffer to have a seat. He opened two bottles of mineral water and offered him one. Kristoffer took a gulp and put the bottle down.

'I have to start by thanking you for an utterly phenomenal lecture. It was so illuminating, absolutely fantastic. It's rare to hear anyone talk about anything important nowadays, it was really liberating.'

Jan-Erik looked down. 'Thank you so much, it's good to hear that you liked it, thanks.'

For a moment Kristoffer thought that Jan-Erik was blushing, but he decided it must be a trick of the light.

Kristoffer suddenly felt at a disadvantage. Something in him wanted to prove his own worth, that he just wasn't any old audience member, but someone whose compliments carried more weight than the words of many others, for he knew what he was talking about. He wanted to impress Jan-Erik, make him feel a little like he had just felt.

'I'm a playwright, so I found it all very inspiring. I'm writing for a theatre in Stockholm at the moment, and if you like I could see to it that you and your wife get an invitation to the première.'

Jan-Erik looked at his watch. 'Oh, so you're a dramatist?'

'Yes, I wrote the play *Find and Replace All*. It was produced a couple of years ago, perhaps you've heard of it?'

Jan-Erik frowned pensively.

'No, I don't think I have. I'm afraid I don't go to the theatre very often.'

There was a moment's silence. Jan-Erik took a gulp of water.

'Do you write too?'

'No, no. I have enough to do with Pappa's works. What did you say your name was? I didn't catch it.'

'Kristoffer Sandeblom.'

'I think I recognise that name.'

'Marianne Folkesson probably mentioned me. I got your name from her. I'm the one that Gerda Persson named as her heir.'

'Quite right, that's where I heard it.'

Kristoffer picked up the bottle and drank some more water to give him a moment to think. Where should he begin?

'The thing is, I didn't know who Gerda Persson is, and as far as I know we've never even met. I have no idea how she even knew me.'

The frown on Jan-Erik's face returned.

'That's odd.'

'Yes, it is. Although I think she must have been the one who sent me money every month for years, at least since I was about eighteen. It wasn't a huge amount, but still. So I don't really know what I'm asking, but I thought you might know something about her that could explain things.'

Jan-Erik slowly shook his head.

'I don't have the slightest idea. You know, I haven't had any contact with Gerda since about 1979, 1980. She worked at my parents' house, but I'd already moved out by 1972. She stayed on another few years, but I was abroad most of the time.'

Kristoffer listened attentively. Nineteen seventy-two. Back then he'd still been living with his parents. The calm he had felt was now gone. As always when he got close to the truth.

Jan-Erik slapped his hands on his thighs as if to say that everything important had been said and it was time to call it a night. But Kristoffer still sat there wondering what exactly he should do. For the first time in his life he wanted to tell someone, reveal his secret to this man who tonight had proved himself worthy. He had finally found a link to what he'd always been searching for; it was almost as though he'd found part of his family.

Jan-Erik looked at his watch.

Kristoffer felt a pang of annoyance at his lack of interest, but he'd made up his mind. Everything was ready and could not be called back, yet he could hardly expect Jan-Erik to understand what was remarkable about the situation before he had explained it.

His heart was thumping.

'It's like this, I . . . This feels especially important for me because I . . .'

He fell silent; what he wanted to say was inexpressible. How could such a little word contain such great anguish?

Jan-Erik looked at him. He had an odd look on his face, and Kristoffer gathered his strength for the inevitable. He closed his eyes.

'I'm a foundling.'

He opened his eyes. A sense of heaviness he'd never felt before spread through his body, and all at once it seemed difficult to move. Jan-Erik sat motionless, only his eyelids blinked occasionally. As if it would help him to take in the information. After a long while he finally spoke.

'So you think this has something to do with Gerda?'

'I don't know.'

He inhaled deeply, trying to counteract the force of the weight that was dragging him down.

'I know nothing about my origins, but of course it struck me when I heard she wanted me to inherit her estate. But, as I said, as far as I know I've never met her.'

'So you think Gerda may have been your mother?'

'No, she couldn't have been – she would have been fifty-eight when I was born. But somehow

226

she must have known that I'm a . . . a foundling. I lived with my adoptive parents from a very young age, so it's not something that people know, and it's nothing I've ever really talked about.'

He lowered his eyes.

'This is actually the first time I've told anyone.'

Jan-Erik, who had been leaning back in his chair, abruptly shifted position.

'What year were you born?' His voice had taken on a new tone.

'Seventy-one, I think. Possibly seventy-two.'

'What do you mean, you *think*?'

'No one really knows how old I was when they found me.'

'But you couldn't have been born as late as seventy-six?'

'No, I went to my foster family in 1975.'

For some reason Jan-Erik looked relieved. He got up and found his briefcase, opened it and took out a bottle of Glenlivet.

'This calls for a drink. Would you like one?'

Kristoffer looked at the bottle. Jan-Erik set out a little tray with two glasses and poured whisky into them, took one and handed it to Kristoffer.

'Well, it's a strange story. I don't really see how I can help you, though. I haven't the slightest idea how it's all connected.'

The fumes from the glass in Kristoffer's hand crept into his nostrils. His whole body was ready to accept the longed-for drink – the one thing that was missing for him to feel complete. Just a little, just a single drink, now that he'd told someone for the first time.

'There aren't many people you could ask, either. As far as I know, Gerda didn't have many friends. She always stayed in, even when she wasn't working.'

Kristoffer looked at the glass. The liquid shimmered, as bright as amber. He was desperate to take a sip; he deserved to be viewed as an equal. He couldn't tell him the truth, couldn't reveal yet another shame to Jan-Erik. That besides being a foundling, he was also an alcoholic.

A sudden fury came to his rescue. Who did he think he was, anyway, this man before him? Sitting there with his whisky puzzling over Kristoffer's background, when he'd soon forget all about it and go to his hotel and have a fancy dinner with his wife. This man who because of his sophisticated family tree could travel about basking in the glow of his surname. And he couldn't even write; he was only mimicking what his father had once created. So simple, so fucking privileged.

The glass in Kristoffer's hand was so tempting soon he wouldn't be able to resist.

'What time is it?'

'10.35.'

He put down the whisky and stood up.

'My train is leaving soon, so I'll have to be going.'

Jan-Erik knocked back the last drops, stood up and offered his hand.

'Best of luck, then.'

'Same to you.'

Kristoffer couldn't get out into the fresh air fast enough. At the same time he felt a weariness so overpowering his legs would hardly carry him. He went out the way he'd come in, across the stage and through the auditorium to the foyer. Outside the doors he stopped and filled his lungs with air, trying to convince himself that he had done the right thing. Because now he regretted it. He had placed his secret in someone else's hands, but instead of feeling unburdened he felt exposed. He wanted to go inside and take it all back, tell him that what he'd said was a lie. He didn't want Jan-Erik Ragnerfeldt to know he was a person who had been discarded like old rubbish.

He fished out his mobile, wanting to ring Jesper and hear his voice, to experience something ordinary, something that belonged to the time before his confession. Four rings. The voicemail picked up. He didn't leave a message.

Across the street was the park he had to walk across to get to the station. Full of shadows and hidden secrets, it felt threatening. He made it halfway across the street before his fear of the dark took over. But he had to get to the train. He wanted nothing more than to get home. He stood on the pavement and lowered his head. On the street in front of his feet there was a dark spot on the tarmac, an oval shape that he suddenly imagined looked like an eye. Without knowing why he stood on the spot and closed his eyes. In the next moment he realised to his astonishment that he had begun to sing.

'Twinkle, twinkle, little star, how I wonder what you are.'

He opened his eyes and looked towards the park.

The dark didn't scare him any more.

He was no longer afraid.

CHAPTER 18

When Axel woke up he was alone. Some time during the night she'd had the good taste to avoid a farewell that would detract from their experience. There was nothing left to say that hadn't been said already. He felt gratitude over what had happened, yet right now it felt hard to believe. With his hands clasped behind his head he recalled the experience. It was so extraordinary that during the night he'd been the object of a woman's desire, that his presence had aroused her lust. Now it aroused only disgust with Alice. He did not wish anything undone. On the contrary, he felt exhilarated by what had happened. He'd thought that desire had left him, that it had gone after all those years spent in sexual deprivation. He hadn't even been aware that he'd missed it; he'd directed his passion towards his writing, which became his surrogate lover. He already knew that it was only this one time, and he felt no wish for a repeat performance. They had met by accident and taken advantage of the occasion, there wasn't anything more to it. Now he would return home and continue working on his book in the hope that what happened would give him inspiration.

He got up and went into the bathroom. Filled a glass with water and drank. Despite a slight headache he felt in excellent spirits.

He skipped breakfast, deciding to have a coffee at the train station. He wanted to retain the memory of the night as it was, pure and unspoiled. Like when he was a boy and had experienced something special that only he knew about, and then could safely carry his treasure about in his heart.

It was walking distance to the station, and he said goodbye to no one before he left.

He strolled through the park towards the station. The night had been cold, and in the shadows a thin layer of frost covered the ground. For weeks it had been grey and dark, but today the autumn sun peeked out from its hiding place. The air was so clear his eyes watered. He wanted to go home to his work. He had waited so long for the spark to be ignited. Now it was back, he could feel it, longed for and welcome.

The train was just about to depart. He was sitting alone in a compartment for eight and had gratefully pulled shut the door to the corridor. He looked at the glass carafe in its holder on the wall and wondered when the water had last been changed. On the table before him lay his pad and pen, but he hadn't written a word. Then the door was shoved open and Torgny and Halina stepped in.

'There you are!' exclaimed Torgny. 'Where did you go off to last night?'

He heaved the bags onto the luggage rack, and Axel's and Halina's eyes met. He couldn't say a word. Torgny threw himself down on one of the seats and took off his scarf. His eyes were blood-shot and he stank of stale alcohol.

'Oh, curse this bloody headache, I don't know what it is. I've got to cut back on the cigarettes.'

He grinned and patted the seat next to him.

'Come and sit down, sweetie.'

Halina hung her jacket on one of the hooks. Torgny caught sight of Axel's writing pad.

'Don't tell me you're sitting here writing?'

Axel collected his things and put them back in his leather briefcase.

'No, I was just about to make some notes.'

'Damn it, Ragnerfeldt, you're going to have to learn to relax and let go a little. Come down to earth with the rest of us once in a while, and pull out that stick you've got up your arse.'

Torgny laughed and sought approval in Halina's eyes. Axel realised that Torgny was still drunk. Even though his language was occasionally improper, this was a bit coarse even for him. Halina pushed open the door.

'I just have to go to the toilet.'

She pulled the door shut behind her and turned

to meet Axel's eyes through the glass before she vanished.

'Well, what do you think?' Torgny smiled and nodded towards the door.

'She seems very nice.'

'Damn it, Ragnerfeldt, come on. I saw the way you were looking at her last night. I sure as hell didn't realise there was such a horny little devil inside you.'

Axel said nothing. The language Torgny was using was the kind that Axel had left in his childhood. This side of Torgny's personality was as new as it was disgusting. Even if the situation had been different Axel would have had a hard time joining in this sort of conversation.

Torgny leaned forward.

'She's a real animal, just between you and me. I didn't sleep a wink last night, well, maybe a little on the sofa at the party but that hardly counts. The only complaint I have is that I don't get much writing done since she moved in, but I suppose I have to take the bad with the good.'

For a few seconds Axel fumbled for a bearable interpretation. Then he had to acknowledge one that made him feel sick.

Torgny is my friend, but not my man. We're not a couple or anything, if that's what you're thinking.

She had lied, duped him into doing something that lay far beneath his dignity. To betray Alice was something he had chosen to do; it may not have been very honourable but it was acceptable at the time. But one never touched a colleague's woman. Suddenly he was in debt to a man he detested. Who sat there reeking of alcohol, contaminating the air with his repulsive words. From his higher ground he had slipped and become inferior to Torgny, since he was the one who had committed a base act in their relationship.

The thought was repellent.

Halina came back and Axel avoided looking at her. Their experience had been transformed into something crude and perverse; what he'd done was the opposite of everything he'd ever been taught. Loyalty, morality and a conscientious life.

He got up and began gathering his things.

'If you'll excuse me I'm going to sit in a different car.'

Torgny objected but Axel didn't listen. He just wanted to get out of the compartment and never have to see either of them again; he couldn't get away from them fast enough.

'Wait, you dropped something.'

He was already standing in the corridor, about to pull the door shut. Halina picked up something from the floor, and without meeting her eyes he took what she had in her hand and stuffed it in his jacket pocket. Then he went to the last carriage on the train and stood in the corridor until the train pulled into Stockholm Central Station.

* * *

When he got home he went straight to his office and closed the door. On the way there he'd encountered Gerda, who took his bag and told him that his wife was resting and his daughter was in her room; she had a cold and had stayed home from school. He didn't feel like seeing either of them, and he asked Gerda to say that he was not to be disturbed.

He didn't leave his office all afternoon. Just before six he went to the kitchen and asked Gerda if she could bring him dinner at his desk. He didn't get one word written; all his thoughts were circling around the events of the night before and how he could repress them. At nine o'clock he gave up, took his empty plate and went out to the kitchen. Annika was sitting at the kitchen table with a pen and a piece of stationery. He was amazed to see how grown-up she looked. No longer a girl, but soon a woman.

She looked up when he came in.

'Hi.'

'Hello, dear.'

He put down his plate, took a glass and filled it under the tap. He tried to work out how old she was. Was she fourteen at her last birthday?

'What are you doing?' he asked her.

'Writing a letter to Jan-Erik.'

He drank the water. Gerda came in and curt-seyed when she saw him. He no longer knew how many times he'd asked her not to do it, but eventually he'd given up.

'Excuse me, sir, but I found this in your jacket pocket, and I thought it might be important.'

He set down his glass and went over to her. She handed over a little folded piece of paper. He opened it and read:

In all haste . . .
Thank you for a wonderful night.
I'll be in touch as soon as I can.
Your H

He quickly crumpled up the note and glanced at Gerda. She didn't return his gaze, and her impassive expression was impossible to interpret – he couldn't tell whether she had read it or not. Without saying anything more he left the kitchen and went back to his office, tore the note into tiny pieces and flung them in his wastepaper basket. Then he thought for a moment, got up and opened the door.

'Gerda!'

He waited a few seconds before he called again.

'Gerda! Would you please come here?'

In the next instant she appeared. Her shy gaze swept past his a couple of times before fixing on the wall behind him.

'I just want to say a few words. Come in here, please, for a moment.'

He tried to make his voice sound kind but saw that she was afraid. He held the door open for her and closed it when she stepped over the threshold.

She stopped just inside the door, and he went to sit behind his desk. Her obvious anxiety diminished his own, but he still needed the power conferred by the desk.

'I just want you to know that Torgny Wennberg is no longer welcome in this house. If he shows up, please tell him I'm not available.'

Gerda curtseyed.

'Yes, sir.'

'And for God's sake stop all that curtseying!'

In sheer fright she looked up and their eyes met. This time he lost his patience. She was more than ten years older than he was, and yet she looked like a browbeaten schoolgirl.

'Yes, sir.'

Axel regretted it at once. He knew that she had worked as a servant since the late twenties, when other customs prevailed; it was only natural that she would behave the way she did. Yet he felt uncomfortable when he witnessed her submissiveness. It reminded him of his parents, the way they always hunched over when faced with authority figures. Even with him, nowadays, as if he were a stranger.

'Gerda, please forgive me, it was not my intention to raise my voice.'

Gerda didn't respond. Just stood there inside the door with her eyes fixed on the carpet.

'Was there anything else?'

He hesitated. Should he mention the note? If she had read it, anything he said would only draw attention to it. If she hadn't read it, what he said would be a form of confession. He decided to let the matter rest. If Halina got in touch he would clearly and unequivocally declare his lack of interest, and Gerda would know nothing more about it. The whole thing would be over, and everything could carry on as usual.

'No, that will be all.'

Gerda curtseyed and quickly left the room.

Axel sat there looking at the closed door. Gerda, and all she represented, was a reminder of a vanished era. In the present day it was considered inappropriate to have a housekeeper, especially in left-wing intellectual circles where the gap between classes was supposed to be non-existent. But the truth was, they couldn't get along without her.

Four days passed. Four days of writing nothing. The piece of paper that met him each morning was still a blank blinding white when he gave up in the evening. Alice had a few good days when nothing in particular provoked her, and she mostly stayed in the library. In the evenings the sound of the TV seeped into his office. Sometimes he would emerge and try to keep her company. Silently they would watch *Columbo* until he could no longer stand it and went back to his office. He knew that she missed Jan-Erik and was sad that they rarely heard from him. Whenever a letter arrived it was always addressed to Annika. Sometimes he got the feeling that Alice was more attached to the children when they were out of sight. As far as he knew, she didn't devote many hours to the teenager who was still living here. He couldn't understand why Alice didn't try to write anything again. When the children were small she'd complained that she didn't have time, but her excuse was no longer valid. Sometimes, staring at the blank page, he envied her. Her right not even to try.

When he went to bed she was still up. As he waited for sleep to come his thoughts flew to his night with Halina. Not to her personally; her face was robbed of all its features. His fantasies followed the path of his hand over skin, a woman's skin. He recalled how his hands had grabbed greedily for her, how she willingly opened up, the sounds she made. How she gave herself without reservation in a way Alice had never done, not even long ago before it had all mouldered away. Now he wondered whether he'd made a fatal mistake by awakening an urge he had no longer missed. Because how could he satisfy it now? With Alice downstairs in front of the TV? The thought was implausible, almost repulsive. But what if? Could he find the courage necessary to take the initiative after all these years? To risk being rejected? Was it even possible to reawaken the passion he'd once felt for her, which had long since been submerged by all the quarrels, all the indifference, all the silence? He remembered how he'd felt in their early years together. When they had made love and lain close to each other and listened to each other's heartbeat. The feeling that no one could ever be less alone than this.

He realised it was more difficult to have sex with his wife than with a strange woman at a hotel. The thought intrigued. Maybe he could use it in his book.

The feeling of guilt had begun to dissipate. Once in a while a memory would flit past, but it was easy enough to ignore. What was done was done, and only time could dilute his mistake. But on the fifth day after his night with Halina a thick, oversized, unstamped envelope was lying on his desk when he returned to his office. He turned it over. His fury was instantaneous when he saw the single letter H. Just an H. As if they had a secret intimacy. He went out to look for Gerda. He found her on her knees in front of the tile stove in the living room.

'Where did this come from?'

Gerda stood up quickly and smoothed out her apron. He held out the envelope.

'It was hanging in a bag on the front door. It must have come by courier, although I didn't hear anyone ring the doorbell.'

Through the doorway to the library Axel caught sight of his wife sitting in one of the easy chairs reading a book.

Without taking her eyes from its pages she asked, 'What is it?'

'I don't know.'

'What do you mean, you don't know?'

'I haven't opened it yet.'

'Well, why don't you? That might explain things.'

He said no more and headed back to his office. With the door closed he hurriedly ripped open the envelope and pulled out a wad of paper. He knew at once it was her manuscript. Handwritten on lined paper. A typed letter was fastened with a paperclip to the first page, and he quickly scanned the words.

> *Axel, the hours that have passed have not been lonely. You are still with me in my thoughts. Since I've had a hard time getting away I thought I'd just send you my book anyway. I'd be grateful to have your wise views on it. No one else has read it (as you will see, it's far above Torgny's head). My book longs only for your lovely eyes to read it.*
>
> *Your Halina*
>
> *P.S. I'm so glad that we finally met! H*

At first he couldn't decide what angered him more. Her intimate tone, which assumed her interest was reciprocated or her shameless demand on his valuable time. If he'd wanted to be an editor he would have taken a job at a publishing company; nothing could interest him less than the desperate ambitions of a first-time author.

He stuffed the letter and the manuscript back in the envelope and unlocked the door to the cupboard. He put it on top of a pile and went back to his typewriter.

It was twenty past two.

By evening he still hadn't written a single word.

The low pressure that had settled in during the summer was stubbornly hanging on. For four days it had been raining, and the sky was so dark they had to turn on the lights in the morning. Water had leaked in through the letter-box, but Axel could clearly read the writing on the card that Gerda delivered to him when the post arrived. Written in ink and open to public gaze.

Prinsen Restaurant 17.00 today. Your H

Gerda had left, and again he sat bewildered. He couldn't quite work out why it was so important to him to know whether Gerda understood or not. She would never tell tales to Alice, so that couldn't be the reason; it must be something else. There was something in him that sought Gerda's approval. He had heard the happy laughter from the kitchen whenever his parents were visiting, easy-going conversations that faltered when he tried to partici-pate. The community from which he was now excluded. He wanted to have Gerda on his side, to assure himself that what she told them about him was well-intentioned, what she said to the two people he could no longer reach. She was his link to what had been taken from him.

243

He turned over the card. A picture of a little kitten on a pink cushion. The key to the cupboard lay in his desk drawer, and he opened it up and put the card in a box of fan mail.

Naturally he wouldn't go to the restaurant, but her boldness had ruined his concentration. Anything other than ignoring her would be meeting her halfway. For a long time he'd been used to having people around him respect his orders, and if anything bothered him, measures were immediately taken. Now he was being subjected to her unwelcome approaches. She kept cropping up in his thoughts; she had acquired a power she had never been granted. The whole situation was untenable, and at the present moment it was intolerable.

The rain continued. It was reported on the news that the record had been broken. Never before had so much rain fallen in eastern Svealand as in these two months.

His publisher called, proposing a meeting. Some of his older titles were going to be reissued, and they wanted him to look at cover designs. Reluctantly he left his office and took a taxi into the city. He needed to ask for more advance money, which was always humiliating. Alice didn't know, but there was good reason to worry. If he didn't get something written soon, the situation could well become alarming.

He was received with coffee and rolls, and not

until the end of the meeting did his publisher ask how it was going with the new book. He lied and said everything was going well. He might be able to finish by spring. He regretted the remark at once, as he realised the consequences. But an additional advance was approved.

When he stepped outside, it had finally stopped raining. He stood in the entrance for a moment, wondering whether he should take a little walk. Perhaps all the way down to Slussen and then take the commuter train home. He was just setting off when he felt a hand on his shoulder. It may have been the cigarette smoke, maybe just his instinct, or maybe he had been expecting it the whole time, but he knew who it was before he even turned round. He was greeted by her smile. Nothing of what he'd planned to say to her remained, not a word would pass his lips. The strength of his displeasure gave him a feeling of inferiority. Even the note slipped into his pocket on the train had felt like an infringement. All the days of dreading new attempts at contact came as an assault.

She dropped her cigarette and made a move to embrace him. He fended her off and took a step back.

'Listen to me, Halina, I . . .'

'Sshh.'

She put her finger to his lips and he was caught off guard.

'Just let me look at you for a moment.'

He noticed the smell of tobacco. He removed her hand from his face and dropped it as if wanting to be rid of something unpleasant. Her smile faded as abruptly as she had appeared.

'What is it? Why are you acting so strangely?'

The door to the publisher's opened and two men came out. Axel recognised one of them and nodded in greeting, doing his best to seem nonchalant. The whole time he was watched by Halina, who seemed to be reconsidering the situation. She fished around in her handbag for another cigarette, lit it and took a quick puff.

'Shouldn't I be the one who's angry? Do you know how long I sat waiting for you at Prinsen?'

'I never said I'd come.'

'Oh, I see. So you didn't even think you could take the time to ring the restaurant and let me know you weren't coming? That would have saved me a lot of bother.'

He changed the subject and tried to assume a conciliatory tone.

'Halina, I don't know what you were hoping for, but you have to stop contacting me. You know I'm married.'

She snorted. 'It didn't seem to matter in Västerås.'

'No, I know. I was . . . it was stupid that things turned out the way they did, but I thought it was understood that it didn't . . . that it only . . . that it was just then . . .'

'That you wanted to have a sneaky little fuck?'

Axel closed his eyes and put his hand over his

face. The situation he was in was so absurd that despite his profession he was at a loss for words. Forty-eight years old and he was standing here in the street trying to break off a relationship he had never started. In the hope of making himself understood he threw out his arms.

'I'm sorry if I led you to believe there could be anything between us, I really am. I don't usually behave that way but, well, things just turned out the way they did. I assumed that we both knew it was a one-off. I have a family and children and I, well, I really do beg your forgiveness.'

She smiled, but now it was another sort of smile.

'So that's all it was?'

'Yes, unfortunately, that's how it has to be.'

She gave a flat little laugh.

'So, you, Axel Ragnerfeldt, the famous fucking author with a pole up his arse, you think it's okay just to screw me a little and then throw me away like an old towel?'

'Halina, please,' he appealed to her, but she just shook her head.

'How the fuck could I be so stupid?'

He suddenly got the feeling that he was dealing with a child.

'Halina, please, I sincerely apologise for what happened. Can't we just try to part as friends? Can't we at least do that?'

She took a drag on her cigarette.

'Do you know what I do when I get angry with myself?'

He sighed.

'Can't we just . . .'

'This is what I do.'

She stretched out her arm. He couldn't stop her. With a sizzling sound she pressed the tip of the cigarette onto her bare wrist. He slapped away her hand and looked in horror at the reddish-black hole the burn had left behind.

'Are you mad?'

She stood quite still, as if the pain had numbed her. He looked around to see if anyone had seen what happened, but there was no one nearby. The sleeve of her jacket fell down over the wound and he gently took hold of her arm. She wrenched it free and stepped back a couple of paces, turned round and walked away. Axel stood there watching her go, utterly at a loss. She crossed the street and he still stood there, incapable of understanding what had just happened. What scared him was not only what she had done, but also what he had seen in her eyes. Something in her look that had escaped him the first time, but this time he had seen it clearly. He wanted to get out of her consciousness. He didn't want to be a part of what occupied her thoughts.

On the other side of the street she suddenly stopped and turned to him.

'Hey, Axel!'

He watched her, waiting.

'You with the great imagination, why don't you go home and wonder about what I do when I get angry with someone else?'

CHAPTER 19

Jan-Erik woke up alone in room 403. His only company in bed was an empty bottle of Glenlivet and some colourful miniatures from the minibar spread helter-skelter over the flowery bedspread. He realised he'd fallen asleep with his clothes on. The key he had so ingeniously handed over in the theatre dressing-room had been returned to the reception desk when he arrived at the hotel; the delay had apparently made her change her mind. Now he was grateful, but the dreary hotel room had driven him to empty the minibar. He hated hotel rooms. The anxiety-filled isolation; the claustrophobic feeling of being cut off from the world. He always checked all the emergency exits so he'd know which way to run if a fire started. Tried to convince himself that the probability of the hotel catching fire on the very night he was there was negligible. On the other hand hadn't all hotel guests that died in a fire thought the same thing just before being engulfed by the flames or suffocated by the smoke that prevented them from finding their way out?

With great effort he propped himself up on his

elbow and looked around for some water. There was a bottle on a little side table, but the distance seemed insurmountable. He fell back onto the pillows and closed his eyes. He wanted to be somewhere else, at some other time. It couldn't be a hangover, this was something else. He must have come down with some illness. His heart's laboured beating seemed audible throughout the room. The anxiety lent each thought sharp barbs. Every molecule in his body was trying to fight the poisoning. He couldn't possibly have caused this himself, it couldn't be self-inflicted.

He lay utterly still and tried to convince himself that his condition was not life-threatening.

It was ten minutes to six.

His drunken state wouldn't even allow him to sleep.

He fell into a restless doze and managed to kill forty minutes. Then he was involuntarily back in reality. Cautiously he broached the thought of the day before. Sporadic memories arose, gradually trying to arrange themselves in some sort of order. He had woken up at home. Morning in Stockholm. Louise and Ellen had already left. He had thought about Annika, about the choice she'd made, about the new grief that had to be endured, and how he would handle his parents' thirty-year-old lie.

Then came the newly discovered fear that Louise might leave him; in the morning light it had still felt real. He had promised himself that he would change his behaviour. Never again come home feeling guilty, never again wake up in the straitjacket of a hangover. He would show that he really wanted to fight, though he didn't actually know for what. All he knew was that he couldn't stand having such a crucial decision taken over his head. On the way to Central Station he had passed by Louise's boutique. The 'closed' sign was on the door, and she hadn't answered her mobile. With a nagging sense of uneasiness he had taken a seat on the train and swore to himself to be a better father, a better husband, a better person. He had even considered ringing the therapist, if that's what it would take.

But then he had stood there on stage in the spotlight. Felt how every pore opened up and gratefully absorbed the unconditional admiration that came rushing towards him from the audience. Felt the adrenaline racing through his veins, the power of approbation. And she had sat there worshipping him, unable to get enough of what he had to give. It was so simple, so impossible to resist.

And once again he'd fallen to temptation.

He thanked God that she had changed her mind.

He would become a better person. He really would.

It was his mobile ringing that woke him the next time. In the hope that it was Louise he fumbled about looking for the phone. He had rung her several times the day before without getting an answer. She hadn't returned his calls.

He cleared his throat in an attempt to sound less groggy.

'Yes, this is Jan-Erik Ragnerfeldt.'

'Oh, forgive me, this is Marianne Folkesson. I didn't wake you, did I?'

He cleared his throat again.

'No, no, not to worry, I just have a slight cold.'

He sat up with an effort. Some of the little bottles fell to the floor with a clatter.

'I just wanted to ask if you'd managed to find a photograph for the funeral. Time is getting short, so I really need to know.'

'I looked all over the house but unfortunately I couldn't find one.'

He wanted to be of help. Especially this morning. So that not a single person could think ill of him.

'But I'll look again. I'm in Västerås right now but I'll be home this afternoon. Is it all right if I let you know tomorrow?'

'Yes, of course. It'll be a bit of a rush but I think there'll be enough time.'

He was going to go straight home. Buy some groceries on the way and have coffee and sandwiches ready when Ellen came home from school.

'I should also tell you that I gave your phone number to Kristoffer Sandeblom, the one who's named in the will. I hope that's all right. He wanted so badly to get in touch with someone who knew her.'

Jan-Erik suddenly remembered the visit in his dressing-room. The strange young man and the awkward circumstances. The absurd notion that he might be Annika's child, that it had something to do with her suicide. Crazy perhaps, but the stranger's story had got tangled up in the thoughts that were uppermost in his mind. Thankfully he had worked out that the years didn't match. With the clarity of distance, he realised what his preposterous idea said about his confidence in his parents. It filled him with sadness.

He cleared his throat again.

'I've already talked with him. He came to meet me yesterday after a lecture, and I must say it was a strange story. Unfortunately I wasn't much help to him. He is apparently a foundling, but I haven't the slightest idea what connection he might have had to Gerda.'

'A foundling, you said?'

'Yes, that's what he told me.'

There was silence on the other end.

'But I promise to let you know tomorrow when I've had another chance to look for a photo. I think there must be one somewhere, the question is where. I promise I'll do my best.'

They said goodbye. There were seven minutes left till checkout time.

He managed to shower but not much more. Embarrassed, he checked out and paid for wreaking havoc with the minibar. He explained to indifferent ears that he'd had some friends visiting and they'd even drunk the small bottles of liqueurs.

His hand was shaking when he signed the bill.

★   ★   ★

He took the path through the park to the train station. Tiny stones caught in the wheels of his rolling suitcase, and kicking it did no good. He picked up the bag and ran to catch the train, his body protesting at the strain. Thirsty and sweaty he made it in time and found his seat in the first-class carriage. He sat down to catch his breath and noticed at once that he could see into the restaurant car. The feeling of being poisoned was still strong, and he knew very well what would help. The method was well-proven and he would feel so much better if he took a little nip, merely as an antidote to help his body.

He took out his mobile and tried to ring Louise, but he still got no answer. The Swedish Railways magazine lay on the table before him and he leafed through it half-heartedly, without taking in what he read. The door to the restaurant car opened and closed when a passenger went through. He drummed his fingers on the armrest, looked out of the window and then at the restaurant car again. He took out his mobile for a second time and began keying in a text message, but stopped and deleted it. He drummed his fingers some more, looked out of the window, flicked through the magazine. Maybe he ought to buy something to eat; the thought wasn't appealing, but still. In any case he could see what they had. If nothing else, he could stretch his legs a bit.

He looked out of the window again and continued drumming his fingers.

★   ★   ★

Lasagne, vegetarian pizza, pancakes. He did a thorough job of reading the entire menu. Chicken salad, tortellini with meatballs. He spied some sandwiches wrapped in plastic near the cashier and went to inspect them. Below them stood the drinks, and he scrutinised all the juices and at last decided on a beer.

Purely medicinal, he argued to himself when he got back to his seat. Even the sound of the bottle cap coming off made him feel better.

Four beers and fifty-seven minutes later he stepped off the train at Central Station. It was two o'clock and the day was young. He felt melancholy. He wished he could go home and be greeted by someone who understood him, secure in the knowledge that he wouldn't immediately be interrogated by someone who always demanded the impossible. She couldn't even answer her mobile. She was punishing him, even though he was trying to do his best. Why couldn't she see him as the person he was? And Ellen, little Ellen, the years that had gone by so fast. He remembered her as a baby, toddling across the floor; those days were gone for ever. He felt tears well up in his eyes as he hurried towards the waiting taxis.

Do your duty, be a good person.

Gerda had died utterly alone, and he hadn't even been able to find a single photo of her for the funeral. So many years she had spent with him, dear Gerda, the solid anchor of his childhood.

What could be more important right now than honouring her with one last effort?

He climbed into the back seat of a taxi and asked to go to Nacka.

When the taxi stopped outside the gate he no longer felt quite as confident. He paid the driver and got out, checking to see whether, unlikely though it was, there might be something in the post-box. All he found was a flyer from a charitable organisation. It was twenty minutes to three.

He looked at his childhood home. Empty windows. Four point two million kronor taxable valuation but with no soul and no purpose.

On the path through the garden he scrolled to Louise's number but ended the call before it went through.

Enough was enough.

Now it was her turn to ring him.

There was nothing to drink in the downstairs kitchen. There had never been a drinks cabinet in the house. He went upstairs to what had been Annika's room but was later converted to Alice's kitchen. All he found was an unopened box of rice and a packet of old cocoa.

Axel's office looked the same as the last time he had been there. The cupboard door was open, and the raw cold had spread into the room. He stopped in the doorway and looked at the lamp hook in the ceiling. How had it been possible for his father to continue working in here afterwards?

The box in which he'd found Annika's death certificate was still on the desk, and he quickly looked through the rest of the contents. No picture of Gerda.

Maybe he should go home. Now he regretted coming back here. His restlessness had returned.

He carried the box back to the cupboard and almost stumbled over the black rubbish bag. He stood there drumming his fingers against his thigh. The jumble of piles on the floor and shelves, all the boxes and cartons, the whole thing gave him the creeps. A whole life collected in a few square metres, filled with success and uncertainties. What he had already found was betrayal enough.

A picture of Gerda. Where was that bloody photo? Why had the old devil been so disorganised?

He pulled out a cardboard box and went over to the desk, sat down and opened the lid. Boring paper, boring paper, boring paper, newspaper review, boring paper, letter from his publisher, boring paper, magazine article, invitation to the Finland–Sweden Literary Society, boring paper, boring paper, boring paper.

He lifted out the whole mess and let all the papers slowly flutter back down. Not a photograph to be seen. He went into the cupboard and chose a different box. Boring paper, boring paper, review.

Photographs.

Somewhat encouraged he took them out but was soon disappointed. Axel receiving a prize from some unidentified person at some unknown location.

Gerda was obviously not a popular subject for photos.

He returned to the box. Under another boring paper lay about fifty unopened letters. Different colours and shapes, some thicker than others, but all with the same handwriting. He turned one over to read the return address. Simply a tiny H. They were all the same. For a brief moment he hesitated before his curiosity took over. He was the one who would have to sort through all this eventually, so why not start now? He carefully slit open the envelope. It contained only a small note. He pulled it out to read it.

The shackles – they burst – they fall off me.
The darkness is dispelled. I let love triumph!
Your H

Flabbergasted, he put the note back in the envelope and leaned back. The stamp was postmarked 17 March 1975, but he was the first to read the cryptic lines. He lifted the lid of the box and emptied out the letters onto the desk. One of the envelopes had been opened. He picked it up and unfolded the paper.

Thank you for your message. I promise to be there. Finally, my love!
Your Halina

He read the lines three times with increasing astonishment. His father was the one person on earth in whom he truly believed – although naturally it wasn't all positive. But here was something he never in his wildest dreams would have suspected: his father had had a lover. Although he knew his father must have made his mother pregnant at least twice, the thought of Axel Ragnerfeldt as a sexual being was absurd. And unfaithful? Could it really be possible? That he would dare risk appearances – the very basis for the meaning of life?

And with the power of a sudden detonation he was then struck by a terrible thought.

Imagine if Axel's lover, sometime around 1972, had borne his child.

CHAPTER 20

*A*xel, Axel, forgive me, forgive me. Let me pour out a thousand pardons over a thousand pages before I try to convince you that I deserve your forgiveness. With complete confidence I appeal to your magnanimity and beg you to give up the aversion you feel for me. I can't change the place from which I came, only the place to which I am on my way. There I will be able to carry your benevolence like a smooth stone in my hand, a consolation when memory plagues me. How could it happen? you must have wondered. I beg you to read my words without judging. To admit a mistake, after all, is only to admit that one is wiser today than yesterday. All I want to accomplish is a farewell that allows us to part as friends, as you so sensibly said back then, when I was in no condition to listen.

A thousand and another thousand times I beg you to forget what happened outside the publisher's, because the person you saw was me and yet it wasn't. Since my teens I've suffered from a number of problems, the doctors say that the explanation lies in my experiences in the camp during my childhood. As long as I take my medication I'm the Halina you met in Västerås, the Halina *to whom you gave such a beautiful memory. Our experience enriched me. It's so easy to believe that everything is whole when the heart is joyful. Unfortunately it made me careless about taking my medication. And I ended up taking it out on you, to my great dismay. It hurts so much to be rejected, when a feeling of worthlessness already fills every part of me.*

Axel, none of it was your fault. I would like so much to say farewell with these lines and tell you that everything is fine. You're a wonderful man and writer, and I wish you all good fortune with all my heart.

Halina

Axel read the letter four times. The relief he felt made him euphoric. Since the incident, he had gone around in a daze, not knowing what was up or down, and with each day his feeling of helplessness had spread. Each time he left the room he was afraid of seeing Gerda with yet another letter; when he heard the telephone ring he feared that it was Halina. He peered out of the windows when he thought he heard unfamiliar sounds. But Halina had not got in touch again. The letter was a liberation. He had already worked out that she suffered from some sort of mental disturbance. He hadn't been able to forget what he'd seen glinting in her eyes, and during sleepless nights he had wondered about her personality change.

Three weeks had passed, and the whole time he'd

had the feeling of trying to balance on a slack rope.

Christmas came and went with its usual frenzy. The problem that had been lifted from his shoulders gave way to other concerns, and he had actually written a little, nothing very good but at least he'd managed to get something down. On Christmas Eve they had rung Jan-Erik, a brief conversation considering the cost of long distance calls to the States, but it had been worth every krona. Alice blossomed after hearing her son's voice, and for once the Christmas holiday was quite enjoyable. On Christmas Day his parents came to visit, but his sister refused to participate, as usual. He asked about her sometimes. He knew that she lived in Farsta and was on a disability pension because of all the heavy lifting she had done in the nursing home. She had no children, and he had no idea if there was a man in her life. His parents didn't volunteer much information, even though he knew they were in close contact with her. Once a long time ago he had asked to come along, but his sister had let him know that he was not welcome.

Twelfth Night passed and the regular routine returned before everything was ripped up again. On the ninth of January the snow came down heavily as a storm moved in over Stockholm. He was standing in the library, listening to the house resisting as the wind picked up and came in through all the cracks, causing sounds he had never heard before. As soon as he heard Gerda's footsteps he suspected the worst. She handed him a small envelope, and without a word turned and left. There was something about her expression. He knew at once who it was from, and now he had confirmation of what he'd suspected – Gerda had known all along. He went straight into his office and ripped open the envelope so that the little H was torn off in the middle.

Thank you for your message. I promise to be there. Finally, my love!
Your Halina

He opened the cupboard and put the letter in the nearest cardboard box. Then he went to the kitchen.

'Gerda, could I see you for a moment, please?'

He didn't wait for an answer, just turned and went back to his office. At the door he stopped to let her pass. She entered the room, and the procedure from the previous occasion was repeated. Gerda cowering just inside the door and Axel enthroned behind his desk. Gentry and servant. Axel Ragnerfeldt and his father and mother. He didn't know how he should behave to break the class barrier. He needed her services and she needed his money; they shared the same house. Why in God's name couldn't they behave

263

as equals? He had attempted to use the familiar form of address with her at first, invited her in as a member of the family, but he'd soon been forced to realise that his behaviour was unwelcome. With almost fifty years of experience in her profession she wanted respect for her abilities, and that involved certain conditions. She had clearly demonstrated that she did not intend to become part of the family.

'What I tell you now will remain between the two of us, and I don't want you to discuss it with Alice because there's no reason to upset her. Recently I've been contacted on several occasions by a woman, but I want nothing to do with her. She is a complete stranger and I've never even met her. Presumably one of my readers. You've probably noticed a number of strange letters arriving?'

'I don't know if I have.'

'Well, in any case, I would like you to know about it. I'm rather worried that the woman in question is not in full possession of her senses.'

He wished that she would say something, ask a question. Show that she appreciated his trust and shared his concern.

But Gerda said nothing. Not a word passed her lips, and when her silence continued he realised that she had no intention of saying anything.

'That will be all. Thank you.'

Gerda curtseyed and turned to go. At the same instant the front doorbell rang. Their eyes met and for a second he felt that they were united in some sort of conspiracy. Then the moment passed, and she was gone. Axel followed her but stopped halfway, filled with misgivings. The doorbell was rarely used; no one came to the house unannounced.

No one except Torgny Wennberg.

He heard Gerda's voice trying to be heard over the storm.

'I'm sorry but I can't let you in. Mr Ragnerfeldt is busy and has asked not to be disturbed.'

'Oh really! You mean that randy old goat Ragnerfeldt? Get out of the way. I have to talk to him.'

His voice was enough to reveal the alcohol in his bloodstream. Axel was afraid that Alice might hear him so he hurried out into the hall. Torgny was white, covered with snow. Gerda was holding onto the door handle with both hands, and the snow was whirling through the gap in the doorway. Torgny grabbed hold of the door and forced his way in. With great difficulty he managed to close the door behind him.

'Well, look here, if it isn't the gentleman himself, down here on earth like the rest of us.'

He bowed and threw out his arms flamboyantly. Axel shook his finger at him.

'You need to calm down. There are people sick in bed in this house.'

Torgny squinted histrionically.

'Is that your dick or your little finger? I can't see any difference from here.'

'It's all right, Gerda. Thank you for now, I'll take care of this. We're just going to step outside and have a little chat.'

He hastily pulled on some shoes and a coat as Gerda left the hall.

'You're scared that Alice will hear, eh? That dried-up old cunt. Doesn't she let you get any, or is she out somewhere else getting some cock? She probably gets plenty out here in this posh part sucking off the neighbours.'

'Shut up. Let's go outside.'

'Aren't you getting any grease on your prick anymore, Ragnerfeldt?'

Axel reached out his hand and pressed down the door handle behind Torgny's back. With a crash the door flew open as it was caught by the wind, and the hall was filled with even more snow. Axel shoved him outside and pulled the door closed. They stood on the steps in the storm, huddling as best they could against the lashing snowflakes. The feeling that his life had become absurd came over Axel once again. What had happened recently was beyond his usual experience. Here he was standing with Torgny Wennberg in a blizzard outside his house, realising that they would have to have a discussion to put an end to all this misery, but he also knew that they couldn't stay there. The wind was so strong they had to hold on to something. The only good thing about the storm was that it had finally shut Torgny up; he hadn't said a word since they'd come outside.

'Come on, let's go over to the woodshed.'

He started walking and Torgny followed him. With one hand gripping his coat collar and the other shielding his eyes, Axel trudged towards the little shed. The snow had settled in a drift in front of the door, and Axel pushed it aside with his foot while undoing the lock. He let Torgny inside along with a flurry of snow and closed the door behind them. They stamped a few times, brushed off the worst of the snow, but the raw cold in the shed cut through their clothing and shoes. Torgny's beard was white and his face blazing red, his breath billowing like smoke from his mouth. Axel rubbed his hands. Neither of them said a word. The hostile tone had lost its way somewhere out in the storm; now they were two freezing men with a common foe. Of course, the feeling of 'we' was never greater than when the powers of nature were threatening. The cold had sobered up Torgny and he suddenly looked embarrassed.

What Axel wanted could take many forms. More than anything he wanted to put an end to the entire episode, but not if it meant that he'd have to admit what he'd done in Västerås. The memory was now associated with so much denial he was no longer sure it had really happened.

Torgny shivered and sank down on a pile of wood that was stacked against the wall.

'Couldn't you at least have let me come into the

house? Do I have to sit here and be humiliated in a shed?'

The wind whistled through the cracks in the wall, rising and falling in a desolate wail, echoing their mood. Torgny looked around, grabbed hold of a log and absentmindedly weighed it in his hand. He was so cold he was shivering, but was feigning nonchalance with bravura.

'That would have been more proper, considering the circumstances, don't you think? But what the hell. You win, brother, I give up. Are you finally satisfied? Or is there something else you want to steal from me?'

Axel stuffed his hands into his coat pockets and pressed his arms to his body.

'You understand, don't you, that I couldn't let you in. Not while you were ranting like that. Yes, I admit that I didn't want Alice to hear the way you were carrying on.'

'So she doesn't know yet? When were you planning to announce the happy news?'

Axel said nothing. Torgny dropped the log to the floor and folded his arms. With his head cocked he stared at Axel as if evaluating an incomprehensible art object.

'I never would have believed it of you, Axel, that you were capable of acting like an ordinary human. I thought you were happy out here in the suburbs, with your elegant house and your old lady, your perfect kids and maid and all that. She really must have turned your head around.'

'What do you mean?'

'All the success, your reputation, you've got everything. I never would have thought you'd give up all that just because your bollocks twitched a bit.'

'Why don't you come out and say what you mean before we both freeze to death?'

Torgny snorted a humourless laugh and picked up another log.

'So, when are you going to tell the family?'

Axel felt that his limit had been reached.

'Tell them *what*? Say what it is you want, because I'm going back inside.'

'You're going to have hell to pay, you know that? When she doesn't take her medication it's like she's possessed by the Devil. Good luck is all I can say, I'm glad to be rid of that bit.'

Axel could no longer feel his feet. The more Torgny kept talking, the more he realised the conversation was going to be lengthy. He sized up the situation and decided.

'I presume it's that Halina or whatever her name is we're talking about? You make it sound as though we were planning some sort of future together. I don't know what you two are up to, or what she may have told you, but I'm completely sure I don't have the slightest thing to do with any of this.'

What he said was not, strictly speaking, a lie, and the truth gave him courage. When he saw the confusion appear on Torgny's face, he grew even more confident.

'I find this situation incredibly unpleasant, and I wish you would explain to me once and for all why I'm standing in my woodshed about to freeze to death.'

'What are you saying?'

'You heard me.'

'You mean you haven't proposed to Halina?'

'No, I certainly have not.'

Torgny was silent for a moment.

'But you have a relationship?'

'Good Lord, Torgny. No, we do not. If you promise to keep your voice to a normal level, we can go inside and talk some more.'

Torgny was lost in thought. Axel assumed that he was doing his best to re-examine the situation. When he spoke again he did so softly and deliberately.

'If you're lying to me, I swear I'm going to kill you the day I find out the truth.'

Axel swallowed. But his words would always carry more weight than those of a woman with mental health problems. No matter what sort of claims she tried to make.

'What more do you want me to say? Come on, let's go inside.'

'No, I'm not going inside.'

Torgny closed his eyes and rubbed his hand over his beard.

'Christ, she said that you two had it off back in Västerås while I was asleep on the sofa.'

Axel said nothing.

'Then she's sick again, running around somewhere. She packed up her things and took off. She said you were going to meet each other somewhere. She's been going on about you ever since we were at that Book Day event in Västerås, so I believed her. I should have known there was something wrong. The other day she imagined that she'd got some sort of message in the newspaper. She didn't want to say what it was, but she was convinced it was for her. I tried to make sense of it but I couldn't find anything.'

He shook his head slowly.

'And she has the boy with her too.'

'What boy?'

'She has a son a few years old. He's not mine or anything, but I've grown quite fond of him. She doesn't treat him very well when she's ill.'

Axel no longer had any feeling in his hands.

'We have to go in before one of us catches pneumonia.'

'Damn it, Axel, I think I should apologise for what I said in there. Can we go inside and I'll explain. Then there won't be any more trouble about this whole thing.'

Axel's immediate instinct was to turn down the offer, but he realised it might solve all his problems. If Alice had heard what Torgny said, nothing Axel could say would help. On the other hand, she would surely listen to Torgny. And Gerda would be given proof of his innocence.

'Actually I'd be grateful if you would.'

★   ★   ★

271

Gerda and Alice were sitting on the sofa in the living room. Gerda perched on the very edge after being persuaded to sit down. It was Axel who insisted that she be included. Axel sat in the armchair with a blanket draped over his lap, and Torgny stood before them and made his little speech. Deeply humiliated, he apologised for his behaviour, begging them to forget what they'd heard in his unforgivable outburst in the hall. Alice's expression was inscrutable. Axel glanced at her occasionally but couldn't work out how much she'd caught of the insults. Torgny stumbled on, fumbling unhappily for words that would make amends for overstepping the mark.

'It was stupid of me. Now I see that I got everything back to front. I was stupid enough to believe what she said. Unfortunately she has problems with her nerves. She's a wonderful woman, but the past haunts her sometimes, and she has been known to imagine things. I didn't think it was true this time, but I'm ashamed to say I did come to believe her. I realise that I accused Axel with no justification whatsoever, and I sincerely beg his forgiveness.'

Torgny took a deep breath, and Axel could not help being impressed by his recapitulation. He knew how hard this was for him, to be forced to denigrate himself. A vein in his temple pulsated, revealing his inner turmoil.

Only now did Axel understand how strong Torgny's love must be, since he was prepared to undergo this humiliation and still defend her. The depth he had never suspected in Torgny was suddenly exposed, the need for love from which all creativity issues.

Alice, who so far had been fidgeting restlessly, stood up.

'If I've understood this correctly, right now a mentally ill woman is running around who is in love with Axel and thinks that they're a couple. Is that right?'

'She isn't seriously ill, and I have no idea why she said this about Axel. Maybe it was simply to hurt me.'

'Either way, I think we should call the police. I have absolutely no desire to sit here waiting for some madwoman to show up. Who knows what she's capable of doing?'

Axel put a hand on Alice's arm.

'Now, now, calm down.'

'There's no need to call the police. She'll probably be at home by the time I get back, and if not I promise to find her. You don't have to be the least bit afraid. There's a greater risk that she might injure herself.'

Alice sat back down.

'But why Axel, in particular?'

Torgny shrugged.

'Perhaps because we met him in Västerås, I don't know.'

Alice turned to Axel.

'So you have met her?'

'Yes, we talked a bit during dinner, that's all.'

Axel looked at Gerda. He realised at once he'd made a mistake. For the first time during the conversation she looked up and stared straight at him. He lowered his eyes, but the damage was done. From her expression he was clearly able to read what she was thinking, and it had nothing to do with what he'd said. He had given himself away with his anxious glance.

'As I said, I simply want to apologise. I should probably go straight home and see whether she's turned up.'

Gerda jumped up from the sofa and preceded Torgny out to the hall. Axel stood up to follow them, but Alice stopped him.

'If I see any sign of that woman I'm going to call the police. What does she look like?'

'Quite ordinary-looking, dark brown hair, average height. It'll all work out, Alice, she obviously just needs to take her medication. When she takes it she's apparently as normal as anyone else.'

Alice snorted.

'As anyone else? As if that's supposed to be reassuring.'

Axel said goodbye to Torgny and for safety's sake locked the door. The blizzard seemed to have abated, but the wind was still blowing hard. Through the hall window he saw Torgny struggling through the snow. Alice disappeared upstairs, and he wondered whether he should follow her, but he decided not to. He could hear sounds from the kitchen, and after a brief pause he went in and sat down at the kitchen table. Gerda stood with her back to him, busy with something on the worktop. Her hands moved efficiently after many years of practice.

'I have a feeling you don't really believe what I said.'

Gerda spun round as if she hadn't heard him come in.

'Gosh, you gave me a fright.'

Axel sighed and gave her a little smile.

'Can't we start talking to each other as friends, once and for all, after all these years?'

Gerda didn't reply; uncharacteristically she turned her back and went on with her chores. She pulled out a drawer and grabbed a whisk. She cracked two eggs on the edge of a bowl and began expertly whisking them.

'We're equals, you and I, Gerda. I don't see why we can't just treat each other that way. I'm good at writing and you're good at what you do, so why do we have to make it so difficult?'

Gerda didn't answer, but he could hear the motion of the whisk slow down slightly. Once again he felt the similarity to the conversations he'd had with his parents, as if his words were no longer comprehensible but took on a different meaning in their ears than they'd had in his mouth.

'Gerda, please, won't you at least talk to me?'

The whisk stopped abruptly. Axel looked at her back.

'We're not equals.'

She spoke so softly he had to strain to hear.

'Yes, Gerda, we are.'

He saw her shoulders rise and fall with her breathing.

'I know what I have to do, and I do it the best I can. That's that.'

'There, you see? That's the way it is for me too. I just do what I do the best I can.'

In the silence that followed, everything lay open. For eighteen years they had shared this life. For the first time they were having a real conversation. He couldn't quite grasp why it felt so important, but it did.

'We're not equals.'

'What do you mean by that?'

She still had her back turned away from him.

'Because I'm content and you're not. You're always chasing after what you imagine you could become.'

Gerda went back to whisking, marking the end of their talk. Axel sat speechless, contemplating her words. And he realised that he'd received the most serious insult of his life.

A week later and they all resumed their respective roles in the house. Everything returned to normal. Gerda took care of the housekeeping. Annika did her schoolwork. Axel struggled on with his novel, to no avail. What Alice was doing he had no idea, but she mostly stayed in the library, dressed in her customary dressing gown. They didn't hear a peep from Torgny. He'd promised to ring as soon as he knew something, but apparently Halina was still missing. Then, on the seventh day, another letter appeared, and it turned out to be the beginning of a daily routine. Each morning a new envelope landed in the letter-box, and Gerda delivered them to his office without comment. Alice was not informed. On a few occasions she asked whether there had been any word from Torgny, and Axel was able to say truthfully that there had not. He put the letters unopened in his cupboard. If anything untoward were to happen, it was a good idea to save the letters as proof of her madness. And as with anything that goes on long enough, the whole thing soon became a habit; the letters were received with the same matter-of-factness as the morning paper.

February turned to March, and the world went its way.

Israel attacked Palestinian guerrillas in Lebanon, and in Mjölby 14 people died in a train crash. The king appealed to the media to respect his private life, and Iraqi forces put down the Kurds' fight for freedom. U.S. Secretary of State Kissinger tried to mediate in the Middle East, but Egypt refused to go along with any demands as long as Israel occupied Arab land. Researchers feared that we were heading for a new ice age, Ingemar Stenmark won the World Cup, and it was claimed that the

CIA had compiled a hit list of foreign heads of state, with Fidel Castro at the top.

Nothing much new under the sun.

It was April 1975.

CHAPTER 21

*T*oday we are facing an acute threat to the environment, with the greenhouse effect and climate change. Today's environmental destruction threatens our entire globalised world and in the long term could lead to the annihilation of our civilisation. By looking at prominent extinct civilisations, such as the Mayans, scholars have been able to show that what begins as environmental degradation risks ending in civil war and the total collapse of society.

It begins when population growth causes an increase in the demand for food and other resources. Forests are cleared, the soil erodes, plants and animals are wiped out to make room for agriculture and the breeding of livestock. The result of depleting the environment and using up resources is starvation, and finally the population begins to wage war over the shrinking supplies. In the end the total population drops drastically because of starvation, illness and war. The ability to adapt to new living conditions becomes the difference between life and death. Finally, the total collapse of society is unavoidable, and a civilisation goes under.

Today we are heading towards a repetition of this mistake. We decimate the forests, empty the seas of fish, deplete the soil and fight over the resources that are left. The difference is that we take it another few steps – we pollute the air and water, which causes global warming and destroys the basic prerequisites for our own life.

Earlier in history it was a matter of individual, isolated cultures that went under. Today's environmental destruction threatens the whole of our globalised world. The only thing to our advantage, and which distinguishes us from earlier cultures that were wiped out, is that we have the opportunity to learn from others' mistakes. But are we human beings capable of doing that in depth, or do we personally have to experience the consequences in order to avoid them? New generations seem to keep repeating the mistakes of history, despite research and extensive documentation of the results. What harms us is our tendency to choose most often to do what works best for ourselves in the short term, even though in the long run it turns out worse for all of us.

Kristoffer put down the book and looked at the clock. It was five past three, which explained why he wanted a cup of coffee. He got up and went over to the window. The rain was falling diagonally, and the bare tree branches in Katarina cemetery were shaking in the wind. Kristoffer, who'd been considering taking a walk over to Café Neo, decided to stay in.

He still hadn't heard from Jesper, despite the fact that he'd rung him several times, sounding more and more urgent in his messages. Finally he revealed that he had something important to tell him, because after having admitted the truth to Jan-Erik Ragnerfeldt he felt lonelier than ever. He wanted to ask Jesper to come with him to Gerda's funeral. After the experience in Västerås he realised that he needed a friend at his side, no matter how hard it was to admit. He was used to managing by himself, and it bothered him to have to ask for something that weakened his independence, tied him to an obligation that he might be forced to reciprocate at any time.

His laptop was closed, and books and magazines were strewn across the table. He was determined to let his work tear his thoughts away from what awaited.

The deadline for his play came closer and closer. But writing was easier said than done when all his thoughts were elsewhere. They kept returning to the funeral, where he would meet Gerda's friends, and the mixture of anticipation and fear spoiled his concentration. He resorted to watching the rain, doing his best to find inspiration. He had to include that in the play. The fact that the weather was no longer what it had been. That madness was rampant. The idiocy of short-term thinking. From time immemorial the climate had been one of the few things that refused to submit to human-ity's need for power and was impossible to influence. Those days were gone. Now it had been proven that our amazing planet had finally been forced to yield; it could no longer put up resistance. The monumental victory of market forces. The stupidity of human beings in all its glory.

He would get the play done in time. It was his duty to wake people up, since so few seemed to understand that there was a real urgency.

He went back to his computer and sat down.

FATHER: So what have we decided? Are we going to Thailand or Brazil?

DAUGHTER: What about a camping trip?

FATHER: Camping?

DAUGHTER: Do you know how much CO_2 emission our family would produce on a trip to Thailand by air? Five point four tonnes.

MOTHER: Good Lord, how tedious you are! I don't understand how you got like this.

DAUGHTER: I know, it's unbelievable.

MOTHER: That plane will spew out just as much junk even if we stay at home and have a boring time. Just because we happen to be environmentally aware, do we have to give up our lovely holiday in the sun? Not on your life. I really need a few weeks of sunshine this time of year just to keep going.

SON: We could buy carbon credits then. To offset what we're emitting.

DAUGHTER: We'd be emitting just as much crap anyway! You can't buy everything. Especially not freedom from your own responsibility.

FATHER: Sweetheart, it's good that you're so involved, but now you're just being foolish.

DAUGHTER: Foolish?

FATHER: Surely you realise that someone else is going to come along and buy our tickets even if we don't go. The Svenssons, for example, are going to Bali on holiday, and I don't intend to sit here and listen to their damned travel stories when the only place I've been is camping.

He got up and went to the kitchen for a glass of water. His thoughts strayed once again, edging their way out of the isolation of his flat. If only Jesper would ring. He filled the glass and went back to his desk, sat down and read what he'd written. Placed his hands above the keyboard, but again his thoughts roamed. He made a quick note of the idea he'd just had before it too managed to disappear.

But when the occasion arises, all are equally intent on applauding role models like Joseph Schultz, convinced that when the chips were down they would be equally heroic.

He folded down the screen. It was futile even to try. It was as if all his thoughts had been loaned out from the place where they actually belonged. Restlessness kept forcing him out of his chair, and he'd lost count of how many useless walks he'd taken around the flat. It was like an itch inside him. On several occasions he had caught himself counting his pounding heartbeat. It frightened him, since he knew that it resembled something he'd experienced before. During those first wretched months in the flat, when he was tortured by the loss of his life's companion. The one thing that had helped him simplify reality. He let his gaze wander up the bookshelf and over to the bottle of cognac. Purchased on the day of the première of *Find and Replace All*, to stand as an unopened monument to his achievement and his indomitable character. It had fortified him, made him feel invincible.

He got up again and went to check his mobile, to see whether he might have missed a call or message, but the display was blank. He dialled Jesper's number but was met at once by his recorded voice.

He sighed in annoyance.

'It's me again. Call. It's extremely important.'

He disconnected and tossed the mobile on the sofa. It landed next to a piece of paper: the article about Torgny Wennberg he'd printed out a few nights ago. He sat down and read through it. Astonished once again at the tragic headline. *Forgotten proletarian writer.*

No survivor here.

At the bottom was the phone number he'd found online. He looked at his phone, pondered for a moment. Born 1928. Fourteen years younger than Gerda. He wondered how well they had known each other. Maybe they'd even been related. The only thing he knew for sure was that he wouldn't get anything done until he found out why he'd ended up in Gerda Persson's will. The fact that he kept glancing at the cognac, feeling that he was no longer invincible, made him pick up the mobile and punch in the numbers.

He didn't have a chance to think through what he was going to say before he heard a raspy voice on the other end.

'Yes, who is it?'

'Hello?'

'Yes?'

'Is this Torgny Wennberg?'

'Who is this?'

'I don't know if I have the right number, but I'm looking for Torgny Wennberg, who was an author?'

'What do you mean, "was"?'

Kristoffer picked up the printout he had put down earlier.

'No, I just mean is this the Torgny Wennberg who wrote *Keep the Fire Burning* and *The Wind Whispers Your Name*? Among others,' he added, when he got no reply.

'Yes. That's me.'

Only now did Kristoffer hesitate and wonder what he should say. He wished he had planned the conversation better.

'If you're one of those fucking salesmen, then I'm not interested.'

'No, no, it's nothing like that.'

He hesitated again. Torgny Wennberg sounded irritated, and he didn't want to risk being dismissed on the phone. He decided to take a chance.

'I was wondering if I might possibly interview you about what it's like to be a proletarian author. I'm a playwright myself, and I read about you on a web site. I'm working on a piece right now and it would be a great help if I could meet with you. If you have time, of course. I would appreciate asking you a few questions.'

There was silence on the line. He realised that further coaxing was required.

'I'd be happy to buy you dinner or lunch or something, near where you live, so it won't be so much trouble for you.'

'No, damn it, we can't even go to the pub now that smoking is no longer allowed. So you'll have to come up here if you're interested. I'll be at home tonight if it's that urgent.'

With relief Kristoffer said that would be fine, and they agreed on a time. He asked if he should bring anything, and Torgny suggested picking up a pizza for him. There was a pizzeria right around the corner.

Everything felt suddenly lighter. It was the passive uncertainty that was so taxing; now he was on his way again.

Not until he pulled on his shoes did it occur to him that he hadn't mentioned his name.

He took the path across the cemetery and continued towards the bus stop. There were no seats on the bus but he was happy to stand. It made his restlessness less obvious. A mother with a child in a pushchair stood in the crush by the central doors. The boy was shrieking and kept trying to climb out of his prison, to his mother's increasing exasperation. She looked tired and had dark circles under her eyes; the boy was bright red in the face and the hair sticking out from under his cap had stuck to his sweaty forehead. Finally the mother's patience ran out; grabbing the boy roughly by the arm, she shoved him back down in the pushchair. A man with a briefcase gave the woman a disapproving look. The boy stopped screaming at once and rubbed his arm where his mother's hand had grabbed it.

Why not like fish roe? thought Kristoffer. Or tadpoles? Why did human offspring have to be dependent on and at the mercy of their progenitors, marked for life by their mistakes?

He got off the bus and looked for the pizzeria. He ordered two pizzas and sat down to wait. Although it was only five o'clock, several of the tables were occupied. Two people at one table, two at another, a party of four – scattered throughout the room, all the customers sat with invisible barriers between the tables. In the endless space-time of eternity they all happened to be gathered right here, right now. For one single moment. Kristoffer imagined a scenario. What if a madman came in the door and took them all hostage? In an instant everything would change – the barriers would be torn down and together they would form a unit. United by a common threat they would quickly organise themselves into a group and do everything possible to work together. But as long as no threat was in sight, they sat there and did their best not to notice one another.

'Your pizzas are ready.'

Kristoffer stood up and paid for them.

He cast one last look at the diners before he walked out the door.

Clearly the threat of climate change was not scary enough.

★　　★　　★

Torgny Wennberg had given him the code to the front door, and he balanced the pizza cartons on one knee as he keyed in the numbers. The lock buzzed and he pushed open the door. A list of residents informed him that Torgny lived on the third floor, and since it was difficult to pull open the grille of the lift with his hands full of pizza, he decided to take the stairs. He pressed the doorbell and the next moment the little point of light in the middle of the peephole turned black, and Kristoffer knew that Torgny was looking at him. He smiled, and the next moment the door was opened. Kristoffer smiled a little more.

'Hello, here I am with the pizza.'

Torgny Wennberg stood quite still and stared at him. He didn't move a muscle to indicate that he was going to let him in, and his expression made Kristoffer unsure.

'I'm the one who rang you before, a few hours ago. I wanted to ask you a few questions.'

He got no reply. Instead Wennberg clapped a hand to his mouth. Kristoffer was confused. Maybe the man was sick or something. The deep furrows in his unshaven face testified to a hard life. His hair was grey and bushy, and the hand he'd put to his mouth shook in a disturbing way. A stale smell of old cigarettes infiltrated the pizza aroma, and Kristoffer began to regret that he'd come. Torgny looked like somebody Kristoffer might turn into if he weren't made of sterner stuff.

As always, when faced with someone else's obvious weakness, he felt a slight contempt.

Torgny lowered his hand.

'Is it really you, Kristoffer?'

In the moment that followed, all his senses took on a sharpness he had never felt before. Everything froze.

'How do you know my name?'

And when Torgny replied, the door he had always searched for opened up wide. He dropped the pizzas and wanted nothing more than to run away from there.

'Because you look just like your mother.'

CHAPTER 22

Fearing tranquillity I upheld chaos, unaware
of the deep domicile of joy in my sheltered breast.

Axel read the words he had written. He didn't know where they had come from, he just wrote them all of a sudden, and for a short while he thought he was back. Such a long time had passed since the spirit of creativity had granted him a rewarding day of work. To fix the words to the paper had seemed like hard physical labour, since none of them voluntarily wanted to find their place. The story he was trying to tell faltered through thirty pages; stacked on the desk they constituted an insult if the time it had taken to write them were taken into account. None of his characters wanted to settle down in the life he was trying to give them. The delivery date he had rashly promised the publishers was fast approaching, and Gerda had informed him yesterday that someone from the bank had rung looking for him. He still hadn't rung back, well aware of what they would tell him. With the money from the Society for the Promotion of Literature prize, the advance from the publishers, and the Swedish Church writers' grants, he had kept the household running since the summer, but now the money was starting to run out. He had asked for a reprieve on his mortgage interest and the bank had granted it – with compound interest on the interest he was already unable to pay, naturally. Conscious of his profession and its irregular income, the bank had regarded the house as sufficient security, but now the deadline had passed and he knew the banker would want to discuss a solution to the problem.

With hindsight it was plain to see that he and Alice had had delusions of grandeur when they bought this desirable home. Everything it seemed to represent had blinded them, since it fitted so perfectly into their vision of the future. Back then in the mid-fifties Alice had still been writing, and with the relatively steady income from two writers the monthly mortgage had seemed reasonable. But reality had brought a different future than the grandiose one they had envisioned for themselves. He was now expected to support the whole household while she moped about like a martyr, drowning her sorrows in other people's books, vintage wine and TV. Soon he would need to have a talk with her about money. Explain that they would have to let Gerda go and possibly sell the house and buy something smaller.

That conversation was not something he was looking forward to.

He heard the telephone ring. A single ring before it stopped. He glanced at the clock. It could very well be the bank looking for him again. Only a minute passed before there was another ring. He shoved back his chair irritably and got up.

Gerda was still on the phone when he entered the kitchen. She was standing with her back to him and didn't hear him come in, which gave him a chance to listen in.

'I can leave him a message, but unfortunately he can't be disturbed right now because he's working . . . No, I'm sorry, that's not possible.'

There was silence for a few seconds before Gerda with a repeated 'no' tried to get a word in edge-wise. If it was the bank she was talking with, their persistence was highly alarming.

'She is unfortunately not available at the moment, either. I'll have to take down your number and ask him to call you back . . . Yes, in that case you may ring again. Yes. No, that's not possible. I don't know, but I'll tell him that you asked. Goodbye.'

Gerda hung up with a heavy sigh. She crossed out something on her notepad and put down the pen.

'Who was that?'

She gave a start before turning round.

'I think it was that woman. She didn't give her name but asked for both you and Mrs Ragnerfeldt. She doesn't have a telephone so she didn't leave a number.'

'She asked for Alice?'

Gerda nodded. How could he possibly create anything under these conditions? Four months had passed since Torgny's startling visit, but aside from the letters that arrived periodically he hadn't heard a word about what had happened in the meantime. Torgny hadn't contacted him, and Axel had been grateful for his absence.

'How did she sound?'

Gerda thought for a moment.

'Furious is probably the best description. She wanted to know if you had read her letters.'

Both of them fell silent and looked at the doorway as they heard Alice coming down the stairs. She still knew nothing about all the letters and had stopped asking whether he'd heard from Torgny about the fate of the lovesick woman. She came into the kitchen and gave them an indifferent look on her way to the refrigerator. She had decided to get dressed for a change.

'I see everyone's as cheerful as usual. Did somebody die, or is it just the normal afternoon chatter?'

She took out a jug and went over to the cupboard to get a glass.

Axel and Gerda looked at each other. If the circumstances had been different he would have enjoyed the moment. For the first time he encountered an empathy in Gerda's glance, and he was willing to convince himself that it had happened voluntarily; that meant a lot to him. But now the circumstances were different, and the situation evoked anything but pleasure. It was time to tell Alice, before Halina rang again and Alice picked up the phone. If she mentioned the letters Axel would have to admit that he had kept the truth from her, and then run the risk that Alice would demand to read them. She was well aware of his inability to throw anything away.

'Alice, could we sit down for a minute? Let's go into the library.'

He didn't want to talk about it here in the kitchen in front of Gerda. He might have to omit certain details, which Gerda would consider lying.

Alice looked up when she heard the gravity in his voice.

'Nothing has happened to Jan-Erik, I hope?'

'No, no, it's nothing serious, there's just something I'd like you to know.'

She took her glass and headed for the library. Axel gave Gerda a look, but her attention had already shifted elsewhere. She was reaching for the jug that Alice had left on the worktop, to put it back in the fridge.

'It's about that woman, you know the one Torgny was here telling us about, Halina or whatever her name was.'

'Yes?'

Alice was looking at him attentively. She was sitting in one of the library's armchairs, with her

295

back straight and one leg crossed over the other. Axel had sat down in the other one, and it struck him how long it had been since they'd sat here together. They'd bought the armchairs when they moved in. They were much too expensive but hand-picked to fulfil their mutual dream of the future. The library was the first room they furnished, intending it to be the heart that would give life to the house. There, in the armchairs, they would sit together in the evenings when they ventured out of their inspiring conversational rambles.

Now the armrests had been worn by the arms of others, and the conversations had wandered off somewhere and never returned.

'That woman sent me some letters recently. I didn't say anything because I didn't want to concern you.'

'What sort of letters?'

'I haven't read them. I threw them out.'

The glass of juice she was raising to her mouth stopped halfway.

'You did? You threw out letters you received?'

Her voice was full of suspicion, but he intended to stand by his words. And he hadn't read the letters, after all.

'Yes, I did.'

She took a sip and set down the glass.

'Unbelievable. What does Torgny say? He should know if she's taking her medication or not. He said that was all she needed.'

'I haven't spoken with him.'

'Why not?'

Axel gave a deep, genuine sigh.

'Because I'm so bloody tired of the whole affair. I thought that the less I worried about it the better.'

She plucked a little fleck from her trouser leg.

'Then ring and ask her what it is she wants.'

'She didn't leave a phone number.'

'Torgny should know it, shouldn't he?'

He sighed.

'To be honest, I have no desire to ring him about this. You heard for yourself how he stood here defending her. You can say what you like about Torgny, but I actually feel sorry for him now that she's sending letters to me.'

'Didn't you notice anything when you met her in Västerås? I mean, didn't she seem strange?'

Axel shook his head.

'I hardly spoke to her. She was there with Torgny and they sat at the other end of the table after dinner. I don't understand why she decided to latch onto me.'

'No, it's hard to believe.'

She said the words with a thoughtful expression as she looked the other way, apparently unaware of the insult. As if the words had simply come naturally to her.

'So she told Torgny that the two of you had a fling together there in Västerås?'

'Yes, obviously.'

She sat in silence for a moment and then cocked her head to one side and looked at him.

'I take it you didn't?'

'Alice.' He used his most reproachful tone of voice.

There had been a time when a lie would have been fruitless. She used to know every shift in his gaze, every nuance in his voice, every shadow that passed across his face. But the mere thought of lying to her would then have still been unthinkable.

'I had to ask. It would explain her behaviour at least. And I certainly have no idea what you do on all your trips.'

'I actually don't travel that much. I went to five Book Day events last autumn, that's all. You're more than welcome to come along next time if you're interested.'

'No, thanks.' There was both indulgence and sarcasm in her reply.

'I'd be grateful if I didn't have to go, either. You know what I think about that sort of thing,' he said.

She didn't answer, and it occurred to him that she might not know this about him. A lot had happened since they stopped sharing their thoughts with each other.

'Anyway, she apparently rang today and asked for you.'

She looked up. 'For me?'

'Well, for me too, but when Gerda said that I

wasn't available she asked for you. I want you to hang up at once if she rings again and you happen to answer the phone. But hopefully she won't call again.'

'Why did she ask for me?'

'No idea. It's difficult to make sense of any of this. But she's obviously not altogether mentally stable, so maybe there's nothing to understand.'

Alice got up and went over to one of the bookshelves. She took down a framed photograph of Annika and absentmindedly wiped off the glass before she put it back. At that moment Axel realised that he hadn't seen Annika for several days. But then he remembered there had been talk of some riding camp over the weekend.

Alice turned round.

'I think we should call the police. I don't understand why we have to tolerate such behaviour. There must be some way to make her stop. Isn't it illegal to keep on harassing someone like this?'

'I don't think it is. The only thing she's done is send me letters.'

'She rang too.'

'Yes, but that may have been a one-off. We'll have to wait and see what happens. Imagine what the press would do if they got hold of this. The tabloids love this sort of story.'

Alice sat down again. The conversation faded out to silence.

Outside it had begun to grow dark. Neither of them made a move to leave; they just stayed sitting in the armchairs they had splurged on once upon a time in another life. Axel was oddly affected by the memories that came washing over him. All the work they had put in when the dream had still been alive. The person selling the house had owned it since it was built, and the price was relatively low because of the renovations it needed. Axel's father had helped out with things they couldn't do themselves, such as the plumbing and new joists for a ceiling. Otherwise he and Alice had struggled through room after room with tins of paint and wallpaper paste. He raised his eyes and searched the ceiling. He found the little hole where the newly painted plaster had given way to the champagne cork. When they had ceremonially inaugurated their library by candlelight. Just the two of them, as always. Back then, when neither could exist without the presence of the other and the rest of the world intruded like a necessary evil.

He looked at her. Almost twenty-five years had passed.

He had been so convinced that neither of them would ever again have to feel lonely.

An impulse made him reach out his hand and place it gently on her arm. In astonishment she looked at his hand as if she didn't know what it was. Then she put her hand on his and they sat there, two lost souls who had given up all hope of finding their way home.

★　　★　　★

300

At what moment does the process begin? When does the first flake fall that will form the snowball? At what stage does the movement start? Was it the day when he secretly chose the linguistic path, or when he wrote his first book? Was it signing the papers for the house, or the first night they chose to sleep without touching each other? Was it all the years of frustration, or the moment he accepted the invitation to the Book Day event in Västerås? Or was it not until the moment when he let himself be seduced?

By now everything had been in motion for a long time.

There was an hour left until what they thought was theirs would be lost for ever.

CHAPTER 23

The pizzas had remained untouched in their cartons, which were still lying on the landing. Kristoffer was sitting on an uncomfortable Windsor chair in the single room of the flat. The alternative had been to sit down next to Torgny on the unmade bed. There were piles of newspapers, empty glasses, dirty clothes, overflowing ashtrays and things that had been left wherever they'd been put down. Everything he saw seemed filthy and old, and it was clearly a long time since anyone had tried to put the room in order.

With long pauses their conversation had stumbled along; both of them were too overwrought to be able to complete a logical train of thought. Most of what was said had come from Kristoffer's lips, a result of Torgny asking whether it was his mother who had sent him. He had told him the truth, finding no reason to lie under the circumstances. It had been easier this time to talk in detail about his life. About steps inside the entrance to the amusement park. About the fact that he didn't

302

remember anything from his first years, and that he'd always wondered who his parents were and why he'd been abandoned. Torgny sighed and went to fetch two beers. Kristoffer said that he didn't want one. The spectacle of Torgny and his home made abstinence easy.

It could have been him if his character had been any weaker.

Halina.

His mother's name was Halina.

Not Elina as they thought the four-year-old had said. Two letters had made all the difference. A tiny misunderstanding that meant the police had never been able to locate her.

Torgny sat down on the bed again, dazed. He lit a cigarette. Kristoffer shook his head when Torgny held out the packet to him.

He sat staring at an oil painting. In this context it looked like a captured peacock in a junk-shop. He tried to avoid looking at anything except the face, but his gaze kept sliding along the naked female body. Lying indolently with her head resting on one hand and the other half-heartedly hiding her crotch.

He had found his mother.

He didn't want to see her like this.

He dropped his eyes and blushed.

'You can see for yourself how much you look alike.'

Torgny looked at the painting, and although Kristoffer knew that his eyes must have wandered over her naked body an infinite number of times, he still wanted to ask him to stop. He wanted to cover her up, take her down and turn the painting to face the wall.

'It was your father who painted it, the swine. But he could certainly paint.'

Kristoffer didn't know whether he could stand hearing any more. It was dizzying, like standing at the edge of a cliff. Utterly unprepared he had trudged up the stairs with his pizza cartons, and now he was sitting in a flat that looked like a crack den and was expected to absorb the precious information he had always sought.

'So she left you at Skansen . . . Jesus.'

Torgny heaved a sigh and shook his head, taking a deep drag on his cigarette and a swig of beer.

'If only I had known.'

Kristoffer sat in silence.

'So you don't remember living here when you were little?'

Kristoffer looked around.

'Here?'

'Yes, until January 1975. That was when she packed her bags and left. Since then I haven't heard a word.'

'But she didn't leave me at Skansen until May the tenth.'

Torgny seemed not to be listening. Or else the information made no difference. He took a few gulps of beer.

'If you knew how I searched for you. I just about

turned half the city upside down trying to find the two of you, but nobody knew a thing. I found some weird commune where you apparently lived for a month or so, but they didn't know where you'd gone after that. They couldn't keep her there since she was ill, they said, although they seemed screwier to me than she ever was. It was all that sodding seventies new age crap and shit. But she could be really strange when she didn't take her medicine. You could see it in her eyes, like somebody threw a switch or something. Something that had never bothered her before would make her crazy the next time you did it. In the morning she'd be like a pitiful little bird, asking me to promise never to leave her, then in the afternoon she would be screaming that she hated me. It wasn't always easy to cope with.'

He lowered his eyes and plucked at the pull-tab on the beer can.

'But Christ, I really loved her.'

He sniffed and wiped his hand across his face. Then he got up and went over to the bookshelf, searched for a moment and pulled out a book.

'This one is about her; it's the last book I ever wrote. After that there weren't any more.'

Torgny stubbed out his cigarette in a filthy ashtray and handed the book to Kristoffer.

He read the cover: *The Wind Whispers Your Name*. A picture of a woman turned away.

He turned over the book and read the blurb on the back cover.

George is a bitter, middle-aged man who has given up hope of finding love. When he meets Sonja he is forced to re-evaluate his view of life, since this powerful love leaves him no choice. But Sonja is carrying dark memories that slowly take over their lives . . .

With uncanny authenticity Torgny Wennberg depicts a man's downfall after the end of a love affair. In the powerful portrait of George and Sonja he paints a gripping portrait of the difficult art of being human.

'You can have it if you want. I know how it ends.'

Torgny gave a little smile and raised the beer can to his lips but discovered it was empty. He crushed the can and dropped it on the floor, picking up the one he had offered to Kristoffer.

'Maybe she took her own life. She threatened to do it sometimes when she was really bad.'

Kristoffer sat in silence. Why was he the way he was? Was there any family resemblance? What had been influenced by what?

He was getting some of the answers, but he was suddenly terrified of the questions.

He swallowed.

'What was wrong with her?'

Torgny shrugged.

'The hell if I know. When she was healthy she didn't want to talk about it, and when she felt bad she didn't know she was ill. But you have to understand, your mother was a fantastic woman. She couldn't help it if she acted the way she did; it was a disease she had, and most of the time she was well. When she took her medication everything was fine, but sometimes the mare would ride her at night, as they say. I remember she used to cry out in her sleep. Then it was almost impossible to wake her and make her understand she was only dreaming. It could take hours to calm her down.'

He sighed and lit another cigarette.

'I think what she was most afraid of was being abandoned again. She had been through so much shit it's no wonder something broke inside of her. My own crappy childhood was a luxury cruise in comparison. It's fucking shit when you think about it.'

'Tell me.'

And so Torgny told him. That Kristoffer's mother was Jewish and had been born in Poland in 1938. That she was sent to a concentration camp and lost her entire family. That her mother was shot, her father was probably taken to another camp, and that she never found out what happened to him. That her sister died in the camp and left her alone. Only after Torgny had been talking for a while did it dawn on Kristoffer that this was his own family he was talking about. This wasn't someone else's. He came from Poland instead of Sweden, and his whole family had been wiped out. The more information he heard the more confused he became, and finally he had to ask for a pen and paper so he could take notes.

'Imagine yourself as a six-year-old seeing your mother's brains blown out. She told me he'd laughed afterwards, the man who shot her mother. He'd bet another soldier that he could shoot someone in the eye. It was just random that he happened to choose her.'

His grandmother. They were talking about his grandmother. And his mother who had been forced to watch. Kristoffer suddenly thought of Joseph Schultz. From Jan-Erik Ragnerfeldt's lecture. Maybe there was something in him that was especially affected by that story, an inherited cry for justice.

'Someone said that Halina went back to Poland, and maybe that's what she did. She didn't have any family left, but that's where she was from, after all. She still spoke the language fluently, and there was nobody here to keep her. Sadly.'

Torgny took a swig of beer.

'The thing was, she never felt the same about me as I did about her. Otherwise, she would never have left me.'

He fell silent and looked at the floor.

'She seemed to retreat when I showed her how I felt, as if she didn't think she had a right to be happy in any way. I remember that sometimes it felt as though she liked me best when I didn't care as much; that's when she became more loving. But then when I loved her back she would retreat again.'

Kristoffer listened intently. Torgny spoke with ruminative pauses, and something told Kristoffer that these memories had waited a long time to be aired.

Kristoffer looked at the book in his hands. The picture of the woman turned away.

'You mustn't believe that your mother was some sort of idiot just because she had a problem. On the contrary, she was probably the smartest person I ever met. When she was well she was like a . . . I don't know, I can't describe it.'

Torgny smiled and looked around as if searching for a suitable description.

'Damn, what great times we had when everything was good. There was no one else quite like her. I know, because I've looked.'

He stopped talking and fell into a reverie.

Torgny had been quiet for a long time. Kristoffer felt a profound weariness but he knew that the conversation was not over yet. There was more he needed to know. Yet he no longer knew what he was going to do with the information.

'You said that it was my pappa who painted that picture.'

He nodded towards the painting and Torgny snorted.

'That brute. Luckily for him he managed to drink himself to death before I had a chance to kill him.'

'So he's dead?'

'Yes, a long time ago, and you should be glad of that. Karl-Evert Pettersson was his name. An artist, but he evidently drank so heavily that nobody wanted anything to do with him. He was the sort who flies into a rage when he's drunk and wants to fight and cause trouble. He was drunk when he did it.'

'Did what?'

'When he raped her.'

Kristoffer shifted in his chair in an attempt to shake off what he was hearing. Now he didn't want to hear any more. No more.

'She was modelling for that painting, trying to make a little extra money. She wanted to be a writer but she never managed to get anything published.'

Torgny broke off suddenly as if he'd said something he didn't want to talk about.

Kristoffer felt that something was starting to fall apart. His fantasies during his childhood, the dream world where hope was kept alive. The images of how happy his parents would be when they finally found him. How they would be heart-broken and had fought to get him back.

'That was when we met, after she got knocked up. She was desperate because she didn't want to . . . Well, I might as well tell you the truth. She had been raped, but the abortion laws were different then. The new abortion law that gave women the right to choose and all that wouldn't be passed until a few years later, and you should be damned glad of that.'

A feeling of nausea washed over Kristoffer.

'But then, after you were born, she was happy. She was a good mother, she really was. It was only sometimes, when she wasn't feeling well, that she could be a bit harsh.'

Kristoffer tried to get up, holding on to the back of the chair.

'She must have been ill when she left you at Skansen. She would never have done anything like that if she were feeling well.'

With the book in his hand he managed to make it to the hall.

'Kristoffer.'

Torgny was still sitting on the bed, but Kristoffer couldn't speak. He reached for the door handle.

'Why don't you get in touch again sometime, Kristoffer? We could see each other again, the two of us.'

He went out to the landing and managed to pull the door shut behind him. His ears were filled with a piercing scream. His hand shook as he grasped the banister, and his legs felt stiff as if seized by cramps. He barely managed to make it down the stairs.

Everything was in ruins.

His hidden inner world that had always glittered like a distant oasis, enticing him with its promise of bliss. Empty and ravaged, it had dissolved and slipped away. All the endless waiting. All the lost seconds. The hope that had driven him onwards. How could he accept that all the waiting had been in vain?

They had never looked for him; he had never been missed.

From the depths of his being it came surging up – the grief he had never permitted to exist. Like a howl for restitution it came flowing and knocked his feet from under him. With his back against the wall he slid down to the floor.

He hadn't wanted to know any of this!

All he wanted was to get it back.

The hope.

The hope of one day finding an explanation that would bless him with the ability to forgive.

CHAPTER 24

When the doorbell rang they were still sitting in the library. For a while now the smell of dinner had filled the house, and Gerda would soon be here to tell them it was ready. They looked at each other when they heard her footsteps moving down the hall towards the front door. Axel got up, and knew immediately who had rung the bell.

'I'm looking for Axel Ragnerfeldt.'

'I'm sorry, he's not at home.'

'He certainly is, I saw him through the window.'

For a few seconds there was silence.

'Unfortunately he's busy.'

'Tell him I want to talk to him. It's for his own good.'

Alice got up and hissed at Axel.

'Go and help Gerda, for God's sake!'

Axel rushed out. To his consternation he realised that he was afraid. More afraid than he could ever recall being since he was a child.

He reached the hall just in time to see Gerda trying to shut the door. Halina had squeezed herself into the doorway in an attempt to force her way inside. But the commotion stopped when she caught sight of him.

'I want to talk to you.'

He could see the desperation in Gerda's eyes and realised it would be unfair to involve her. He nodded to her and she let go of the door. With her lips pursed, she did not deign to look at him as she walked away.

Halina stepped into the hall.

'Where's your wife? I want her to hear this too.'

Axel glanced over his shoulder and saw Alice standing at the other end of the hall by the living room door. He turned back to face Halina but could barely look at her. Her hair was a mess and her clothes dirty. In her eyes was that look he'd seen outside the publisher's, the look he'd prayed to God never to see again.

'I must ask you to leave. I'm not interested in what you have to say.'

'Did you read my letters?'

He took a step forward to block her path.

'No, I didn't. Now I'm going to have to ask you to go.'

She clutched the door-frame to secure her position.

'I just want to—'

'I'm not interested in what you want!'

He prised loose her fingers and with a hand on her shoulder, managed to push her onto the front steps, a little more roughly than he'd intended. His fear had faded, leaving space for a rising anger;

now she had literally stepped over the line. He locked the door and she was left outside, screaming and ringing the doorbell. Maybe he should call Torgny, ask him to come and get her. But what would they do with her until then? The police were not an option; calling them would only bring more misery. His dread of scandal was even greater than his fear of the woman on the other side of the door.

The constant ringing of the doorbell resounded through the house, and her wails penetrated the walls. Then her face appeared outside the porch window, and he backed out of sight. Alice was still standing with her arms folded in the living-room doorway.

'Let her in so we can finally put an end to all this. The neighbours will hear!'

'Absolutely not! She's not setting foot in this house.'

Alice frowned and headed for the front door with a determined look on her face.

'Then I'll do it myself.'

'Listen to me, Alice! Don't open that door!'

'We have to put an end to this insanity once and for all. We can at least listen to what she wants.'

He tried to stop her as she passed but she brushed his hands away.

The sound of the doorbell stopped abruptly when Alice unlocked the front door. Axel had stayed a distance behind her and saw how the two women sized each other up for a few seconds.

Then Alice opened the door wide and stepped aside.

'Come in. But take off your shoes.' Alice turned and walked down the hall. 'Gerda, could you please serve coffee in the living room?'

Halina stepped into the hall and pulled off her pointed boots, throwing Axel a triumphant smile.

He watched Alice go, her back straight and her steps resolute. He knew precisely what mood she was in; with her verbal artillery she was ready to crush Halina like a troublesome insect.

He closed his eyes and pressed his hand to his temple.

Alice was sitting on the sofa when they came into the living room. She gave a little smile, and in her kindest tone of voice she asked Halina to take a seat. Then she patted the space beside her.

'Come, darling, sit here next to me.'

Axel didn't reply but remained where he was, leaning on the mantelpiece by the tile stove. The situation was so bizarre that a part of him still couldn't believe it was really happening.

Halina looked around the room. Alice followed her gaze as if wanting to confirm what she was seeing.

'I've asked Gerda to bring in some coffee. You do drink coffee, don't you?'

Halina nodded.

Alice's superiority was palpable. With an imperturbable calm she took control of the situation, and Halina sat there dirty and mute in her armchair. Alice smiled and looked at her for a moment before she spoke again.

'I understand that you're interested in my husband. Apparently you've sent him a number of letters.'

Halina said nothing. But it was obvious what she was thinking. Alice remained unmoved by what she saw blazing in Halina's eyes.

Gerda came in with the coffee tray, and no one said a word as she arranged the china.

'I think we have some pastries we could offer, don't we, Gerda?'

Gerda stopped in the middle of what she was doing, then nodded and left the room.

Axel waited for the explosion. At any moment Halina would start speaking, and he knew that he would have to choose his words carefully. The lie was so established that admitting the truth now was out of the question. Her madness was what would save him, the shield behind which he could hide no matter what she claimed.

'What exactly do you do, then? Do you have a job?'

It was Alice's mild voice that continued the conversation. She sounded as if she were talking to a child.

'I'm a writer.'

'I see, so you're a writer too. What sort of books have you written?'

'Among other things, I just finished a short story

317

that I'm going to send to *Artes* magazine. An erotic short story. Actually, that's what I came here to talk about.'

Axel swallowed. *Artes* was a prestigious arts journal published under the auspices of the Swedish Academy. It was highly unlikely that someone such as Halina would ever have a story published there, but it would be bad enough if the editors read what she had written. Because he knew which erotic incident it was that she had described.

'What's it about, then? Well, you know what I mean, I understand if it's erotic, but why do you want to talk to us about it?'

Axel closed his eyes. For the life of him he could no longer understand it. How it had happened. The power, so difficult to comprehend, of that incident. Such a tiny mistake. What had happened had been so meaningless, so utterly insignificant. But it had prompted such unprecedented consequences.

'Because it's about Axel and me.'

He looked at Alice. She was still smiling. He was just about to deny the assertion when Alice beat him to it.

'You mean about your night in Västerås?'

For the first time Halina seemed to waver, but when Alice continued, Halina regained her equilibrium.

'The one you made up,' said Alice.

Halina smiled and looked at Axel.

'Is that what you told her? That I made it all up?'

Axel, who hadn't yet said a word, had to clear his throat before he spoke.

'You know as well as I do that nothing happened that night in Västerås. Torgny was here, and he said that if you'd only take your medication you could get rid of all these illusions.'

Halina leaned back and laughed.

At the same moment Gerda returned.

Halina put her hand in her jacket and pulled out a bundle of folded paper which she handed across the full pastry tray.

'Read this, and then see which of us you believe. He likes oral, but you probably know that already, at least I hope so. And then there's that cute birthmark on his groin, the one that looks like a little heart.'

Afterwards Axel could remember only fragments of what followed. He remembered Alice's face, Gerda's footsteps that stopped short on the parquet floor, Halina enjoying her revenge. He had a vague memory that the telephone rang but that none of them made a move to pick it up. He said nothing. He could have denied everything, countered every accusation by hiding behind the alibi that Torgny had provided. But not the fact that she knew about the heart-shaped birthmark, which had once been his and Alice's most intimate symbol of love.

It was Halina who broke the silence. Gerda's

319

paralysis vanished and she disappeared back to the kitchen.

'Initially I thought I would turn to *Artes*, but they pay very poorly. There are other magazines that pay considerably better, but I haven't really made up my mind yet. I thought you could offer some advice and tell me what you think, which publication you think would be best.'

Axel looked at Alice. She was sitting with her hands in her lap and her back was no longer straight. Gone was the confident aura. She looked crushed, and dropped her eyes as one last confirmation of her humiliation.

Halina had vanquished her.

'Why are you doing this?'

Axel had a hard time getting the words out; he didn't want to lower himself to speaking to her. The repugnance he felt distorted his voice.

Halina got up and stuffed the papers back inside her jacket.

'Because you hurt me, you smug bastard. I've taken enough shit in my life, and nobody treats me the way you did without paying for it. You, with all your beautiful words and elegant phrases. I can't stand it that people regard you as some sort of hero when in reality you're nothing but a cowardly bastard. You're going to feel what it's like to be dragged through the mud, I promise you that, Axel Ragnerfeldt. This is only the beginning.'

CHAPTER 25

Jan-Erik returned the last letter to the cardboard box and leaned back in the chair. He had opened and read the contents of each unopened envelope, becoming increasingly astounded yet ultimately convinced that his father had actually had a lover. None of them was dated, but using the postmarks he had sorted them into a rough chronological order. The early ones were heartfelt love letters, some filled with poetic romanticism, others with burning lust. Some parts made him blush when he pictured his father as the object of the ardent prose. But gradually the tone had changed. A hostile undercurrent seeped in between the lines, and the last letters had been almost threatening – with repeated threats that she was going to publish a short story unless Axel showed up at a certain meeting place.

He wondered why Axel hadn't read the letters. Maybe he was trying to break off the affair by simply ignoring her. Had his mother known about it? It occurred to him that he may have found the real explanation for why his parents were living on separate floors of the house by the time he returned from the States.

But his greatest fear had been confirmation of an illegitimate son born from the relationship. Thankfully he had discovered nothing of the sort mentioned in any of the letters. And yet the anxiety had not gone. Kristoffer Sandeblom's strange story still chafed him. A foundling. Precisely during the years when his father was having an affair. His father who had unquestionably ended it and broken off all contact. The woman's desperate tone in the letters. Gerda, who had written Kristoffer into her will. The money she had sent him all those years, despite not being rich. He pushed away the thought, realised how unlikely that was. Perhaps it was all a strange coincidence. Kristoffer had mentioned it about the same time he'd found Axel's old love letters. His imagination had run away with him. His hangover wasn't helping his thinking, either.

And yet.

He realised what the existence of an unknown half-brother would mean on the day the inheritance was to be distributed. Under no circumstances did he intend to share any of it with some illegitimate guy who had suddenly turned up from nowhere. He was the one who had administered the assets, fought to maintain interest in his father's books, and above all put up with the old devil for all these years. It was bad enough given what had already been willed directly to Louise.

He returned the cardboard box to the cupboard. Once again he had been sidetracked from looking for a photograph of Gerda. Darkness had fallen, and it was high time he went home. He would have to ring Marianne Folkesson and tell her there were no pictures.

He walked through the house to make sure everything was in order. A lamp was on in the library, and he checked that the timer was set properly, sighing at the sea of books waiting to be sorted. Maybe turning the house into a museum would be the best solution: let everything remain the way it was. He stopped at the photograph of Annika. He saw in his mind's eye how, desperate and alone, she had climbed up on the chair in Axel's office. A girl just turned fifteen who should have had her whole life ahead of her.

He stroked his finger over the glass covering her face.

'I miss you, you know.'

In the upstairs bathroom he found some headache tablets and swallowed them, drinking water straight from the tap. His mouth was stale. An ancient tube of toothpaste in which the contents had solidified was of little help, but in the bathroom cabinet there was a bottle of mouthwash. He shook a few drops directly onto his tongue and grimaced at the sting. He put the bottle in his pocket; he didn't want to reek of alcohol when he got home.

Louise still hadn't called.

He was in the taxi when his mobile rang. Hoping it was Louise, he snatched it up but was disappointed when he saw an unfamiliar number.

'Yes, this is Jan-Erik Ragnerfeldt.'

'Hello, Jan-Erik, my name is Gunvor Benson and I'm a representative of the Nordic Council. I hope I'm not disturbing you.'

'No, not at all.'

'I've been given the very pleasant task of ringing you to let you know that you've been unanimously voted the winner of the Nordic Council's literary prize this year.'

Jan-Erik was dumbstruck.

'This is the first time the prize has been given to anyone other than an author, but we feel that what you have accomplished in the wake of your father's unique body of work is so admirable that we want to acknowledge it.'

'Oh, my goodness.'

The taxi was passing the London viaduct, and he stared blankly at a huge ferry.

'The prize money is 350,000 Danish kroner.'

'Good Lord!'

'Perhaps you'd like to hear the citation?'

'Yes, please.'

She read it off. 'In recognition of Jan-Erik

Ragnerfeldt's efforts, through lectures and human-itarian aid work, to transform the achievements of an extraordinary author from the printed page into tangible results.'

'Oh my.' It was all he could manage.

She laughed on the other end.

'You sound surprised.'

'Yes, well, it's a bit unexpected, I have to say.'

'I'll get back to you with proposed dates for the award ceremony itself, but I just want to mention that we won't officially announce your name until just before the award ceremony, so please keep this to yourself for the time being.'

'Of course, I will.'

'I have your postal address, and I'll send you my contact details in case you have any further ques-tions. Otherwise I just want to offer my congratu-lations.'

'Thank you. I really don't know what to say. I'm overjoyed.'

And he was. After they said goodbye he sat there with a big grin on his face. For the first time in a very, very long time he felt a huge, wild happi-ness running through his body.

He shook out a few more drops of mouthwash on his tongue before he unlocked the door to the flat. With renewed courage and hope for the future he was in great spirits. He would tell Louise, share his success with her, see to it that this award marked a turning point. He would get a grip on his alcohol problem and devote himself more to his family.

It was quiet in the flat, but the lights were on.

'Hello?'

He set down his baggage and hung up his coat.

'Hello.'

It was Ellen who answered. Jan-Erik went over to her room and stood in the doorway.

'Hi.'

'Hi.'

She was sitting at her computer. Jan-Erik walked over to see what she was doing. A woman in black with a tiny waist and enormous breasts was massacring enemies in a wasteland. Ellen's fingers tapped on the keyboard at the same speed as the shots firing on the screen.

'Hey, that game doesn't look so nice.'

'Just leave it.'

He clammed up, afraid to provoke his daughter's anger. He moved away a few steps and sat down on the bed. Ellen kept playing and took no notice. The anguished screams emanating from the computer were accompanied by a pounding rock melody.

'Where's Mamma?'

'She went to bed. She's got a headache.'

On the screen blood was spattering everywhere; he was amazed by how lifelike the animation was.

'How was school today?'

'We had a study day.'

'I see. So you had the day off?'

326

Ellen didn't answer. The battle onscreen continued.

Jan-Erik was again struck by how awkward the conversation was. It was so difficult to communicate with his daughter. What did you talk about with a twelve-year-old girl? Her world was as incomprehensible to him as an alien's.

'Do you want to know a secret?'

'Mmm.'

'But you can't tell anybody else.'

Enemy after enemy was mowed down and annihilated.

'I'm going to get a huge prize, for all the work I do with Grandfather's books and stuff. You know, those clinics and things I've started up.'

'Oh, right.'

He might as well have been telling her that he sometimes ate sandwiches. Ellen's total lack of interest seemed genuine. She wasn't even trying to pretend that she was impressed.

'It's called the Nordic Council Literary Prize, a very prestigious award. And 350,000 kronor. They've only given it to authors, before me.'

The music changed tempo. The woman in black was now inside what looked like some sort of church, but it didn't dampen her ardour. The massacre continued.

Jan-Erik got up.

'Have you eaten?'

'Yeah.'

He left the room without another word.

★   ★   ★

327

The bedroom door was closed. He went up to it and listened before he cautiously peered in. She was lying on her side with her back to him. He stood still and waited a moment, but nothing happened.

'Are you asleep?' he whispered.

There was no response.

As quietly as he could he pulled the door shut and went to the kitchen. The table had been cleared after dinner. He opened the fridge; there were no leftovers, but he made himself a caviar sandwich. Only now did the thought of food seem appealing again.

He would never again have a hangover. His promise was sincere. Today's had just passed, but the memory of the torment was still with him.

When he finished eating he sat down in his office. The pile of letters and junk mail had grown, and he spent half an hour taking care of the most urgent items. Fan mail addressed to Axel Ragnerfeldt he set aside; at the moment he didn't feel like being reminded of his father's accomplishments.

He suddenly remembered Marianne Folkesson. It was just a little past nine, not too late to call.

'Marianne here.'

'Hi, it's Jan-Erik Ragnerfeldt. Listen, I'm afraid I couldn't find any photo of Gerda.'

'You didn't?'

'No, I searched everywhere.'

'Okay, then I'll have to use the one I found in her flat, even if it is blurry. Thanks for trying.'

'There's nothing to thank me for, it was the least I could do. Sorry.'

'We did what we could. I'll see you at the funeral then.'

'Yes, okay.'

Jan-Erik said the words slowly. There was more he wanted to discuss but Marianne didn't pick up on his hesitation.

Just as she was about to hang up, Jan-Erik said, 'You know, now that I have you on the line, I'm a bit curious. I was thinking about that Kristoffer Sandeblom who came to my lecture yesterday. You haven't found out any more about why Gerda left her estate to him, have you? What sort of connection they have to each other, I mean.'

'I've no idea, but I did find a letter for him. I went to her flat today to pick up some things for the funeral.'

'A letter?'

'Yes, I put it in the mail today. He should have it tomorrow.'

'So you have no idea what it said?'

'No, no clue. I didn't open it.'

'Hmm.'

'We'll have to ask him at the funeral. I'm rather curious myself.'

Nothing she had said lessened Jan-Erik's unease. He couldn't convince himself that his suspicions were improbable. Annika's suicide had seemed improbable too, until it was confirmed.

A half-full water glass stood on the table. He poured the contents into one of the flowerpots in the window, got up and took the bottle out from behind the books on the shelf.

He had vowed never to have a hangover again, but that didn't mean he couldn't treat himself to a little nightcap.

CHAPTER 26

Alice was sitting on the sofa watching TV. It was a baffling programme about a rich American woman who wanted to get an operation to make herself look like a cat. Since they'd had cable TV installed in the house, she'd gained insight into so many odd things that she no longer knew what to believe about humanity. But in the absence of other companionship the TV was most often on, and occasionally something would come on that was worth looking at.

She had almost given up hope when the telephone rang. She'd been trying to reach Jan-Erik all day to ask him to give her a lift to the clinic tomorrow. This time she was sure. It wasn't her imagination; there was something strange going on in her body. Despite her worry she was looking forward to the examination, as if she were going on an exciting adventure.

'Jan-Erik?'

He got straight to the point.

'I have a couple of questions about some things I found in Pappa's cupboard.'

No greeting, no 'How are you?' Jan-Erik's voice

was curt, and she didn't like it when he sounded that way. Their previous conversation still hovered in the air, despite all her efforts to drive it away. His accusing stare burned in her mind, just as strongly as if he'd put it into words.

You're the one who bears the blame for what Annika did. It's your fault she didn't want to live. As her mother it was your responsibility to prevent what happened.

But what about Axel! she had wanted to scream, why didn't any blame fall on Axel? With his inconsiderate belief in his sole right to existence, he was the one who had created her powerlessness.

He had been given everything.

Simply everything.

An invincible battleship that, unconcerned, steamed forth in the hunt for honour, while everyone else around him went under.

But she had sat there in silence. And the old feeling of guilt, long absorbed, had been drawing in nourishment.

'What are you doing rummaging about in that cupboard? All you'll find is misery.'

'It's about letters from somebody called Halina. Is that someone you know?'

The name hit her like a punch in the stomach. So many years had passed during which it had never been mentioned, an unspoken agreement to eradicate it from their consciousness. But through the silence it had remained, festering like a malignant tumour. Thirty-one years later she still didn't know the truth about their relationship. Whether it was only that one single time or whether it went on for much longer.

Afterwards, when it all became irrelevant, she hadn't wanted to know. As though in a haze they had tried to recreate all the routines in order to contain the truth. A forced need to map out their daily lives in order to expel the consequences. But how did you take up the threads of a life you didn't even know you wanted?

'No, I've never heard that name.'

'The letters are from the seventies. So you've never heard of anyone named Halina?'

'No.'

He kept the letters! So typical of Axel! She would have to go to the house some day and see whether the idiot had saved anything else that should never be found.

'They were unopened, so he can't even have read them. I just thought you might know who she was.'

'No, I have no idea.'

Three times Halina had now been denied. With each time, she came all the more alive in Alice's mind.

Everything had seemed so surreal. One moment of her life had suddenly become decisive. A tiny parenthesis that was lifted out and became the headline.

Until Halina rang the doorbell the whole day had been so ordinary, if one ignored the unusual episode in the library with Axel. Normal time was being counted down, although no one had realised. Soon they would eat dinner, she would watch *Rich Man, Poor Man* on TV; everything had been completely normal.

An instant of madness.

She had been so afraid. So terribly afraid. Not when it happened, not when Axel ran out to the hall after Halina and she remained humiliated on the sofa. Not when she heard Halina's continued threats about what she intended to do to destroy their lives. Not when she grabbed the heavy silver candlestick and headed for the angry voices. Not even when she stood there with the candlestick in her hand, looking down at Halina's lifeless body had she been afraid.

All she had felt was amazement. She had looked at her hands holding the candlestick and was amazed that they were hers. They had obeyed instinct, an instinct as old as humankind – the readiness to kill in order to protect what is ours.

Somewhere inside her she had unknowingly carried the ability.

She had sacrificed so much for the little she had succeeded in achieving. A life in the shadow of the man so admired.

For that little bit she had shown herself capable of killing.

Not even then was she afraid.

Gerda's shrieks of despair. Soundlessly they hit her ears.

Axel, who sank down next to Halina.

'What have you done? What have you done? What have you done?'

Like a mantra he kept repeating the question, and not until she heard the sound of Axel's voice did it come slinking in: the horror of the irrevocable.

Terrified she had looked at his hands trying to shake life into Halina in an attempt to save their future. The blankness that descended when his efforts proved futile.

The realisation entered her consciousness, striking her like a club and forcing her to her knees. What he had done she could never forgive.

That man, whose children she had borne, had turned her into a murderer.

She gave a start when she heard Jan-Erik's voice on the phone.

'Okay, I was just wondering. I'll come and pick you up tomorrow morning at ten past eight.'

CHAPTER 27

When Louise opened her eyes it was already light. She had lain awake for a long time listening to the sounds in the flat, but kept herself hidden behind closed eyes. Not until the front door banged and the silence had settled was she ready to emerge. When there was no one left to encounter.

For a long time she just lay there breathing, finding no reason to get up.

Three days had passed since she'd dropped the mask. When her sorrow had spilled out and overpowered her. Right before the eyes of her fellow actor. The farce they had been playing for so long. All the well-planned lines. The dismay she provoked when she suddenly stepped out of her role.

All she wanted was to connect. She had sacrificed her last ounce of self-respect and pleaded for his attention.

His silence spoke loud and clear.

She was nothing.

Not even worth refuting.

★   ★   ★

She had lain awake all night after quickly turning off the bedside lamp when she heard him in the hall, and then pretending to be asleep when he looked in. She was incapable of facing him in her new subservient position. She simply wanted to get away.

Away from what might have been.

Everything had been amplified yesterday. For the first time in more than fifteen years he had stepped out of her fantasies and was suddenly within sight: her ex, the man who had left her, but not her imagination. During the years with Jan-Erik he had become wrapped in an ever more dazzling glow.

A window table in a restaurant. Two children and a beautiful wife. They were laughing and listening to each other so attentively, sitting together. Like a real family.

While she had stood across the street, hidden in the entrance to a building. Unseen, she had watched, and painfully realised that he'd found what she had always been looking for. What she had wanted to give him back then, if only he'd let her stay.

If only he had wanted her.

Maybe there was something about her. Something she wasn't aware of. Did she smell bad? She took a shower every day. Wasn't what she said interesting enough? She tried to keep up with what was happening in the world. Was her body repulsive? She was in better shape than many women her age.

She didn't know what it was, but there was definitely something. Something that made her impossible to love.

She curled up on her side and pulled up the covers. She tried to convince herself that there was some reason to get out of bed. The only thing she had to look forward to was the glass of wine she usually enjoyed while sitting in front of the TV after dinner. Before that there was a whole day to get through.

She found a note on the kitchen table. He was taking Alice to the clinic. She wondered what it was that had to be examined this time, which part of her body was attracting her mother-in-law's attention now. She was thankful she wasn't the one who had to drive her.

She was standing staring at the coffee-machine when the phone rang. She wondered whether it was worth the trouble to answer it. The cordless handset was lying on the kitchen table. She picked it up but didn't recognise the number. A number in Göteborg. She put down the phone, but it wouldn't stop ringing. Finally she gave up.

'Louise Ragnerfeldt, hello?'

A click on the other end. This was the third time it had happened. Unless there was something wrong with the phone, somebody had been ringing and hanging up whenever she answered. She had heard that telesales people used that trick; calling several potential customers at the same time and taking the one who answered first. Annoyed, she went back to the coffee-machine. On principle she never bought anything from anyone who bothered her in her own home.

She wasn't particularly hungry, but she filled a bowl with cornflakes and milk. She wasn't tempted by coffee or the morning paper, so she sat at the table reading the milk carton:

Words to live by.
Courage: the ability to act without fear of consequences, usually for a good cause and fully aware of the risks.

She put down her spoon and looked up out of the window. If she were a courageous person everything would be different. She would be capable of hauling herself out of the place that had turned her into a shadow of what she wanted to be. All her expectations. All her dreams. All she had obediently packed away and put in a place she could no longer find.

But she was not a courageous person.

She had told her therapist she wouldn't be coming back. She could no longer stand listening to herself talking about what she should do, only to leave the office too cowardly to follow her own good advice.

Again the phone rang. Without looking at the display she picked it up.

'Yes, hello?'

The line was silent but she could sense that someone was there.

'Who's this?'

'I'm looking for Jan-Erik.' A woman's voice.

'He's not home at the moment. Who shall I tell him called?'

Silence again, but not very long.

'Just say hello from Lena in Göteborg. Ask him to ring me.'

Louise was still holding the receiver to her ear when she heard the woman hang up. Lena in Göteborg. Looking for Jan-Erik. Surnames superfluous. Phone numbers already exchanged.

Wasn't Göteborg where he was a few days ago? That time when he missed Ellen's play? She grabbed the phone and pressed the buttons to check the calls from the past few days. Seven times the same number in Göteborg showed up. Seven times Lena had called. Including half an hour ago, when she'd hung up.

She leaned back and wondered about her reaction. She didn't feel anger, or despair. All she felt was a sense of relief that she had finally found an explanation.

It wasn't contempt.

He simply loved someone else.

Louise got up, and armed with her new knowledge went to the bathroom. She had a shower, put on her make-up, got dressed. Something had happened to her mood. Suddenly the air felt easier to breathe and her steps were not as heavy. It was as if the knowledge of Jan-Erik's lover had restored her dignity. She had risen from her position as underdog, strengthened by the fact that she now had a real accusation to use as a weapon. She surprised herself. She felt no disappointment or bitterness. It was no more important than that. Something unusual had happened that had roused her from her drab grey stagnation, and it was worth being rejected in favour of Lena in Göteborg.

She put on her coat and went outside. She decided to keep the boutique closed for another day, she couldn't stand being there any more. The solitary hours spent behind the counter, waiting for a banal conversation with one of the few customers who ever found their way to her shop.

She breathed in the clear air, letting it fill her lungs, and tried to persuade herself that it was there all around her, the courage that she still lacked.

She headed towards the canal. When she reached the pathway she heard her mobile. She let it ring and kept walking, but then her voicemail beeped. It might be Ellen. She pulled out the phone and, seeing that the call was from home, played the message. It was Jan-Erik.

'Hi, it's me. I'm back home. I went to the shop but you weren't there. Where are you? It didn't go so well at the clinic. They actually found something this time, and it's apparently quite serious. She's back home now but will be having an operation the day after tomorrow. Call me when you get this. Bye.'

She deleted the message. Alice ill? Seriously ill? The news shook her. All those years Alice had pestered them with her imaginary pains, but finally she was right. With a pang of guilt Louise stuffed the mobile in her pocket, turned round and headed towards Alice's flat.

She had intended to use her own key but changed her mind as her hand reached the lock. If Alice was in bed she didn't want to surprise her. Their relationship had never allowed such intimacies. Instead she rang the doorbell.

Alice came to the door quickly and opened it.

'Oh, Louise, how nice. Come in.'

Louise didn't know what she'd expected, but it wasn't the image of the woman who stood before her. Brisk and sober and wearing a flowered apron, Alice stepped to one side to let her in.

'Aren't you at the shop today?'

Louise hung up her coat.

'I'm taking the day off. Jan-Erik rang and told me about the doctor's exam.'

'Yes, apparently things didn't look so good. Come in. But you shouldn't have closed the shop for that.'

Louise stopped short. The Alice she saw before her was different. Louise had gone there ready to hear her usual complaint that no one ever believed in her illnesses. She'd imagined Alice triumphantly ensconced in bed, intent on feeling sorry for herself and apportioning blame.

Alice vanished into the kitchen after motioning Louise towards the living room.

'Would you like some coffee?'

'No thanks.'

Louise let her gaze sweep over the mess. Almost everything in the room had been moved from its place, and every flat surface was covered with books, papers, magazines and knick-knacks.

Alice appeared in the doorway from the kitchen with a cardboard box in her hands.

'I've started cleaning up a bit. You should have a look around and see if there's anything you'd like. I thought I'd have someone come over and take away the rest.'

Alice picked up a little glass horse. 'I know Ellen was fascin ated by this when she was little. She might like to have it as a little keepsake.'

Louise watched her, amazed at her energy and the sparkle in her eye.

Alice caught sight of one of the paintings on the wall.

'I think Jan-Erik would want this one. I remember he said he liked it. It was in the living room out in Nacka, and if nothing else I think it might be worth a few kronor.'

'But, Alice, don't you think you're jumping the gun a little?'

Alice put down the box and looked around as if she hadn't heard a thing.

'What did the doctor say?'

'Well, God knows, they use so many big words

that nobody can understand what they really mean. But she looked worried and wanted to go in and investigate the day after tomorrow. And what about this!'

Alice went over to the bookshelf and took down a book.

'Well, here it is! It was one of the first books I ever read. Imagine, I haven't seen it for years. I thought I'd lost it. You have to give this to Ellen.'

Louise was surprised that Jan-Erik had left Alice by herself. Not even he could have helped noticing her agitation.

'So you're going to have the operation the day after tomorrow?'

'Yes.'

Alice went over to the sideboard and pulled out the top drawer.

'Imagine how many things one collects over a lifetime, and only a fraction have been of any use.'

She continued chattering in her cheerful tone. Louise sat down on the sofa, unsure what to do. How should one behave with people in shock?

Alice began taking out silverware and piling it on top of the sideboard.

'If you polish them up, they look really nice. I inherited them from Mother and Father.'

Louise looked at the back of Alice's head. During a conversation long ago she had once mentioned losing contact with her parents early on; she never said why. She never mentioned them again other than on that one occasion, and then it was Ellen who had asked about them.

Louise's own mood suddenly gave her the courage to ask.

'Didn't you ever miss your parents?'

'No, parents are very overrated.'

A statement as if quoted from a psychology book. Even with her back turned it was clear that Alice had no intention of delving any more deeply into the topic. She inspected a tablespoon with extra care.

It occurred to Louise how little she knew about Alice's life, how little she knew her at all. She had lost a child in a car accident, a fifteen-year-old daughter. Not until now did Louise fully realise what that actually meant. As if Ellen right now would have only three years to live. The thought was impossible to grasp.

Alice's hand kept inspecting the silverware in the drawer. Once that hand had written books; Alice had been a writer just like Axel. She had written some novels back in the fifties that Louise had never bothered to read. And neither had Jan-Erik, as far as she knew. She wondered why she had stopped writing.

Alice pushed the drawer back in and headed towards the kitchen with the silverware.

Louise sat in silence, thinking about the contempt she'd so often felt for her mother-in-law. Intertwined with a reluctant wish to win her respect. Maybe it was only fear she'd felt. She had wanted to secure her own position to avoid Alice's verbal attacks, well aware of the way she talked about other people. Like an autocratic judge she evaluated everyone around her. If she found a personality trait she herself lacked, she was quick to make it the object of ridicule.

Louise heard water running. The clattering of the silver in the sink. Louise went out to join her. She stood at the door and watched Alice's attempt to be supremely practical.

'Alice, wouldn't it be a better idea to wait a while and see what the doctors have to say first?'

Alice squeezed out some silver polish onto a white cotton cloth and picked up a fork.

Louise tried again.

'We don't actually know yet, maybe it's not so serious.'

Alice's hand rubbed faster, and the cloth turned black.

'I still think you ought to wait a bit and see what the doctors say, don't you?'

With violent force Alice suddenly cast the fork aside and turned round. Completely unprepared, Louise shrank from the ferocity of her gaze.

'For God's sake, woman! Can't you at least let me enjoy my own obliteration?'

For a few seconds Alice was exposed, and Louise lost her breath at what she saw. A despair so deep it distorted her features. Then the moment passed, and Alice returned with furious movements to her silverware. Louise backed out to the living room and sank down on the sofa.

It was Alice who was standing there in the kitchen, and yet it was herself she had seen.

In a sudden moment of clarity she understood that in forty years it would be her turn to see the meaninglessness of life finally confirmed. Just like Alice, over the years she would spread her bitterness over anyone who came near her, over Ellen and her future family. Passing on to her daughter the futile task of attempting to make up for a wasted life. Illuminated from a different angle, all perspectives had changed, her obligations to her daughter other than she had envisaged. For whose sake had she sacrificed herself? Who was expected to show gratitude? Ellen, who would be sent out into life with a distorted view of what love is? Jan-Erik, whose behaviour she condoned by not telling him to stop? What sort of role model was she for her daughter? Louise realised that her fear of making a move was merely selfish cowardice, for what joy would Ellen gain from a mother who was already dead? A mother who, when it was much too late, would expect gratitude for everything she had given up to keep the family together.

All she desired was to be allowed to surrender. To set free a life that had been imprisoned for so long. She could feel it inside, how it was begging for oxygen, pulling and tearing to be allowed to show its potential.

The instant she made her decision, everything became calm.

The little glass horse was standing on the

window-sill. She reached out and picked it up, placing it gently in her hand. Then she returned to the kitchen. Alice was still standing where she had left her, picking through her parents' silverware. Louise hesitated, wanting to thank her, but as usual couldn't quite find the words. She put her hand tentatively on her shoulder.

'I'm going now, Alice. Good luck with everything you have to do. I'm taking this little horse and giving it to Ellen. I know she'd love to have it.'

CHAPTER 28

Torgny was sitting at his kitchen table holding Gerda's obituary. No poem. No grieving relatives. Just as anonymous as his own would be one day, if someone even took the trouble to put one in the paper.

His black suit was hanging in the hall. Nowadays he only wore it to funerals. Newly brushed but as outdated as himself. A disguise he allowed himself now and then.

He would often look in the newspaper to see who had died, and if a name sounded familiar he would go to the funeral. A chance to get out and kill some time, steal a little sympathy. His tie had once been tied by Halina's fingers. He had never undone it. He simply widened the loop a bit and pulled it over his head, wearing his noose as a symbolic marker.

He struck a match and lit a cigarette, opening the window a crack as he'd promised the landlady when the neighbours complained about the smell of smoke from his flat. For fifty-four years this had been his home, ever since he moved to Stockholm. With youthful enthusiasm he had moved into the city proper, ready for the world to open up to him. A world that had been divided into black and white, where no nuances of grey had yet made themselves felt. The black was everything he had left behind; his childhood and the inherited job as a metalworker. Even as a child he had felt different. Early on he'd learned to hide his pain whenever a schoolmate, one of his brothers, or his father gave vent to their fury because he refused to apologise for his individuality. Short, thin and not very strong, he was easy prey for anyone who felt so inclined. Until he discovered the power of language. With his newfound weapon he fended off every antagonist, and over the years he honed his argumentative technique to perfection. Not that he escaped being bullied; on the contrary, people who are inarticulate are quick to raise their fists, but the beatings were always easier to bear when he knew that he'd already won.

The white part was what awaited him in the future. Stockholm, its cultural offerings, and the writer's life that had begun. He would certainly show everybody back home just who they had been laughing at.

He would soon turn seventy-eight. Twilight had come early, his life had long been moving towards evening. The days were growing more desolate; everyone he'd known was gone or had been lost somewhere along the way. Few people were left who could share his memories.

He looked at the obituary he'd torn out of the paper.

Kristoffer's confession had forced Torgny to concede that an aeon of time had passed, to accept all the wasted days and the fact that his waiting had long ago become meaningless. The little boy was transformed into a grown man, but in Torgny's world he was still a sorely missed four-year-old. What Kristoffer had told him was a final confirmation that Halina was no longer alive.

Torgny hadn't had time to ask for Kristoffer's phone number or his last name. The boy he'd once viewed as his own had surfaced only to disappear once more. Above all else he wanted to be able to see him again.

How strange that he'd turned up just now, when the advent of Gerda's funeral had also speeded up his memories. It was asking too much of him to attend. He couldn't handle it now that the images of what he had done had surfaced, bursting through the thin membrane in which he'd wrapped his shame.

He no longer even understood why he'd wanted to go to the funeral in the first place. Maybe it was so he could take one last look at the man who had destroyed his life. One last look, to reinforce the hatred that had been his only lifelong companion.

He threw the cigarette butt out of the window and closed it. He no longer wanted to remember anything now, and he buried the obituary under a pile of newspapers. It didn't help. Gerda and all that was connected to her memory lingered on. They had barely known each other; they'd merely exchanged an occasional word when he was at the house. On the way in or out he might stop for a moment as she worked in the kitchen or knelt by a flower-bed.

The last time he'd seen her was immediately afterwards. On the verge of vomiting he'd rushed out of the house and, leaning on his knees, tried to throw up all his own wickedness.

He shook another cigarette out of the packet but left the window closed. He got up to fetch a beer but slumped back on the chair when he remembered that he'd drunk them all.

If only he'd understood then that he was genuinely happy. Back then, when Halina and Kristoffer had been in his life and he still had the ability to write. When he didn't have to crouch behind the words after once and for all losing the right to make himself heard. Not until all was lost had he realised what he'd had. His suffering increased by the contrast.

The invisible breaking point.

Not until much later had it become as clear as a beacon.

The moment when Halina had asked him to take her to Västerås.

He should have been suspicious, since she never wanted to come along. Childcare was so expensive, she always said. Wasn't it when he mentioned that Axel Ragnerfeldt was going to be there that she suddenly changed her mind?

As so many times before, the answer had forgotten its question, when everything in the light of what followed had become apparent.

In the period that followed, everything was Axel this and Axel that. Her constant comments about his brilliance. His books that she kept reading, over and over again. They were spread out all over the flat, a visible confirmation of Axel's superiority. Torgny tried to swallow the hurt but she noticed straightaway and used it against him during their arguments. When it seemed that nothing could get any worse, the intimations came sneaking in – that they'd spent the night together in Västerås behind his back. The sly passing of little notes and letters that proved the contact had continued. The excruciating jealousy he'd felt.

Axel Ragnerfeldt, always his superior, demonstrably possessed a greater gift than he had. Who had achieved all the respect that Torgny had always coveted.

In the end also superior as a man and lover.

He thought about the day when Halina packed her bags and took Kristoffer with her. He did nothing to stop them. He had believed her when she said that Axel was waiting for them. He hadn't begun searching until it was too late. When it became obvious that Axel was still living with his family, and Halina and Kristoffer seemed to have been swallowed up by the earth.

He got up and looked at the painting. Her gaze that always followed him. Whenever he looked she was there, her elusive eyes taking in his every meaningless step. Eternally young, constantly present, always within reach. Like a chronic disease she had lodged in his chest and refused to let go. Was it her he still loved, or merely the idea of their love? Had time beautified the colours, toned down her moodiness and unforgivable betrayal? Was she only a stubborn melody playing over and over, bewitching him?

His prison consisted of all that remained unfinished, his longing for an explanation; everything was laid open with no means of closing it up again.

At first he had felt utterly paralysed. When he was forced to give up his search and no longer knew what he should do, the walls of the flat, emphasising her absence, kept creeping closer and drove him outdoors. In the crush of people there was no one like her; each meeting became an insufferable reminder. Then, in his despair, he had begun to write. He shut himself in the flat and tried to recreate her, deep in his heart, hoping that she would return the day she read what he'd written. When she got a chance to see how brilliant he was.

The Wind Whispers Your Name became the best thing he had ever written.

But not even that lured her home.

Once again he was beaten. The glowing reviews had been pushed off the cultural pages. All the news was about Axel Ragnerfeldt and his Nobel Prize; his literary triumph, *Shadow*, which had finally convinced the Swedish Academy. Praised to the skies, the book had been named the novel of the century. At first Torgny didn't want to read it, but curiosity won out. He needed to see with his own eyes what it was that made this man so superior. And made Torgny a nobody.

He remembered his reluctance when he bought it at the bookshop.

And his shock when after only the first page he'd understood.

A year after the terrible day when he'd stood in the Ragnerfeldts' living room and been forced to apologise, he realised the enormity of the lie.

Torgny didn't even bother to ring the doorbell. He just opened the door and walked right in, feeling fully entitled to do so. No more tiptoeing round a man who was worth more contempt than he could possibly muster. Gerda saw him from the kitchen as he passed by, but she was so surprised she didn't say a word. She just came dashing after him as he strode towards Axel's office. Torgny had already opened the door by the time she caught up. Axel jumped out of his chair but managed to control himself. Yet Torgny had time to see the glint of fear in his eyes.

'It's all right, Gerda, I'll handle this.'

He didn't even look at Torgny as he walked past and closed the door in Gerda's worried face. Without a word he went back to his desk, sat down in the chair and folded his hands in front of him on the desktop. For a moment they were both silent, then Axel gave an awkward smile as if to test the waters.

'Torgny, it's been a long time.'

Wary but not unfriendly.

Torgny was still standing by the door. The sight of Axel's discomfort made him want to drag things out for a while. His feigned politeness, a red flush at his throat. Torgny felt a strange sense of calm. With truth on his side, for the first time he had the upper hand. The power he felt was intoxicating. He sipped at the situation as if it were expensive champagne.

'I must congratulate you on being elected to the Swedish Academy.'

'Thank you.'

Torgny held his gaze slightly too long but then released him and looked around the room. He went over to one wall, peering with interest at the certificates and photographs, well aware of the uneasiness his silence was creating.

'Was there something particular you wanted?'

Torgny continued studying the wall with his back turned. He ran his finger along the top of a frame and shook off the dust.

'I think Gerda's missed a bit.'

He turned round and walked slowly across the

room to the bookshelf. With his head cocked to one side he read the spines of the books, and after a while he found *The Wind Whispers Your Name*.

'Well, look here. Have you had time to read such trivial literature? And there I was, thinking you were busy writing your own books.'

'Can I offer you something? Coffee? Whisky?'

'No thanks.'

Silence again, and he ran his finger along the row of Axel's books.

'I assume you've come on some business. I didn't know you were going to drop in, and I do have other plans.'

Torgny stopped.

'So you think I'm here on some business?'

'Yes.'

He looked at Axel. 'And what sort of business do you think that might be?'

Axel didn't answer.

Torgny went back to *The Wind Whispers Your Name* and plucked it from the shelf. For a moment he stood weighing it in his hand.

'Do you know who this book is about?'

'I'm sorry to admit that I actually haven't had a chance to read it yet.'

'No, I can understand that, you've been busy. I'll tell you, so you don't have to waste your precious time. It's about Halina. Perhaps you remember her? The woman we had such a pleasant conversation about out in your woodshed a year ago. Does that ring a bell?'

357

'Yes, I remember.'

Torgny put on a thoughtful expression.

'Now, let's see. I believe I can recall that conversation pretty much word for word. One usually does when an experience is so unpleasant. I remember one detail in particular, since it made me feel so relieved at the time. It was when you said that nothing had happened between you and Halina. Isn't that what you said?'

'And nothing did, either.'

'You said that you hadn't had anything to do with each other.'

'What are you getting at?'

The flush on Axel's throat had spread to his face.

Torgny shook his head.

'You know, Axel, there have been times when I've been jealous of you, when I've been forced to admit that you actually had something special, not only because of your books but because of what I thought you stood for.'

He looked at Axel's clasped hands. The knuckles had turned white. With clenched teeth he let Torgny's words pass without countering them.

Torgny could no longer maintain his poise.

'How the hell can you sit there and keep pretending when you know you've been exposed, that I know what a fucking charlatan you really are?'

Axel's arms began to shake and he thrust his hands into his lap. Torgny put his book back on the shelf and took down a copy of *Shadow*. Axel saw what he was doing but quickly looked away, as if he couldn't bear to see what was happening. Torgny watched him, careful not to miss a drop of his evaporating dignity.

'How does it feel to win the Nobel Prize after having been praised to the heavens for this book?'

Axel didn't move. Then he took in a deep breath, the kind you take before a dive. For several seconds he held it, then let it go; his body fell forward and he leaned his forehead against his typewriter. Torgny stood quite still and watched the facade crumble.

'Where is she?'

Minutes passed. Long minutes. Axel looked as if it was taking all his concentration to stay in his chair. Then he began to gasp for words, but stopped as soon as anything was about to cross his lips.

'You have to help me, Torgny.'

'Tell me where she is.'

With difficulty Axel managed to straighten up, and the face Torgny saw was that of a stranger.

'I don't know, I swear. She said something about going back to Poland. Torgny, please, you have to understand, I was completely desperate.'

He was begging, with despair in his eyes. Torgny was shocked at what he saw. Axel Ragnerfeldt, obsequiously asking for his sympathy. He couldn't say a word. What he saw made him sick. He looked at the book in his hands, let the pages riffle through his fingers. All those letters, all those words, that taken together described the worst hell a human being can endure. The conditions in a concentration camp described in a way that no one but the person who had endured them could describe. Written down in anguish in order to silence the demons. Axel Ragnerfeldt had plundered and robbed everything from her. He had stolen her thoughts, raped her soul.

'She sent the manuscript to me and said I could do whatever I liked with it.'

Torgny erupted.

'She was ill, damn it! You knew that! Do you know how long she struggled over this novel?'

'She didn't want to have anything to do with it, she said. She was going back to Poland to start a new life. She wanted to forget everything that had happened, she said, and . . .'

Axel's shoulders drooped and he looked down at his lap. With the fingers of his right hand he began twisting his wedding ring.

'I hadn't been able to write anything for several years, not a thing, and I was completely desperate. My publisher was hassling me, the bank was putting on the pressure, I had no money to pay the mortgage, I scarcely had enough left to put food on the table. I couldn't wring a single line out of myself, I simply couldn't write at all any more, it was all gone. I had just decided to tell Alice that we would have to sell the house. I was going round here preparing myself, and just then my parents rang and told me that my sister had died, that she'd had a heart attack. I hadn't seen her in almost thirty years. I could hear what a hard time they were having trying to ask me, but at last they managed to get it out. They wondered whether I could take care of the funeral expenses, and I . . . I couldn't tell them the truth, admit that I was broke. Admit that I had failed.'

He hid his face in his hands and for a moment Torgny thought he was crying.

'I began searching through the cupboard to see whether I could find some old pieces I'd written, and that's when I found it. It was just lying there and I . . . She'd told me I could do whatever I wanted with it. I know it was wrong, but just then I couldn't see any other way out.'

'Nobel fucking Prize winner Axel Ragnerfeldt! Jesus Christ! How the hell can you live with yourself?'

Torgny spat out the words, the contempt searing his tongue.

Axel sat huddled on the chair staring into space. The man Torgny saw was someone he had never met before.

'You must have known that you'd be exposed, that I would read it eventually.'

'She said you hadn't read it. That nobody had read it.'

Torgny was speechless. For years he had sat at her side and encouraged her, persuading her to

361

fight on when she wanted to give up. He had commented on every sentence; with eyes wide he had been amazed at her talent and tried to convince her of the greatness of what she'd written.

Hadn't read it!

'I took a chance. Just then I thought that nothing could get any worse. If I'd known that there would be such a fuss about it . . . Never in my wildest dreams did I imagine it would be like this. I just wanted to buy a little time so I could finish writing what I was working on.'

He looked at Torgny but turned away when he didn't find the sympathy he sought.

'Don't you think that I've regretted it? How do you think it feels to me? You know me that well at least. The whole thing has been like one long nightmare.'

Axel got up and walked over to the window.

'I wish I could undo it, Torgny. More than anything I wish that I could, but I can't.'

There was silence in the room. A sound from the hall outside made Axel turn round. He went to the door and opened it, but no one was there. When he assured himself that nobody was listening he went back and sat down.

'I know that I don't have the right to ask you to keep quiet about this, Torgny, but I'd do anything.'

Torgny snorted.

'I'll give you half the prize money.'

The proposal amazed Torgny. A little boy who was caught cheating on a test. With a little more skulduggery he thought he would be released. Torgny's temples were throbbing. The blood wanted to burst out of his veins. The man he had reluctantly admired, whom he had always looked up to, despite his antipathy, was now grovelling before him like the little worm he was. His moral integrity, his strength of character. The whole time the opposite had been kept hidden underneath, eclipsed by his exceptional achievements.

'She told me I could use it.'

Quietly, a final attempt to persuade him.

Torgny looked at Axel. The person he saw was the man who had won Halina's love, who with his dazzling reputation had driven a wedge between Torgny and Halina.

'When did she say that?'

Axel gave him a furtive glance.

'It was in the letter she sent with the manuscript.'

'Come on, Axel. You said you never saw her.'

'She sent it in the mail.'

'So where's the letter now? Can I see it?'

'I threw it away.'

'Right. Why the hell would you think that I'd ever believe a word you say? What happened in Västerås, anyway? Suddenly Halina's version sounds a lot more believable than yours.'

Axel didn't answer.

Torgny closed his eyes.

Axel and Halina. Fucking in secret behind his back. His hands lying there on the desk, hands that had greedily explored her body. And Halina had willingly let it happen.

Axel had cheated him out of everything that had been his. Everything that had belonged to him and Halina, that had taken them years to nurture and polish, that they had learnt from each other's pleasure. The man who now sat there behind the desk, lying, had stripped them of their most intimate secrets.

He saw Halina's face, her lips parted, the tip of her tongue, her mouth closing around Axel's swollen cock; the glint in her eyes, the way she moved her hips, the sound she made when he thrust inside her.

If that had happened he would have to kill him.

'Take off your trousers.'

Axel stared at him.

'What?'

'Take off your trousers, I said!'

'Are you crazy?'

'You have a birthmark there somewhere, don't you?'

Axel closed his eyes.

'Halina described it to me to make me believe her. She even drew it on a piece of paper to convince me.'

During those last days. When all that remained was to hurt him.

'Do you remember what I said there in the woodshed? That I would kill you if I found out you had lied?'

Nothing more needed to be said. He could read the truth in Axel's face.

'You fucking pig!'

'It was only that one time in Västerås. I beg you to forgive me, Torgny. She said that you weren't a couple, that you were just friends. If I'd known she was lying I would never have touched her.'

Axel stood up.

'It didn't mean a thing, Torgny. We drank too much, it just happened.'

It was after Västerås that everything had started going wrong. After Västerås that Halina's illness returned. It had been the beginning of the end.

It didn't mean a thing, Torgny.

He was breathing hard.

Afterwards, during all the years he was forced to relive over and over again what followed, he often thought that it was at this moment he had gone off the rails. When the truth about the betrayal punched a hole in his innermost being and evil was released.

'It was only once, that was the only time, I swear.'

Just one wish.

'What are you going to do now, Axel, with the truth about *Shadow* splashed across the arts pages all over the world? What hole are you going to crawl into then?'

He could hear his own voice, muffled and toneless, as if it were someone else's. Something had taken possession of him. Something that had knotted his fists and fixed his gaze on the man who had ruined his life. The man who had taken Halina and the boy away from him.

Axel must have noticed the change. With a calmer expression he sat down and assumed the same pose as before the revelation. Hands clasped on the desktop, he stared at Torgny, with a new feeling of determination. His excuses had been in vain, and it was clear that he was now thinking of trying a new tactic.

'I'm sorry to have to say this, but you give me no choice.'

He paused for a second before he went on.

'You can't prove a thing.'

'What do I have to prove?'

'What you claim about *Shadow*.'

Torgny snorted.

'So it's not enough for you that *I* know? You can live with this as long as nobody else knows?'

'What choice do you think I have?'

'You fucking hypocrite.'

'I've admitted that I made a mistake. What more do you want?'

'I take it you're going to persist in taking all the praise for her masterpiece?'

'I was on the shortlist for the Nobel Prize long before *Shadow*. You know as well as I do that it wasn't the only book that won me the prize, the award was based just as much on my other books.'

'Your *own* books, you mean?'

'As I said, you can't prove a thing.'

Torgny didn't move a muscle. He was thinking of Halina's sense of inferiority after the degradation in Treblinka, which made her incapable of allowing herself to be loved. For the rest of his life he would be forced to watch Axel in the spotlight, cloaked in honour and fame, and know that the one who should have stood there was Halina. He would have to witness the obsequious flattery of the cultural establishment and watch Axel bow and scrape over the suffering that she had managed to transform into magnificent art.

The lie came as a matter of course, and he hadn't even planned it. The same toneless voice came out of his mouth.

'I have her notes at home. All the letters she received during her research. The rough draft, the whole outline. In her handwriting.'

That did the trick. But Torgny knew that Axel was right. There was no way to get to him. Nobody would believe Torgny without proof. Even if they did manage to find Halina. If what Axel said was true, perhaps she would even deny the truth and choose Axel once again. Like water off the back of a well-fattened goose the scandal would slide off him, and Torgny would be left to bear the shame of his tawdry accusation.

Torgny felt it glowing white-hot inside him. The desire to destroy Axel. To make him suffer the same pain he had caused. Nothing else was important. He was prepared to do anything to achieve it. If he couldn't get at Axel's body of work, then he'd have to destroy his life. The blackness was so powerful it scared him. He fumbled for something that might stop him, but everything had vanished in the darkness. And from a distant place he heard the voice which would set the diabolical plan in motion.

Where did it come from? He didn't know.

'If it's my silence you want to buy, there is one way. It depends on what you're willing to sacrifice.'

Axel sat quietly, waiting for him to continue.

'There's a saying: an eye for an eye, a tooth for a tooth.'

'I don't understand what you mean.'

'You took my woman away from me.'

'Torgny, it was *one time*, and I didn't even know she was yours. Is that what this is all about? A single transgression?'

Tonelessly the voice droned on.

'Once doesn't matter, twice is a habit. Isn't that what they say?'

Uncomprehending, Axel threw out his arms, and Torgny went on.

'One time is enough for me too.'

'I don't understand. What is it you want?'

'To be paid in kind.'

Axel's frown testified to his confusion, until it was slowly erased.

'Is it Alice you're talking about?' Axel snorted. 'I don't think she's particularly interested, but be my guest and give it a try.'

'I'm not talking about Alice.'

Axel's smile disappeared.

Torgny's body felt heavy, positioned between reason and will. He stood perfectly still and allowed the darkness to engulf him. The instant before taking the step towards his own ruin.

'I'm talking about your daughter.'

Axel leapt up from his chair.

'Have you lost your mind?'

To have the power to destroy. To have the power to ruin Axel's life by whatever means he could.

'It's up to you. How much is your reputation worth?'

'Annika has absolutely nothing to do with this, absolutely nothing. How can you even suggest something so . . .' He was momentarily speechless. 'What do you think of me anyway? Do you understand what you're saying? It was Halina who seduced me, if that makes it any better. Why should my daughter be punished for something I did? She's only fifteen years old! Fifteen! I believed a lot about you, Torgny, but this! How low are you prepared to sink?'

Torgny smiled.

'That's exactly what you have to ask yourself, Axel. How low are *you* prepared to sink? You've already gone pretty deep.'

Axel's eyes narrowed to slits.

'I can assure you that I wish I'd never used that manuscript, but I can't undo what is done, no matter how much I may want to. Isn't it revenge enough for you to know what an advantage you have over me, to live knowing that you might some day expose me? You know very well what would happen if . . . I can't imagine that even you, Torgny, would wish such misfortune on me.'

If what was raging inside Torgny were visible on his face, it would have made Axel take back those final words.

'Halina said that I could do whatever I liked with the manuscript, so by what right do you come here with this vile ultimatum? Besides, I rewrote a lot of it. You would have done exactly the same thing in my situation.'

'Would I?'

'It's easy for you to stand there now, all righteous and sincere, but I know you, Torgny. You would have done exactly the same thing.'

'But I didn't. That's the difference.'

Axel sank into his chair again, opening his palms as if that might make Torgny listen to reason.

'Torgny, let's discuss this like two reasonable men. I deserve your contempt, I accept that. I've also offered you half the prize money. Go home and think about it. You're much too worked up now to think rationally. I intend to forget what you proposed just now and forgive you. Go home and think about whether the money is enough to make you want to keep quiet.'

'I don't want Halina's money.'

'What *do* you want?'

'I've already told you.'

'For Christ's sake, man!'

Axel pounded his hand on the desk. Torgny smiled. Swearing didn't sit well with Axel's urbane manner.

'You decide. It's up to you. This time as well.'

Axel shook his head in disgust.

'You can't mean what you're saying!'

'Choose now, Mr Nobel Prize winner. My offer expires in one minute.' Torgny raised his arm and looked at his watch.

'You don't know what you're doing. You're not thinking clearly.'

'Forty-five seconds.'

Axel got up. 'You can't be serious.'

'Thirty seconds.'

Axel closed his eyes.

Torgny felt empty inside. The enjoyable malicious pleasure had dissolved in the dense darkness.

'You're going to regret this, Torgny, when you come to your senses.'

'Ten seconds.'

Axel sank back in his chair.

The second hand completed its fateful circle and Torgny lowered his arm.

'Well now, Axel, it pleases me that you managed to scrape together a tiny ounce of honour from some forgotten corner.'

Axel leant forward with his head in his hands.

Torgny moved towards the door. He had just put his hand on the doorknob when he was stopped by Axel's voice.

'Wait.'

Something in the dark sneered. Torgny turned round. Axel had got up from his chair, and what was burning in his eyes was a worthy rival to what was ravaging Torgny.

'You leave me no choice. I hope you realise that.'

'One always has a choice, Axel. After that it's a whole other matter as to what takes priority.'

Axel looked away. He was breathing heavily.

'How do you intend to proceed?' His whispered tones were scarcely audible.

'Let me worry about that. Just see to it that she's alone here tonight.' He looked at his watch. 'Take your wife to the cinema or something, and make sure that Gerda stays away. I'll wait here in your office until you all leave. And don't forget to bring me that whisky you offered me.'

'You bastard.'

Torgny smiled.

'How does it feel, Axel? Be sure to remember how it feels.'

Axel stood leaning forward with his hands flat on the desk, a shadow of his former self. Torgny's revenge was complete. All that remained was to carry it out.

With a voice that had lost all its resonance, Axel ended the conversation, slowly emphasising each and every syllable.

'If so much as a rumour ever comes out that anyone but myself was involved with *Shadow*, I will hold you personally responsible and make public what you did here today. If I go down, you will go down with me. I also want your promise that you will for ever stay out of my sight. And my last hope is that you will end up in hell, where you have always belonged.'

Torgny sank down onto on his unmade bed. For thirty years he had endured in the darkness which after that day had never left him.

How could he have done it? He didn't know. Only that the darkness had blinded him. For thirty years he had searched, but he had never succeeded in finding any excuse. For a while he had pretended. Kept the outer surface polished and denied any blame.

But even a bell's invisible crack is revealed by a dull peal.

Had the evil always been inside him, as a natural component of his being? Or was it an intruder that had taken over when everything was stolen from him? When all that remained to him was the ability to shatter in order to retaliate.

Too late he realised that he had directed his revenge at himself. That what he had shown himself to be capable of had chained him to a shame too heavy to bear.

Axel's last hope had been granted.

The rest of Torgny's life had become an effort

to live as the brute he had proven himself to be. All intentions produce results in the end, if only one makes a real effort. And that he had done.

And he had succeeded beyond all expectations.

CHAPTER 29

*I*t is early morning. Already before I wake I know that I am happy.

'George,' she whispers, and her lips graze my ear. 'The spring has come, I can smell it through the window. Come!'

Sonja takes my hand and wants to pull me along to everything that is waiting. I open my eyes and she laughs.

If the gods can feel envy, I should be careful.

Don't take this away from me, I pray silently.

But never so that she hears.

We pack the basket and go down to the water. Spread out our blanket and eat breakfast. The boy has left his cap at home and rolls around in what had been brown and dead, places where the green has now awakened to life. I lift him onto my shoulders and gallop through the springtime air till he almost chokes with laughter. She is sitting on the blanket and laughing. A little dot far off in a red dress.

Afterwards he sits on her lap and eats biscuits. I serve coffee in mismatched cups. The boy catches sight of something that only children can see and walks off a little way from us. She keeps a watchful eye on him.

I lack nothing, I think. She is well again and I lack nothing.

But after I have thought this thought, it sits down between us on the blanket.

The thing we never talk about.

She takes my hand as if she too sees the unwelcome guest. As so many times before, she replies before I even ask.

'I never fell,' she says. 'I just sank.'

'I am here with you.'

I stroke her cheek.

'It is through you that I breathe. It is with your legs that I walk. Do not leave me, George.'

'I will not leave you.'

She looks at the boy.

'Man and woman can make promises to each other. They know what the words mean, that they apply to here and now, and can always be renegotiated.'

'Not mine.'

She takes my hand in hers.

'A child believes in the words. I believed my mother when she said that she would never leave me. How can one promise a child something when one does not know if the promise can be kept?'

She looks at the boy again.

'I love him. Why is that not enough?'

Kristoffer put down Torgny's book. He was still in bed, although it was already afternoon. He had been reading excerpts from *The Wind Whispers Your Name*, sometimes just lying still and staring at the ceiling. The text was only bearable in small portions. His hidden world – for all those years it had been available at the library.

Unwillingly he tried to adjust his identity. From half and hopeful to whole and meaningless. For three years he had fought to be deserving of justice, believing that the world was ordered so that goodness would be rewarded. He had tried to set a good example, elevating himself above the average and doing his best to make the world better. Decided who his ancestors ought to be and took pains to live up to them. He had come to terms with his alcoholism, battled his demons, unaware of its hiding place in his own gene pool.

The truth that had sneered behind his back.

Keep fighting, you little fool, soon enough you'll be knocked to the ground.

His megalomania must have provoked the universe. His belief that some people were naturally superior because of their genes. And obviously if that was the case, he was one of them. A gigantic finger had finally landed on his head and pressed him down like a drawing-pin.

He raised the book to his face and inhaled the odour. It stank of cigarette smoke and old dust. His mother had been loved. It was some consolation to know that. Sometimes the words indicated that he had been too, but it was harder to believe, since he had already lived through the end of the story. The reality did not mesh well with what Torgny had imagined.

The injustice he had been subjected to could not be forgiven. Her illness was not sufficient excuse. Someone must have seen how things were, someone who could have chosen to intervene and prevented thirty-five wasted years of uncertainty. Four months had passed between the day they had left Torgny and the day she abandoned him. Many people must have encountered them during that time and realised how ill she was.

No one had come to their rescue.

He heard the letter-box rattle and the post dropping onto the hall floor, but he didn't have the energy to get up. The sound of the postman's footsteps faded away. He turned his head and looked at his computer. Not even his play seemed important any more. The people he most wanted to impress would never be sitting in the audience.

His eyes went to the cognac bottle.

With a heavy sigh he got up and tightened his dressing gown around him. He saw the post lying on the doormat but let it be. Instead he sat down at his desk. For a long moment he sat there with his hands in his lap, then he opened his laptop.

He heard the sound of an incoming e-mail.

Finally a sign of life from Jesper.

He opened it but found only a web link. He clicked on it and the page started to download. It took an unusually long time, and he drummed his fingers impatiently as he waited, then dialled

Jesper's number. This time the voicemail didn't even pick up. All he got was an odd flat tone as if he'd dialled incorrectly.

On the screen the page was finally loaded. He went out into the hall and poked his foot at the pile of mail. A flyer from a takeaway restaurant, a bank statement and a handwritten letter. He picked up the letter and went back to his desk. Kristoffer clicked on play and the video started. An image of Jesper sitting in his flat. Kristoffer recognised the wallpaper in the background.

'My name is Jesper Falk. Thank you for watching this video and confirming my hypothesis that most people have forgotten what obligations are involved when one is born as a human being.'

Kristoffer put down the letter and leaned back. It was good to see him – something reliable amid all that had changed.

On the screen Jesper waved some hundred-kronor bills.

'This is five hundred kronor. I'm going to give it to this guy. Here you are!'

Jesper gestured to someone who was off to the side behind the camera. The next moment a head appeared, face hidden by a black ski mask. A pair of blue eyes looked out from the holes, but Kristoffer didn't recognise them.

'Wave a little and show everyone you're happy.'

The anonymous man waved.

'I bought him for five hundred kronor so that he would put this video up on the Internet. Everybody can be bought. Some are a bit more expensive, others cheaper. Have you thought about your own price? All right, you can go and sit down again.'

The man vanished, and judging by the direction Kristoffer guessed he'd gone to sit on Jesper's bed.

'Now to the topic at hand. I've written a novel entitled *Nostalgia – A Strange Feeling of Manageable Sorrow*. Remember that title. It took me seven years to write, and now an excellent publishing company has decided to publish it. Naturally I'm overjoyed. Because there are some important things in my book. I wrote it because I want it to change the world. Because things can't go on like this any longer. Don't you agree?'

Jesper looked for approval towards the masked man.

'Even he agrees.'

Kristoffer couldn't help smiling. Jesper had finally worked out a way to promote his novel.

'Like all authors I believe my book is particularly important, and like all authors I hope you'll choose to read what I've written. But here, a major problem arises. How can I get you to choose my book over all the others? You can see for yourself, I'm pretty ugly. I'm not going to be livening up any glitzy magazine spreads or TV talk shows. I don't know any celebrities. I'm a damn good writer but terrible at talking, so that's why I have a cue card here that I'm reading from.'

He looked down at something below the frame of the video.

'So, the book will be released on the fourth of March. Don't forget that, the fourth of March. *Nostalgia – A Strange Feeling of Manageable Sorrow.* Write it down. Okay? Now, back to the major problem.'

The cue card was now visible at the bottom of the frame.

'About 4,500 books are published in Sweden each year. So how am I going to get you to notice mine? There's only one way. By getting the media to write about it as much as possible. And how will I manage to do that?'

Jesper paused, as if somebody might answer his question. Then he continued.

'Some people think that newspapers write about what's important, because they have a duty to keep you informed, but that's not true. Most news-papers write about what they know you want to read. That's the only sure way to get you to buy their paper. So you're the one who decides what you want to hear about, what sort of news should take priority. You're the one who has the power. Each time you open your wallet and buy some-thing, you're saying "hello" and "okay" to what you're buying and to the person who will be getting rich from your purchase. So I checked a few tabloid headlines to see what you like to read about. That's when the next problem came up.'

Once again he glanced at the cue card.

'I'm not a hit man or a paedophile, I've never raped an old woman, never tortured any children,

I've never fucked on TV or been on a reality show. I don't have silicon breasts, have never participated in a gangbang, have never run through the streets naked. I don't even take dope. I'm a completely normal guy. Well, okay, I know I'm pretty ugly, but still. How the hell could I manage to become interesting enough in your eyes for the media to want to write about my book? I thought about it for a while, and then I came up with this. I already know that this web site is going to break records for the number of hits, and my novel will be mentioned on every news-stand all over Sweden, because you love stuff like this. All of you watching this right now are the reason why this is the best way for me to get my book out there. All of you who heard the rumour and who know what's going to happen, and still you choose to visit this site and look at this shit.'

His eyes narrowed and he pointed into the camera.

'It's precisely for people like you that I wrote my book. And if you don't read it after you've seen this video, go fuck yourself!'

Jesper paused and leaned back.

'Don't forget I'm doing you a favour. I'm doing this to remind you of what it is you've forgotten.'

He raised his hands to his throat.

'The only thing that could go wrong now is if Paris Hilton buys another Chihuahua and my book gets knocked off the front page, but I have to hope for the best.'

He fiddled with something inside his collar, and

when he took his hands away he had a thin plastic band around his neck. One of those used to seal packages. One end went into a little opening at the other end, and little ratchets along the plastic prevented the band from being loosened once it was pulled tight.

'Remember now, *Nostalgia – A Strange Feeling of Manageable Sorrow*. On sale fourth of March. My name is Jesper Falk and thanks for watching.'

Jesper pulled on the band as he stared into the camera.

Kristoffer jumped up so quickly his chair tipped over backwards.

The camera zoomed in. The plastic band cut into Jesper's neck. His eyes burned like lasers into the camera lens and into the viewer. Frantically Kristoffer's hands raced over the keyboard in search of the button that would stop what was happening. He grabbed his mobile, rang the familiar number, but got the flat tone again. On the screen Jesper's face had become distorted, the determined look gave way, and after he blinked repeatedly the camera lens released him and turned in the direction in which the masked man had gone.

Kristoffer began to sob. What he was seeing was unbearable. Jesper had asked for his help, had wanted to talk about his panic about promoting the book. Kristoffer had brushed him off; in his jealousy he had deleted his message. He hadn't even let Jesper in when he was standing outside his door. He covered his face with his hands and closed his eyes, but they opened of their own accord, and he was forced to see the terror of death in Jesper's eyes as his fingers vainly tore at his neck, trying to get the plastic band off.

The wail from Kristoffer's throat could not be stopped. He was exploding inside, and all his pent-up despair ripped loose. To the sound of his moans, Jesper's head slumped forward and hung there. The picture went black and all was for ever too late.

A car horn beeped in the street. A neighbour flushed a toilet.

The last thing that had remained intact had now cracked.

Nothing he thought, nothing he felt, was important any more.

Four steps to the bookshelf. With fingers that had never forgotten, he yanked the cork out of the cognac bottle. No matter what the cost, he appealed for mercy.

CHAPTER 30

Jan-Erik heard the front door open and hurried to the refrigerator to take out the bottle of champagne. The glasses were already set in place on the kitchen table next to the candlesticks. He struck a match to light the candles. He had been waiting for several hours. When he had gone out to buy the champagne, Louise had apparently been at home, judging by the tube of caviar that was left out on the worktop, but when he returned the flat was empty. She hadn't answered her mobile.

For a while he had debated the appropriateness of celebrating now that Alice was so seriously ill, but there was too much to lose if he held back. For once he intended to put the focus on him and not on her. She was not going to be allowed to take this moment away from him.

He was going to surprise Louise with champagne and Ellen with Appletiser and tell them about his prestigious prize. Maybe suggest that they take a holiday together. Put a stop to the disintegration that he'd been worrying about ever since Louise had collapsed in tears and voiced her doubts. The power of his reaction had surprised him. Realising how important it all was, and how much he had taken for granted. Their marriage must remain intact at any price; it was the base from which he proceeded and to which he must always return, the skeleton supporting his life and the foundation for everything he did. He would do everything he could to keep the three of them together. But he had not thought through everything that entailed. He had cleverly avoided the thought of certain marital components. The consequence of this line of thinking would make his efforts impossible. Having sex with Louise was unthinkable. That's why Ellen had to be there at the celebration. He had consulted her school schedule on the refrigerator door, and she would be home in half an hour. What still felt unthinkable must not be allowed to happen, however Louise might interpret his initiative.

He noticed his hand was shaking when he lit the last candle. He had refrained from easing his nerves with a few drinks while preparing the surprise. Even though he conducted most of his drinking outside the walls of the house, he sometimes grew afraid that Louise still knew how much he drank. But right now they were going to toast with champagne, a natural and legitimate way of celebrating.

When he looked up she was standing in the doorway.

He blew out the match.

'Hi.'

Her gaze went right past him, over all his celebratory efforts, and wandered on out through the window.

'Come and sit down, we have something to celebrate.'

He grabbed the bottle of champagne and tore off the foil, thinking she could at least say hello. He undid the wire, popped the cork and filled the glasses as quickly as the foam permitted.

She remained motionless in the doorway and clearly needed persuading.

He raised his glass to lure her to him.

'Come on.'

Something about her was different, but he couldn't put his finger on it. Three days had passed since he'd last seen her awake. That was when he'd left her crying at the kitchen table which he had now decorated with champagne and candles.

He went over and handed her the glass.

'Now listen to this – I've won the Nordic Council Literary Prize. It's the first time they've ever given it to someone who isn't an author.'

'Congratulations.'

She couldn't even be happy about that. He saw it clearly in her face. But he knew what would persuade her, something she was good at squandering.

'The prize is 350,000 kronor. Danish. So it's worth even more.'

Without touching the champagne she went over

and placed her glass on the worktop. There she stood with her back to him, and during the ensuing silence he grew angry. Never to receive any appreciation from her. Never to get recognition when he did something good. He worked like a dog and just once he ought to get a kind word or a little encouragement. He had even made a special effort, champagne and everything. He was trying to make her happy, trying to make an overture after their bitter conversation three days ago. But, as usual, it wasn't enough. Sulky and unforgiving, she was now going to force him to make even more fuss over her.

'I thought you'd be happy. I was going to suggest we take a trip together somewhere. But that's probably not good enough, as usual.'

He emptied his glass and filled it again. The champagne foamed over and ran down his hand, and he shook off the worst of it. Seeing her back turned was driving him crazy. He blew out the candles and didn't give a damn if tiny drops of wax landed on the table, which would annoy Louise. Then he grabbed the bottle, went out to the living room and sat down on the sofa. But he got up again and went instead to his office, kicked the door shut, and sat down behind his desk. He put down the champagne bottle among the piles of unopened fan mail for Axel Ragnerfeldt.

It was impossible to please her, he might as well admit it. She was a black hole into which all positive energy was sucked and obliterated.

He refilled his glass and ran his hand over the damp ring that had seeped onto the oak desk. Without knocking she opened the door, walking in determinedly, and sat down in his reading chair. He looked the other way. He didn't intend to be nice to her; now it was her turn to try. He sipped a little champagne; this time he was without guilt and had every right to be angry.

'I've asked Ellen to sleep over at a friend's house tonight, because you and I have to talk.'

For a few seconds his anger remained entrenched until the gravity in her voice made him pay attention. Treacherously it came slithering with its foul breath. When he looked at her he realised that something really *had* changed. Her face was open and her gaze unwavering, and the minefield that usually surrounded her had dissolved.

'I'm sorry this is such bad timing, because you're so excited about the prize and surely worried about Alice, but I might as well come straight out with it.'

His senses held their breath.

'I want a divorce.'

The air in his lungs emptied out as if he'd been punched in the stomach. She sat calm and composed in the easy chair as if what she'd said was entirely normal.

'Both of us know it's the right thing to do.'

What scared him most was her decisiveness. As if everything had been fully discussed before they even spoke. He gritted his teeth and tried to hide his panic, grasping for the one fact he had relied on in the muddle of thoughts that had passed through his brain in recent days. She was dependent on him, destitute without access to his wallet. Only until the day his father died, of course, but Axel could live a long time yet if all went well. That circumstance was his best defence. The fact that she knew nothing about the provisions of Axel's will.

He gave a little smile, rested his elbows on the desk and leaned his chin in his hands.

'And how do you intend to make ends meet, Louise? You don't have any money.'

'It'll all work out somehow. I'm going to go back to university and finish my degree, so I'll take out a student loan. Then I'm going to go back to work as a civil engineer.'

He swallowed. It was all planned out.

'Where will you live?'

'I talked to Filippa. I can sublet her flat for the time being, then I'll have to see.'

Plans forged and executed behind his back.

'Ellen will be staying here, just so you know.'

'Maybe. She's twelve years old, and at that age children usually get to decide where they want to live after a divorce.'

He took a deep breath and could hear that it gave him away; he raised his glass but set it down again when his hand shook. Their roles were now reversed. So many times he had been the target, cleverly dodging her missiles, refusing to fall no matter what she threw at him. Her composure frightened him, the self-confidence she radiated. He fumbled for something that would break her supremacy, neutralise her advantage and give him control. Her sheer will-power was evident. No threats from him would alter her decision. She had slipped beyond his control and landed out of reach. Suddenly he felt terrified. She really intended to leave him, leave him all alone.

'It doesn't have to be this way. Every marriage has its problems, but we can solve this together, Louise. I promise I'll change, I can go to that therapist if you like. Just tell me what you want me to do.'

'Jan-Erik, please.' She cocked her head to one side, pleading as if with a child. 'Don't you see that we're destroying each other?'

'No, I don't. We can't just throw away everything we have together because things are a bit difficult right now. Damn it, we have to fight back a little.'

'Haven't we been doing that long enough?'

He tried to find something to say, but the words weren't part of his vocabulary. Her impossible questions. Having to plead. Having to put into words what he felt. What she was demanding was unreasonable. All he wanted was for this whole thing to be over. Go back to the way it was. When he could still choose.

'But what about Ellen?'

'Ellen will always be our daughter even if we're

divorced. Seriously, Jan-Erik, we may live at the same address, but that's *all* we have in common.'

She shifted in the chair, clearing her throat a little, as if only now did she feel uncomfortable.

'Lena rang for you. She wants you to call.'

There was no anger in her voice. She was merely stating a fact.

'Lena who?'

'Lena in Göteborg.'

At first he didn't know what she was talking about. As far as he knew he didn't know any Lena in Göteborg. But then he remembered, and to his dismay he felt himself blushing.

'I don't know any Lena in Göteborg.'

But his gaze had slid along the wall however much he tried to keep it steady.

On the rare occasions when he gave his phone number to women he met, he always used his mobile number. As a final precaution he would change one digit to give them a hint of how little he wanted to hear from them.

'It doesn't matter, Jan-Erik. It's odd, but I even feel happy for you.'

Her comment amazed him.

'What do you mean? You think I've been having an affair with some woman named Lena in Göteborg?'

'Yes, I do.'

He snorted.

'But I haven't. I have no idea who Lena in Göteborg is. Probably someone who heard one of my lectures. Is that why you want a divorce, because you think I'm unfaithful?'

'No, that's not why.'

He couldn't understand how she was managing to stay so calm. How could she sit there unafraid, facing the dreadful change she was setting in motion? She must be getting her strength from somewhere. And all at once he knew. There was someone else. There was a man who had taken his place and was driving her to do all this. Her path was already staked out. When she broke up their marriage, all she would have to do was to follow the straight line. All the fruitless searching had already been done, any threatening loneliness had been precluded; all that was left was for him to be pushed aside and replaced with a better model.

'Ah, now I understand. You're trying to blame all this on me and on some bloody Lena in Göteborg, when it's really you who've met someone else!'

Louise lowered her eyes. Then she looked at him with the hint of a smile, neither spiteful nor indulgent.

'Admit it! Admit you have someone else!'

'No, Jan-Erik, I don't.'

He didn't believe her. He knew she was lying in order to cast herself in a better light. But then she continued, and the words shattered his brilliant conclusion.

'If you only knew how much I wish I did have someone else.'

He clenched his fists, letting himself be attacked by images of how his territory was about to be stolen. He would have to witness the invasion, incapable of repelling the attack. For ever more unwelcome in the very domain he sought to defend.

'You are Ellen's father and you always will be. I don't want to hate you, Jan-Erik, but I will if I stay here. I was at Alice's today. You know, I've never seen her so happy before, now that she believes she's about to die. I realised that I'm starting to become just like her, and I don't want that to happen. And you're becoming more and more like your father with each passing day.'

Her insult cut straight to his heart. Rage came rushing in from every direction to staunch the leak and prevent what was inside from flowing out and drowning him.

'If we share custody of Ellen you'll see her every other week. The two of you will finally have a chance to get to know each other.'

His throat hurt. A lump was blocking his vocal cords. He pushed out the chair and got to his feet, left the room and pulled his suitcase from the hall cupboard. In the bedroom he threw into it whatever clothes he could grab. On his way back through the living room he stuffed in some bottles without bothering to look at the labels. The only thing that mattered was how much was left in each one.

She was still sitting in the chair. He saw her legs as he passed on his way to the front door.

With his hand on the door handle he finished the conversation.

'I'll sleep at the house tonight. When I come back tomorrow you have to be gone. If there's anything else you have questions about, call my lawyer.'

CHAPTER 31

With what right?

Kristoffer pulled another length of books off the bookshelf.

With what right was everything taken from him? Another gulp burned his throat, but like a rejected lover it refused to come to his rescue. The image of Jesper was scorched onto his retina, refusing to be dissolved by the solvent he was pouring into himself.

He had rung Jesper's parents and received confirmation of his death. Two days before they had found him in his flat. A police report had been filed and a search had been launched to find the masked man. What crime he might be charged with, the police couldn't yet say.

Another length of books crashed to the floor, and when he was finished with them he knocked over the bookshelf too. Gasping, he looked around for something else he could pull over. Nothing could be allowed to stand, pretending to be whole. All these books at his feet that he was ploughing his way through. Written by smug scholars who had fooled him into thinking there was a logic to existence.

He raised the bottle to his mouth. The liquid he'd been longing for ran down his throat, but all he sensed was a shrill ringing in his ears.

He turned to the desk and swept the computer to the floor. The screen went blank and he gave it a kick to make sure that it would never light up again.

Jesper was gone.

Jesper had left him.

Jesper was dead and had taken with him all that he had meant to Kristoffer. The closest thing to love he had ever dared feel.

Outside the window, Katarina Church still stood there. The branches of the trees were still attached to the trunks. No windows were blown out in the surrounding buildings. And down in the cemetery someone was walking as if the air were still fit to breathe. Only in his flat was the catastrophe apparent. The rest of the world seemingly intended to go on as if nothing had happened.

He was gone. Would never exist again. All that he'd had ahead of him would never happen now. His brilliant power of observation had in the end been beaten by cynicism. Evil had been permitted to triumph.

Exhausted, Kristoffer sank down in a chair. He sat there, listening to the sound of his own breathing. The involuntary repetition. The prerequisite for his survival. The instinct to keep himself alive.

Gratefully he felt it take over. The feeling of

liberation when his brain went numb. When he was no longer capable of comprehending the depth of his pain. Why weren't human beings born this way? With their blood spiked from the start with a small percentage of alcohol. With the defence mechanism disconnected and the soul in a state of peace.

Was survival really so important that it outweighed all suffering?

He took another gulp from the bottle. On the desk before him lay a letter. He had picked it up from the hall when Jesper was still alive. Having a reason to reach out his hand felt like an achievement. *Sender: Marianne Folkesson.* He tore open the envelope. Inside was a note and another letter.

I found this in Gerda's flat. See you at the funeral.
Yours truly,
Marianne

A white envelope with his name on it. Written in a flowing script.

To be delivered after my death.

He opened the envelope lethargically and began to read.

CHAPTER 32

'I plan to ring Ellen and tell her about this. You're not going to convince her with a bunch of lies that this is all my fault!'

'I have no intention of doing that. Jan-Erik, please, don't ring her tonight. She mustn't find out by telephone. We have to sit down with her and tell her face-to-face.'

'No chance. I'm not going to help you cover up your sick decisions. You're going to have to do it yourself.'

'Jan-Erik, please . . .'

But he had slammed down the receiver, and as he'd threatened to do, he rang Ellen's mobile.

'Ellen? Ellen, this is Pappa. I just wanted to call and tell you what's happening before your mother beats me to it and deludes you into believing a bunch of lies. She's decided that the two of us should get a divorce, that we won't live together any more. She says you should live with each of us every other week, but I think you should just stay with me. We'll stay in the flat, you and I, so she'll have to manage as best she can. You should know that she's the one who decided all this. I tried to talk her out of it, but she's only thinking of herself. But we'll stick together, Ellen, you and me.'

It was Louise's fault that Ellen had cried on the phone. Louise's fault that he was drunk and wandering about in the dark like a lost soul in his childhood home.

The heating was turned up all the way, but nothing could prevent the cold from eating its way in. He didn't want to be here, walking about among all the memories that saturated the walls. He hated this house down to the tiniest piece of it, hated every nail and every board that held its walls together. The atmosphere penetrated his skin and spread through his veins. He wanted to fight yet there was no one to hurt, scream yet there was no one to scare.

By God, he would show her! Even if she had bewitched his father to write her into the will, he was the one who would continue to manage the funds. He would raise the fee for his lectures, invest wisely in an account out of the reach of her greedy fingers, and work out a way to transfer all the copyrights exclusively into his name. He would see to it that her share of the inheritance would be as small as possible, and he would have his plans ready for the day the old devil finally died. Louise's brief triumph would rapidly turn into bitterness when she realised how much she had lost.

He stopped outside his father's office. As usual, his body involuntarily hesitated before stepping over the threshold. His eyes were drawn to the lamp hook, but he looked away at once. Annika had also let him down. She was one of those who had left him.

He looked at the cupboard. It was in there he would find the solution. There must be unpublished texts he could use as a tribute after Axel Ragnerfeldt's death. The income would replace the part of the inheritance stolen by Louise.

He went over and opened the door. Darkness welled out and he picked up the pocket torch that was still lying on the desk. At the entrance to the cupboard he stumbled on the black rubbish bag. Furiously he tore it open and went back to the office, where he emptied the contents on the floor. Papers flowed out over the carpet. He squatted down but lost his balance. Sitting on the floor he ran his hand through all the documents, and a tiny spark of excitement unexpectedly came over him when he discovered a thick manuscript. Something his pappa had discarded, but which would probably be considered good enough in Jan-Erik's eyes. There was a little note attached to the title page, and he scanned the lines.

Axel, the hours that have passed have not been lonely. You are still with me in my thoughts. Since I've had a hard time getting away I thought I'd just send you my book anyway. I'd be grateful to have your wise views on it. No one else has read it (as you will see, it's far

above Torgny's head). My book longs only for
your lovely eyes to read it.
Your Halina
P.S. I'm so glad that we finally met! H

He swore to himself. The lover again. Everywhere in the cupboard she kept popping up as if she'd rented part of the space. Without much interest, he was leafing through the handwritten pages when a sudden sound made him snap to attention. It didn't come from inside the house, but from somewhere nearby he could hear a rhythmic, ringing sound. He put down the manuscript and got up from the floor. Outside the window it was pitch dark, and he hurried to switch off the overhead light so he could see better. Nothing moved in the dark garden. He took his pocket torch and went through the darkened rooms. From each window he peered out at the yard, but nowhere could he find an explan ation. He could see nothing from the living room, nothing from the dining room, nothing from the kitchen. He opened the door to the room where Gerda had once lived, went over to the bureau and looked out of the little round window above it. Something was moving outside. A black silhouette on the lawn way over by the bushes. In the spot where the greenhouse had once stood but which on his return from the States had been turned into a flagstone patio. He stood still and watched until his eyes adjusted to the dark. Only then did he realise what the sound was; the blade of a shovel hacking at the flagstones.

At first his mind was blank. What he saw could not be explained. But in the next moment he was overcome by rage that someone was destroying their patio. He switched on the pocket torch and directed the beam of light at the person moving outside. The black silhouette became a man, and when the glare focused on him he turned to face the light. Jan-Erik recognised him immediately. The foundling who was going to inherit from Gerda Persson.

He opened the window.

'What the hell are you doing out there?'

The man didn't answer. He turned his back to Jan-Erik and kept digging.

'Do you hear me? If you don't stop I'll call the police!'

He got no reaction.

Jan-Erik slammed the window shut and went out to the hall, put on his shoes and a jacket, and made sure he had his mobile in his pocket, in case he had to ring for help. He flipped the switch for the outside light but nothing happened. Annoyed, he slammed the door and stumbled down the stairs and across the lawn. The light from his torch played over the ground, and he avoided the bushes and unweeded flower-beds until the light reached the hole that Kristoffer had dug. The flagstones lay spread about under a layer of dirt.

'What do you think you're doing? This is private

property, and if you don't stop right now I'll call the police.'

Kristoffer sniffed and wiped his hand across his face before he resumed digging. Jan-Erik reached for the shovel, but Kristoffer knocked his hand away.

'Did you know the whole time?'

Jan-Erik shone the light at the young man's face. His eyes were red and swollen, and tears were running down his cheeks. Kristoffer put his hand up against the blinding light and then continued digging. Jan-Erik was baffled. The absurd situation, the intruder's obvious mental instability, Louise wanting a divorce, all the alcohol he had downed: everything was a maelstrom. He lowered the torch, suddenly exhausted.

Because he didn't understand. Nor did he know if he really wanted to understand, really wanted to know why the foundling who was Gerda's heir was digging a hole in their garden.

Kristoffer stopped and took a folded piece of paper from his pocket. He held it out across the hole to Jan-Erik, who was incapable of raising his arm. He was about to contract a deadly virus; a chronic disease that would never leave him.

Kristoffer shook the paper at him.

'Read it!'

Now it would be proved. That this stranger standing in front of him was his half-brother. That yet another part of the inheritance would vanish to someone who hadn't lifted a finger to deserve it.

But that didn't explain the digging. The dread awakened inside him was unthinkable.

The paper was burning his fingers. In the light of the torch Gerda's flowing handwriting took shape, curling along the lines like an ornamental work of art. At a quick glance it all looked so harmless. But slipped in under the innocent surface he understood that something terrible was hidden. If he allowed the words to form into sentences, something would be destroyed that could never be restored.

To the sound of earth being shovelled he began to read.

> *My dear Kristoffer,*
> *I don't know whether it's the right thing to do to write this letter, but I blame myself so much that I just can't leave it be. I believe I'm doing this to try to put right what I was once forced to take part in. Many years have gone by, but not a day passes that I don't think about everything that happened, and now I'm old and can feel that the end is approaching . . .*

Why does the eye follow the line that it doesn't want to read? Why does the brain interpret the words it doesn't want to understand? With each word he read, something was lost. Silently the secret had slunk after him through all the years. Disguised behind their misleading behaviour his parents had allowed him to build his conceptual world and his life on something that had actually never existed.

Underneath the gilt cover was nothing but a hole. The very root of his existence was pure fantasy.

. . . and the morning after the terrible event, I found you in the woodshed. Mrs Ragnerfeldt was in bed and had taken a sedative, so she knew, and still knows, nothing. Mr Ragnerfeldt didn't know what to do, but then he told me to drive into the city and leave you somewhere where someone would find you, and I didn't dare refuse. I saw all the evil happen, but I was brought up in a home where I was taught not to talk back to my superiors. I hate that man for everything he's done and for what he made me do . . .

'But this is total madness. Gerda must have been struck by dementia. Anyone can see that. You can see that someone senile wrote this, can't you? She claims all these things about Axel Ragnerfeldt. Don't you know who he is? You have to understand, it's totally impossible he would do something like that!'

Kristoffer stopped, breathless with exertion.

'So your sister didn't kill herself?'

'What?'

'Did you read all of it? About why she did it?'

Something heavy and impenetrable slammed down inside him. A defensive wall surrounded his soul. A few seconds passed and by then, without even realising it, he had taken sides.

'My sister was run over by a car!'

. . . outside Mr Ragnerfeldt's office there was a broom cupboard. From there I could hear everything that was said in his office, and sometimes I stood there listening, because it seemed easier to bear if I understood what was going on in the household. I know it was wrong of me, but that's what I did. Some months after Mr Ragnerfeldt received the Nobel Prize, the writer Torgny Wennberg came to visit, and since I knew he had known your mother, I was afraid he had revealed everything and I would be held responsible. I listened in the broom cupboard and heard when . . .

In front of him Kristoffer had fallen to his knees. Jan-Erik shone the light from the torch down into the hole and felt the horror spread through his body. Kristoffer had found what he was looking for. All at once Gerda's words were confirmed and could never be denied again. Jan-Erik turned off the torch to make what he'd seen in the hole disappear.

'Turn it back on!' Kristoffer yelled. 'Turn it on, I mean it!'

Jan-Erik turned on the torch, suddenly afraid that someone would hear them.

For a long while Kristoffer just sat there breathing hard and staring down into the dark hole. Time after time he wiped his nose on his sleeve, and his wet cheeks glistened in the faint light.

'You never abandoned me.'

Jan-Erik needed something to drink.

With difficulty Kristoffer got to his feet.

'Do you know what a survivor is?'

Jan-Erik didn't reply. Everything that had mattered before now had suddenly been obliterated, and it was impossible to comprehend what had taken its place.

'A survivor is someone who does something so unique that the memory of him always lives on. Someone like Axel Ragnerfeldt was to me. But if it's the last thing I do, I'm going to make sure that he goes down in history as the fucking bastard he is.'

Inside himself Jan-Erik heard his own voice. The words he had repeated so many times in the spotlight. *My father realised that our actions are like our children; they live on, independent of us and our will. Joseph Schultz and my father belong to the minority who realise that the reward for a good deed is the very fact of having done it.*

His lectures were over. Never again would he stand on a stage and feel the flood of applause. Never again would he see the respectful glances when he mentioned his surname. From here on he would carry the name like a disfigurement. He would never get his literature prize from the Nordic Council. Louise would never regret that she'd left him.

Everything would be taken from him.

Kristoffer grabbed the letter out of Jan-Erik's hand. After a last glance down into the hole he started walking towards the gate.

'Wait a minute!'

Kristoffer kept walking.

'Really, wait a minute, can't we talk?'

Jan-Erik was blameless, yet he was the one who would be forced to endure the punishment.

'I'll give you money. Three hundred and fifty thousand kronor. Danish.'

Kristoffer stopped short and turned round. Jan-Erik couldn't make out his expression, but the tiny hope that had glimmered was extinguished when he heard Kristoffer's reply.

'Fuck you!'

Then he kept walking towards the gate, with the white threat fluttering in his hand. Outside that gate Gerda's words would spread like pollen.

Jan-Erik didn't have time to think. Not when he bent down and his hand gripped the handle of the shovel. Not when his legs began to run to catch up. Not even when he stood a few metres from the gate and looked at the motionless body on the gravel path. The only thing he felt was surprise. The light of the street-lamp fell on the hands holding the shovel, and he was amazed that they were his. They had obeyed instinct, an instinct as old as humankind – the readiness to kill in order to protect what is ours.

Somewhere inside him he had unknowingly carried that ability.

During all those years when he had fought for what little he'd been able to achieve.

A life in the shadow of the man so admired.

For that little bit he had shown himself capable of killing.

The hole was already dug. The ground had been broken by those who had gone before.

Thirty-one years later it had fallen to the next generation to transform the place into a family plot.

CHAPTER 33

Lovely is the earth, lovely is God's Heaven,
beautiful the pilgrimage of souls.
Through the fair realms of the earth
we march unto paradise with song.

Marianne Folkesson sat alone on the church pew with a hymnbook in her hands. She knew the hymn by heart, she had sung it at so many funerals. The magnificent tones of the organ resounded between the stone walls where there was nothing to muffle the sound. Nothing but herself, the pastor, the cantor and the funeral director. No Kristoffer Sandeblom, no one from the Ragnerfeldt family, no Torgny Wennberg.

Gerda Persson would go to her eternal rest as alone as she seemed to have lived her life.

Epochs may come, epochs may fade away,
generations follow one by one.
Never muted is the tone from Heaven
in the soul's joyful pilgrim song.

She looked at the white casket, decorated with red roses as Jan-Erik Ragnerfeldt had suggested. It was not an extravagant flower arrangement, but as usual the florist had done a fine job. The blood-red colour framed by green gave dignity to the scene and alleviated her feeling of failure.

Just before the church bells began to toll and the doors were closed, she had stood on the church steps and called Kristoffer Sandeblom. No one had answered. She wondered whether it was the letter from Gerda that had made him change his mind, if that was why he had decided not to attend. Her curiosity about what the letter had said, whether it contained the explanation of the will, had remained with her since she had posted it.

Disappointed that no one had shown up, she took her place at the front of the church and nodded to the young pastor. Sadly there was no reason to wait any longer.

Souls rejoice, the Saviour is come.
Peace on Earth the Lord has proclaimed.

The tones of the organ slowly died out. The pastor went up and stood next to the casket.

'In the name of God the Father, the Son, and the Holy Ghost.'

She heard the cantor moving about in the choir. The sound was amplified in all the emptiness and blunted her sorrow. In front of her the pastor unfolded the paper she had sent him. Some brief information about Gerda. She had written down the little she knew but hoped that he could still come up with a suitable eulogy. She had done what was expected and perhaps a little more besides, but still it didn't feel adequate.

The pastor raised his eyes from the paper and began to speak.

'We are gathered here today to say farewell to Gerda Anna Persson, who left us on the fourth of October, 2006. A long life has ended, and much has happened in the world during her lifetime. Ninety-two years have passed since 1914 when Gerda was born in Borgholm on the island of Öland. After six years in school, at the age of thirteen she went into service as a housemaid with a family in Kalmar. Four years later she moved to Stockholm, and here she would remain. For all those years since then she worked as a housekeeper for various families in and around Stockholm. She remained longest with the renowned author Axel Ragnerfeldt and his family, where she worked until she retired in 1981.'

He lowered the paper and put it in between the pages of the Bible he held in his hand. Marianne fingered the rose she would place on Gerda's casket and hoped that the pastor intended to say something more. That he would make an effort for Gerda's sake. She was just about to give up hope when he looked out over the deserted pews and began to speak as if every seat in the church were full.

413

'When we imagine Gerda's life, it is easy to resort to platitudes. I must admit that I did so myself when I was faced with this task. According to the standards of our day, we find at first glance nothing enviable, nothing we would wish for ourselves or our children; on the contrary, Gerda's life appears monotonous and quite arduous. But what do we actually know about a human life? About the things that happened every day. About sorrows and joys. About the dreams she had and those that were fulfilled. We know little about Gerda, except that she now belongs to those who in the end found the answer to the eternal mystery of life. Let us then ask the question: can she teach us anything here today, by reminding us of the transience of life?'

Marianne leaned back. He had understood and shared her desire to honour Gerda at the last opportunity that remained.

'Nowadays people often talk about happiness. Books are written about it, courses are taught on it, and some of us even try to buy it. Feeling happy has become a right, and we chase after it, convinced that once we have found it we will also find the solution to all our problems. Not being happy has come to be equated with failure. But what is happiness, after all? Is it possible to be happy each waking minute, day after day, year in and year out? Is it actually something worth striving for? For how can we conceive of our happiness if we have never experienced any pain?

414

Sometimes I think that today we have trouble finding happiness because of our deep fear of suffering. Perhaps we have forgotten the lessons that can be learned from our own darkness. Is it not there that we must go sometimes in order eventually to distinguish the light from the stars? To understand how the happiness we so assiduously pursue actually feels? A life without sorrow is a symphony without bass notes. Is there anyone who can truthfully claim that he is always happy? I have never met such a person. On the other hand, I have met apparently happy people who said that they were content. I looked up the word in the *National Encyclopaedia*, and it describes the feeling of having obtained or achieved what can reasonably be desired. And when I read that, I thought that perhaps we have gone astray in our pursuit of happiness, that what we should actually be seeking is the ability to feel content. Something has made us believe that it is the rapture of the moment and the ecstatic rush of the senses that leads to happiness, but perhaps it is instead the courage to settle down and dare to be satisfied with what we have.'

He turned towards the casket.

'How you felt, Gerda, we will never know. We know only that you lived your life and did the best you could with the circumstances that were given to you. I want to thank you for causing me to meditate on happiness as I wrote this eulogy.'

Marianne smiled. When their eyes met she

nodded her sincere thanks. He smiled back and went to stand at the head of the casket, where he picked up a handful of earth.

'From earth are you come, and to earth you shall return.'

Three times she saw the earth scattered and she knew they had done the best they could.

The key to Gerda's flat was still in the Jiffy bag. She had stuffed it in her handbag, intending to take Kristoffer there after the memorial service. Now she hesitated on the church steps and again dialled his number. After the first ring the connection was picked up by his voicemail and she left a message asking him to please get in touch. The flat had to be emptied so she decided to begin the work without him there to watch. If she found anything she thought he might want, she would set it aside for the time being.

At the bottom of the escalator in the underground station she went into the kiosk to buy something to eat. It was late afternoon and she knew herself well enough to realise that soon she would be hungry. The billboards for the evening papers reminded her of the Ragnerfeldt family, and once again she felt angry about the empty church. That Gerda's passing was so unimportant to them that other things had taken precedence. Not even Jan-Erik, who had shown such interest, had taken the time to show up.

She bought a sandwich and some fruit and tore her eyes away from the lurid headlines.

WRITER FILMED
HIS OWN
SUICIDE
Posted it on the Net

When she reached Gerda's flat, she hung up her coat in the hall, sighing when she saw what a huge amount of work remained. Decisions had to be made about Gerda's belongings, what was valuable and what should be thrown away. She decided to start with the wardrobes in the bedroom. Anything that was clean and in good condition would be given to charity, and the rest consigned to the dustbin.

The first wardrobe was full of clothes; she inspected the garments one by one and sorted them. A black rubbish bag was quickly filled, and only a coat went into the charity carton. The next wardrobe had shelves full of handkerchiefs and ironed sheets. Stacked in neat rows, they soon joined the lone overcoat in the charity box.

It was when she cleaned off the top shelf that she found them. Right at the back lay a stack of black notebooks. Even before she looked inside she knew what she had found. The first diary entry was dated 4 August 1956. She climbed down from the chair. She cursed the fact that she hadn't discovered them before the funeral; it might have made her search for relatives much easier.

Standing in that bedroom with all Gerda's life secrets in her hands, Marianne asked herself whether she had the right to read them. What would she herself have wanted if she'd written diaries and someone found them after her death? Pensively she put the stack of books on the nightstand and went back to the wardrobes. The black notebooks drew her like a magnet as she absent-mindedly took a dress from its hanger. The person who would inherit Gerda's estate had not even shown up at the funeral, so could he possibly be interested in reading them? If Gerda absolutely had not wanted them to be read, she should have thrown them away. If they were intended for someone in particular, she should have left a note as she did with the letter to Kristoffer Sandeblom. Right now only Marianne was interested in Gerda Persson and how her life had turned out. Once again the question went through her mind: what would she herself have wanted? The answer came instantly. The day she died nothing would bother her any longer. Those who were left behind should do as they thought best.

With her mind made up, she laid aside the dress and took the diaries with her to the kitchen, where she sat down at Gerda's table and began to read.

CHAPTER 34

A little strip of moonlight seeped in between the drawn curtains in Axel's room. They had laid him on his back, and he could follow its path across the ceiling with his eyes.

What will your eye want to look at, when you know that it's the last thing you will see? The question was posed in his first novel, written at a safe distance from the moment that now awaited him.

With the door closed it had silently slipped into the room. Gratefully he had sensed the presence of what he had so long yearned for. The one who had finally come to free him from his prison. All afternoon he had sat like this, elatedly looked forward to what he thought would now happen.

Then the day had turned into evening and darkness slowly fell. But his anxiety grew stronger, keeping pace with the darkness descending over the room. As he waited, dread crept in and gave life to an intense premonition. A tremendous fear struck him. The grace he had imagined he would be allowed to enjoy had been transformed into a threat of dissolution. A warning of chaos and putrefaction.

When the nurses came in and lifted him over onto the bed, he wanted to scream for them to stay and not leave him alone with the thing lurking in the corners, the one thing he couldn't see. Unsuspecting, they laid him under the covers and forced him to listen to their heedless conversation. He watched them go, leaving him in lonely desperation.

He didn't want to die. He was no longer ready. For five years he had called on death, and when it finally sought him out he realised that he was not prepared. Eye to eye with the inevitable it was not death he saw, but himself.

It became harder and harder to breathe, his chest was being pressed down by an enormous weight. His body struggled furiously to maintain the life it did not want to relinquish. Far off he could see the red alarm button. The inaccessible connection to those who could come to his rescue.

His chest felt heavier and heavier, and there was a foul smell in the room. All he could see were shapes, but he no longer knew what it was he was seeing.

He wanted to call for Alice, ask her to come and save him. But she just sat over there at the desk with her back turned, not paying him any attention. He heard the sound of her typewriter; he wanted to go over and put his nose on the back of her neck and inhale her scent.

He was falling, faster and faster, but his useless arms refused to protect him. He needed the consolation of meaning, a real purpose to the life he had lived and the death he was about to face. He wanted to be able to leave his life with accomplishment, and not as an escape. Pushed from his hiding place he was falling helplessly through whispering voices. All the events he had silently ignored came rushing past.

He was freezing and begged for someone to warm him.

Only now did he understand that death was unavoidable. That all roads led away from what his senses had known. His mind raced through his life, grasping for memories that might alleviate his terror.

His name was known all over the world. He had shaken hands with kings and presidents. He had assumed his place in history.

To what benefit? All that awaited was annihilation.

He was admired by millions of strangers, but not a single one could offer any solace.

What was it that he had always searched for?

And when his chest sank and his heart stopped, one last question echoed.

To what purpose did I need all those honours?

Through the canopy of branches overhead a sunbeam found its way and blinded him. He was lying on the little patch of grass underneath the

421

apple tree. He heard the sound of steady blows from his father's hammer and his mother pottering about in the garden.

He was back at Bliss.

The happiest moments of his life.